W9-BST-332

Dear Reader,

Spring is on the way, and the Signature Select program offers lots of variety in the reading treats you've come to expect from some of your favorite Harlequin and Silhouette authors.

The second quarter of the year continues the excitement we began in January with a can't-miss drama from Vicki Hinze: *Her Perfect Life*. In it, a female military prisoner regains her freedom only to find that the life she left behind no longer exists. Myrna Mackenzie's *Angel Eyes* gives us the tale of a woman with an unnatural ability to find lost objects and people, and *Confessions of a Party Crasher,* by Holly Jacobs, is a humorous novel about finding happiness—even as an uninvited guest!

Our collections for April, May and June are themed around Mother's Day, matchmaking and time travel. Mothers and daughters are a focus in *From Here to Maternity,* by Tara Taylor Quinn, Karen Rose Smith and Inglath Cooper. You're in for a trio of imaginative time-travel stories by Julie Kenner, Nancy Warren and Jo Leigh in *Perfect Timing*. And a matchmaking New York cabbie is a delightful catalyst to romance in the three stories in *A Fare To Remember* by Vicki Lewis Thompson, Julie Elizabeth Leto and Kate Hoffman.

Spring also brings three more original sagas to the Signature Select program. *Hot Chocolate on a Cold Day* tells the story of a Coast Guard worker in Michigan who finds herself intrigued by her new downstairs neighbor. Jenna Mills's *Killing Me Softly* features a heroine who returns to the scene of her own death, and *You Made Me Love You* by C.J. Carmichael explores the shattering effects of the death of a charismatic woman on the friends who adored her.

And don't forget, there is original bonus material in every single Signature Secret book to give you the inside scoop on the creative process of your favorite authors! Happy reading!

Marsha Zinberg

Marsha Zinberg
Executive Editor
The Signature Select Program

Signature Select™

MINISERIES

Julie Elizabeth Leto

NEW ORLEANS NIGHTS

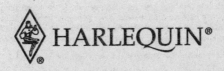

HARLEQUIN®

TORONTO • NEW YORK • LONDON
AMSTERDAM • PARIS • SYDNEY • HAMBURG
STOCKHOLM • ATHENS • TOKYO • MILAN • MADRID
PRAGUE • WARSAW • BUDAPEST • AUCKLAND

ISBN 0-373-83706-2

NEW ORLEANS NIGHTS

Copyright © 2006 by Harlequin Books S.A.

The publisher acknowledges the copyright holder of the individual works as follows:

PURE CHANCE
Copyright © 2001 by Julie Leto Klapka

INSATIABLE
Copyright © 2001 by Julie Leto Klapka

www.eHarlequin.com

Printed in U.S.A.

CONTENTS

For the Leto brothers, Chris, Tim and Jason,
who are just as good-looking and adventurous as any
romance hero I've written—and even more fun!
Thanks for being proud, protective and supportive,
for recognizing the importance of family and
for realizing that having a tough, not-easy-to-intimidate sister
isn't so bad in the larger scheme of things.
I love you guys!

PURE CHANCE

PROLOGUE

"WHAT DO YOU THINK you're doing?" Serena Deveaux demanded of her sister. Then she groaned as a wicked grin spread across Samantha's face like a lazy curve in the bayou—the kind with a hungry gator on the other side of a cypress, lying low until he could chomp off your leg for lunch. The devilish smile remained as Samantha drove past the corner of Dauphine and Esplanade, then double-parked while a woman with an armful of packages loaded her burgundy Mercedes.

"I'm waiting for that space," Sammie answered, drumming on the steering wheel with nervous energy. "You didn't think I was just going to drop you off? That wouldn't be neighborly."

"Neighborly?" Serena may have spent most of her childhood separated from her sister—she living with their mother in New Orleans and Sammie with their father in California—but she knew her sister didn't care two flips about being polite. "You're from Los Angeles. What do you know about neighborly?"

In the past, Serena wouldn't have teased her younger sibling about her Hollywood lifestyle. Their relationship had been too strained by their parents' rancorous divorce to handle good-natured ribbing. But twenty-five years after the judge said, "Enough, already," and two months after Sammie abandoned her rental home in Pacific Palisades and her job as a movie stunt double to return to the French Quarter, they finally had a chance to be sisters again—teasing and all.

"If New Orleans is going to be my permanent home, I need to start thinking Southern. Listen to this." Sammie shoved her car into park, unbuckled her seat belt and turned to face her passenger. "Hey, Serena, where y'at?"

Sammie's expertise with accents made her traditional Quarter greeting sound completely convincing. Serena couldn't help but laugh. Unfortunately, her mission this morning wasn't about laughter or teasing. It was about desperation and subterfuge and ridding herself of a dearly loved, but desperately unwanted, fiancé.

Drew Stuart, her unsolicited intended, had been her best friend since kindergarten. As she thought back over the years of scraped knees and quilted forts and stickball games in the street, she couldn't imagine how their friendship had taken such a dramatically wrong romantic turn. Just over a year ago, Drew started getting all mushy. Sending her potted plants with frilly ribbons. Buying her Valentine cards that didn't contain the usual rude joke or harmless insult. Talking about marriage. Marriage!

As if he didn't know that walking down the aisle with anyone was the last thing she'd ever do.

No thank you. She was only six when Devlin and Endora Deveaux split their family in half, separating Serena from her sister and her father, except for brief visits when the mood struck him. Heck, Drew barely survived the parting of his own parents just after high school. But one very determined bee had invaded Drew's marital bonnet and he was walking around with a ring in his pocket, waiting for Serena to lose her mind long enough for her to say yes to his proposal. She'd already said no, several times. He'd ignored her and booked the church. She'd tried refusing to speak to him until he came to his senses. He'd pouted until she relented, then chose their china pattern.

Well, enough was enough.

Serena wished her plan could be less complicated. Like the hand-painted tile hanging above her desk, Emerson's mantra of "Simplicity, simplicity, simplicity!" usually ruled her thinking. Once she discovered that transcendental philosophy in college, she'd clung to the idea in every aspect of her life. She worked for love, not money. Simple. She had an occasional lover, but no long-term boyfriends. Simple. She played hard and lived happy and planned to be single and unfettered for the rest of her life.

Apparently, not so simple.

"You'll be making crawfish étouffée and singing 'Iko, Iko,' any day now." Serena's compliment notched Sammie's smile from haughty to dazzling. She hated to tarnish the shine, but she really couldn't afford Sammie tagging along. "But could you think Southern tomorrow?"

Serena grabbed her thermos and a basket from the back seat, a homemade breakfast of café au lait and beignets. Suddenly, her offering seemed paltry for a man she was about to trick into becoming her accomplice in showing Drew the light. "I need to see Brandon alone."

"You? Alone with Brandon Chance?" Sammie's deeply set blue eyes widened. "As I recall, the last time you two tried that, things didn't turn out so well."

Serena squeezed her eyelids shut and winced. Had it really been fifteen years? She remembered the glittery streamers hanging from the gymnasium rafters. Balloons stamped with "Congratulations, Graduates" floating above the crowd. Zach Doucet spiking the punch his mother served from her best crystal bowl.

And **Brandon Chance**, her *other* best friend since the second grade, luring her into a dark corner and kissing her—a kiss that changed her forever—a kiss that mangled the one friendship that had always mattered most.

If she learned one thing from the incident, it was that friendships—like hers with Drew—were too precious to lose over romantic nonsense.

"That was a long time ago," Serena insisted. "I've practically forgotten all about it." If Sammie bought that lie, Serena would consider selling her prime real estate in the Bayou St. John.

"Brandon groped you, Serena. He was drunk and treated you like 'a Bourbon Street whore,' I believe you said…or perhaps I should pull out the letter you wrote to me shortly thereafter? I kept it, you know."

Serena shifted in the passenger seat, moving the warm basket of pastry from one side of her lap to the other. "You're a packrat, you know that?"

"So are you. Comes in handy sometimes."

"So do old friends. Brandon apologized. I accepted."

Too bad the damage had already been done.

Sammie shook her head, bobbing her neat, blond ponytail. "But you haven't had a conversation with him since that happened, have you? He was your constant companion from age seven, more so than even Drew. You have a mountain of unresolved feelings for the guy, Serena. You'd better deal with that before you go waltzing into his office offering him…whatever you're offering."

Literally, she was offering him breakfast. Figuratively, she was offering way more than he'd ever accept—if not for the ace up her sleeve.

When Serena had heard that Brandon Chance had moved back to New Orleans and opened a bodygaurd service, she finally saw a way to convince Drew that his one-sided romance would destroy their friendship—something she wasn't yet willing to let happen. Drew had been there graduation night. He'd seen what Brandon's fumbling, artless kisses and grabbing had done to her, the long-term price she'd paid. Drew had warned her countless times over the years that Brandon was the reason she refused to form long-term, intimate commitments. If she became involved with Brandon again, Drew would be the first one to warn her off.

He'd be the first to tell her that friends should never become lovers. The first to remind her of the pain and heartbreak of a one-sided attraction.

Hopefully, he'd finally see the light and drop his own fruitless pursuit before she had to cut out contact with him altogether.

All she had to do was hire Brandon as her bodyguard and then make the world—and Drew, in particular—believe that they were lovers. She didn't allow herself time to mourn the fact that fifteen years ago, he would have helped her just because she asked. Now, she had to resort to deception.

"I need Brandon's help with a professional matter," Serena said.

As the burgundy Mercedes finally vacated its spot, color drained from Sammie's California tan. "Serena? Tell me this isn't about Brandon's new business. Has something happened to scare you?"

Scared? God, yes, she was terrified! Not of Drew and his proposal. She'd hurt him if she had to, sacrifice his friendship if he wouldn't back down. Marriage simply wasn't an option, though she'd try anything to avoid losing yet another cherished friend.

What scared her was the man in the office above. The one who'd taken her teenage crush and turned it into something heartbreaking and humiliating. The one who'd given her the sincerest of apologies, then abandoned her for fifteen years.

The one she had to face. Today. This morning. Now.

"Brandon's bodyguard business doesn't have anything to do with this."

Brandon Chance's retirement from the military had shocked more than a few Quarter residents who figured this particular native son to be an army lifer. The fact that he'd returned to open a personal-protection service incited gossips from the banks of Lake Pontchartrain to the Moonwalk. Even his Aunt Tillie, still best friends with Serena's mother, didn't know the nature of the career switch, though she lamented that he'd simply swapped one dangerous endeavor for another.

Serena didn't really care why he'd chosen to become a bodyguard. She just factored his new profession into her plan.

She had to remove marriage from Drew's agenda and restore the casual comfort of their friendship. She'd tried everything she could think of to do so without resorting to mind games, but buoyed by the support of everyone who knew them, her own mother included, Drew remained firm.

She had only one option left. Convince him she'd fallen in love with another man. But not just any other man.

Brandon Chance.

She couldn't remember now the precise moment she'd started fantasizing about Brandon, but the memory of making out with her pillow and pretending the soft, fluffy down was Brandon, stuck in her head. She was, what? Fourteen? With her double promotion into Brandon's class, she saw him every day—watched him flirt and tease girls who were obviously smitten with him—then he walked *her* home. Spent his free time with *her*. Yet even then, she'd known that initiating a romance would spell certain disaster.

She'd been right then. She was right now.

Unfortunately, Brandon's apology for his horrible behavior included a goodbye he obviously meant. He'd humiliated her with his clumsy kiss, but she'd paid him back by wounding more than just his pride that night with her muffled scream and resounding slap. She'd cursed their friendship, saying she wished they'd never met. And he'd made her wish come true. Since then, he refused to be more than a passing acquaintance.

If she wanted Brandon to help her, she'd have to hire him as her bodyguard. And to that end, she'd created the "Cliché Killer."

Her sister grabbed her hand. "Are you sure this is a good idea? You've been acting weird the past few days. I haven't been around you enough to know if that's unusual."

Serena chuckled and squeezed her sister's hand tightly. "Depends on who you ask."

Sammie rebuckled her seat belt and glanced into the rearview mirror, a sure sign she would give Serena the privacy she needed. "So I'm not supposed to worry? You want a private meeting with the boy—now the man—who broke your heart and I'm not supposed to be concerned?"

Serena opened the door and swung her legs out of the car, then tossed a sly glance over her shoulder. "Nope."

Sammie's mouth twisted with apparent disbelief. "Reassure me again *after* you've seen Brandon."

With that, Sammie rolled up the window and sped away. Serena watched until her sister's taillights whipped around the corner. Behind her, Brandon's office building loomed. Stepping toward the hewn stone stairs, she put down the thermos and basket and took a deep breath. Her heart slammed against her chest so violently, she felt sure she'd get the hiccups any minute. Or she'd pass out.

Fifteen years since he'd lured her to dance in a dark corner of the gym. Since she'd nearly fainted from overwhelming passion—a desire so incapacitating, her brain stopped working. For the briefest of moments, she'd thought he loved her. Like she loved him. That he wanted her. Like she so wanted him.

Then he'd kissed her. The alcohol on his breath had immediately quashed her raging hormones and made his motives clear. When his hand fumbled up her shirt, the last of her romantic notions deserted and her instincts kicked in. She'd slapped him. Then she'd run, straight to a chaperon who then dragged Brandon away by his collar.

All night long, she'd refused his phone calls, ignored the pebbles he'd flung at her window. She'd run like a coward. Away from the boy who'd befriended her on the playground and taught her about winning. From the teenager who'd driven her to her first nightclub and taught her how to dance the two-step.

From the young man who'd made her crazy with wanting.

The next morning, she'd accepted his apology. After a terse goodbye, he'd left only a few days later for a summer internship. He returned to New Orleans on an occasional holiday, and though they'd exchange small talk, Serena wasn't dense. Her fear and his screw-up had destroyed their relationship forever. He wouldn't help her salvage her friendship with Drew or take her job offer if she promised him all the money in her bank account. Nothing could undo the distance between them.

Nothing but the one thing Brandon couldn't resist…

CHAPTER ONE

LIKE TINY SOLDIERS snapping to attention, the hairs on the back of Brandon Chance's neck stood rigid and straight. The undeniably female form, visible but muted through the frosted-glass door between his bare reception area and his office, raised her arm to knock again. A jangle of bracelets accompanied her staccato rap, followed by a voice he'd know anywhere—a voice smooth like fine Kentucky bourbon, yet hotter than any Louisiana pepper sauce.

"Brandon? I know you're in there."

He watched the colors of bare flesh and bohemian clothes shift and writhe. She had her hands on her hips. She was probably curling down that bottom lip and deciding if he was worth the effort.

She knocked again.

He shook his head, wondering who he possibly could have pissed off so royally that they'd send Serena Deveaux to his office so early on his first day in business.

He considered blaming God, knowing He most definitely had a questionable sense of humor and a love for irony. But Brandon had been a relative saint over the past year and, so far as he knew, hadn't broken a single commandment. He'd watched his drinking. Given up cigarettes in the interest of healthy lungs. Hadn't even had a date that didn't end with a chaste kiss on the cheek—or worse, a businesslike handshake that made him wonder if he hadn't stayed in the army *way* too long.

But someone was getting a serious chuckle out of this morning's turn of events. Serena Deveaux, on the other side of his door, demanding entrance to his celibate life after years of deliberate separation.

"Brandon, open this door!"

"No Chances Protection is not yet open for business," he barked. "Call later and make an appointment."

Or better yet, don't call. Leave me alone. You're trouble, woman. The kind of trouble I'm going to avoid, even if it kills me.

True to the bold little girl he'd first met on the playground when she'd climbed too far up on the monkey bars to get down safely on her own, Serena grabbed the doorknob and turned. Luckily, he'd locked the door.

"If I didn't know better, I'd think you were *hiding* from me, Brandon."

He shoved out of his chair. *Chance men didn't hide.*

"I'm busy, Serena."

"Too busy for breakfast? A friendly peace offering?"

He didn't reply. In moments, he could see her frustration as clearly as if she stood right in front of him rather than on the other side of the door. At least from here, he didn't have to watch the way her wavy, caramel hair curved around her face and brushed her shoulders. Didn't have to contend with wide green eyes that could set his heart pounding with a single sidelong glance.

"The sooner you let me in, the sooner I state my business and leave. I have a friend who needs a bodyguard. Right away."

Brandon shook his head as he rounded the desk, wondering why he bothered delaying the inevitable. New Orleans, for all its various neighborhoods and outlying parishes, wasn't a big place—the French Quarter even smaller. Serena and her family—headed by her mother, Madame Endora, the foremost psychic in this booming colony of con men and swindlers—were relative fixtures in the Vieux Carre as much as the wrought-iron scrollwork and the Mardi Gras beads that dangled from them long after Fat Tuesday.

And since Serena now owned her own business in the heart of the Quarter, he accepted that he couldn't avoid her for long. Better to face her right here and now—in his office and on his terms. Surely he could trust himself to keep out of trouble long enough to hear about her friend.

He flicked the lock and pulled the door open, pasting on the stern expression he usually reserved for new recruits.

She countered with a grin that could boil sugarcane down to clear, hot syrup. Folding her arms, she caused her breasts to pout beneath a tank top tighter than a turn maneuver in enemy airspace. When she'd first knocked, only the hair on the base of his skull had sprung to attention. Now, other parts of his body followed suit, making him incredibly sorry he'd tucked his black T-shirt inside his equally dark jeans.

"You don't make it easy for a body to be friendly," she complained, her voice only half-annoyed as she turned to reclaim a basket and thermos from where she'd perched them on a tower of boxes near the door.

He returned to his desk and picked up an empty file folder. "I didn't come back to New Orleans to renew friendships."

At least, not ours.

He didn't need to share that sentiment aloud, and apparently, she didn't care one way or another. She shrugged and waved her hand in front of her as if she was clearing his negative karma from her path.

"You'd best rethink that strategy. Making a business work in this town is all about who you know." She dropped the basket in the center of his desk, unlatched the wicker and flipped back the top. A smell as sweet and light as pure heaven wafted past the dusty odor of half-unpacked boxes and freshly used gun oil.

"Beignets?" he asked, his tone entirely too wishful. "From Café du Monde?"

She grinned and shook her head. "Better. From Miss Lily's iron skillet. She told me to tell you she expects a proper visit from you before the week is out."

Brandon's mouth watered at the aroma of the hot French doughnuts. Mixed and fried by Serena's mother's lifelong cook and companion, the treats, their smell, instantly transported him back to the lazy days of his youth, back when he and Serena had been inseparable friends. They'd stirred up and then avoided as much trouble as they could, running wild in the Quarter in the hot summers or caged in the halls of St. Simon's parochial school during the fall, winter and spring. She held the basket toward him, luring him into her personal space—space that just a minute ago had been *his* sanctuary. Serena invaded his office with the ease and confidence of a military leader staging an uncontested coup.

He just had to decide if he still possessed the ability to put up a potent resistance. He took a beignet from the lacy interior, then grabbed the whole basket just to show her who was boss.

Gesturing toward the thermos, he took a ravenous bite. "Is that café au lait?"

She twisted off the top with a similarly crooked grin and poured a generous helping into his army mug. "I added sugar before I left. You still drink it sweet, don't you?"

He answered by blowing on the coffee and taking a hearty

swig. The bittersweet taste of coffee, chicory and milk heated his mouth, awakened his tongue and slid down his throat into a belly already blanketed by the doughnut. He could get used to such attention and culinary delight. In fact, he had an ironclad plan to find a wife as soon as possible who could whip up beignets and coffee that would beat even Miss Lily's in a taste test. Luckily for him, Serena's kitchen skills were limited to boiling water for tea.

"Tell me about your friend, the one who needs the bodyguard."

A tiny frown tilted her coral-tinted lips, then flitted away. "All business, huh?"

"That's why you're here, isn't it?"

She screwed the top back on the thermos and looked around his sparse office. He didn't have much to offer by way of seating. A metal folded chair sat in front of his secondhand desk and battered leather seat. A stack of boxes. A pile of books. She settled on the windowsill, her hands cushioning her thighs, her psychedelic wraparound skirt tousled by the breeze filtering in from outside.

"It's a fairly challenging case," she said.

"I'm listening."

"It may well be over your head, you being new and all."

Willing himself not to betray his emotions, Brandon leisurely leaned back in his chair and crossed his legs at the ankles. Inside, he raged with a simmering mix of anger, guilt and cynical suspicion—emotions only this woman could stir. Without much attention to subtlety, never her forte anyway, Serena was laying a trap. And since she knew him so incredibly well—fifteen years of relative estrangement notwithstanding—he wondered if he had the maneuvering power to steer clear of her snare.

Well, a Nightstalker pilot always had at least *one* option.

A bluff.

"You're probably right. I'm too new. You should find someone else."

He bit into a second beignet, careful not to breathe too hard unless he wanted a coating of powdered sugar all over his desk.

His easy retreat didn't phase her. She knew him better than to buy his sudden reluctance to take on a challenge beyond his ability. She dangled her sandals, watching her brightly painted toes as they swung above the baseboard.

"Nice try, Brandon."

"You don't know me anymore, Serena. Maybe I'm tired of danger and long-shot odds."

She snorted. "Maybe. But I'll *bet*—" she emphasized the word with just enough certitude to show him the direction of her strategy "—you won't be able to say no."

"Never make a bet you can't win, Serena. Didn't I teach you anything when we were kids?"

"Oh, yeah. You taught me a lot of things." For an instant, he thought he heard recrimination in her voice, but when he turned to look into her eyes—an error if ever there was one— he saw nothing but fiery challenge in her bottomless, gulf-green gaze. "Like the fact that you can't resist an honest wager, if the stakes are high enough. Are those darts?"

From her perch on the sill, she toed the brass case on the corner of his desk, drawing his gaze to the silky smoothness of her tanned leg and the glittering crystal dangling from her ankle bracelet.

He cleared his throat. "Yeah. So?"

"I bet you one bull's-eye, shot in our traditional manner, that you'll take this case."

He swallowed the last of his beignet and chased the doughy delectable down with half a cup of coffee.

"Do you think it's wise to gamble with your friend's safety?"

She leaned back against the window jamb, her hair catching the breeze and fluttering all too attractively around her cheeks. "I know what I'm doing. Do you?"

Brandon grumbled, certain he hadn't known what he was doing since he opened the door to let her inside. He'd spent fifteen years trying to keep Serena Deveaux out of his life. They were too alike—too reckless, too rash, too willing to throw caution to the wind and fly straight into disaster. He decided long ago to surround himself with people who would anchor him, keep him grounded and sane and out of trouble. For most of his adult life, that meant his army regiment, members of the elite Nightstalker squad—men who relished danger as much as he did, but had the discipline to pull back when ordered or when a battle couldn't be won.

Now that he was a civilian, Brandon had to find a new means to tether his wild ways. He certainly couldn't turn to his parents or brothers. Even Aunt Tillie had a devilish streak and a rap sheet. What he needed was a wife. A sensible, practical woman who would teach him the comforts and pleasures of home and hearth.

And though he hadn't done much by way of wife-shopping since his retirement or his return to New Orleans, he certainly planned to make it a priority soon. The sooner the better. But certainly not this morning. Serena Deveaux, beautiful and sexy and undeniably fun, was the most impractical, insensible woman he'd ever known. She would make his life interesting, definitely. But she'd also make his life hell if he gave her an opening.

On the other hand, if he played his darts right, maybe he'd turn the tables to his advantage, have a little fun before he got down and serious. He was a Chance, after all. Games and bets and high-risk ventures were his family's specialty. While he most definitely had his eye on a future with a stay-at-home wife, three kids and a huge mortgage, he'd long given up trying to *entirely* resist the thrilling lure of unknown outcomes.

He smoothed his hand beneath his collar, his scalp suddenly itchy and his shoulders tight. Of all the people in the world, Serena should have known better than to mess with him. A person didn't make a bet—any bet—with a Chance unless they were completely prepared to lose.

Brandon eyed the polished brass case on his desk as he considered her offer. "I don't think this is a good idea."

Her sea-green eyes glittered with sunlight from the window, then crinkled deviously.

"A Chance backing down from an honest wager? There's an ancestor or two rolling around in their graves." She flattened her hands against the windowsill. "I can feel them."

Brandon shook his head, trying to remember if he'd ever met a woman who could pull off such swaggering self-confidence and still manage to look as fresh as a newly bloomed magnolia. Someone was definitely having a grand old laugh over this one. Here he was, hell-bent on starting a respectable life, and who sashays into his office but the playful, unpredictable sprite who'd taught him at a young age never to underestimate a woman.

"There are a lot of bodyguards in New Orleans, Serena. I'm sure you can hire someone else without resorting to games."

She shoved off the sill, clapping her petite, sandaled feet on his scuffed wood floor. She crossed her arms, adorned with swirling gold armbands that caressed her just above the elbows and a set of bracelets around one wrist, and jutted her slim hip to the left, her standard stalwart stance.

"That sounds weird coming from a man who's always

treated life as a big competition. You don't like to lose, which should make you a perfect bodyguard." She picked up his appointment book, flipped the blank pages without comment, then set it aside. "Look, you don't want to work with me, but I want to hire you. You need the job, my friend has money to burn and I *know* you can't resist the opportunity to beat me, even if it is just darts."

She opened the lid to the brass case, fingering the stiff blue-and-red feathers, raking her orange-tipped nails along the slim, shiny body of the dart, nearly pricking her finger on the razor-sharp tip. "I guess I'll just have to dare you."

He forced his gaze away from her and her haughty, naughty smile and judged the distance to his target. As much as he wondered why Serena insisted on spurring his competitive nature—and if he wasn't dreaming, his libido as well—instead of simply finding another agency, he wasn't about to ruin his perfect record by forfeit.

He'd just hung the dartboard this morning, directly across from his desk. He expected customers to be scarce until he drummed up interest in his protection agency. So he'd brought some toys along—the dartboard, two decks of cards and a handheld flight simulator—to ward off boredom while he worked on a business plan and made some calls. He had no idea Serena would drop in with a basketful of hot beignets, a thermos of café au lait and a challenge.

His grin widened with impending victory. "What are your terms?"

She matched his smile with a self-assured beam that was hers and hers alone. "Simple. When I win, you take the case. No arguments."

"And when I win?"

She shook her head as though the notion was as ridiculous

as them ever rekindling the friendship they'd lost long ago. "Name your prize."

She stepped back and waved her hand as if she controlled the very air they breathed.

He ran a finger over the boxed darts, imagining he could feel the electric sizzle of her touch still crackling around the metal casing. "If I win, you're willing to do whatever I ask you to?"

Serena snatched a steaming French pastry from the basket. "Last time I lost to you, I had to sing four verses of 'When The Saints Come Marching In' while dressed like Sister Mary Claire during the mayor's visit for Catholic Schools Week. Doesn't that prove I'm willing to do *anything?*"

Despite his every effort to remain aloof, he chuckled at the memory. The scene seemed as fresh as the breakfast she'd brought—Serena dressed in full black habit, singing off-key while Father Michael chased her around the cafeteria—all because Brandon's team beat hers in a Sunday game of corkball.

Unfortunately, dressing her in a nun's habit would seem like a crime against humanity today.

"I can be very imaginative," he warned her, closing his eyes against the images of Serena dressed in nothing but artfully woven feather boas, the kind she'd collected for years. "Still want to take the risk?"

She took a bite of the beignet, tearing a powdered, sugar-coated corner with straight white teeth, then licked the snowy remnants with a stiff, pink tongue. Hands on hips and eyes blazing, she locked her gaze with his.

"I triple-dog dare you."

His eyes widened. She'd skipped the double dare and had gone straight to the ultimate challenge. The armor gauntlet tossed at his feet. The line drawn in the sand.

A feral growl vibrated in the back of his throat.

"Stand aside." He stretched his arms, hoping to send her scrambling back to give him some much-needed breathing room. He'd be damned if he missed this shot. He would *not* lose to Serena Deveaux, even if winning meant briefly letting her back into his life.

But she didn't succumb to intimidation easily. She never had. Gracefully, she twisted to avoid his stretch, but didn't budge an inch.

"Am I making you nervous?" She polished off the rest of the beignet in three ravenous bites, then licked the sugar dust from her ringed fingers. "I thought that secret military force you were in required nerves of steel."

She cleared a spot on the corner of his desk and slid her hip atop it—half sitting, half leaning so that her wraparound skirt flared enough to give him a second, longer glimpse of her smooth, tanned legs. The distinctive scents of magnolia and cinnamon wafted from her sun-kissed skin, scents he'd assumed until now had come from outside. The fragrance of the French Quarter surrounded her like her best feathered boa, all at once genteel and wanton. Lazy and sweet, but simmering with spice.

He cleared his throat and chose his dart.

"Stay where you are and watch how it's done."

Turning to face the window, he balanced the blue-feathered, silver-tipped dart over his left shoulder. He had to shoot backward—that was their traditional manner—but aiming placed her firmly in his peripheral vision. He closed his right eye. It didn't help. He took and held a long, deep breath, angling his elbow and forearm for optimum velocity and marksmanship. He cocked back, focused on the bright red dot at the center of the board and…waited.

He knew Serena. First, she'd try to distract him by coughing or sneezing.

She rewarded his suspicion with a mischievous grin.

Okay, maybe she'd graduated beyond uncontrollable noises to break his concentration.

So he waited for her last-minute question, the inevitable "Shouldn't you twist your shoulder a little lower?"

Thirty seconds passed. She pressed her lips together while she admired the condition of her fingernails.

Brandon found it hard to fathom, but perhaps Serena no longer stooped to juvenile antics.

Confident once again, he turned completely away from the target and prepared to shoot. That's when she combed her fingers through her wavy hair then let the caramel curls float in a breezy mass around her shoulders.

The dart found its home at the center of his unframed picture of Rush Limbaugh—a gag gift from his brother Kell, who insisted early retirement from the military would turn Brandon into an ultraconservative ditto-head. He winced and felt a phantom pinch in his groin in response to the throw. Too bad the photo wasn't just a head shot. Well, actually…

"Ha! I win." Serena's squeal and victory dance, a sweet little shimmy, increased the ghostly ache in his lower body to a very real pain.

"You haven't won yet." He should have guessed she hadn't abandoned her modus operandi. She'd just changed her mode of distracting him to one he wouldn't anticipate. "You still have to shoot."

"All I have to do is make sure I don't emasculate Rush further," she taunted.

She licked her lips again, her grin crooked, but swallowed whatever indelicate comment invariably danced on the tip of her tongue—a very moist, very inviting tongue, Brandon thought as he watched her dampen her coral lips one last time while she picked a dart from the case on his desk.

The possibility of beating him polished her skin with a warm glow and rocked her hips in a slight but rhythmic swing left over from her victory dance. She could hardly contain her excitement. Brandon scowled, refusing to be drawn into her wicked web of mirth.

He stood his ground—though he did defer two steps to the right to allow her a fair angle—and tried not to think about what had changed so drastically about Serena Deveaux.

The smattering of freckles that once dotted her cheeks and nose had faded beneath the power of her sun-kissed skin. That night when he'd touched her in what must have been the sloppiest grope a teenage boy had ever attempted, her body had resembled the rigid grid of the French Quarter streets, all straight lines and sharp corners. Now, her arched cleavage, slim waist and rounded hips brought to mind the lazy curves of the Mississippi River and made him glad he'd come home.

Betting Serena would have ended up this gorgeous is one challenge he would have willingly lost.

She still brimmed with a love for life he'd never known anyone to match. She still simmered with a fiercely competitive spirit she'd probably deny till the day she died. What he didn't know was how she, simply by filling out, could have him thinking about hot sweaty sex at ten o'clock in the morning. Especially after she'd left him cold all those years ago.

She winked at him before glancing briefly over her shoulder and firing the red-feathered dart with hardly a moment's preparation. The tiny thud of metal hitting crimson wood bloomed her Cheshire-cat grin.

CHAPTER TWO

BULL'S EYE.

She didn't even have the decency to make the shot look difficult.

"You've been practicing." He attempted a neutral observation of her improved skill, but still managed to sound surly. She rolled her eyes and retrieved the darts, crossing the room with the same flow of movement as her tie-dyed skirt.

He'd lost. At least now he'd find out the nature of his first assignment.

"I play a game or two when I eat at Rollo's," she explained. "He serves a mean oyster po'boy and reserves a board for Drew and me on Wednesdays." She leaned over to return the darts to the velvet-lined case, seemingly unaware of how the heady mix of spices clinging to her skin made him hunger for a lot more than a fried oyster sandwich.

He drained the rest of the thermos into his mug and downed the milk-and-chicory coffee in two large swallows. Aunt Tillie had mentioned the swirling rumors that Drew and Serena were planning to marry. For once, he'd doubted his aunt's usually impeccable sources. Serena had eschewed the institution of marriage her entire life, choosing her parents' high-profile divorce as a prime example that certain men and women had no business taking vows. She'd included herself in that list. He had no reason to think she'd changed her mind.

But apparently, she and Drew still hung out together. He shouldn't have been surprised. The three of them had spent more time together than some brothers and sisters he knew. The fact that the threesome had continued as a twosome after he left rankled more than it should have. Was he jealous? Please. He was just being nostalgic.

"Drew Stuart? You still hanging out with that geek?"

For the first time that morning, Serena's cocky grin faltered. "He's not a geek. He's just not a goon like you."

Brandon grabbed his gut and feigned an expression of pain. "That hurts."

She straightened her spine and impaled him with a no-nonsense glare that would have made his commanding officer proud. "Grow up, Brandon. I won the bet. I need a bodyguard and you're the man."

She punctuated her assertion with an orange-tipped fingernail, painted like a…sunset, he guessed, attempting to decipher the miniature scene upside down.

She glared at him until he met her stare with his.

"*You* need a bodyguard?"

"For my friend." She picked up his day planner again, attempting to hide her momentary fluster behind the faux-leather book. "Write in 'Serena's—seven o'clock.'"

"Your place? Serena, what are you trying to pull? If you're the one in danger…" *If you're the one in danger…what?* He would refuse to help her? He would let a fifteen-year-old wound to his male pride prevent him from protecting her from harm?

She hurriedly gathered the remnants of breakfast and tossed them in her basket. "Don't sound so hopeful, I'm just the 'contact.' Is that the word? It sounds so…intriguing." She wiggled her eyebrows and fingers, mocking the cloak-and-dagger element of his new job—the same rudimentary risk that drew him to the profession in the first place. After putting his life on the line for eleven years and sustaining himself on the rush, he'd chosen his new profession precisely because of the intrigue and danger.

Of course, not having been keen on taking orders during his former army life, he'd gone into business for himself.

He wondered if he would have made the same choice to start his new career in the French Quarter if he'd known Serena would be at the heart of his first job. She offered the last beignet to him, which he took, though he'd already eaten two. A deep-rooted craving stirred in his belly that had nothing to do with food. But since Serena was, well, Serena, he had no choice but to satiate himself with freshly fried and sugared dough. "So who's this *friend?* Criminal? Celebrity?"

She stuffed the thermos into the calico and lace-lined basket. "Just your average French Quarter business owner."

"Like you?"

She eyed him warily. "You know what I do?"

Aunt Tillie hadn't been stingy in her updates about Serena. Though he figured she would have used her multiple science degrees to discover a cure for the common cold or invent a vehicle that could travel at light speed, Serena operated some sort of beauty salon that catered to both the New Orleans elite and tourists alike.

"I heard you run a massage parlor." He couldn't resist teasing her. The instinct, as natural as blinking, imbued him with a vigor he hadn't felt in years.

"I have a *spa* on Toulouse Street." She pursed her lips, either cutting off a retort to his massage-parlor crack or fighting her urge to embellish her statement with more detail.

Brandon sat back in his squeaky new office chair, attempting to keep his assessment nonchalant. As long as he'd known her, Serena rarely answered direct questions without more minutiae. But replaying their short conversation this morning, he realized she'd been unusually tight-lipped.

Which meant, of course, that she was up to something.

Curiosity stirred. Serena Deveaux had never effectively told *him* an untruth. "A spa? What, like a gym?"

She shook her head and scooted his single folding chair nearer his desk. Turning the chair around, she sat sideways, one knee tucked beneath her, one leg jutted lazily to the right and her arms folded over the backrest. Except for the fact that she wasn't blond, she resembled an old black-and-white photo of Jean Harlow his grandfather had kept since the war. Her wide green eyes seemed weighted by her glorious fan of lashes. Her cheeks glowed with a natural color that bloomed as she spoke.

"No. Like a spa. Massages. Herbal wraps. Facials." She wiggled her fingers at him, making music with her bangle bracelets. "Nail art. I have a holistic dietician and massage therapist on staff and a signature line of natural teas and aromatherapy scents." Little by little, her intrinsic enthusiasm crept into her voice. He hadn't seen Serena in a long time, but he knew she wouldn't do anything every day unless she loved it.

"And you make money doing that?"

She rolled her eyes at him again, this time leaving them in a heavenward position for a long moment to express her exasperation.

"Let's just say I'm not starving."

He snickered. "That doesn't answer my question."

"Since when are you the fiscal patrol?"

"Since I left the service and have to pay for room, board

and three squares. I've got a business to run." Adjusting to civilian life really wasn't as difficult as Brandon implied, but he did intend to make this business work on his own terms. "I can't waste my time watching one of your crazy pals burn incense unless I'm paid in advance, expenses included—bet or no bet."

When she slipped those blazing nails down the front of her V-necked tank, Brandon felt as if he'd just swallowed a desert sandstorm. His attention riveted to her breasts, she produced a small rectangle of green paper from beneath her purple top.

His gaze followed the treasure when she tossed it on his desk. From the visible corner, he recognized the check made out for fifteen hundred dollars. His fingers itched to caress the paper, still softened by the warmth of her skin.

"Will that hold you over for a few days?"

The ache in his groin, undoubtedly visible through the worn denim of his jeans, made him grateful he was sitting. He scooted closer to the desk, just in case. This woman was not the same Serena he used to play hide-and-seek with. Thinking about finding her in a dark, secluded space rushed a torrent of moisture into his mouth—until he remembered the last time he'd lured her into a dark, secluded space.

Guilt nagged at the edge of his consciousness. He hadn't exactly given her much warning, coming on to her on what should have been the best night of her life. Friends didn't paw each other behind the bleachers. But friends also didn't slap each other and run off to hide.

"I'll manage," he answered. He pocketed the check quickly, before his brain could fully register the effects of the moistened paper on his libido.

She stood and stared at him for a moment, the slight indentation in her cheek telling him she was biting the inside of her mouth. Like gnawing her nails, her habit was an old one and, obviously, one she hadn't overcome. He decided she wasn't lying to him. But she was holding back details—details that might make him decide not to honor their bet. Of course, he was a Chance, one of the last descendants of a long, infamous line of gamblers, speculators and die-hard risk-takers. He'd honor the terms or die trying. That was in the family creed.

And damn it, Serena knew that long before she'd come knocking on his door.

"Good. My house, tonight, at seven." She wrote her address on the back side of a New Orleans Events flyer he'd brought up from his mailbox. "We'll have dinner and discuss your…assignment."

"I need to know more before then."

She pondered his request a moment. "The assignment will probably last two weeks. Yeah, that ought to do it." The last comment, clearly meant to be thought, not spoken, engaged his internal radar.

"Serena, what aren't you telling me?"

She stood and straightened her skirt. "We'll talk tonight."

"Why not here and now? What are you trying to pull?"

"Pull? Me? Gosh, Brandon, don't you remember what a bad conniver I am?" She masked her face with a fake glaze of innocence and backed toward the door. "Remember that time I tried to trick you into eating those super-hot chilies?"

"You ended up eating them yourself. And drinking an entire gallon of milk out of my fridge." The memory, once again, made him chuckle. "I couldn't have my Wheaties the next morning."

His physical condition back to a relatively normal state, Brandon stood, sensing a crack of weakness in the confident air she'd surrounded herself with all morning. He edged around his desk, his gaze locked with hers.

"You survived," she reminded him. "I had heartburn for a week." She felt around behind her for the doorknob.

He took a few more steps in her direction. An underlying panic flashed in her eyes. He was making her uncomfortable. Good. Since she'd come into his office, he'd experienced a lack of balance and control that was entirely her fault. "You deserved it. It was a dirty trick you tried to pull."

"I had a good reason."

"As I recall, you always have a good reason."

She turned to open the door. She glanced over her shoulder, her eyes bright and her smile sincere. "That's one of the things you can count on with me, Brandon. I have good reasons for the stuff I do."

She slipped out before he had a chance to reply. *Good reasons.* Like when they were nine and she roped him into playing Prince Charming in her children's-theater production by promising he could use a real sword and kiss Renée Perkee on the lips. Or when she volunteered him to teach the entire faculty of St. Simon's High School how to play craps for Casino Night, a talent your average eleventh-grader wasn't supposed to have. Or the night he was so far out of line, he should have slapped some sense into himself.

Serena Deveaux, for all her strange ideas, then and now, never failed to make his life interesting, unpredictable. Much like his missions with the Nightstalkers. Toying with the eyeglass case on the corner of his desk, he wondered if the corrective lenses inside would have given him the edge to beat Serena at darts. He'd become adept at compensating for his failing eyesight, until his fuzzy vision nearly cost him his life and the lives of his crewmen. So he'd retired. And after eleven years in the service, he could use a little temporary fun. He could definitely use the fifteen hundred dollars.

Serena knew anybody and everybody worth knowing in the city and beyond, thanks in part to being the child of New Orleans' foremost psychic medium and a famed Hollywood director. She had more contacts than the security system at the Pentagon and could be just the ticket to launching his business with a bang.

That she'd transformed into a sexy minx made the prospect all the more challenging. And a Chance *never* backed down from a challenge.

AT THE BOTTOM of the stairs, Serena slid down and put her head between her knees, lifting her eyes once to smile at the sour-faced glare from some woman with horrendous taste in hats. But even the purple chapeau with silver ostrich plumes couldn't distract Serena for long. Had she owned smelling salts, she would have taken a big whiff right about now— anything to undo the unexpected effects of being alone with Brandon Chance.

She settled for a vial of lavender oil she wore around her neck. Dabbing two drops in the palm of her hand, she took a deep whiff. She could barely breathe. Panic remained twisted around her lungs.

Panic and something she didn't want to acknowledge— raw, lustful desire.

Brandon, like all the Chance men—younger brothers, Kellan and T.J., included—had always been a looker, but until sometime in her junior year, she'd never allowed herself to think of him as anything more than a surrogate older brother. Little by little, her feelings for him became what she'd thought was a harmless crush—a teenage attraction that wouldn't amount to anything more than a pleasant memory. That's why she'd reacted as she had all those years ago. He didn't have any business touching her like that, kissing her like that, making her feel things a girl not yet seventeen shouldn't feel.

The remnants of her reactions rushed back. When he'd lured her into that darkened corner of the gym, her heart had beat more furiously than a summer rainstorm on a tin roof. Then, he'd grabbed her, kissed her, sloppy and drunk and fumbling with her clothes, until she could do nothing but fight to get away. His apology the next day had been hard to hear, and even harder to accept. But she had, unwilling to lose her best friend over a stupid mistake.

Yet she'd lost him anyway. And no matter the sizzling attraction and sexual awareness that had assaulted her in his office, she couldn't allow chemistry to cloud her thinking. Her "affair" with Brandon would be a fake one, for the sole purpose of forcing Drew to see that his marriage quest was ruining their relationship.

She ran her hands through her hair, realizing that with any other man than Brandon, she would not ignore the messages her body was sending. She had never denied herself the pleasures of romance, the intimacies of adult interaction. But Brandon was everything she wasn't, even if they'd once had so much in common. He'd always been somewhat cynical. Inherently competitive. Driven. More inclined to conquer the world than make peace with it. As anxious to discover puzzles and contradictions as she was to avoid them and just enjoy the moment.

Simplicity, simplic…

Emerson's mantra died before she reached the third repetition. Simplicity and Brandon Chance didn't coexist. The man was complication personified.

Yet, here she was, nearly thirty, not inexperienced, and the man had her heart doing back flips. Not to mention her liquid, hot reaction to his thick black hair, piercing gray eyes and broad, square shoulders.

She was a real sucker for big shoulders.

Maybe this was all a very bad idea.

Lord, Brandon Chance was one gorgeous hunk of man.

No.

She stood up, took a deep, cleansing breath, fluffed her hair and willed her heart to stop doing gymnastics. She'd protected herself from his misguided magnetism on graduation night; she'd do it again.

Reinvigorated by her resolve, she stepped into the sunlight and down the stone steps. Sniffing her palm again, Serena headed toward Esplanade Avenue on her way back to the spa. She needed something stronger than aromatic oil to restore her balance—she'd mix up a cup of her special brew, maybe schedule a massage.

The side street was quiet. Cars lined the stone curb, and at least one idled nearby. With a quick glance left and right, Serena stepped in front of a parked sedan and started across the street. She was halfway to the other side when a black car peeled off the curbside and barreled straight toward her.

CHAPTER THREE

BEFORE SHE COULD react, a body, hard and lean, half tackled, half carried her onto safe ground. She landed in a circular bed of ivy with Brandon Chance and his gorgeous mass of male muscle firmly atop her. The roar of the speeding car died away, leaving only the sound of her heartbeat and panted breaths—intimately commingled with his—to break the sudden silence.

That, and Brandon's muttered curse. "Does the word *ditz* mean anything to you?"

Wind absent from her lungs, Serena coughed into the green leafy vine and threw her elbows back until Brandon grunted and shifted to the left, allowing her room to steal some air. But not much. His shoulders and chest and stomach and hips pressed against her like a living brick wall, hard and hot and heavy, in a way that wasn't entirely unpleasant. Not unpleasant at all.

"No, but *oaf* is suddenly crystal clear." She struggled beneath him, shoving against him with her backside without thinking of the consequences. Sexual awareness jolted through her and rooted her to the spot. His erection pressed against her bottom sent a surge of pure lust to every erogenous zone in her body—a few she hadn't realized existed until right now in the grass. The yin and yang of basic need—

his hard to her soft, his male to her female—grabbed her at the core and held her captive.

She willed herself to speak. "I know you hate to lose, but isn't this a bit extreme?"

He rolled over, grunting when his back met the chiseled stones separating the ivy from the grass. She rediscovered her ability to breathe.

"In case you didn't notice, I just saved your life." His tone demanded her undying gratitude.

Men.

"Delusions of grandeur," she mumbled, pulling herself onto her knees. "I would have made it out of the way on my own."

A cool spring breeze drifting up her thigh brought her attention to the state of her skirt. Treating him to a view of her panties furthered the indignity of crouching on all fours in a pile of foliage. She yanked her skirt down and growled at him all in the same breath.

That arrested his attention. His gaze immediately caught her dash for modesty, and she didn't miss the cloud of disappointment that darkened his eyes from silver to thundercloud gray. "And what if you didn't?"

"The car would have swerved."

Except that it hadn't. The fact obviously occurred to Brandon at precisely the same moment. His gaze turned from skeptical to accusatory.

She moved to stand on her own, but he grabbed her elbow and pulled her up with him instead. With a tiny bounce, she landed inches from him, her nose even with the base of his throat.

"*You* need the bodyguard, not some friend."

Serena glanced back at the road, quiet now that the car was long gone. She just hadn't been looking where she was going.

The driver probably wasn't paying attention. And she'd been distracted by the unwanted and unexpected return of her adolescent lust for Brandon. She'd looked both ways, but hadn't checked for cars pulling out of curb spaces. No one was *really* trying to hurt her.

Unfortunately, she couldn't tell Brandon that just yet.

"I'm fine," she insisted.

"That's not an answer, that's an evasion. Are you in danger?"

She slapped the clinging ivy leaves from her elbows and knees, then plucked wayward twigs from her hair. "No. I mean, no, I don't think so." She shook her head, realizing this incident could help her cause. She needed him to believe she was in danger, just not until tonight when she'd had time to prepare. "Not at this precise moment," she amended.

"Not at this precise moment." He repeated her words exactly as any disbelieving, retired military-commander-turned-bodyguard would. Understated annoyance clung to his clipped tone. Then he bit his tongue and growled much as she had earlier, though the guttural grumble rumbling from his throat made him a rottweiler to her Chihuahua.

He tugged her by the elbow out from under the tree, and quickly surveyed the area, holding her close. His cologne—musky without a hint of spice or sweetness to offset the overwhelming masculine scent—nearly kept her from noticing he was now in bodyguard mode. Except she didn't want him on the job. Not now. She had work to do this morning. A lunch date with Drew she simply couldn't cancel, not when she planned to set the wheels of progress in motion after dessert. Brandon could start tonight. After work. After dinner.

After I have time to squelch my raging hormones.

She tried to wrench her elbow free, but quickly learned the power of his grip. "What are you doing?"

"You paid for three days' worth of protection. Consider the meter running."

"I don't want the meter to run." He glanced at his watch as if noting the time. She tugged at the nylon band. "Turn it off! I'm fine. The car was a fluke."

He twisted his wrist from her grasp, yet kept her firmly in his. "But you did hire me for yourself, didn't you?"

She refused to answer. Couldn't answer. The feel of his hands on her—of his body on hers—overrode her ability to contain a situation that had already gotten out of her control.

"Have you received threats before today? Before that car tried to mow you down?"

"That car didn't try to mow me. It was an accident." She struggled against his grip again, huffing when her actions proved fruitless. She'd have to try reason, which as far as she could remember never worked with Brandon once he made up his mind about something. "I wasn't paying attention. I must have stepped into the street without looking. It happens all the time. Well, not to me, but to other people."

Brandon half listened to her attempt at rational logic while he scanned the street for any sign of danger. Determining the immediate area secure now that the dark-colored, older-model Chevy Corvette Stingray was long gone, Brandon turned his attention squarely to Serena. She wasn't biting the inside of her mouth, and her eyes, liquid and lucid and green as the gulf, fairly begged him to believe her.

She could be right. He'd been so intent on catching her to return her frilly basket, he hadn't noticed the Corvette, either, until he'd stepped between parked cars. His crack observation skills allowed him to recognize the make and model. He might have caught the license plate if he didn't hate wearing his glasses so much.

"Maybe the car was an accident, but that doesn't explain why you went to such interesting lengths to hire me." He released her arm, wincing inwardly when he noticed the ring of red his fingers left on her skin. "'Fess up."

Stalling, she made a production of ensuring the straightness of her clothes. "'A deal is a deal and a bet is a bet.' Isn't that your family motto?"

He couldn't contain a crooked grin. Serena remembered the damnedest things from their childhood. "Something like that. So you didn't think I'd help you unless I put Chance honor on the line. Why not?"

She shrugged, then proceeded to pluck leaf bits and mulch from his shirt. "Do I have to remind you?"

Her fingers were quick and nimble, her eyes entirely focused on him and his chest, reminding him why they were no longer friends. He took a step back and divested himself of foliage remains with two large sweeps of his hand. "That was a long time ago, Serena. I got over you."

She glanced aside, silently chagrined. "Of course you did."

But had he? Really? He couldn't deny that Serena didn't fit into his carefully crafted plans for his future, but he also couldn't ignore that since she'd walked into his office, he'd never been so aware of a woman in his life. That cognizance acted like a current of electricity, imbuing him with an energy he hadn't felt in months—if ever. Except for that one infamous instant years ago, Brandon had always been better, smarter, stronger because of Serena.

He wouldn't let her down now, even if it meant spending every minute of his free time in a cold shower until he got to the bottom of her problem. "What kind of threats have you been receiving?"

She hesitated and Brandon immediately saw her intention

to weave a tale. With a hard glance, he convinced her other-wise. She breathed a reluctant sigh.

"Just notes and stuff," she admitted.

"What kinds of notes? Do you still have them?"

"I threw them away."

"No, you didn't. You're not that dumb."

"I threw the first one away."

"That's natural. But the others?"

"Printed on a computer. Inkjet. Standard paper in a plain business envelope. They were slipped into my newspaper after delivery. None of my neighbors saw a thing. The threats are impossible to trace."

"I'll be the judge of that. Where are they?"

"At home."

"Let's go."

"I have a staff meeting and a client appointment in an hour. I can't be later than I already am."

Brandon closed his eyes to keep her from seeing them roll upward. He had no right to belittle what she did. Despite her wacky ways, Serena had the brain of a rocket scientist. She could have joined NASA or gone to MIT and graduated with honors had she wanted to. But if she preferred brewing weeds and mixing mud masks for rich socialites, who the hell was he to judge?

"We'll go to the spa first and then head to your house. It will give me a chance to check security at your work."

"I don't want you scaring my clients. I worked very hard to create a clean, relaxing atmosphere."

Brandon could practically hear the wind chimes and koto music and smell the smoking incense. Not his kind of hangout, even for a brief stay. Places like that made him jumpy, as if the atmosphere could melt through the carefully crafted walls he'd built around his private thoughts. To avoid the place, he would have challenged her to a rematch at the dartboard…if not for one important detail.

Serena might really be in danger. Though she insisted the near miss with the car wasn't intentional, the fact remained that she'd hired him as her bodyguard. Serena was a do-it-yourself kind of woman. She wouldn't ask for help—especially from him—unless circumstances left her absolutely no other choice. He'd seen her get herself into and out of trouble more times than a petite little brainiac like Madame Deveaux's oldest daughter should have. Between "Cyclone" Serena and "Dippity" Drew, her eternal sidekick, Brandon's childhood had never been boring.

Why she'd come to him was baffling, but he couldn't contain the slight but warm puffing of his chest. He'd always been her ace in the hole. He wouldn't let her down.

Not this time.

"No one will know I'm there," he insisted. "Where's your car?"

"I don't have one. I caught a ride here with my sister. I planned to walk back."

He fished his car keys out of his pocket and pressed them into her hand. "Mine's the black Jeep parked on the corner. Start it up while I lock my office."

Her palm and fingers, soft and warm and smelling of something floral and sweet, felt small in his hand, but strong. Powerful, even. Yet hers was a power he knew and needed to avoid.

"I'd prefer if you came by later tonight." Her suggestion, clearly a last-ditch effort and accompanied by a tilted grin, cured his momentary lapse. He dropped her hand. Keeping her in his grasp this time had nothing to do with protecting her or ensuring her safety…just plain old sexual attraction.

"Go start the Jeep, and lock the doors. I won't be two minutes."

Serena accepted his decision with her usual aplomb, twirling toward his parking place with grace. He watched her walk to the car, every sultry step down the entire block. When she disengaged the alarm and slid into the driver's seat, he remembered he had something to do.

Back in his office, he loaded his gun, slid into his shoulder holster, pulled on a light sports coat and engaged the answering machine. Before locking the door, he slid his glasses onto his nose and stuffed the case in his pocket as he headed toward his car. Knowing Serena as well as he did, he'd have his work cut out for him figuring out who'd sent the threats. Notwithstanding the few times he'd wanted to wring her neck himself, he couldn't imagine anyone wanting to hurt Serena.

His investigative training was still fresh. His mind quickly but methodically ran through the procedures he'd learned from the intelligence officers he'd worked with, as well as from his training at his former commander's protection agency in Miami. Serena would be a reluctant client, the hardest type to protect. If he had any brains, he'd ditch her at her office and make a run for it to save his fledgling career.

But he wouldn't. A Chance didn't retreat.

He grabbed the car latch, silently cursing the damn family-honor code. *A deal is a deal and a bet is a bet.* Several generations of gamblers and risk-takers had imbued Brandon and his brothers with the inability to back down from a challenge—especially when wild cards were thrown in, making the outcome that much more unpredictable.

And Serena Deveaux was the wildest card he knew.

She unlocked the door when he knocked on the window. In an off-pitch voice, she sang along with Heart's "Never" playing on a classic-rock radio station, while drumming her palms on the steering wheel.

"Get in." She squeezed the words in between two lines of the verse.

Leaning against the open door, he watched her bob to the bass beat, wondering how the heck he was going to survive the next hour, much less the three days to two weeks she planned to employ him.

"No way. You ride shotgun."

Turning up the volume before she exited the vehicle, she slid out of the seat and bopped to the beat all the way around the back of the Jeep. Brandon quickly glanced around, but the surrounding block was clear. He'd talk to her about being less conspicuous later.

They'd be safe once they reached the heart of the Quarter. Serena was weird, but would blend in with the oddballs he'd seen hanging around Jackson Square. Seems Serena, once only privately goofy, had overcome her reserve on all fronts. *Lucky him.*

He didn't have the heart to lower the radio volume until a commercial for potato chips provided a break to the music. He'd stopped at a light on the corner of Dauphine and Toulouse and watched the tourists crossing one block up at Bourbon. The Quarter hadn't changed all that much since he left after high school, except the tourists were more plentiful and enjoyed their hurricanes and daiquiris a little earlier in the day. Serena didn't seem to notice the crowd, though she did roll down the window to shout to a hansom cabdriver and his mule, both by name and with separate salutations.

She directed him up Toulouse, then jumped out of the car

before he had time to pull into a coveted parking space near the corner at Royal.

"I'm late. Meet me inside."

She disappeared into the storefront of Serena's Spa and Scents without incident, so Brandon parked and cased the block on foot. He'd seen no sign of the Corvette during their drive or as he walked the distance from the antiques shop on the corner to Decatur and back. Maybe she was right. Maybe the car incident had nothing to do with the threats she'd received. Of course, he'd never know until she filled him in, something she seemed oddly reluctant to do.

Brandon tucked his glasses back in their case and yanked open the shiny black, glass-paned door into Serena's shop. A soft jingle brought him to the attention of the college-age guy manning the reception desk.

"Welcome to Serena's. You Brandon?"

Brandon bit down his impulse to tell the kid to stand straighter and get a haircut. "Me Brandon."

"Cool. Serena said to fix you a cup of tea and show you round." His voice was an odd mix of California surfer-dude and high-country Creole. "Chamomile or green?"

"Excuse me?"

"Tea. Don't drink it, right? I didn't either till Serena recruited me, man. Can't live without the stuff now. Clears the brain." He mimicked the cleansing effect with a waving sort of gesture, then reached out to shake Brandon's hand. "I'm David."

Brandon resisted the temptation to show him the grip of a man who started his morning with strong Cajun coffee not girly tea, but the boy was young, no more than twenty. No longer responsible for breaking in new recruits, Brandon cut him some slack.

"Work here long?" he asked. Might as well start his investigation with her employees. Even without knowing the nature of the threats, he could store any information away for later.

"Over a year. Since I started Loyola. Serena schedules work around my classes, and she, like, guilts me into studying when things are slow. She's ultra, you know?"

He'd never heard the expression, but understood the meaning implicitly. *Ultra.* Beyond the ordinary.

A perfect description.

"Yeah, I know." Brandon declined the tea and proceeded to look around. As he left the waiting area through a drape of crystal beads, he relegated David to a low slot on his so-far empty list of suspects. The boy's admiration for his boss was fairly obvious. He had no observable reason to threaten her.

In the main spa area, shafts of prismed sunlight broke through the beveled skylights, some stained blue or green, and dappled the thick white carpets and shiny marble floors with the colors of sky and sea. Mirrored walls on three sides reflected the sylvan artistry of the garden outside, fully visible through floor-length windows and a double set of French doors.

Unlike many of the gardens tucked behind the homes and businesses in the Quarter, this one had been totally refurbished, scrubbed clean and polished to a New Age glow. The lawn—short, cropped and green enough to make the caretakers of Augusta similarly colored with envy—sported walkways of smooth granite and trimmed topiaries. The privacy wall was tiled with massive squares of marble. The central fountain, white as genuine alabaster, trickled drops of clear water over an abstract shape Brandon immediately found erotic. He stepped closer to the French doors, trying to determine what exactly in the fountain's shape made him think about sex, when Serena's lilting purr beckoned from the threshold to her office, a small room in the far-left corner, partially hidden behind a mirrored door.

"Soothing, isn't it?"

Soothing wasn't the word he'd choose. For the fountain or its owner. She'd tidied up since their nosedive into the ivy. Her hair shined as if recently brushed, the curls softer, the natural gold highlights brighter. Her lips glistened like the water slithering over the polished, curving shapes of the fountain—stirring images of tongues and flesh and wet, wet heat.

"Captivating."

"You think?" She moved toward him, her walk rhythmic, her voice soft, as if they discussed some intimacy rather than outdoor art. "I had it commissioned last year. It's an interpretive piece. The artist claimed it would intensify the feelings and emotions foremost in the viewer's mind."

That explained the eroticism. Since this morning, he'd had little on his mind other than sex and Serena.

"My clients seem to believe it works."

He dug his hands deep into the pockets of his jeans. "And these clients…what? Ask you to conjure up a gris-gris to make their troubles disappear?"

His comment came out more belittling than he intended, but from the way she stuck her tongue out at him, she hadn't taken the jab to heart.

"I run a spa, not a voodoo shop. That's Endora's realm. And I'm not telling you anything more about what I do if you're going to make fun. You can just do your security check and wait for me in the lobby."

Feeling appropriately chastised, Brandon considered her suggestion, then decided he genuinely needed to know more about her business—for the sake of his investigation, of course. A little "bad mojo," as his aunt called it, could make a client very angry. And since Serena's mother, Endora, was still the reigning queen of New Orleans mysticism, Brandon suspected Serena's tearoom and massage parlor dealt with more than ginseng blends and aromatic oils.

"I didn't mean to make fun. I just never thought you actually believed the mumbo jumbo your mother makes her living with."

"I don't." She folded her arms as if to cross them, but forced them to her sides with a huff. "Not entirely." Taking a deep breath, she closed her eyes, paused, then reopened them and spoke with a serenity she was wildly trying to cling to. "My methods are scientific to the greatest extent they can be. Herbs and teas have the power to positively affect different parts of the body. A lot of your run-of-the-mill psychological or emotional problems can be eased this way. They help a person cope better."

"You're not a licensed holistic doctor."

"No, but I have one on staff. My specialty is teas and aromatherapy." She crossed her arms over her chest, abandoning her battle with defensiveness. "And I do hold a degree in chemistry, in case you forgot."

And one in physics. And one in accounting. Serena bit down hard on her tongue, causing a stabbing sensation that ran straight to the center of her indignation. And anger. And more than a little annoyance. All negative emotions she tried daily to purge from her life. She hated justifying herself to anyone as much as she abhorred throwing around her degrees to gain credibility. It wasn't her style.

She entered the garden, slowly inviting the warmth of the spring sun to bathe away the negative karma Brandon brought with him. Without sunglasses, she squinted into the late-morning sky. The sun, currently angled into the spa's garden, lit the tiny specks of glass imbedded in the granite walkway into flames of cool fire.

She loved the garden this time of day, before the rush of lunchtime clients. She glanced at her watch, noting that she didn't have much time today before she had to meet Drew at the Court of Two Sisters for a meal with a potential client of Drew's and his wife. She'd have to cancel. Either that or bring Brandon with her. No time like the present to set her plan in motion, right?

"I'd like David to run me a list of your clients," Brandon said. With his shoulder propped against the doorjamb, he crossed one black sneaker over the other in a pose of perfect manhood-at-ease. Perfect, *sexy* manhood-at-ease. Brandon's presence in close proximity to the sculpture she'd found erotic since the artist delivered it nearly threw her into carnal overload.

"What for?" She sat on the fountain's ledge and dredged her hand through the water, sparkling sapphire and emerald as the sun above met the small mosaics below the surface. The sculpture behind her was set so the moving water caressed the curves and then dripped into the turquoise pool from smooth points of stone…that suddenly looked like nipples. When Brandon pushed off the doorjamb and joined her, her body temperature rose at least two degrees.

"Suspects. I won't know what I'm looking for until I see the threatening letters, but I should get the ball rolling. I offer a full-service plan—investigation *and* protection." For an instant, he spared the sculpture a quick glance, then sat with his back to the fountain and stretched his long, lean legs across the narrow walkway. He either wasn't affected by the marble's sensual curves, or she just didn't inspire the same arousing thoughts that he did for her.

She fought the urge to splash him. She fought the urge to splash herself. She'd asked him here. Heck, she'd triple-dog dared him right into the center of her personal life. She had no right to complain, no matter how dizzy he made her.

"Suspects, huh?" Exposing her clients to his merry wild-goose chase hadn't been her intention, but Brandon couldn't make a case out of something that didn't really exist. She'd gone to great lengths to make sure her faux threats could not be traced to anyone in particular—especially her. "Tell David what you want. He's a whiz on the computer. Consolidated my entire database over Christmas break."

"David seems to like you a lot. Maybe a little too much?"

She dramatized her smirk with a grunting sigh. He wasn't serious, was he? "He's a kid. Like a little brother."

"To you, maybe, but what about to him?"

Well aware of the dangers of unrequited lust, Serena shook her head. "I'm one hundred percent certain that David's feelings for me are completely platonic. Leave him alone. Unlike you, he wouldn't threaten a flea, even to help the dog."

"Unlike *me?*" Hostility deepened the furrow in his forehead.

"I didn't mean it that way." Serena nearly reached for his hand, but fought the urge. Touching him would be a mistake of epic proportions. "Just don't waste your time or your suspicions on David. He and I have been alone a million times. If he wanted to hurt me or come on to me, he would have."

She glanced at her watch, then stood and smoothed away the imaginary wrinkles in her skirt. "My client will be here soon. Can you make yourself scarce for a while?"

He shook his head, his smile fixed. "You didn't pay me to be scarce. You'd better get used to me, Serena. Until I find out who threatened you, you bought yourself a shadow."

CHAPTER FOUR

SERENA SAT, hands firmly beneath her thighs, trying desperately to keep her attention on Drew's clients, and her fingernails out of her mouth. She could feel the heated weight of Brandon's gaze along the side of her neck. As far as she could tell, he hadn't taken his eyes off her. Not once. Not to order his meal at the table hidden by the lighted ficus to her left. Not to eat. Especially not when Drew draped his arm across the back of Serena's chair. The possessive gesture suddenly made her feel guilty, as if she was doing something horrid, like perpetuating a lie—which she was, on so many different levels her head spun.

Just yesterday, the idea of resorting to half truths and a few bald-faced lies had seemed a small price to pay in pursuit of the greater good. Now, Serena wasn't so sure. Brandon wasn't the average, easily distractable male. Her flirting this morning might have helped her achieve an easier victory with darts, but she couldn't count on feminine wiles now that Brandon was on the job and in such close proximity. In fact, unless she wanted to invite some serious trouble, she had to figure out a way fast to rein in her instinctive responses to his potent masculinity.

If not for the heavenly scents wafting from her barely touched plate, she'd probably still smell that musky essence of his. She still strongly recalled the warmth of his body engulfing hers when he'd tackled her to the ground. The memory of him pressed hard and firm against her made her want to wriggle right out of her skin…and right into his.

"Serena, are you all right?" Drew cupped her shoulder and she nearly jumped out of her chair, bobbling her water goblet so that four pairs of hands reached out to catch it.

She uprighted it first, then dabbled a few wayward drops with her napkin.

"What? Oh! Sorry. I'm not hungry today. Tough morning."

Drew's clear blue gaze followed hers to the lighted plant. He leaned back so his line of vision could bypass the ficus tree to what was drawing Serena's attention on the other side. Silently, Serena prepared an explanation for Brandon's presence. But when Drew turned around, his boyish grin was a mixture of patience and relief.

Serena bent forward around Drew and peeked past the tree herself.

Brandon was gone.

She glanced apologetically at the Smithfields, the New York couple sitting across from them, probably wondering if they should invest in Drew's company when his supposed girlfriend was more interested in decorative foliage than his pitch.

"Would you like a mimosa? Or a Mai Tai?" Mrs. Smithfield held up her drink and shook it, as if the swirling pink liquid could chase away any and all ills.

Serena might have believed a double-bourbon straight up could do the trick, but not today.

"No, thank you." She replaced her napkin on her lap, fiddling with the angle across her skirt. "I don't drink on Tuesdays." She picked up her ice water and took a deep swig. It was sound reasoning not to drink on Tuesdays, though she regretted her vow today. Designed to keep her out of trouble during Mardi Gras, dry Tuesdays were suddenly a risk to her mental health.

Obviously, Mrs. Smithfield didn't grasp her logic. "Why not Tuesdays? Is it your religion?"

Drew capped his hand on her shoulder again, a little roughly this time, to stop her from answering. "Just a quirk. Serena's got a million of them. It's why I love her."

Except that he didn't love her. He just didn't realize it. Just as he wouldn't admit that he'd silenced her to keep her from beginning the inevitable debate on the topic of religion. If he had the gumption, Drew could make himself a millionaire by writing a book on how to effectively avoid conflict and still get what you want.

"That's me." She smiled dopily. "Quirky ol' Serena."

The relief on Drew's face sparked her ire nearly as much as the unexpected return of her attraction to Brandon Chance. Men! Nothing but trouble since that day in the Garden of Eden.

"Excuse me, Miss Deveaux?" A green-jacketed waiter interrupted with a slight bow. "You have an urgent message at the bar."

"Probably something at the spa. Mother must be late for the afternoon readings again. Excuse me, please." She laid her napkin across her seat, grabbed her bag and wove through the heavy lunch crowd of business executives and tourists, leaving Drew to explain her cryptic comment to his guests.

Just as she expected, she found Brandon leaning impatiently against the bar to the right of the maître d's stand, his arms crossed leisurely over that impressive chest of his, his sports jacket hugging his incredible shoulders with a delectable snugness.

"If you wanted to talk to me, you could have come by the

table." Her fervent whisper was nearly lost under the merriment of the crowd. "Why be so secretive? It's just Drew."

He eyed her narrowly and she used every ounce of her grit not to look away. Before they entered the restaurant, he'd explained why his job required he blend into the shadows at this point. While his course of action didn't bode well for her plan to convince Drew that she and Brandon were involved again, he didn't know that—yet.

"I'm trying to be inconspicuous, remember?"

Serena sniffed and gave him a very conspicuous, very complete appraisal of his new attire. Dressed in black jeans, a black polo shirt and matching sports coat, he looked like the devil on a mission of seduction—a mission he might succeed at if she didn't prevail over her hormones.

"I hate to break this to you, Brandon, but you can't do inconspicuous. It's invisible or nothing for a guy like you."

"Is that a compliment? Or a come-on?" He shifted his weight, releasing his arms and adjusting the angle of his shoulders and hips so she suddenly felt as if he'd closed the space between them, though he'd barely moved.

She swallowed the measly amount of moisture in her mouth and decided her best defense was selective hearing and a quick change of subject. "Is something wrong? Or do you have to leave?" she added hopefully, crossing her fingers in full view, until she noticed her hands shaking and tucked the gesture behind her back. She'd been away from him for over an hour, and yet even at a distance, he'd invaded her personal space like bead-seekers on Fat Tuesday. Now, pressed closer by the crowd in the bar, his scent and warmth enveloped her once more, along with that infuriating cocky grin.

"I want to get to work," he answered. "I'm not learning

anything about your stalker by listening to Dippity Drew spout Internet projections and cost estimates."

Dippity Drew. She hadn't heard that in a heck of a long time. "Name calling? Haven't you outgrown anything?"

Other than your clothes? And me?

"I'm kidding. The Drew-boy wouldn't take me so seriously."

She frowned, knowing he was right—and worse, knowing there was a time when she didn't take him so seriously, either. Drew always laughed at Brandon's jokes, no matter how raw they sounded to her. Boys operated on a different level sometimes, a lower level.

"Well, the 'Drew-boy' doesn't know you're here."

"Brandon? Brandon Chance?"

Her indignation caught in her throat like a wad of caramel-coated popcorn. And she hated popcorn.

"Drew-boy!" Brandon reached past Serena and grabbed Drew's outstretched hand, pumping with an enthusiasm that engaged Serena's dishonesty radar. "Didn't know you were here."

And from the look on his face, Drew's radar clicked on as well. "Serena's having lunch with me and some clients," he explained. "Didn't she tell you?"

"He knew." Resignation tinged her retort. "He's teasing."

Drew smiled boyishly and swept aside a constantly unruly lock of his blond hair, reminding Serena how she missed the old days when being Drew's friend meant sharing her new pack of baseball cards or telling Sister Frances Patrick that *she* shot the spitball at the blackboard to keep him out of trouble.

Sometimes, being an adult sucked.

"Haven't changed much in that department," Drew answered, still smiling, still unaware of how Brandon's return was about to disrupt his life. "Heard you'd retired from the service. Opened a detective agency or something?"

Brandon didn't elaborate, but engaged Drew in harmless talk about computers, Drew's family and the Saints' most recent losing season. Serena tried to find her soft place, a comfortable mental zone of blooming gardenia and trickling brooks and no men in any proximity, especially not these two, acting like long-lost brothers and dashing her plan to hell. Then Brandon grabbed her fingers, jolting her back into the restaurant with an electric flash.

"Then Serena brought me breakfast this morning and I finally felt at home again. I have to thank you one more time." He looked at her as if no one else in the world existed. He was flirting, shamelessly. Unfortunately for her ego, Serena knew his attention was only meant to annoy. And though his teasing aided her plan to convince Drew that she and Brandon were destined to reunite, she couldn't help rolling her eyes, knowing only Brandon could see her reaction.

"So you *did* know Serena was here." Drew's lightning-quick glance at her hand, entwined with Brandon's, formed a marble-size pit in the back of her throat.

The seed had been planted—her plan was now in motion. *No turning back now.*

"That's why I came." Brandon's smile tilted with such mischief, he reminded Serena of the time he tied her training bra to the flagpole on the back of his bike. If she didn't tread carefully, she'd end up just as humiliated as that day on the playground.

Drew wasn't a fool. He knew her very, very well. Knew Brandon well and the long history of their fitfeen-year-old acrimony. That's why she'd chosen Brandon, she reminded herself, no matter how much risk she took with her own heart.

No risk, no gain. No risk, no gain. The chant wasn't exactly Emerson, but it had seen her through more than a few tight spots.

"Brandon, Drew and I are having lunch with—" She started to put an end to his charade when he winked, effectively cutting her off.

"I really have to talk to you, Serena. Privately."

His words could have meant a thousand things if not for the sultry rasp in his voice. In a tone meant for candlelit tables in a back corner booth, he established an intimacy between them more effective than anything she could have concocted.

The question was, Why? Still, she played her part by matching his seductive whisper.

"I really can't. Drew's clients…" She shrugged, implying she'd rather not return to the table.

Drew didn't miss the hint, but he continued genially. "If I handed them a pen and a contract, they'd sign right now. Talk to Brandon."

He squeezed Serena's shoulder before he stepped away, then turned back and kissed her on the cheek. Pressing his lips against her skin hard, he startled her with the intensity. Usually, she and Drew parted with a brief sweep of mouth to skin, barely touching, the contact not as important as the gesture.

This time, her friend attempted to brand her, and the desperation in it nearly broke her heart.

"I'll call you next week," Drew said to Brandon. "We'll have a beer after work?"

When Brandon agreed, Drew disappeared into the dining room without a backward glance.

Though he had no way of knowing her plan, Brandon's intimate capture of her hand and rumpled-sheets whisper had helped her cause. Drew *never* engaged in public shows of affection. Because normally, she'd deck him if he did.

Brandon's presence evoked exactly the response she'd hoped for, but she'd arouse Brandon's suspicions if she didn't act at least a little irked. He didn't, after all, know that she wanted him to play the part of her lover.

Did he?

"What was that?" she asked.

"I want to see those threats."

"That's not what I'm talking about." She raised her hand to his eye level, so he could clearly see his fingers still clutching hers.

His pupils grew larger, darkening his eyes to the same pewter hue of her grandmother's antique musket. The effect was just as deadly. When he increased the pressure from his callused fingers, Serena swallowed deeply, then rooted her feet into an even-keeled stance—so if he did something unexpected like kiss her hand, she wouldn't faint right there on the polished stone floor.

He drew her arm closer. She stepped nearer. His gaze lingered on her trembling hands, then he met her breathless stare with another wink. "It *is* a sunset."

"Sunset?"

"On your nails. The manicure you probably paid too much for." He dropped her hand with disinterest.

She may have paid five dollars a finger, but she'd risk destroying them for one good swipe across his smug face. Lord, this man provoked her violent nature without hardly trying!

"You were flirting. Was that just to annoy Drew or were you trying to make him jealous?"

"I'm just your bodyguard, Serena...." Grabbing her elbow, he wound them through a party of six toward the door. The hallway between the restaurant and the street was wide and dark, with smooth stone walls on either side that made the short space cavernous and private all at the same time. Once the doors to the restaurant shut, he swung her back against the stones and blocked her body with his. "I'm not your lover. Why should Drew be jealous?"

She blinked as her eyes adjusted to the sudden darkness, but she could do nothing to make her body adapt to having him so close physically—and mentally. He was on to her. Somehow, in typical Chance fashion, he'd figured out her scam. Either that or he was fishing.

Time to turn the tables with the most powerful weapon in her arsenal—the truth.

"He'd be jealous because he knows how I felt about you— once."

"What? That you hated me for treating you like a cheap slut on graduation night? I apologized for that, Serena. I meant every word."

She saw the self-recrimination in his face, deeper and darker than it had been fifteen years ago when he'd sobered up and then bit out an apology. His words then had undoubtedly soothed his conscience more than they had her hurt feelings. He was a guy, after all. She hadn't expected him to understand the depth of his betrayal. And she'd never had the opportunity to explain.

Until today.

"Brandon, I only hated you for about fifteen minutes. You broke my heart that night, you know? Not the way a lover does. After a while, girls learn to chalk that up to experience. I lost a friend that night. That's worse. *That* stays with you."

He nodded, then hung his head for an instant before glancing back up at her with eyes of pure silver, cleared of the gray storm clouds that shadowed them all morning. When he licked his lips, her heart slammed against her ribs so hard, she felt certain she'd shaken the stone she leaned against. His face inched toward hers, mouth slightly open, wet and warm and inviting.

"Yeah," he agreed. "That does stay with you."

She flattened her palms on the cold, jagged wall, grasping for a handhold to keep her from falling—back into the web of his mystique, back into the desire she thought she'd beat so very long ago.

Too late.

Her lips parted to suggest they leave, to insist they take this somewhere private, but she caught the words with a gasp when the door from the street swung wide, allowing a bright gleam of outdoor light to stream into the dusky hallway. He pushed off the wall.

The air around her instantly changed, even before three tourists walked between them to go inside. Like a curtain tugged partly aside, the hurt from the past had eased, but the attraction most definitely had not. It just jumped up a notch from instinctual to inevitable.

Brandon dug his hands into his pockets, his back flush with the opposite wall—as far away from her as he could manage in the enclosed space. "I acted with my hormones and not my head that night, Serena. That was wrong."

She grinned, knowing from personal experience how hard apologies were for Brandon. "Your head wasn't exactly clear, either, if I recall." She laughed lightly, hoping to abate the tension a bit more.

His smile revealed her success. "No, it wasn't."

Then the humor disappeared. His mouth tightened. His eyes squinted, as if his facial expression alone could convince her of his new resolve. "But I'm thinking clearly now, Serena. I shouldn't have flirted with you back there. And just now…"

"Just now, what?"

Serena had to know. If the attraction between them was not one-sided as she'd first believed, she had some serious decisions to make. Like whether or not to go on with her scheme at great risk to her heart. Or whether or not she should explore her desire for Brandon—to find out if it was just a physical attraction born from what-ifs, or a simple chemical reaction that could be sated then forgotten.

"You almost kissed me, Brandon. Why?"

He shook his head, grabbed her by the elbow, roughly this time, and pulled her toward the door. "Because you make me crazy, you know that? Let's get out of here. We have a stalker to find."

Serena contained the thrilling wave of triumph bubbling inside her. *She made him crazy.* From anyone else, the words might have offended her. But from Brandon, the admission was inherently self-satisfying. Maybe he hadn't written her off so easily when he'd left New Orleans. Maybe his kiss-and-grope fifteen years ago wasn't just a drunken, nonsensical mistake. Maybe, just maybe, he'd wanted her. Like she'd wanted him.

Like she still wanted him, she finally admitted.

She followed him into the sunlight, digging her sunglasses out of her bag. This was a turn of events she hadn't expected. The stakes in her little game just rose to high-roller level, but Serena decided she wouldn't cash out just yet. The jackpot was too tempting, the prize too alluring, to ignore. She might not be the one with Chance for a last name, but she certainly enjoyed risks and payoffs as much as he did.

And very soon, she would show him how much.

ONLY SERENA COULD make unlocking a door erotic. She bent over to peer directly into the antique keyhole, then shimmied her bottom while she worked the skinny key into the lock. She'd twisted her hair into a loose knot atop her head secured with a chopstick she'd found in her purse. Soft caramel curls kissed the back of her neck, in precisely the spot Brandon would choose to kiss if he was ever insane enough to come on to her again.

He had no idea what had come over him at the restaurant. Maybe it was his lifelong rivalry with Drew for Serena's attention, maybe the quaint atmosphere of old-fashioned romance at the Court of Two Sisters. Maybe he'd just been without a bedmate for way too long.

And maybe the same unalterable attraction that had led him to grope her that night in the high-school gym had returned, with a vengeance.

He shifted to the left, shoving the cooler she'd asked him to pick up from the spa onto the scrollwork railing of her front steps. Dredging up old, better-forgotten memories wasn't going to help him with his first order of business: finding out who was threatening her life.

"I'll upgrade the locks on your doors tomorrow morning. If someone was chasing or following you, you wouldn't have much luck getting inside quickly and safely."

She stood up and brushed aside her bangs, her forehead gleaming with moisture.

"This is the original doorknob. And key." A long red tassel twisted around her wrist as she held the key aloft. "Do you know how many people have handled this? No one's lost it in one hundred years. That has to mean something good."

"It'll mean something better if your place is secure. I'm changing the locks first thing tomorrow."

"There's no—"

She cut off her argument by swinging around and manipulating the metal mechanism until he finally heard a loud click. Brandon had the distinct impression the lock wasn't the only thing Serena was manipulating. More than once today, she'd insisted she wasn't in any danger, despite that she had several threatening letters and had shelled out fifteen hundred dollars as a retainer for his services. She was up to something. And he had no doubt he'd soon be finding out exactly what.

She used her shoulder to shove the solid oak door open. Tossing her large, hand-woven bag onto an antique secretary in the front hall, she waved him inside.

The walls were pink. Not little-girl pink, Brandon decided as he strolled over a genuine wool carpet much like the ones he'd bought for his mother in Istanbul, but a berry shade that reminded him of lipstick. A Tiffany lamp worked with the stained-glass sidelights to bathe the front entrance in a muted rainbow of jewel tones. Antique portraits, some framed in gilded squares or fruitwood ovals, covered the entire wall. The faces were young, old, male, female, aristocratic and common—all hung together in a haphazard collection of portraits.

"Your relatives?"

Serena had already made it to the back of the house. Situated in a double-shotgun style, the house allowed her a quick beeline from the foyer through the parlor into the kitchen. Unlatching the back door, she turned to see what he was talking about.

"You like my gallery?"

"A motley bunch."

"That's what I like about them. I collect portraits from antique shops and estate sales. Some belonged to clients."

"You don't know any of these people?"

"My great-aunt Aggie is the second in the third row."

"The rest are strangers?"

"They welcome me home every day, so I don't really think of them that way."

Brandon shook his head, wondering if Serena really knew what a stranger was. Even when they were young, her mother let her wander the Quarter with little-to-no supervision. She made friends with the shop owners, surrey drivers and street performers, who looked out for her as if she were their own. She sought out the tourists, trading directions for descriptions of their hometowns or tales of their travels. She was an irrepressible mix of charm and sociability and intelligence. How could anyone want to hurt her?

Then again, he'd hurt her once, but not intentionally. When he'd made his sloppy attempt at seduction, he'd wanted nothing more than to please her—pleasure her in ways a boy of seventeen had no skill in doing. What resulted was her shock, her humiliation, her anger. Then she'd forgiven him the next day without berating or badgering. And he'd repaid her by staying away.

At the time, his motives had been honorable. He and Serena, since they'd met as children, brought out the devil in each other. They tempted fate and pushed the rules, creating a childhood of fun and frolic that he'd never forget or regret. But as an adult, he saw that her influence on him wouldn't help him attain his goals, or vice versa. They each needed someone to balance and ease their adventurous natures.

That's why the teasing, the flirting wouldn't happen again. Beyond protecting her, beyond keeping her safe, he refused to relive the disasters of the past. And short of welshing on his bet, he'd do everything in his power to maintain a safe distance between this woman and his heart.

If such a goal was possible—even for a Chance.

When she opened the back door, a flying mass of four-legged fur bounded in from the screen porch. Wet-tongued and panting, the long-haired mutt of massive size and questionable parentage tackled Serena to the floor. Brandon tensed at the threat, then relaxed. Of course she had a dog. She probably had an entire kennel in the backyard.

After scanning the street once more for curious eyes, he closed the front door and set down the cooler. He watched her roughhouse with the dog, it yelping and her squealing, and decided she was as wondrous now as she was when they were kids—even more so. She twisted his hormones into a badge-winning knot with her heady blend of childlike enthusiasm and subtle seductiveness. One afternoon with her, and it was oh-so-easy to pretend that they'd never been apart.

As Brandon stepped out of the foyer, the dog immediately stopped playing and stood alert. Brandon halted. The dog might act like a puppy, but his jaws looked as powerful as the row of teeth he'd suddenly started to bare.

"Maurice, out!" Serena commanded.

With a canine "harrumph," Maurice closed his mouth and sat, a body full of long, straight hair flowing up, then settling onto the floor like a carpet with a dog underneath.

"Brandon, meet Maurice. Maurice, this is Brandon. He's a friend." She called Brandon over with a wave of her hand. He approached warily, his left hand extended.

Obediently, Maurice sniffed Brandon's hand, then his leg, then panted a doglike smile.

"He likes you," she concluded.

"What is he?"

"Part sheepdog, that I know."

"You rescued him from the pound, no doubt."

"Nope. He showed up at the spa one day. I gave him a bath, a bowl of vegetarian chili, a doggie massage and a home.

We've been best pals ever since." She fluffed his ears while she talked, and the dog leaned his full weight against her as his back paw tapped the floor with growing speed. He nearly knocked her over again until she pushed him aside.

"Big baby. Find the cat, Maurice." He cocked his head at her request, paused a moment as if to translate English into dog-speak and then tore off toward the front bedroom.

Brandon glanced around the kitchen. Done in wood only slightly lighter than the mahogany and cherry in the foyer, the space had been brightened with flowered wallpaper on a field of white and a forest of houseplants hanging from copper baskets and perched atop expertly carved cabinets. Lace covered her kitchen table and hung around the large windows that looked onto a whitewashed back porch. From front to back, this house had a woman's touch—more like a woman's punch—on each and every surface. He never would have expected such domesticity from her. "Nice place."

"Thanks. Miss Lily decorated it for me."

That explained the hominess.

"You live by yourself?"

Funny, he hadn't thought to ask until he found himself alone with her.

"Always have."

"The dog's good for security."

"He's a marshmallow."

"Doesn't matter. A big dog is a big dog. Do you keep his bowl in plain sight?"

"It's on the porch. He stays there most of the day and can go in the yard through a doggie door."

"A doggie door? They make them that big?" He considered the security risk of a man-size flap entrance until he realized what it advertised. "I guess someone would have to be suicidal to try to come in that way. Are there any other entrances to the house other than the front and back doors?"

She shook her head.

"Good. That'll make securing this place easier."

"Is all that necessary?" she protested, then added, "I don't want to change the house much. It's on the historical register."

"Didn't the notes all come to the house?"

"Yeah."

"Then it's necessary. Can I see them?"

Twisting her mouth in a wary expression, Serena gestured toward the parlor. He followed her into a room brimming with antiques. Floor-to-ceiling windows allowed muted, natural light—but more importantly, showed him that the alleys on either side of the house were securely gated. Her home faced a quiet street in a residential corner of the Quarter. Either Serena or a previous owner had torn down the inner walls of the original two-family home to create additional space inside, but the close proximity to the houses next door would make an unnoticed stranger highly unlikely.

"How long have you known the neighbors?"

She sifted through the contents of a wooden box she'd slid from a bookshelf, digging until she found a folded sheet of plain white paper, just as she had described. "Since we were kids. They all know my mother, too. In fact, every house on this block has at least one family member who's a satisfied, return customer of Madame Endora's."

He unfolded the paper, miffed that exploring that angle would probably end up fruitless.

"'Life is short?' That's it? You consider that a threat?"

"Read the back."

Brandon flipped the paper over. This time, the words weren't typed in a plain, computer-generated font like the main message on the inside. They were done with elaborate color graphics—small, block letters dripping with blood. "'For you.'"

He nodded and refolded the paper. "When did you get this?"

She tapped her toes and studied the carpet, shrugging rapidly as if she wanted to dance—or leave. "Last Monday."

Again, she answered his question without detail. Either the threats scared her more than she would willingly admit or she wasn't being entirely truthful. Both scenarios made his job more difficult.

"And you found it…"

"Tucked in with my newspaper."

"Did you question your delivery guy?"

"Armando? Yeah. He didn't know anything about it. He folds and throws the papers himself."

"What time does Armando deliver?"

"Around six."

"What time do you bring it in?"

"Probably seven. After walking Maurice."

"Where are the others?"

Not once during the entire exchange did she look up from the antique casket brimming with colorful cards, flimsy pink and yellow receipts, assorted news articles and envelopes stuffed with licenses, certificates and warranties. Not exactly the most congruous place to store threats on her life. Yet Serena had always been a living, breathing lesson in irreconcilable differences. Just look at the two of them.

She scratched the back of her neck, then kneaded the muscles before diving back into the wooden box. She found two more notes, both similarly folded, on exactly the same paper. He read the threats, starting with the typed phrase on the inside and following with the bloody punch line.

"'Time flies…when you die.' 'All's well…that ends in hell.'"

She shut the box and put it back on the shelf. "I guess he likes clichés."

"The Cliché Killer. How perfect for the media."

Serena rubbed her hands up and down her arms. "He hasn't killed anyone."

"You don't know that. You also don't know that this psycho is a man. You don't know anything about this creep at all. Serena, this is serious. Are you sure you've told me everything? Shown me everything?"

"I hired you as a bodyguard, not a detective."

"Some agencies, like mine, specialize in both. I can't do a very good job of protecting you if I don't know the nature of the threat. And unless you want to pay my fee indefinitely, I should try to find out who's sending these, don't you think?"

She nodded, then wordlessly slipped back to the kitchen to unpack the cooler, avoiding his gaze from start to finish. He tapped down his growing frustration with a deep breath. He couldn't remember Serena ever avoiding trouble, much less ignoring it completely. Why would she start now, with her life on the line?

Tossing the threats back into the casket, he crossed to the kitchen and watched her prepare dinner. At first, her movements were jerky and quick, but slowly, the tension eased from her shoulders. She stopped twice, her back to him, and paused just to breathe. He couldn't tear his gaze away.

Right then, Brandon knew, he was in big, big trouble.

She slipped the chopstick from her loose twist of hair and the soft curls spilled onto her shoulders. Combing nimble fingers through the waves of sunset brown, she sighed. The sound, barely audible yet brimming with a lethal mix of fear and frustration, tugged at a piece of his heart he'd tamped down a long time ago. He still cared about her. Still wanted her. Still craved the one prize horrible timing and horrendous manners had denied him.

His keen desire tugged him, urged him nearer. When she began massaging her temples, he longed to slip into the space behind her, his hips pressed to hers, his fingers tangled into her hair as he commandeered the circular motions with his own hands. Unlike this morning in his office, Serena wasn't flirting to distract him—and yet he couldn't keep his mind focused on figuring out the cryptic threats or enhancing security or anything except touching her again. What a sap he was! Here he was lusting like a green cadet after basic training and she didn't know he was there.

Or did she? Brandon grinned, then cleared his throat and scowled with all the severity he could muster.

"I don't think you should stay here alone tonight."

Serena winced when she should have rejoiced. Just as she'd schemed, Brandon was about to become her roommate. With him under her roof, she'd quickly convince Drew that she and Brandon were mad, passionate lovers. She didn't doubt that Drew would then rush to warn her about her infatuation with Brandon in the past—how mistaking friendship with romance had set her up for tremendous heartbreak—and she'd throw that illustration right back at him and force him to face the truth.

"If you really think that's necessary," she conceded, too overwhelmed to argue, even for the sake of appearances. Brandon was about to stay the night, in her house. He'd shower in her bathroom, sleep just a few feet away in the spare room. Would she sleep at all, knowing he was near enough to touch?

"Absolutely necessary," he declared. "So, should you call Drew, or should I?"

CHAPTER FIVE

"CALL DREW?" She banished the squeak from her voice by clearing her throat while she wiped her hands on a clean paper towel. She scooped up the oversized bowl she'd just filled with Asian chicken salad, and with every ounce of calm nonchalance in her burgeoning supply, carried their dinner to the table. "I don't need Drew's permission for you to stay the night."

He paused before he spoke, causing Serena's spine to vibrate with anxiety. Just how much did he know about her and Drew and her "situation"? Likely more than she bargained for.

"You sure about that?" he asked.

One look into Brandon's suddenly unreadable gray eyes told Serena to proceed with caution. A tinge of suspicion, coupled with a teasing lilt that had none of the playfulness or humor she'd once grown accustomed to, made her believe that Brandon wouldn't see the brilliance of her plan too easily—especially since she'd gone so far as to show him the fake notes.

"Are you afraid to stay with me? That's gotta be hard on the bodyguard business."

His scowl motivated her to grab a knife and begin slicing bread at the kitchen sink. She tried to concentrate on cutting the crusty loaf in equal, even portions—anything to fend off the haunting feeling that she'd just kicked a hornet's nest with a sharp-toed shoe.

"That line doesn't work anymore, Serena."

He pushed off from the doorjamb and approached. Serena felt each and every noiseless step as if the space between them stretched with an invisible, elastic force. Taut yet pliant. Supple and subtle and sizzling with an undercurrent of volatile energy. He stopped not two inches away from her. His words accompanied a breeze of hot air that singed the curls at her nape.

"You're hiding something," he whispered, his fingers barely touching the small of her back. "We may not have seen each other in a long time, but you've always been an open book to me." He slid his hand from her back to the curve between her shoulder and neck. Fingering her hair, he teased her earlobes with the intimate strokes of his hand and heated breath. "What aren't you telling me?"

Serena slowly placed her serrated knife back on the cutting board. Her hands shook. Attempting to cut even crusty bread could be dangerous. Though at this very moment, she could think of nothing more perilous than standing in her kitchen with a man who exuded sexual energy with the same unstoppable force as the Mississippi River during a flood. Sheer stupidity and fear had allowed her to fend off that attraction once.

What could possibly save her now?

"I've told you everything you need to know," she insisted, hoping a degree of honesty would stall him.

He snatched a chunky slice of bread and took a hearty bite. "And I don't need to know that you and Drew are engaged?"

Anger fueled by familiar annoyance gave her the strength to push away from him to retrieve a breadbasket from the hutch. "Who told you that?"

His eyebrows raised at the tastiness of the whole-grain bread, and he popped the rest into his mouth, chewed and swallowed. "My aunt scorched more than a few fiber optics delivering that news. None of those rings you wear are diamond solitaires, but I figured you to pick something less…conventional."

Serena looked at her hands before shoving them onto her hips. "I'm not wearing a diamond solitaire because I'm not getting married. To anyone. Ever."

He didn't react in the least to her claim. He'd heard it before, years ago, but with enough repetition that she felt certain he hadn't forgotten. Still, she would have felt better if he reacted a little. A smile, maybe? Relief?

"Have you told Drew?" he asked.

Serena gnawed the inside of her mouth, putting aside her own ridiculous fantasies to deal with the here and now. Here she had the perfect opportunity to come clean. To be honest. To seek his help without lies and half truths and open-to-interpretation excuses. "Yes. Several times, as a matter of fact."

"And…?"

The expression he wore gave her absolutely no clue as to how her admission had affected him. In fact, she was certain her marital status meant nothing to him at all. She shouldn't be surprised. She definitely shouldn't feel disappointed.

But she did.

She risked approaching him again long enough to fill the basket and place it in the center of the table. Breaking through a decade and a half of Brandon's indifference toward her wasn't going to be easy, but Serena knew she was going to have to try. And not because of her kooky plan. Because she wanted him to care, darn it! The way he used to.

"Drew doesn't believe me," she explained. "He thinks I'm just being stubborn."

"Stubborn? You?"

"Coyness doesn't become you, Brandon." She grabbed plates and glasses and set them on the frilly place mats she kept on the table. Usually alone, she rarely ate without a newspaper or book to distract her. What she wouldn't do for a nice thick copy of *War and Peace* right about now. "He's known me as long as you have. I have a certain reputation for being true to my convictions."

"You mean for being pigheaded."

"You're impossible, you know that?"

"I've heard. From you, as I recall. On more than one occasion just today, as a matter of fact."

She turned to the refrigerator and yanked a tall amber bottle from the wine rack inside, remembered today was still Tuesday and cursed before sliding the Chardonnay back in place. She rummaged instead for a can of soda, grateful Samantha had left one of her caffeine-loaded, artificial-coloring-and-flavoring favorites behind the remnants of the cheesecake they'd shared last week. She preferred alcohol at times like these, but would settle for sugar.

Grabbing the largest goblet in her eclectic collection of stemware, she poured a generous serving of a chartreuse carbonated drink. Only after she swallowed a quarter of the glass did she have the urge to offer some wine to her guest.

"Not while I'm on duty, thanks."

She shrugged and swallowed a few more gulps before she felt the muscles in her chest and stomach relax. The headache lingering at the corners of her eyes melted away.

"Do you want some with dinner?"

"I'm invited?"

"I thought I was stuck with you. My shadow, remember?"

He approached the table and surveyed her offering. "I got the distinct impression you weren't happy with that arrangement. That's why I suggested you call Drew. I didn't know that was a sore spot. I'll take iced tea, if you have it."

She grabbed a pitcher from behind the milk, surmising that Brandon had indeed been traveling the world too long if he thought there was a Southerner alive who didn't keep a fresh pitcher of sweet tea in the back of the fridge. As she poured him a glass, she also realized Brandon probably expected more from a meal than lettuce leaves dotted with poached white meat, mandarin orange segments and carrot, and drizzled with spicy ginger dressing. She pulled a Tupperware of Miss Lily's fried chicken out of the refrigerator and plopped the cold, golden-brown contents onto a platter. Her mother's cook and constant companion had an annoyingly wonderful habit of using her key to fill Serena's cupboards and fridge with more than the healthy fare she served at the spa.

"Drew's not a sore spot. I care about Drew more than anyone. He's my best friend."

Like you used to be.

Brandon slid himself into a chair and filled his plate with two chicken legs, three wings, a breast and a thigh, apparently not bothered by the future of her marital status enough for his appetite to be dampened much. When she shook her head with disbelief, he scooped some salad onto the side.

"Have you told Drew about the notes?"

"No," she answered forcefully. "I didn't think it was necessary."

"He's your best friend and wants to marry you, but you don't tell him when your life is threatened?"

She filled her plate with a generous helping of salad, then speared a mouthful with her fork. While she chewed, she decided that now definitely wasn't the time to admit she'd fabricated the notes to enlist his help. Despite their intimate con-

versation in the hallway outside the restaurant, the gulf
between them remained as wide as the waterway between
Louisiana and Florida, with just as many rough waves and
swirling storms. She needed time to figure out the best way
to navigate without swamping her future entirely.

"I didn't tell anyone but you. I don't want everyone over-
reacting. It's all a hoax. Someone's idea of a joke."

"What makes you so sure?"

He didn't wait for her to respond. Instead, he took a bite
of the cold chicken and then closed his eyes to savor the combination of spices and breading and juicy meat that made
Miss Lily the best cook in all of New Orleans.

A knock at the door waylaid Serena's answer, but she hesitated nonetheless. Lying wasn't her forte and contradicted her
daily goal of achieving simplicity and balance in every aspect
of her life.

So just what was she doing having dinner with Brandon
Chance? Pretending to be a damsel in distress—of all
things—in a nonsensical, if not potentially faultless, scheme
to divest herself of an unwanted suitor while retaining a cherished friendship? Maybe two?

Maybe everyone was right. Maybe she was crazy.

She scooted out her chair, responding to the second, more
insistent rap on the door.

Brandon tore off another mouthful of chicken and stopped
her with a greasy hand. "Let me."

She didn't argue. She was too stunned by the direction of
her own thoughts to protest what was essentially a smart move
for a professional bodyguard.

"That's probably Samantha," she called. "She left a message
at the spa saying she'd be stopping by with some stuff."

When the knock sounded again, Serena leaned around

from her chair to see Brandon still in the living room, coolly assessing the best way to get around Maurice, who stood sentinel in the foyer, his tail furiously swiping a spot of hardwood and his front paws dancing on the rug. He was better than a peephole. No bark meant the person on the other side of the door was someone he knew. The wagging tail further indicated that the knocker had once, and would probably again, engage the dog in some sort of play.

She left the table, squeezed by Brandon, grabbed the dog's collar with one hand and reached around his mass of fur with the other to open the door. "Hey, Sammie, come on in."

Serena stepped back and held the door wide, and the dog in place, while her sister struggled with an armful of packages.

"I could use a little help," Sammie groused.

"I'm holding the door, aren't I?" Serena answered.

"Here, let me."

Brandon moved between Serena and the wall, his body sliding against hers so quickly and efficiently, she shouldn't have noticed. But she did notice. She and every nerve ending from the tips of her breasts to the rings on her toes. That scent that was his alone, now mixed with the spicy aroma of fresh fried chicken, made him the ultimate comfort food. Her mouth watered. Luckily, Sammie made such a production out of carrying in her boxes, no one seemed to notice her reaction but her.

"Brandon?"

Sammie slid the boxes into his arms, retaining a small flat one on top to carry herself. She assessed him from head to toe, not bothering to hide a wide-eyed reaction of feminine approval.

"Damn," Sammie concluded. "You sure as hell grew up nice."

"Samantha," he acknowledged with a wry grin, shifting the

boxes into a straighter, more manageable column. "Now I can be *bewitched* by both Deveaux sisters."

Samantha snorted. "I haven't heard that joke since before Daddy moved out. And there was a good reason for that."

"Not funny?" he answered, grinning.

Samantha pulled out her straightest face. "Not unless you want me to start calling you Derwood."

Serena released Maurice, who bounded over to Sammie joyfully. Brandon had greeted each old friend he'd run into with the same enthusiasm—first Drew, now Sammie—everyone except her.

"I'll pass." He shifted the boxes to the side, facing Samantha as he spoke. "When did you swim back upstream? Aunt Tillie claimed you were going to be the next Linda Hamilton or Sigourney Weaver once your father found you the right part."

"*Your* aunt Tillie listens too much to *my* mother." Samantha gave Maurice a nip of a kiss on the nose, then picked up a brightly covered ball from beneath the secretary and flung it into the kitchen. The dog bounded away, nearly clipping Brandon at the knees. "I never intended to act. My screen time was limited to stunt work."

"Sounds exciting. Why are you back here?"

"Let's just blame it on one too many broken bones and leave it at that, okay?" She tucked her box underneath one arm and balanced a fist on her hip. "Unless you want to end all the speculation simmering through the Quarter and tell us both why you retired from the army?"

His answer was a noncommittal, yet decidedly negative grunt. Then his mouth curved into a friendly smile. "Welcome back."

Samantha grinned. "Right back at you. So, what are you doing hanging around my sister? Hungry for trouble so soon?"

Brandon's chuckle so rankled Serena she hoped he threw out his back standing there with an armful of boxes. Or got a hernia. When he dropped the cardboard containers onto the floor near the kitchen, she realized they were neither heavy nor cumbersome enough to cause this man to even break a sweat.

"Trouble and Serena do go hand in hand, don't they?" he surmised.

"That's what I'm told." Sammie slid her lone package onto an end table and headed toward dinner. "Heard today that she nearly got run over after I dropped her off at your office."

"Who told you that?" Serena asked, protest grinding her voice. She should know better than to think no one witnessed her and Brandon's tumble.

"Mother. Who else?" Sammie answered.

"How did she find out?" Serena threw a suspicious glance at Brandon.

"Don't look at me." Brandon shoved his hands in his pockets. "The last person I'm going to call is your mother, unless I want to hold a séance to figure out who's threatening you."

"Threatening you?" Samantha shot back into the room, gripping a drumstick and licking grease from her lips. "Serena, you told me nothing was wrong."

"Nothing is wrong!" She threw up her hands, swung past her sister and returned to her place at the table. "Unless I count the two of you jumping to conclusions and assigning nefarious intentions to my carelessness. I simply wasn't looking where I was going."

Serena waited for Brandon to tell Sammie about the threats, or that she'd hired him to be her bodyguard, but he did neither. Instead, he sidled over to the casket she'd put on the shelf, surreptitiously shut the lid and came back into the kitchen.

Sammie eyed them both, took another bite of her chicken,

chewed and then concluded, "I didn't come over to lecture you on street safety." She swallowed and then licked her fingers. "But don't be surprised if Endora pops in later."

Serena groaned, and pushed away from the table to quickly grab the phone. The last thing she needed tonight was her mother. Actually, the last thing she needed tonight was her mother knowing Brandon was staying in her house—provided that she didn't already know, either through psychic means or because the neighbors felt obliged to give her a call. The citizens of the French Quarter would by no means be morally outraged by her choice of guests, but they sure as heck wouldn't be able to let such a scintillating tidbit pass without spreading the word to their latest and most beloved queen since Marie Leveau.

Serena couldn't lie to her mother in person. Endora LaCroix Deveaux was a force to be reckoned with in just about every dimension she claimed to visit. And while Serena wasn't sure if Endora's reputed "powers" were more than a heightened sense of intuition or a true psychic phenomenon, she did know without a doubt that Endora *always* knew when she was up to something. And she wouldn't have any qualms about calling her on it in front of Brandon. With no illusions that she could keep her plan secret if Endora walked through the door, she punched in her mother's number.

As Serena dialed, Sammie slid into the chair next to Brandon, eyed then dismissed the salad that didn't have nearly enough sesame oil or clumps of cheese to pique her appetite. She fished a wing from beneath a breast on the platter while Serena thanked Miss Lily for the chicken and asked to speak to Endora.

"You're calling me so I won't come over," her mother said by way of greeting.

"Yes, ma'am, I am." No sense in arguing that point. "I

wasn't looking where I was going, but I'm fine. No scratches, no bruises. But if you'd like, I'll stop by and show you."

Endora's laugh was light. "I'd be delighted if you came by, but I know you're fine—physically. I'm not so sure about what's going on in your head."

That makes two of us, Serena thought.

"My head is fine, too." She ran her hand through her hair as Sammie and Brandon looked up from their food. "I'm in the middle of dinner, though, so can I come by in the morning?"

Endora chuckled. "Miss Lily is peeling potatoes as we speak. Tell Brandon not to fill up too much on chicken or he'll miss out on his favorite hash."

Serena winced. Having a psychic for a parent was something she should be used to by now, but she wasn't. Lying and keeping secrets weren't something she did on a daily basis. She hung up the phone after saying goodbye then took another long draught of soda.

"So, how is your mother?" Brandon asked.

"She said not to fill up on chicken 'cause Miss Lily is making that andouille hash you like so much."

"But you didn't tell her…" His protest died off and he shook his head with a resigned frown that slowly turned into a reluctant grin. He picked up a fried thigh and took a big bite.

She and Sammie filled the silence with conversation, mostly about Samantha's quest for gainful employment that didn't require her to prop her eyes open with toothpicks. After a lifetime of jumping off high-rise buildings and driving flaming cars off bridges while the cameras rolled, arranging shoot schedules for the local film board wasn't cutting it.

"Are you going to quit?" Serena asked.

Sammie rolled her now-bare chicken bones into her paper

napkin. "As soon as I find something better. I do have to pay the bills."

"A Deveaux in need of money? That's a first." Brandon scooped another helping of Serena's healthy, yet surprisingly tasty salad onto his plate. Growing up in a family of gamblers and speculators, Brandon learned very young not to rely on his parents for money and to keep a rainy-day stash somewhere safe. The military had paid him well for his piloting skills, and with the addition of "danger pay," and no family or household to support, he'd created a hefty portfolio he now needed to learn to spend. But the Deveaux clan controlled a fortune that dated back to the Louisiana Purchase and hadn't stopped increasing since. "Your father is loaded and your mother's not exactly panhandling at Jackson Square."

"You left out the part about me being an adult, Brandon." Samantha explained. "Their money is their money. I need my own."

Serena and Sammie exchanged a quick but meaningful glance that stirred Brandon's interest for an instant—until he pushed the curiosity aside. He had enough Deveaux mysteries to unravel at the moment, not the least of which was the reemergence of his desire for Serena.

Thankfully, he'd learned in the service to present an emotion-free veneer. Piloting helicopters into dangerous territory on covert missions, he knew success depended on him keeping his natural apprehension shielded from his men. The skill served him well when Serena not only admitted she wasn't engaged to Drew, but that she considered his old rival just a friend. He'd felt a leap in the pit of his chest that shocked even him. Given a little time and the distraction of finding out the identity of Serena's cliché-loving pen pal, he'd squash his emotions back into submission where they belonged. But until then, he was having a hell of a good time watching Serena eat and talk and laugh. She was a captivating, beautiful woman, an innately feminine creature that men like him couldn't help but watch.

Looking was all he would do. All he was paid to do. Touching was most definitely out of the question. He'd done so only briefly when she was slicing the bread and again when they answered the door, and his body still thrummed from the feel of her warm skin against his. Touching her again would most definitely lead to kissing, which would inevitably progress to lovemaking. They weren't kids anymore.

But one thing still hadn't changed. He wanted to marry and settle down. Serena wanted to remain free and unfettered. And while he neither envied nor belittled her plans for her future, he knew that making love with Serena would mean something—a promise of sorts. A promise he couldn't keep.

"Sammie knows I'll loan her money if she needs it," Serena said, interrupting his thoughts and giving him a much-needed distraction. "That's not the point. She needs to do something she loves."

"Like?" Brandon asked, suddenly anxious for more chatter.

Sammie tabled her hands and leaned her chin on her knuckles. "Being a bodyguard sounds interesting." She batted her eyelashes with complete and utter abandon. "Need a partner?"

"Ha!"

Serena and Samantha tag-teamed him with serious, pointed stares, jabbing the humor of her suggestion right out of him. "It's not you, of course," he began by way of damage control. The last thing he needed was an argument—in deluxe Deveaux surround-sound—about sexism or selfishness or lack of lifelong loyalties. "I'm too new at this to train someone with no experience."

"Who says I have to be trained? Bodyguarding isn't brain surgery. I know how to shoot a gun, I have a third-degree black belt in tae kwon do and I'm very observant," Sammie concluded. "I had bodyguards around me all the time in L.A."

It was Brandon's turn to frown. She really didn't think his job was a piece of cake, did she? Sure, his first job in New Orleans hadn't exactly gotten under way enough for him to talk about the dangers and intricacies of his career, but he had some stories from Miami that would curl that California-blond hair of hers into tight little ringlets sure to yank her scalp.

"The state of Louisiana says you have to be trained," he told her. "And I'm not just hired muscle. This job requires several licenses and courses. I'm an investigator as well as a personal-protection specialist. Why don't you look into it? Do some research?"

"And then get back to you?" Samantha asked hopefully. Her cat-in-the-cream expression made him wonder if she hadn't just baited him on purpose. Sisters! Obviously, their separate childhoods hadn't diminished their mutual love for manipulation.

Anyway, Brandon didn't need a partner. And he most certainly didn't need a partner whose last name was Deveaux. Though he hardly knew Samantha since she grew up with her father on the West Coast, he felt qualified to draw conclusions based solely on her sibling. Deveaux were unpredictable. Resourceful but unreliable. And flighty as all get-out. Once he discovered who was threatening Serena and neutralized the danger, he'd be done with her *and* her insane pack of relatives.

"There's no harm in us having a talk, but don't get your hopes up. After working in a regiment for eleven years, I'm actually looking forward to going this venture alone."

Samantha's smile dimmed, but didn't diminish enough to

let him think for one minute he was off the hook. Her eyes, a dark, sapphire blue, still glimmered with plans-in-the-making.

"Well, on that note, I'd better leave you two to whatever you were doing." She slid away from the table, tossed the napkin in the trash under the sink and washed her hands. "Do I want to know what you're doing?" she asked while drying her fingers with a crisp paper towel.

"We're having dinner," Serena answered way too quickly. Brandon saw the light of interest brighten in Samantha's eyes, but she shrugged in acceptance and waved goodbye.

Brandon had no intention of buying Serena's pacifications so easily. If she was indeed lying to him about something, as he suspected, then his attraction to her was blinding him more than failing eyesight ever did. And he was going to do something about it. Right away.

BRANDON LEFT SERENA alone with Maurice at her side, rummaging through the boxes Sammie had delivered, while he hurried to his new apartment to grab clean clothes. As promised, he returned in less than fifteen minutes, hardly enough time for her to sort through her conflicting thoughts and instincts. The Quarter was a relatively small place and the room he'd rented above an old friend's bar on Bourbon Street wasn't more than a quick jaunt from her house on St. Philip. By the time he returned, she still didn't know when or even if she was going to come clean.

"Find anything interesting?" He dug his hands into his pockets, eyeing the mounds of clothes and trinkets she'd spread across the sofa. An odd mix of confusion and intimidation painted his expression while he watched her pick through the treasures. Women's clothing did that to men, especially the kind Sammie was obviously anxious to get rid of. Beaded gowns worn once and only once to various award ceremonies. Trendy designer duds with tags still tucked in the sleeve.

Serena lifted a completely see-through sheath of the filmiest chiffon she'd ever seen. She held it up and eyed Brandon through the swirling shades of burgundy, rust and gold dyed into the fabric. "Define *interesting*."

Brandon cleared his throat and started poking in a box of hats and purses that looked decidedly safer. "Your sister has *interesting* taste in clothes."

Sensing a chink in his indifferent armor, Serena held the incredibly alluring dress up to her body. The spaghetti straps were little more than woven thread and the hem just breezed over the top of her thighs when she sat up onto her knees. Where her sister wore this was beyond her, until she spied the tiny tag hanging from beneath the arm.

Probably another designer "donation" she never got around to showing off. As the daughter of Hollywood's hottest director, Sammie had often been treated like a star herself. The situation wore on her—and Serena totally understood. Living in the shadow of a legendary parent was no easier on the banks of the Mississippi than it was on the shores of the Pacific. But Serena couldn't just up and move. New Orleans was part of her blood, part of her soul.

Just as Brandon once was.

"She does, doesn't she?" She couldn't resist baiting him further, hoping a little teasing would restore her perspective. Old habits were so hard to break. "How do you think I'd look in something like this?"

Brandon's eyes narrowed. "Like a naked woman who paid too much for her dress."

Serena laughed and draped the dress into her "keep" pile.

She didn't know why, exactly, but suspected the brief glint of discomfort she'd witnessed in Brandon's expression had something to do with her stashing away the ready-to-not-wear haute couture creation. "You have no imagination, Brandon."

When she glanced up a second later, she was shocked to see the dark intensity in his gaze. Though the dress was nothing more than colored film, she suddenly felt the urge to use it as a shield to block Brandon's incredibly hungry stare. She'd changed into her favorite pajamas—an oversize Mardi Gras T-shirt and leggings—yet for the entire duration of his visual perusal, she felt naked and exposed.

She cleared her throat. "I take it back. Your imagination seems to be working just fine."

Expecting him to laugh at her words, she was met with no reaction. She scooped up the clothes she had no use for and shoved them back in the box. After folding the flaps down, she turned to face his sudden silence and unreadable mien.

"So?" She forced airy brightness into her tone, trying to dispel the discomfort that now hung between them. "Want to help me go through the box of board games?"

His hand snaked out and ensnared her wrist so quickly, she couldn't contain a gasp.

"No. No games. It's time for the truth, Serena. From both of us."

CHAPTER SIX

BRANDON IMMEDIATELY released her. Was he nuts? If he wasn't before, touching her definitely knocked what was left of his good sense right out of him. The heated, silky skin of her wrist was scented with oils that now clung to his palm, branding him with an essence of lavender, eucalyptus and mint. He ached for more contact.

And that was out of the question.

"Sit down," he ordered, knowing the minute he spoke that he'd chosen the wrong tone. Her dancing green eyes froze midstep.

"Serena, please. Let's just get comfortable."

She chewed on the inside of her lip while she considered his rephrasing. When her eyebrows peaked, she'd clearly decided she was satisfied. She tossed her sister's throwaways aside to make a spot for both of them on the couch.

"Don't you want to shower first?" She eyed the duffel bag he'd leaned against the wall between the kitchen and living room. "Get into your pj's?"

He slid onto the fringed cushions beside her. He should have showered at his apartment. Getting naked in Serena's space had trouble written all over it. "I don't wear pj's."

Watching her for a reaction, he was silently disappointed when she only smirked. "I'd hate to be your neighbor who came knocking in the middle of the night."

"Neighbors shouldn't knock in the middle of the night."

"You're back in the Quarter now. Strange things happen."

"Like threatening notes in your newspaper."

She drew her bare feet up onto the cushions and wrapped her arms around her knees.

Her toenails had sunsets, too.

"Stranger than that. What Mrs. Sevilla got on her doorstep from her new husband's first wife…*that* was strange."

Brandon shook his head. He didn't want to know the details. About her neighbors. About her life in this neighborhood. He wanted the facts. The information he needed to finish this job and get the hell out of her life.

Before he started to *really* care for her again. More than he did already. Before he started waking up every morning anticipating when he'd see her or automatically reaching for the phone to call her when he faced a tough challenge or reached a particular milestone. Before he started going to bed at night with her and only her on his mind so that she haunted his dreams with scenarios that could never be real. Like the two of them sharing a future, sharing a life.

After a year in college, he'd convinced himself he was over her forever. Now he realized that separation had simply allowed him the luxury of self-delusion. He still believed he was better off without her—and vice versa—but that logical, commonsense assumption didn't do a damn thing to lessen his desire.

"Serena…the notes. We have to talk about this."

Serena opened her mouth as if ready to answer him with all the detail and minutiae he'd once grown accustomed to. Then she popped her lips together with a smack. "What's to talk about? You find out who sent them, tell them to stop, end of story."

"What about Drew?"

The mention of his name made her twitch. He probably wouldn't have noticed if he hadn't been sitting right beside her. Little by little, she'd crept into his awareness. She couldn't curl her hair around her ear without him noticing. Or chew her bottom lip. Blink. Breathe.

God help him.

"You think he's sending the threats?"

He shrugged his shoulders, thankful to actually talk business for a minute and take his mind off the way her caramel curls caught the amber light of the Tiffany lamp.

"He has motive," Brandon argued.

She grabbed a throw pillow and slipped it between her folded lap and her chest. "Come on, Brandon. Drew wants to marry me, not kill me…though I'm not certain the experiences are all that different."

Brandon stood and walked a few paces away. The coziness of conversing on the couch, her all casual and comfy in her oversize T-shirt and no bra—a detail he couldn't help but notice—didn't lend to focused questioning.

"What do you have against marriage? Your parents divorced a long time ago. Aren't you over that by now?"

She looked up at him, somewhat startled by his bluntness. She answered him in a clipped tone.

"Spoken by a man whose parents are still together." She shifted her position on the couch, pulling the pillow closer to her chest. "I'll admit my parents' divorce instigated my negative appraisal of marriage, but I know that some marriages work wonderfully. I'm happy for people like your parents who truly share each other's lives. Maybe I'm just selfish, but I can't see myself in that situation. Can you?"

With this insurmountable difference of opinion out in the open, Brandon felt safe enough to return to his seat beside her.

"Yeah, I can. I'd like the American Dream. Wife, kids, two point three dogs," he joked.

"Don't forget the fence," she added, smiling as she spoke. "White picket is still all the rage, though we don't use them here in the Quarter."

"I don't plan to live in the Quarter."

"Just another thing we don't have in common." She nodded silently, then added, "Isn't it weird? We used to have everything in common."

"Yeah, weird." He mulled over the word and decided *weird* did not accurately describe the situation at all. That he and Serena were so alike—still shared attractions to excitement and thrills and, admittedly, each other—yet held such different visions for themselves was a downright crying shame.

He cleared his throat. "So, Drew knows you don't want to marry him, or anyone, but he's planning everything anyway. Isn't that strange, even to you?"

She smirked at his undisguised insult, but didn't bother to refute it. He'd made it clear long ago that he thought she was odd. For a long time, he'd been drawn to her purely because she saw the world through glasses swirling with bright neon colors and skewed perspectives.

Her annoyance was only for show—just like his teasing.

"Very strange. But I still don't think Drew would send me threatening notes."

"Being in love can make some men desperate," he answered.

She grabbed the wooden casket containing the threatening notes and shoved it at him. "Leave Drew alone. Why don't you look over these again? Dust them for fingerprints or do some fancy paper analysis."

"I might finally have a motive behind these threats and you want to back off? Why?"

"Because this line of thinking is ridiculous. Drew is the guy who flunked biology because he couldn't bring himself to dissect the frog."

"Just because he's threatened you doesn't mean he intends to follow through. Maybe he's trying to scare you, make you think you'll be safer if you marry him."

"That's ridiculous," she muttered.

"Men do ridiculous things sometimes to get what they want, especially when they're in love."

"Drew's not in love with me."

Brandon clutched the inner linings of his pockets and twisted hard, trying to ease some of the frustration her declaration caused. He hated when women assumed they knew everything in a man's heart just because they watched talk shows and read books about Venus and Mars.

"How do you know? Have you ever been in love, Serena?" He bent so close, she had to tilt her head up to meet him eye to eye. "Do you know what love feels like?"

She looked up at him, defiance enhancing her features so he couldn't look away, even if he wanted to. Her eyes caught the dim light of the nearby lamp and turned the golden glow into pure, green fire. Her chin tilted upward; her cheeks flamed. Her mouth, so generous and soft only moments before, now featured lips drawn in an obstinate line.

"Do you?" she demanded.

He struggled to keep his hands in his pockets—no matter how much he wanted to grab her and shake her. Or worse, kiss her. "I asked first."

LOVE FEELS something like this, Serena silently decided. Her heart pounded like a drum in her chest, her nerves thrummed like freshly picked strings of a jazzman's double bass. Standing so close, she couldn't help but breathe in the scent that was decidedly Brandon—pure unfettered musk and man. Basic. Primal. Delicious. Coated by the musty odors of the Quarter's hot asphalt, ancient bricks and fiery spices, he was once again a part of the Vieux Carre—and part of her, like it or not.

"You asked me first? That's an infantile evasion," she pointed out, equally childishly resorting to pointless bickering rather than facing the truth. She could blame Brandon and their lifetime of similar interactions for her response, but that wouldn't be fair. They'd both grown up. They both knew better.

Now they just had to admit it.

He stared, waiting for her response.

"No, Brandon. I don't know what love feels like. Do you?"

Brandon pulled his hands from his pockets and ran them through his hair. She watched the gesture with hungry fascination, her hands anxious to comb through the midnight-dark strands, to brand the texture onto her palms.

"I thought I did. Once," he admitted.

"When?"

As his gaze locked with hers, she knew exactly the moment he referred to. That night. In the gym.

"I was a kid. I didn't know how to show…the girl…how I felt."

"Do you know now?" she asked, closing the space between them. She placed her palm against his chest and marked the time of his beating heart, grinning inside when the rapid tempo matched her own. She and Brandon had decidedly different plans for the future, but denying leftover feelings from the past wasn't going to make them go away.

Confronting those feelings might. And not with words. With action.

"Kiss me, Brandon. Like you should have so long ago."

His pupils dilated, adding a dark shadow to the intensity of his gaze. "You don't know what you're asking."

"Yes, I do. I'm asking you to do what I know you want to. Kiss me," she demanded, then closed her eyes to await his next move.

First, he caressed her cheek with such gentleness, Serena imagined he'd plucked a feather from one of her boas and now used the soft down to tease her skin. She inhaled sharply to keep from gasping, but the added friction of padded callus to her sensitized flesh accelerated her heartbeat and stole her captured breath away.

"We were so young," he whispered. "I was so stupid. But I never told you…even before I got drunk, I wanted to be with you. More than I'd wanted anything."

Don't look. Don't look him in the eye. Her good sense fell deaf to her curiosity. Intending only to take a quick peek to gauge his honesty, she was immediately held prisoner by his intense stare.

"Why didn't you tell me?" she asked. "Then? Or after?"

He licked his lips to cover a bashful grin, but the action only brought more attention to his mouth—a mouth she craved as she craved no other. "How does a guy keep an ounce of pride and admit that to the girl he groped?"

"You're doing it now."

"Time changes things."

"Like you wanting me more than anything?" she asked. She'd asked him to kiss her and still he hadn't. Yet. Maybe he wouldn't. Maybe he no longer wanted to.

He crooked a finger beneath her chin. "Time and distance didn't do much to change that. Damn them both."

He lowered his lips slowly, tentatively, briefly brushing his mouth against hers. He tasted like spicy ginger. Like hot fire.

"Tell me *no,* Serena." His words were a whispered command, and she knew he would stop if she asked him to. He wouldn't betray her trust a second time, just as she wouldn't let a second opportunity pass to explore the connection between them.

"I can't," she answered, raising herself onto the balls of her bare feet to swipe her lips across his again.

"Good."

He pressed harder this time, enough for her to feel the slick warmth of his lips, the moist heat of his mouth. She slipped her arms around his waist. Hunger beat a path from the pit of her belly to the edge of her tongue. He eased one hand behind her neck, one to the small of her back and met her halfway, pulling her as close as he could while they learned what they'd missed all those years ago.

He was a natural-born leader, a man in command. But not here, not now. He let her set the pace. She snuggled closer, her unbound breasts beneath her T-shirt flush with the hardness of his chest. She made no secret of her responses, moaning softly from the back of her throat.

The instinct to explore, the primal need to feel his skin against her palm and learn the planes of his body, couldn't be denied. She spread her fingers over his chest, then brushed her palms downward.

When she skimmed the top of his waistband, he broke the kiss. Before they went too far? Felt too much? But he didn't release her. Instead, he turned his head aside and buried his nose in her hair.

"You're dangerous, woman."

Serena unfolded herself from his hold and stepped aside. "You're not exactly a day in church yourself." She drew her fingers to her mouth, marveling at the thrumming heat still firing her lips. She couldn't allow this to go any further—at least, not until she'd told him the whole truth.

If he'd been honest with her fifteen years ago, told her how he'd really felt about her, their lives might not have turned out any differently, but Serena knew she would have made other choices in the past few days. She certainly wouldn't have lied to him this morning or schemed to rope him into the mess that was her personal life. She wouldn't have had to.

"I've made a huge mistake," she said. "I shouldn't have hired you to be my bodyguard."

He nodded, smiling, obviously aware that she'd pulled some sort of scam on him. "No, you probably shouldn't have. Care to tell me why you did? And no more bull, Serena. The truth. All of it."

Truth was, she'd used him—or had schemed to— without knowing how he'd truly felt all those years ago, without realizing she might hurt him in precisely the way he'd hurt her. But now wasn't the time to rehash the past. He'd asked about now.

She crossed her arms over her chest and admitted the most basic truth in one breath. "I chose you so Drew would see us together and think we were involved again. He'd be the first person to remind me that mixing friendship and romance leads to disaster."

Brandon grew silent. All expression, all reaction disappeared from his eyes. He'd always had a first-rate poker face, but this one nearly made her shiver.

"Not a bad plan, actually." He stepped aside and grabbed his duffel bag, fingering the canvas strap for a moment before he swung it over his shoulder. "This one, at least, I understand. If Drew warned you away from me, he'd have to see the parallel to his own foolishness. Not a bad plan at all."

Without another word, he headed toward her guest room.

Serena reached out to stop him, to explain the rest—from the fake notes to her honest response to his kiss—but stopped. He wasn't going anywhere except to take a shower. She needed time to regroup. Recover from the kiss she'd waited for her entire life.

Immediately after he closed the bathroom door, Serena got to work, determined to clean up the mess she'd created before she went to bed. And she wasn't just thinking about the scattered boxes and strewn clothing. She was thinking about lies and mistruths. Omissions. Things she should have told him this morning. Things she should have told him fifteen years ago, if her wounded pride had only let her. Perhaps the whole truth was better aged, when they were mature enough to appreciate the depth of their adolescent feelings—and knew the limitations of any future they might have.

Brandon wanted a wife and kids and a house in the suburbs. Serena couldn't imagine ever leaving the Quarter or giving up the freedom to dance until daybreak at Restoration Hall or close up the spa on a whim to take a friend to the bayou.

They were the same, yet as different as Lake Pontchartrain and the Mississippi River. And they had no canal to connect them, nothing but the attraction that had only heightened with their kiss.

It was late, near midnight. She let the dog out and watched the clock until the hour hand went one minute past midnight, declaring the end to a dry Tuesday. She fished two glasses from the back of her liquor cabinet and filled them both with a finger of fine, aged bourbon.

She was sitting on the floor amid a neat pile of old board games, sipping the liquor to give her courage and leaning her back against the couch for strength, when Brandon emerged from the bathroom ten minutes later. The edges of his jet-black hair glistened with moisture. His skin radiated the heat of his shower. He wore gray sweatpants that hung low on his waist and a crisp white T-shirt over that military-muscled chest of his.

"Find everything okay?" she croaked, then loosened the walls of her throat with another sip of bourbon.

"Remind me to pick up some unscented shampoo."

"Ylang-ylang is very relaxing."

His smirk denoted his disbelief. "Sleep is relaxing. Don't you think you should be getting some?"

"I'm a night owl. That's why the spa doesn't open till ten."

He tousled his hair once more with a towel, then folded it in sharp thirds and draped it over the bathroom's doorknob. "An advantage of being your own boss."

She lifted the second glass to him. "One of a few."

He shook his head at her proffered drink.

"Tuesday's over, Brandon. One drink. Don't tell me you can't hold your bourbon anymore."

He snorted and reached for the glass. "I can hold my bourbon *and* your bourbon, thank you very much. Still drink it straight up, I see."

"Great-aunt Aggie insisted that real ladies drank their bourbon two ways—in a julep or straight up. I was too lazy to crush the mint."

Though his T-shirt wore its crisp, bleached whiteness like a full-braided dress uniform, his sweatpants were soft and somewhat sloppy. She couldn't help but follow the curves of muscle beneath the athletic gray. Her fingers itched to touch him, to explore and learn about the man she'd thought she knew so well, when in reality she didn't have a clue.

When he turned and squatted to sit beside her on the floor, she drew the drink to her mouth and watched from behind the glass, thankful the odor of strong alcohol would offset—at least temporarily—the powerful essence that was Brandon Chance.

She took a long sip of her drink, savoring the burning flavor as it first assailed her tongue, then her throat and belly. *To fortification,* she silently toasted.

Brandon slid a pile of board games closer and pawed through the collection, all obviously old but surprisingly intact right down to the pewter shoe in Monopoly and the sand-filled timer in Scrabble.

Brandon looked around and took a hearty swig of his bourbon, downing half the serving in one gulp. "What are you, the Salvation Army of the Deveaux clan?"

Serena smirked as she pulled a dusty version of Clue from the stack. "I like old stuff. Sue me."

He smiled when she removed the lid to check the contents. "That brings back a lot of memories." He leaned back against the couch and stretched his legs, causing his impressive thigh muscles to tighten the loose sweatpants. "Miss Scarlet. In the library. With the handcuffs."

"There aren't handcuffs in Clue," she said, pulling out the wrinkled directions from beneath the playing board.

"You sure?" He leaned sideways to look over her shoulder. "I could have sworn I played a game with Miss Scarlet where she used handcuffs."

When she forced herself to think beyond the effects of his nearness—hot-shower smell and bourbon-laced breath and all—she realized he was teasing her. "That was a fantasy, Brandon. You can't kill a person with handcuffs."

"No, but you can make them beg for mercy."

He wiggled his eyebrows suggestively. His blatant innuendo, coupled with the intoxicating effects of the liquor, made her laugh out loud. He chuckled along with her. The sounds of their laughter imbued the air with a familiarity and comfort Serena hadn't felt in years. Placed alongside her earlier admission that she'd hired him to dissuade Drew, she realized the man had an incredible capacity to forgive.

"Will they help a person beg for absolution?" she wondered, her voice small and unsure. She swallowed the last of her drink and suddenly wished she hadn't put the bottle back in the cabinet. But she hadn't relied on alcohol to give her courage before now—she certainly didn't need it tonight.

"Absolution? For what? For hiring me to help you with two troubles at once? I would have preferred you told me everything from the beginning, but you had good reason to think I wouldn't help you."

Her chuckle lacked humor. "That's an understatement."

The grin slowly faded from his face as he watched her struggle with her conscience.

"Serena, why do I get the feeling you're not telling me everything?"

"It's about the notes," she said.

"The threats on your life?"

She nodded, wincing as he sat up straighter, grabbed her empty glass from her quivering hand and put it beside his on the floor. He still believed her life was in danger. And apparently, he *cared*.

"You're holding something back. Tell me. It could make the difference between life and death. *Your* life and death."

She drew her knees to her chest as her stomach plummeted into the soles of her feet. Fighting the urge to scoot out of his line of reach, she chewed her bottom lip and considered how exactly she should phrase her admission—but all she could think about was the wording of his plea: life and death?

Oh, yeah. Because he was going to kill her.

CHAPTER SEVEN

"The notes aren't real. I'm not in danger. I made it all up."

Brandon listened to her tumbling confession, then huffed out his pent-up exasperation in a rush of breath. Now wasn't the time for her to have second thoughts about hiring him! He shouldn't have kissed her. He shouldn't have once again surrendered to temptation, no matter how willing she'd been or how sweet she'd tasted. He'd hoped the kiss would show her that he cared—then and now—despite his best efforts not to. He certainly hadn't intended to…what? Scare her? Force her to lie now about the notes just to get out of their deal?

"Serena," he said softly, fighting to keep his irritation in check, "forget that you had to dare me into taking this job. Forget that I told you I didn't want it. I wouldn't trust this assignment to anyone else. You don't have to lie to me."

She drew her thumbnails into her mouth and nibbled, then pulled them out quickly before she bit through the acrylic. "I'm not lying. I mean, I'm not lying *now*. But I was. This morning. Two minutes ago, to be accurate."

This time, he listened. Forced himself to process her admission and all the implications. The signs were all there. The averted eyes. The tasty nails. He could only imagine what her teeth were doing to the inside of her mouth.

Grabbing her ankles, he scooted her around to face him.

"Say that one more time," he demanded.

"I made up the notes myself," she answered.

She was telling him the truth—now—and she wasn't enjoying the experience.

"Why?"

"So you'd become my bodyguard."

"You got me with the dare and the bet."

Her eyes grew glossy. She wasn't going to cry—Serena wasn't the type to pull out tears for sympathy—but she was fighting like hell to keep herself together. He knew then that he'd better believe whatever crazy tale she told. Her voice was small, but clear and honest. "I got you to come here on the dare and the bet. I thought that without the notes, without proof, you would have left and not looked back before we had a chance…before…"

The kiss.

He suddenly realized he was touching her. His hands encircled her slim ankles; his palms rested on her smooth, bare insteps. With the reflexes he'd honed in the service, he shot back and forced a safe distance.

No. This could not be happening. Not again. He'd been roped into some convoluted Serena Deveaux scheme unaware and guileless. He'd already accepted that she'd chosen him rather than another bodyguard to make Drew face the futility of his marriage quest, but Brandon had still believed the threats were real. She'd lied about *everything.*

Had she lied about wanting him? About wishing things had turned out differently for them?

About caring?

But why? For revenge? For kicks?

"Thanks for telling me," he said, swallowing his anger, but

not his pride. "I'll be going now." Before he wrung her slim, sexy column of a neck.

"No! Brandon, you can't!" She didn't stand, but reached up and grabbed his hands. "Not until you hear why I lied. You know I don't do things without good reason. Never in my whole life have I enlisted your help with something that wouldn't eventually serve the greater good. Think of one time I did—one time—and you can go without another word from me."

Words didn't appeal to him at the moment, but growling served him damn well. He didn't bother trying to think of an instance where her lunacy was for the sake of ill will or simple amusement. He wouldn't find one. Of the two of them, the only one who'd ever acted selfishly was him.

"Why?" He forced the response out on a heated breath and pulled his hands from her grasp.

She swallowed, then stood, lithe and limber in her slim leggings and oversize shirt. Now wasn't the time for him to notice how truly lovely she was—sprightly, alluring, full of the carefree outlook that alluded him all his life—but he couldn't help himself, not when she wore contriteness with all the skill of a penitent schoolgirl.

"I needed you to help me dissuade Drew. I told you that. But there was more. Much more. Something I'm certain I didn't realize until…"

She glanced over her shoulder at the spot where they'd stood when they kissed—when they'd shared an intimacy borne from a long-simmering, age-old desire.

Neither of them wanted to want. Neither of them wanted to feel.

But they had.

Brandon crossed his arms over his chest, grasping for fortification against her shimmering, ocean-green eyes, her cinnamon and magnolia scent. He'd already taken one sucker punch. He braced himself for the rest of the assault.

"Why grift me? To make me pay for what I did to you?"

Her laugh was less than comical, but she didn't waver under the weight of his accusatory glare. Instead, she stepped closer and laid her hands on his crossed arms, tucking her fingers against his chest. "I don't do revenge anymore, Brandon. I did pull a scam, but believe me, I pulled it on me more than you."

Of their own volition, his muscles eased. His ire cooled a notch while the surface of his skin—precisely where she touched him—ignited with instant fire. He struggled to hold on to his anger, clenching his fists tighter and grinding his teeth.

"What is that supposed to mean?"

She stared at him intently, as if he should know the answer to that question without thinking, as if it was something as obvious as the color of the sky or the name of the city in which he now lived.

"I know Aunt Tillie told you all about my social life while you were gone. Didn't you ever wonder, just once, why I never had a serious relationship?"

As she spoke, she skimmed her fingers over his skin, plucking the dark hair on his arms, imbuing his flesh with her body heat, her scent. His nostrils flared. Need stirred in his groin, but if she felt him harden when she brushed her belly against him, she didn't reveal an ounce of surprise.

"You've never been big on commitment," he answered, knowing that wasn't entirely true. Serena shunned the institution of marriage, but she knew all about loyalty and unconditional love and friendship. If he'd stuck around after graduation, or if he'd just given her the opportunity, she would have found a way to restore the trust they'd lost that night. It was her way, her nature.

With ease, she uncrossed his arms, grazed her palms from his biceps to his wrists, then wrapped his hands around her waist.

"I couldn't want anyone when I still wanted you."

So simple. So honest. Brandon stood there, shell-shocked. Unable to move, even when she raised her lips slowly, tentatively, briefly brushing her mouth against his in an exploratory sweep—a recognizance sortie of the most dangerous kind. The scent of spice and flower and pure, unfettered woman swirled around her, catching him like a tailwind, sending him into a spiral he didn't know how to maneuver.

"Touch me, Brandon."

"No," he answered.

His heart chopped in his chest like the blades of his favorite Little Bird aircraft. Hard and strong, yet deceptively silent. She wouldn't know how excited she made him, so long as he exercised the full breadth of his self-control.

"Why? Because you won't marry me in the morning? That's your dream, not mine. I just want you. I always have."

She pressed against his mouth harder this time, unafraid, bold, acting on pure want and desire. She paid no heed to the consequences. She lived for the thrill. And he might have broken away had she not slipped her arms around his waist and up beneath his T-shirt, pressing him closer, opening her mouth and teasing his lips with her supple tongue.

She was willing to take a risk. How could he, a Chance, do anything less?

Besides, he needed to touch her, taste her, make her his— even temporarily—as he'd never needed anything in his life.

He folded his arms inward, releasing her waist and sliding his hands up and across her cheeks, then into her hair, bending her back as he moved, taking control of the kiss. The taste of bourbon lingered in her mouth, the distilled fire intensified by the heat of her tongue and lips clashing with his. She kissed him with no reservations, opening her mouth wide, teasing his teeth with her tongue, gripping him closer and closer until they nearly lost their balance.

She should have been born a Chance the way she tempted fate and good sense in pursuit of pure, unadulterated lust and need. How could he deny her? How could he deny himself? He wanted her, always had. And now she offered herself, with no strings, no promises.

But he knew too well the consequences of acting on impulse, on sheer need. He'd touch her—yes. He was powerless to stop himself. But he'd draw the line…somewhere.

With a careful spin, he lowered himself onto the couch and drew her down with him, folding her onto his lap. She whimpered when he settled her sideways, so she no longer pressed against his erection. He'd done that for his own sanity, but she didn't appreciate the gesture. Instead, she whipped her leg around and straddled him.

"What are you afraid of?" she challenged.

He tilted an eyebrow and considered disclaiming any fear at all, but then decided she knew him too well to believe him.

"Once I start, I won't be able to stop."

She scooted closer, pressing her breasts to his chest and raking her hands through his hair while she bathed his face and neck in hot, wet kisses. "Then don't stop."

Serena appreciated Brandon's innate sense of honor, but if he didn't touch her soon, she'd go mad with wanting. She'd fought her lust for him and lost. Deveaux dealt with failure much better than Chances did. True to her own family name, she'd make the most of this defeat, then sustain herself on the memory long after he walked out her door.

Grabbing the hem of her T-shirt, she moved to toss it over her head, when Brandon stopped her. He slipped the material out of her grasp and guided her hands to his shoulders.

"Going too fast got me in trouble last time, *chère*."

She gripped his shoulder hard at the sound of the endearment, at the unexpected return of that subtle Cajun accent he'd abandoned at West Point. She searched his eyes, dark and pewter and stormy, and witnessed the return of the boy he once was—wild and unpredictable as the bayou—packaged in the body of a man who had more control than a fifteen-foot-high levee and more power than the Mississippi itself.

He slipped his hands beneath her bottom and eased her upward, brushing his lips against her breasts through her shirt, exhaling his hot breath so her nipples flared and gave him his target.

He flicked his tongue across the tight nub. She gasped at the mixed sensations of moist heat and soft cotton. Sliding her hands around his neck, she snuggled closer, offered more. "Slow is all well and good, but you're making me crazy."

His grin was unadulterated pleasure.

"Seems fair, under the circumstances, don't you think? You *did* lie to me."

The feel of his hardness between her legs, thick and accessible beneath his elastic waistband, made her want only to touch him. To explore this explosive sensuality unhampered by talk or excuses or explanations.

"I lied to you because I didn't know the truth. I didn't know how much I wanted to be with you—still. And unless you can come up with a damn good reason why we shouldn't, could you please just shut up and kiss me?"

So enticing. So tempting. Brandon did as she asked, slipping his hands beneath her shirt, running them up her back, then beneath her arms, teasing the outer swells of her breasts with his thumbs while their mouths mated. She cooed and hummed, letting him know what pleased her, urging him to go farther, touch deeper, with the sounds of her gratification, with the grinding of her hips to his, with the full breadth of her luscious mouth.

On a second sweep beneath her shirt, he allowed himself to graze her nipples. She cried out, so sensitive, so tuned with her body, with her needs. Before he could stop her, she ripped her shirt away.

The sight of her stole his breath. She was lovely. Round and soft, yet slim and hard. Beyond any teenage fantasy. Beyond any adult dream.

And she was his for the taking.

But for what? One night? One evening of pleasure? And then? Brandon mentally shook himself. What the hell was he doing? Hadn't he spent years relearning, harnessing his natural instincts, mastering the art of looking before he leaped.

"Brandon? What's wrong? You don't like what you see?"

She sensed his hesitation. Attempted a joke. He smiled in natural response, kissed her, and as much as it tore him in two, slipped her off his lap and handed her her discarded shirt.

He couldn't do this. It wasn't right. Not in the way that counted. Pandering without thought to his own wants and needs—even if she seemingly wanted and needed the very same thing—was wrong. Serena was his client. And more than that, she was his friend again. His first responsibility was to keeping her safe. Her Cliché-Killer threats may have been bogus, but he posed a danger all too real.

He'd hurt her once before by not living up to her expectations. And since he knew they couldn't have a future together, he couldn't cause that same pain again. She may have claimed to want nothing from him, but she'd been wrong about her own heart before. They needed time, distance.

"I'm your bodyguard, Serena. My job is to protect you."

She crossed her arms, barely covering her breasts, barely hiding the dark, aroused peaks of her nipples or the dark, aroused desire in her eyes.

"I made up the threats, remember? I'm not in danger."

He stood up and spun, pointing both fingers at her, shaking them for a moment while he formulated his argument. "You're wrong, Serena. Dead wrong. If you weren't in danger before, you are now. And I have only one maneuver to stop it."

Turning, he scanned the room and reestablished his bearings, growing angry as he realized the full impact of their kiss on his ability to function. He'd gone too far, risked too much. Even for a Chance.

"Where are you going?" she asked, though thankfully, she didn't follow.

He forced himself out of the living room, into the guest room to retrieve his duffel bag then back toward the front door and sweet, sweet freedom. She didn't need his services. And he didn't need this complication. As he scooped the tan canvas strap onto his shoulder, he focused on his future—and her future—and how the two would never work as one.

"I'll rip up your check first thing in the morning." He turned and faced her, wanting to say more but knowing no words could possibly suffice. She'd been right when she said that her deception to break her engagement was born of good intentions. But he couldn't be a part of it. Serena represented everything he'd worked for fifteen years to gain in his life: control over his basic instincts, a taming of his natural need for danger and risk and uncertainty. And what he couldn't subdue, he channeled into positive undertakings, like his time in the service or his new job.

But nothing good could come of his kissing Serena again—nothing positive would result from him learning where to touch her to make her moan or where to kiss her to make her shout his name in ecstasy.

Nothing but complete and utter bliss…along with complete and utter disaster.

"I can't help you," he said, just to make sure she understood.

Her eyes narrowed to slits of glossy green. She shrugged back into her shirt, leaving her hair in sexy disarray and nearly distracting him from seeing the anger in her glare.

"Keep the money, Brandon!" She dug her hands onto her hips, daggers of betrayal darkening her gaze. "If you're half the idiot I think you are right now, you're going to need that cash to find a new line of work."

"Idiot? Me? Walking away right now is going to be the smartest thing I've ever done." He jabbed the air with his finger. "You know it! Do Drew a favor, Serena. Break his heart. In the long run, he'll thank you. Trust me."

The sound of crashing glass, immediately followed by Serena's high-pitched scream, stopped his tirade. He tossed his duffel and shot toward her in one movement, glancing over his shoulder to see the sparkling shards of her front window rain down onto the parlor furniture.

"Get down," he ordered, even as Serena covered her face and ducked beside the couch. He curved his body over hers until he heard the last tinkle of glass fall on the hard wood.

Then nothing. No car engine. No footfalls on the sidewalk. Just silence until Maurice started barking from the back porch.

"You okay?" he asked, scanning the room.

"What was that?"

"Stay down."

He remained crouched as he explored the floor, glad he'd thrown on his shoes after his shower or else his feet would be bleeding from remnants of glass. He found the projectile quickly—a large red brick, wrapped with brown paper.

"What do you see?"

He ignored her question while he snapped the rubber band that held the torn piece of grocery bag around the brick. He read the message and shook his head.

Not surprisingly, Serena had scooted as near as she could in her shoeless feet. "What is that?"

He turned, careful to keep his balance amid the jagged glass. Holding up the note, he watched her eyes scan the per-fectly placed vinyl letters.

"This is impossible," she claimed.

He turned the paper and read the words aloud. "'Better safe than dead.' Sounds like your Cliché Killer to me."

"But there is no Cliché Killer!"

Moving to the window, he scanned the street. Except for a few neighbors emerging from their homes to investigate the ruckus, nothing suspicious caught his eye. Whoever delivered the message was more than likely long gone, leaving him with not only Serena and his rejuvenated attraction to her to deal with, but a mystery as well.

"Obviously, there is now."

CHAPTER EIGHT

BRANDON CLOSED the door behind the police sergeant, once again promising to apprise him of any developments, including new threats. Though the seasoned officer had first distrusted Brandon because of his profession, the Quarter-born officer gave him the benefit of the doubt when he realized he'd once won a huge amount of money at a gaming table when his Aunt Tillie was dealing. The French Quarter was a small community peopled with tourists and drifters at all hours of the day and night, but strangers were difficult to find among the locals.

"I should call my mother," Serena announced. She'd sat in the same spot on the corner of the couch throughout the entire parade of neighbors and police, answering questions just as he'd instructed her—revealing only what had happened with the shattered window and nothing about her ruse with the fake notes. Brandon couldn't see any point to such explanations except to prove that Serena was indeed as wacky as most people believed her to be.

Personally, Brandon no longer cared if Serena was certifiably insane. She was in danger. That's all that mattered.

"Let your mother's spirit guides tell her in a dream. I'm going to clean up this mess and you're going to take a shower."

She wrinkled her nose at him, her sense of humor damaged but not destroyed. "Why? Do I smell?"

God, yes, he thought. Like cinnamon and magnolia and the spicy, exotic essence of a woman born and bred amid the voodoo influence of the Quarter. The elixir was the most powerful magic Brandon had ever encountered, and something deep inside told him there was no gris-gris to ward off the effects.

"You need to relax while I tape up that window."

He watched her walk toward her bedroom, looking like a scout that had somehow stumbled into a secret enemy camp. Stunned. Frightened. Uncertain of what had happened before and what would happen next. When he heard the click of her door, followed by the bang of a few drawers and then the running of water, he went looking for a broom.

By the time he'd finished sweeping and vacuuming, then had cut the boxes Samantha had brought to cover the windows, Serena emerged from the bedroom dressed in a similar T-shirt and leggings as she'd had on before, though she looked decidedly more exhausted and slightly damp. She padded silently to the kitchen, opened the back door without looking first and whistled. Maurice bounded onto the porch, but she grabbed his collar before he bounced over the threshold.

"Is that glass all cleaned up?" she asked.

"Did the best I could," he answered, "but maybe he shouldn't come in here until we have better light."

She nodded and led the dog back onto the porch where he heard her lock the doggie flap on the screen door.

"It's a cool night," she declared when she returned. "He can sleep outside. Have you seen the cat?"

Oh, he'd seen the cat all right. After he finished vacuuming, he'd heard a scratching in the front bedroom. When he investigated, he'd come face-to-face with a massive Himalayan—a ball of beige and brown fur with eyes so blue they practically glowed in the dark. If his aunt Tillie hadn't reported last summer that Endora's cat—the feline he'd shared mutual hate with his entire childhood—had finally kicked the old-age bucket, he would have thought he'd seen a ghost.

"She fled to the pantry about ten minutes ago. I take it she's related to that monster your mother tormented me with as a child."

The comment succeeded in tugging a small smile from her sullen expression.

"Tabitha wasn't the friendliest cat in the world. Tabitha II is much more people-oriented, once you get to know her."

"No, thanks. I don't trust cats."

"That says more about you than I think you want to, Brandon," she teased. Her smile faded the minute she saw the cardboard-covered windows. Without another word, she turned back into the kitchen.

With almost mindless automation, Serena took a small bowl from the cupboard, filled it with one tablespoon of canned cat food mixed with a generous helping of kibble. She set the food just inside the pantry, a walk-in space separated from the kitchen by a coordinating floral-patterned drape, then washed her hands and the spoon, finally turning to look at Brandon with vacant expectation.

Tell me what to do next was written all over her face, and this wasn't an expression he was accustomed to seeing on her—ever. Serena took care of herself. She made her own choices, her own decisions. Anything he convinced her to do was usually based on a strong presentation or an irresistible dare.

He glanced at the wall clock hanging above the sink. Midnight had come and gone. No matter how much he wanted to begin unraveling the twisted web of Serena's initial plan and this new, unexpected episode, he couldn't ignore the utter exhaustion stooping her shoulders and darkening the skin beneath her suddenly sunken eyes.

She was afraid, an emotion Brandon bet big bucks she'd never truly felt before. And the experience had wiped her out.

"Why don't you go to bed? I'll turn off all the lights and check the doors and windows. We can talk in the morning."

She nodded, wordlessly scuffling in her fuzzy black-cat slippers toward her bedroom. She turned before entering and forced a small smile. "Does this mean you're back on the job?"

"I didn't get a chance to rip up that check," he answered, leaning against the vacuum he hadn't yet stored in the front closet. "But I'm just a bodyguard, Serena. Nothing more."

She nodded again, the shock of actually experiencing an unexpected threat against her life obviously kicking her desire for him right out of her. For that, Brandon was glad. He had enough on his plate protecting her from the threats. Protecting her from *him* seemed above and beyond his capabilities.

SERENA AWOKE to the aroma of freshly brewed, strong chicory coffee and spicy andouille sausage. Sounds of whispered conversations and the sizzling of breakfast disappeared when she closed the bathroom door, but when she reemerged scrubbed and brushed and looking a lot better than she expected after only a few hours of fitful sleep, she heard her mother's distinctive Creole accent echoing in the kitchen.

"And exactly what are you going to do about this?"

Disguised by understated annoyance, Brandon's reply simmered with a childhood's worth of conflict and disbelief. "Why don't you look in your crystal ball and tell me, Endora?"

"Disrespectful! It's a wonder the military didn't teach you some manners."

"Isn't this just like old times?" Serena hurried into the

kitchen, leaned over her mother and kissed her forehead then did the same to Miss Lily, who kept watch over the stove. She avoided greeting Brandon. How does one say good morning to the man who haunted you nearly all night—asleep and awake?

"You'd think they'd learn to like each other after all these years," Miss Lily lamented, her dark-coffee skin stretched over a wide, indulgent smile.

Serena inhaled the heavenly scent of Miss Lily's cooking. The mingled scents of the trinity—onion, green pepper and celery—mixed with potent garlic, meaty sausage and hearty potato, created a breakfast delicacy Serena indulged in only on special occasions. Since her mother and Brandon had been in a room together without her to referee for nearly a quarter of an hour and they were both still alive, Serena deemed a party was definitely in order.

"If they ever learn to like each other, I'm certain the universe will implode and leave the rest of us adrift in space." Another point to add to her growing list of reasons why tricking Brandon into becoming her bodyguard was the worst idea she'd come up with since she convinced the drama department to stage *The Best Little Whorehouse in Texas* as the senior musical at her Catholic high school. She'd stayed awake half the night composing that list in her mind, the other half wondering who'd thrown the brick through her window. Growing up in the Quarter, Serena had come to consider most strangers as potential friends. She enjoyed people, trusted them—and trusted her ability to sort the good from the bad.

Still, the fact remained that in order for someone to copy her fake threats, they'd have to have broken into her home, sorted through her personal belongings, then decided to take up where her ruse left off—all for reasons she couldn't fathom. Last night, the idea terrified her. In the light of day, she was madder than hell.

But for now, she had her mother and Brandon to worry about. Keeping them from strangling each other was inherently more important than catching the maniac who'd tried—*tried,* she emphasized—to unravel her hard-earned sense of peace.

She leaned over the sizzling cast-iron skillet and took a great big whiff, hoping to dispel the disquiet churning inside her. "I don't suppose you could figure out a way to make tofu smell that good? I could make a mint at the spa."

Miss Lily laughed as she always did, shaking her head and undoubtedly wondering how Serena, after growing up on her old-style Cajun cooking, could possibly have developed an actual liking for healthy fare. They'd had this conversation a million times, and the familiarity of Lily's perplexed expression banished some of Serena's lingering fear and confusion.

But then she had Brandon's kisses to deal with. The first kiss had been so gentle, so soft and sensual and sizzling with years of unrequited desire—his and hers both. With one brief touching of lips, he'd transported them back to the night of graduation and undone all the heartbreak and anger and hurt.

Then like a fool, she'd spurred him to go farther, to risk more than the new Brandon could—more than was wise and controlled and part of his master plan. He'd pulled away, and it was her fault for going too far too fast. If not for some sicko making a real threat on her life, he would have left, the opportunity to explore the fullness of their passion gone forever.

She shrugged, determined to find means to remedy his reluctance just as soon as they figured out who the heck had sent her that threat. Like it or not, Brandon would insist he solve her mystery before dealing with the attraction still simmering between them.

But they would deal with it. She'd make sure of that.

"So, Serena," her mother sang after a long sip of coffee, "when were you going to tell me you were being stalked?"

Serena grabbed a mug from the cupboard, glancing over her shoulder at Brandon, who rolled his eyes. He'd obviously given up that piece of information in his explanation of his presence in her house so early in the morning.

"None of the threats were real—I mean, really danger-ous—until last night." She grabbed the aluminum pot warming on the stove and poured a full serving of café au lait. "I didn't want to worry you."

"Feed that line to someone else, child. Mothers have a God-given right to worry. Don't you go thinking yourself too grand to deny me my rights."

Serena slid into the seat beside her mother and shoveled two teaspoons of unrefined sugar into her drink. "You had enough on your plate with Sammie moving home and Daddy cutting her off."

Endora's huff had a grunt behind it that was terribly unat-tractive, unlike her mother's appearance even at this early hour. She sat coiffed and coutured and ready to take on the entire spirit and human realms at seven o'clock in the morning. Her dark hair, streaked with gray in a perfect pattern to add credence to her paranormal profession, didn't have a strand out of place. Her dress, full-length with a swirl pattern that covered the complete spectrum of blues from powder to midnight, didn't have a wrinkle and draped attractively over a body only slightly larger in size than it had been when Serena was born. Her makeup, worn slightly thicker than in years past, gave her an otherworldly wisdom that Serena had seen in action on more than one occasion.

Her mother was all things most mothers were, and more:

eccentric, intrusive, demanding. But she loved Serena. She'd proven that more times than Serena dared count lest her guilt overcome her.

"I'll be fine," Serena said, touching her mother's hand in a gesture meant to be soothing. "Brandon's here."

Her mother surveyed her beneath thick lashes. "I *wasn't* too worried about *that* until he met me at your back door with a handgun."

Serena took a sip of coffee and pictured the scene. "And he didn't shoot? They *did* teach you restraint in the army, didn't they?"

Brandon bit back a smile. "You ain't whistlin' Dixie, sister."

Endora glared at both of them until Serena felt a pang of remorse. Her mother endured enough disrespect and doubt from naysayers who questioned her psychic gifts. Like Brandon. She didn't need such sass from her daughter.

"I'm sorry, Mother. We're just teasing you. Brandon was protecting me. He wouldn't have drawn his gun if he'd known you were coming. I thought we were going to meet at your place."

"Yes, well, I changed my mind when my phone rang at five-thirty this morning with Tillie spreading some tale about a brick through your window." She pointed a finger at Brandon. "Your aunt is a terrible gossip. Your uncle gives her what-for about that every time we talk to him."

Brandon's eyebrows slanted over disbelieving eyes. His uncle Hank had been dead for twenty-seven years.

Endora continued her rant. "But she's accurate, that I'll give her." She turned to Serena. "I'm sure this Chance boy had something to do with you not calling and telling me yourself."

Serena never had been a snitch regarding Brandon and her mother. She wasn't about to start now.

"I wasn't hurt. I didn't see any reason to wake you up and have you rush over here just to tuck me into bed."

"So you had him do it?"

Miss Lily cleared her throat as she swung the cast-iron griddle off the gas burner with more steadiness and strength than her seventy-year-old arms should have. "Where's the platter, Serena? That young man looks hungry and my arms are tired of stirring."

Serena jumped up and obediently slid a platter from a lower shelf, laughing to herself at Miss Lily's well-timed interruption. She knew Serena's kitchen better than Serena did. She just wanted to put a stop to the bickering and sniping. Good thing, too, or Serena would have a headache ten times stronger than the one currently being chased away by French-roasted caffeine.

Her mother resumed an air of utter dignity, snapping a napkin onto her lap, as Serena placed the hash in the center of the table alongside a steaming basket of freshly baked buttermilk biscuits and a bowl of fruit compote. Brandon did the same with his napkin. Serena could practically hear the thrumming rumble of a snare drum in the background, keeping time for the duelers as they bowed politely before walking ten paces and firing again. The delicious aromas of Miss Lily's breakfast battled with the air of conflict in the kitchen.

"Brandon, honey." Miss Lily's voice, a musical mix of New Orleans local and old-time Southern belle, broke the tension as she folded herself into her chair. "What about those brothers of yours? Tillie's been stingy with her tales of those two, what with you comin' home and all."

Serena relaxed when she watched Brandon's scowl melt into a reluctant grin. He never could resist loving Miss Lily as much as she did, no more than he could hide his love for his brothers. As they ate, he recounted Kellan's glorious exploits as a decorated Navy SEAL and told, with only a little concern showing through, about T.J.'s new obsession with extreme sports.

In the truest Southern tradition, they avoided discussion of the threats on Serena during the entire meal. When Serena rose with Miss Lily to start clearing the table, Brandon cleared his throat and addressed her mother pointedly.

"Endora, I want you to know I not only intend to make sure no harm comes to Serena, I plan to find out who was responsible for that brick through her window. You may not trust me much, but you have to admit that I've been keeping Serena out of trouble nearly as long as you have."

Endora folded her napkin and placed it squarely beside her. She assessed Brandon with eyes both visible and invisible—the eye of a mother and the eye of a woman guided by things others couldn't see.

"You've caused her a great deal of trouble, too, Brandon Chance. And I don't think you're through yet."

Brandon held her gaze. "No, ma'am, I'm probably not. But the kind of danger I pose won't get her killed."

Standing, Endora waved at Lily, indicating she was ready to leave. "You see to that, young man. Or you'll have me to deal with."

"THAT WENT BETTER than I expected," Serena said after walking Endora and Miss Lily to the vintage Duesenburg her mother drove around town. Brandon had already started to fill her sink with water and soap and stacked the dishes to soak. He turned off the faucet when she closed the front door, and met her in the living room, the added shade of the boxed-up window reminding both of them that they had no time to waste.

"Time to talk, Serena."

"I have to let Maurice out."

"Already done. Filled his water dish, too. The breakfast plates can wait. Who has a key to this house other than your mother and Miss Lily?"

Serena shook her head, wondering who could have possibly gained entrance to her house without her knowledge and then shuffled through the papers in her casket to find the fake notes. She'd carefully hidden the notes beneath at least three years' worth of warranties, birthday cards and receipts.

"They have one key between them. Miss Lily uses it to fill my fridge. Mother rarely comes over when I'm not here— she's too busy."

"What about your sister?"

Serena concentrated, trying to remember if she'd given Sammie a key over the past month—not because she believed her sister had anything to do with the brick through the window, but because she wouldn't waylay Brandon's suspicions in any other way.

"She's only been in town a month. I'd remember if I gave her a key. I haven't."

"And you didn't tell her about your scheme to break your engagement with Drew?"

Serena shook her head and plopped onto the couch. "Sammie wouldn't have approved."

"She wants you to marry Drew?"

She couldn't contain her laugh. "Uh, no. But she's a direct-approach kind of person. When she wants something, she just goes after it until she gets it. She'd want me to do things and say things that would crush Drew. I won't do that," she said one more time for emphasis.

Brandon only shook his head.

"You've never sent David here on an errand with a key, or any of your other employees?"

For the sake of cooperation, she thought carefully about his question. Besides, she really did want to know what the heck was going on. "Not since I created the notes and shoved them in the box."

"Where did you make the notes? At the spa?"

"I'm not stupid, Brandon." She'd been extremely careful to ensure that no one found out about her plan. "I went to a copy center in Metairie, where no one knew me. I rented a computer and I didn't save the files."

He thought for a moment. "The machine could have had an automatic save feature. Someone could have stumbled onto your work after you left, maybe followed you home."

Serena wanted to deny the possibility, but her knowledge of computers was limited to the style she'd used in college, now long out of date. She knew just enough about current technology to function well in her business, maybe a little more than most people because of her friendship with Drew, who owned an Internet company. But she wasn't certain of her knowledge, that was for sure.

"I don't think so, Brandon. But I could be wrong. I'm not sure of all the features on the new operating systems, but I can't see how finding a file on a rented computer would lead someone to me. I logged in under a fake name. I chose a machine in a corner where no one could look over my shoulder."

He nodded, obviously impressed. "After you get dressed, we'll go over to Metairie. You can show me the shop and which machine you used." He slid his hands into his pockets, and for the first time this morning, Serena noticed how snug his jeans were and how very nicely he filled them out. Even his dour expression couldn't dispel her silent sigh.

"Last question, Serena. What about Drew? Does he have access to your house?"

Serena rolled her lips together, fighting not to bite the inside of her mouth. While she'd never given Drew his own copy of her back-door key, he'd used hers on hundreds of occasions—to grab her extra clothes when a customer ran late and they had an engagement after work, or to feed Maurice and Tabitha when she'd gone out of town. If memory served, he'd run such an errand for her on Saturday, when the spa was overbooked and she'd run out of fresh aloe. But despite Brandon's conjecture last night giving Drew a tentative yet plausible motive, she couldn't imagine he'd stoop to such measures to convince her to marry him.

Her uncertainty, however, must have shown on her face. Brandon ran his hands through his hair and sat beside her on the couch.

"He does have a key."

"No, but he's borrowed mine a million times." And Drew was just the type to make a copy for emergencies. And he most definitely knew that any personal paper of the slightest importance was stored in her antique casket. "Brandon, he just can't be behind this. It's not like Drew to do something as dangerous as throwing a brick through my window. He could have hurt me, or one of the animals. Tabitha could have been sitting on that sill."

"Does she usually sit there at night?"

"Cats don't have schedules, but no, she's usually in bed with me at that time…or in the pantry. But Drew wouldn't know that. He's never…"

Her words trailed off, but Brandon took great pleasure in filling in the rest of the sentence. *He's never stayed here that late.* Or better still, *He's never stayed here overnight.* Since

Serena claimed not to be in love with Drew, not to want this marriage to go forward, he'd hoped they hadn't been intimate—not that her sex life was any of his business.

But he'd make it his business. After last night, he didn't have much choice. And conveniently, his investigation gave him the reason to ask.

"You and Drew haven't slept together here?"

Any other woman might have been shocked by his forthright question. Serena just smirked.

"You've been wanting to ask that question, haven't you?"

Suddenly, trying to convince her he was just working on a case didn't seem as plausible as it had a moment ago.

"Since you walked into my office yesterday," he admitted. No sense in lying to her when he wanted nothing less than the whole truth in return.

She licked her lips and fluffed her hair, leaning back into the pillows of the couch and staring up at him with eyes weary from lack of sleep, but still sparkling with the irony of his concern. "Drew and I haven't slept together, Brandon. Not here, not anywhere. I told you, I don't want to marry him. I'm not a tease. When I want a man, he knows."

Brandon inhaled, then held his breath for a long moment before blowing it out through his mouth. He knew, all right. And he was in serious trouble. He watched her swivel ever so slightly and drape her arm over the overstuffed cushion beside her. Sensuality and Serena went hand in hand. Her signals were as clear as a radar blip in the center of the screen, her weapons as dangerous as AMRAAM missiles on a MiG.

In the interest of keeping her safe, he'd fight the good fight to resist her. Their make-out session on the couch had kept him awake all night. He could only imagine what making love with her would do to his ability to function.

"I've made a mental note of that, thanks." With one more fortifying breath, he stood, swiveled on his heel and marched to the kitchen. "I'll tackle the dishes. You get dressed. I want to get to the bottom of this today."

He plunged his hands into the steaming, sudsy water, not bothering to glance over his shoulder. If he knew Serena, and unfortunately he did, she was grinning from ear to ear. She'd just won a small but significant battle. She knew without a doubt that he wanted her more than he would admit.

But he wouldn't lose the war. He'd sworn to protect her— and that he would do. From her stalker. And from himself.

Especially from himself.

CHAPTER NINE

THEY DROVE BACK from Metairie in silence, no closer to figuring out who'd threatened Serena than before. After conferring with the copy-shop manager, Brandon was convinced that no one could have seen Serena's notes once she deleted the documents. Even the printer she'd used was directly beside the terminal she'd rented. Her alias had indeed shown up on the company's records, but neither the manager nor his college-age assistant recognized Serena in her normal clothes.

Though "normal," Brandon noted, was a relative statement with Serena. The night she'd made the notes, she'd reportedly worn a baggy Tulane sweatshirt, cap and jeans. He wished she'd adopt the same mode of dress every day, but instead she'd wrapped herself in another of her slenderizing sarong skirts, topped with a snug, V-necked tank top and an unbuttoned, tied-at-the-waist blouse. With gold sandals and enough rings and bracelets to stock a jewelry cart on the Square, Serena wasn't exactly a woman any red-blooded American male could miss.

And he'd never felt the simmering effects of his own red blood more than he had over the past two days.

"We've fairly eliminated a stranger from being responsible," he pointed out, trying to waylay his attraction, trying to remember that Serena could be nothing more than a client, and an old friend, but definitely not a lover.

"I can see why we might think that," she replied.

Her reluctance to see the obvious succeeded in tamping down his unbidden desire to pull off the interstate and kiss the anxiety off her face.

"Can you see why we might not? Come on, Serena. This has *inside job* written all over it." Actually, Brandon was quite certain it had *Drew Stuart* written all over it, but he wasn't the type to go accusing a man without real proof. Proof he intended to get—today.

"I want to go to the spa." Her change of subject didn't surprise him. Neither did her choice of retreats, though he wasn't sure taking her to a public place was a good idea.

"I'm not…"

"Don't say no, Brandon. The brick went through the window of my house. The spa is completely booked today. I can't leave David and the rest of my staff shorthanded, not after dropping Maurice and Tabitha II off there for safekeeping."

Serena had insisted on removing both animals from the house if they were going to be gone all day. With her mother and Miss Lily out visiting clients and Samantha's tiny new apartment pet restricted, they'd had no choice but to drop them off at the spa before heading out on their fact-finding mission. As Brandon maneuvered his Jeep off I-10, he reevaluated his initial reluctance to leave Serena at the spa. She would indeed be safe, at least for an hour or two.

And an hour or two was all he needed to find Drew and get the truth—even if he had to beat it out of him.

For some reason, the prospect of physical violence against a guy he used to call a friend didn't rub against his grain the way it should. Brandon was a risk-taker, had been a certified daredevil in his youth, but he'd never been particularly violent. And yet, just the thought of Drew presuming some warped type of ownership over Serena made his knuckles itch to pound on flesh.

"What's your sister doing today?" he asked.

"Working if she didn't already quit. Why?"

He shrugged as he took a left onto Chartres Street. "I'd feel better if she could come by the spa and stay with you."

That perked her up. She sat up straighter in her seat and turned to face him as much as her seat belt would allow. "Really? You mean you might actually consider letting Sammie work with you?"

"Don't jump to conclusions. I still want her to do her research and get her licenses before I make a decision. But I wouldn't mind her help today—if she's really as observant as she claims and wasn't exaggerating about her black belt."

Serena leaned her cheek against the headrest. Through his peripheral vision, he caught the weariness in her body language and his insides heated with the renewed fire of anger and frustration and plain old caveman protectiveness.

"If she says she's good, I believe her," Serena responded. "She's not a braggart. She tells it like it is."

"Is that why your father cut her off?" He'd wanted to ask that question since this morning when Serena had made the cryptic statement to her mother. Devlin Deveaux's fame rivaled Steven Spielberg's, or at least Martin Scorcese's. He had money coming out of his ears. Brandon couldn't imagine why he'd withhold anything from the daughter he'd raised.

"*Cut her off* is misleading, but that's how Mother sees it."

Brandon was suddenly glad he'd asked. He liked the sound of the ire in her voice. Any fiery emotion was preferable to the quiet, fear-laden resignation he'd heard before.

"How so?" They had a few minutes until they reached the spa. He might as well get the whole story.

As expected, Serena obliged. "Samantha had her own money from working. Unfortunately, she most often worked for my father, and he preferred to pay her with interest in his movies, then talked her into reinvesting in the next one. He's over budget this time and she hasn't seen a dime since a few months before she left California. He *says* he's made her a producer and that it'll be his biggest hit yet, but since production won't be done for a while, Sammie's purse has been a little empty. She used all her savings just to move back here."

"And she doesn't want handouts from Mom or sis?"

"Not if she can help it. It's not her style."

Turning on Toulouse Street, Brandon maneuvered the Jeep down the narrow brick road, watching for a parking spot. Serena and Samantha may not have been raised in the same household, but both women were as fiercely independent as any of the guys he'd ever served with, maybe even more so. He'd be damned if he let Drew, or whoever was responsible for the brick, take that away from either one of them.

He found a spot and parked, commanding Serena to stay in the Jeep until he got out and surveyed the area. Satisfied no one or nothing suspicious was occurring beyond the regular midmorning mayhem of the Quarter, he opened her door and helped her out. In the process, he was treated to a quick flash of thigh from the split in her skirt.

He really did have to solve this case fast.

The minute the doors of the spa jingled open, Brandon watched Serena put on her best professional face. She greeted customers waiting in the lobby with familiarity and genuine warmth, even the ones she was meeting for the first time. He remained near the door, watching David answer a string of calls with his headset while serving tea to patrons.

"Mr. Chance," David greeted after handing out the last

porcelain cup and saucer. "I brewed a killer oolong this morning. Want a cup?"

Brandon shook his head and watched Serena disappear beyond the beaded drapes, her massage therapist in tow.

"I'm not staying. Do you know how to get in touch with Serena's sister?"

"Yeah, she's in Serena's office trying to keep Maurice from eating the cat." He grimaced and glanced down, drawing Brandon's attention to the pet fur coating his jeans. "They supposedly get along, but Serena once told me she'd designed the spa to bring the most basic emotions to the surface." He swiped impotently at his pants. "I'm starting to believe her."

And in that case, he really should be getting the hell out, Brandon acknowledged with a nod. "Can you ask Sam to keep an eye on her sister for me? I have an important errand."

"I think that's why she's here," David confided. A gentle chirping indicated another call coming in, so he pressed a button hooked onto his belt loop and answered, "Serena's Spa and Scents, may I help you?" He listened for a moment, then catching the impatience on Brandon's face, he asked the caller to please hold.

"Thanks," Brandon said, liking the boy more and more by the minute. "One last thing. Do you have a business and home address for Drew Stuart?"

David's expression revealed a mix of surprise and suspicion.

"He's an old friend of mine, too. And I'd like to pay him a visit."

SERENA WANDERED INTO the garden, watching the shadows elongate as day surrendered to night. Thank God for a busy schedule. She'd been so wrapped up in her customers and their needs, she'd been completely unable to think of her own troubles for more than an instant. Invariably, even those brief thoughts were interrupted by a problem with Maurice, a call from a supplier, a joke from her sister or the message that Brandon's errands would take a little longer than he'd planned and he wouldn't be back to fetch her until closing time.

Which had come and gone. At nearly eight o'clock, the space she'd so lovingly designed for clean comfort now echoed with an emptiness she'd never before experienced. She could hear the gentle tapping of David's fingers on his keyboard out front, working on a paper for his rhetoric class here instead of at his dorm because he didn't want to leave her and Samantha alone until Brandon returned. *Men.* Though David wasn't exactly a grunt-and-bang-his-chest type, he couldn't fight his natural instincts any more than she could. And those instincts had been on superpowered overdrive all day.

Little by little, the horror and fear of the brick through her window and the copycat threat faded to the background. She'd never let fear rule her life and she wasn't about to start now.

Brandon vowed to protect her and she believed him implicitly. She didn't even worry too much over his suspicions of Drew. The more she thought about it, the more she realized how ridiculous that notion was. Though she didn't have an alternative suspect even after racking her brain as much as the day would allow, she trusted that the truth would come out soon enough.

All the truth. Particularly the truth about personal wants and needs. And she was going to be the first to start.

She'd admitted quite a bit to Brandon last night—more than she'd planned to—more than she'd known herself until she'd felt the fire in his kiss and the passion of his touch. But because Brandon was convinced he had to protect her in more ways than she'd paid for, the desire had gone unexplored.

Well, she'd spent way too much spiritual energy trying to achieve simple balance in her life to let this frustration undo her. Until she and Brandon explored and dealt with everything simmering between them, finding out who'd threatened her wouldn't do much but restore an illusion of personal safety and freedom. An illusion because as long as Brandon was still in New Orleans, her heart was at risk.

So the first thing she planned to do was confront their overwhelming, all-encompassing, hot-fire desire. He'd only kissed her a few times, yet the pressure on her lips, his taste on her tongue, still lingered, still smoldered deep inside her, ready to flare with renewed heat the minute he glanced in her direction or brushed against her skin.

Tonight, she'd sate this hunger, explore this all-too-real magic. If she didn't, she feared she'd go even more insane than Brandon already thought she was.

"Serena?" David poked his head through the beads.

Startled, Serena jumped, then tapped her chest to remind her heart to beat. "I'm out here." She stepped closer to the spa entrance. Unlike other gardens in the Quarter, hers had no street access except through the spa.

"Brandon's back," David told her. "He's helping Sam put Tabby and Maurice in her car."

Serena marched to the doors, but lingered at the threshold, not yet wanting to go inside. "She's taking them home?" *She's gonna fit Maurice into that tiny car of hers?*

David shook his head. "Your mother's home and said she'd take them until you got there. She offered your old bedroom for the night." He glanced over his shoulder, indicating to Serena that whoever was behind him wasn't too thrilled with that idea.

Brandon pushed through the beads like a bull through a red drape. "That won't be happening."

Serena grinned. She didn't want to stay with her mother. She wanted to stay with Brandon.

"Tell Sammie to promise my mother I'll call her in the morning," Serena said. "You should go home, David. Can you lock the door on your way out?"

"Sure thing." David hesitated for a moment, watching Brandon with questioning eyes, then gave up trying to decipher his unreadable expression, an expression even Serena couldn't decode. "Good night."

Neither one of them replied. They stood there staring at each other until they heard the rustle of David's backpack, the jingle of his keys and the tinkle of the front bell, followed by a click of the dead bolt.

Brandon took a single step toward her, then stopped again. She'd turned off all the lights in the spa before venturing into the garden, wanting nothing more than the glow of the stars and the Quarter to guide her pensive wandering. A sliver of light slashed across Brandon's face, throwing even more silver into the mixed hues of black and gray of his gaze and putting his mouth and jaw in shadow.

She captured her bottom lip between her teeth. "Did you find out what you wanted?"

"Not exactly."

"Wasn't Drew at his office? David told me that's who you were going to see."

"He was there."

"You don't look happy about whatever he told you."

"He didn't tell me anything I didn't already know."

Brandon clenched his fists at his sides, curling his fingers tightly, then releasing them in a stiff stretch to alleviate the sudden tension in his muscles. Drew hadn't shed any new light on Serena's troubles. Their "man-to-man" conversation did nothing more than confirm facts Brandon didn't want to face.

Like the unmistakable truth that Drew didn't love Serena, even if he thought he did. He valued her. He needed her and cared about her welfare as an old, good friend would. But his love sprang from a fear of being without her much more than from a passion he couldn't control.

And Brandon knew about that passion, knew firsthand.

He clenched his fists again.

Serena slipped away from the door and disappeared beyond his line of vision. "Do you still think he's behind the brick?"

Her voice receded. He'd have to follow her to answer, and the shadowy, intimate setting of her erotic garden wasn't the safest place for him right now…or for her.

The danger they now faced came solely from each other.

His eyes adjusted to the muted light and he spotted her walking barefoot around the back of the fountain. The water dripped and dribbled over the sensuously carved marble, providing a gentle music that offset the late-night echoes of the Quarter on the other side of the high walls.

"No, it's wasn't Drew. That couple from New York had him playing tour guide around the city until well after midnight."

"Couldn't he have hired someone?"

She played devil's advocate with a mocking lilt in her voice. She knew as well as he did now that such a nefarious plan wouldn't occur to a guy like Drew. Brandon had talked with Drew for hours. They'd reminisced, shooting the breeze until Brandon had established a comfortable rapport that led men like Drew into admitting more than they wanted to, more than they sometimes knew themselves. And while Drew had convinced Brandon that he had nothing to do with the threats on Serena's life, he'd also clued him in to the most shocking revelation of all.

"He's not the one," Brandon concluded. *He's not the one behind the threats. He's not the one who should be your husband. And he's definitely not the one to love you.*

That job's already taken.

Brandon experienced another jolt of utter disbelief at the notion that he loved Serena Deveaux, something he'd realized over a beer with Drew and had been grappling with as he wandered the Quarter considering what to do next. She most certainly wasn't the wife he'd envisioned finding when he left the service. Someone who'd cook meals and have babies and lull his restlessness into calm content when his reckless spirit threatened to take control. Someone who'd talk sense into him when he felt the urge to take to the skies in a biplane he'd rebuilt in his garage or embark on a rappelling trip to the Andes with his baby brother, T.J.

Serena wouldn't be a voice of reason to remind him he wasn't getting any younger. She wouldn't tie him down with stern looks or even sweet kisses that reminded him of his responsibilities. If Serena loved him, she'd fly the plane with him so they could make love as they soared, or she'd pack her own climbing gear so they could reach the pinnacles of sensual pleasure on one of the world's highest peaks.

If she loved him.

The possibility seemed ludicrous. Crazier than she was. Crazier than she made him. But he couldn't forget that just last night she'd kissed him with more willingness and more desire than any woman he'd ever held in his arms. He was able to forget that she had pushed him away fifteen years ago, when he was young and foolish and didn't know how to treat her right.

But he knew now. And she knew that he knew.

Her voice rolled toward him with a soft echo over the deserted garden path. "Drew's not the one for me. You are. You always have been."

His eyes caught sight of Serena in a cloak of shadows as she emerged from behind the fountain. Though they were separated by the circular pool and gurgling water, he heard her blatant feminine need—could feel the heat of her desire with the same magnetic tug that urged him to forget about his plans and his vows and do only what she was inviting him to do. The urge to resist was strong. He couldn't make promises. He couldn't change his life direction after all he'd done to lay the groundwork.

"Serena, you don't know me anymore."

"Don't fool yourself, Brandon. I know you better than you think. And I know me. I know what I want. I know what I deserve. I've always known. Always."

He watched her lift her arms behind her head and release the clasp on the bulky necklace she wore. The crafted gold dropped into the water with a gentle splash. She took off her bracelets next, laying them in a stack on the fountain's edge.

"You deserve a man who can love you forever." His platitude sounded entirely too personal, so he amended himself. "Every woman deserves that."

Her laugh was bittersweet. "Yeah, we all do. But you know what? I'll settle for a man who will love me tonight. With all his soul." She stepped over the stone edge and into the pool, her fingers working the knot on her skirt as the hem floated in the water.

"Serena…" He spoke her name to stop her, but didn't move an inch.

Her head tilted ever so slightly, just enough for her eyes to catch a gleam of starlight and reflect her intentions. "Do I need to dare you again, Brandon?"

She unwrapped the skirt, revealing her slim, bare legs and panties so pink and translucent he could see the clear outline of feminine curls as if the beam from a street lamp focused exclusively on the apex of her thighs. His groin grew tight and hot. God, he wanted her. And she most certainly wanted him. Tonight, here, would be nothing like he imagined, nothing like he'd ever planned, even when he used to fantasize about Serena beneath the covers of his bunk bed. In the flesh, willing and wanting, Serena Deveaux transcended any *Playboy*-inspired teenage dream.

Especially since he'd tasted her. Knew the abandon of her kiss, the potential freedom of her embrace.

He stepped closer as she tossed the sarong onto the ground. He kicked off his shoes when she slipped her fingers beneath the hem of her tank top, then splashed into the fountain just in front of her when she tore the shirt over her head. In a tangle of hair and bare breasts and eyes dark with desire, she revealed herself to him, offered herself, with a fundamental freedom of spirit that was hers and hers alone.

Brandon caught her elbows before she brought them down and stood, motionless, his lungs aching for something more than air, his entire body throbbing for something beyond a spontaneous seduction.

"This isn't a good idea," he said.

"Do you really want to waste time trying to convince me, which you won't…or do you just want to make love with me?"

She tugged her elbows from his grasp, threw her top aside and took his hands in hers. Turning them, she examined the breadth of his palms, the length of his fingers, the roughened texture of his skin. His legs grew heavy as his jeans saturated water from the pool. His groin thickened with long lust. How was he supposed to resist her? Here? Like this?

"You have great hands, Brandon." She met his gaze straight on—no shyness, no fear—nothing but unadulterated need and utter concentration. On him. As if he was the only man who existed in the world. As if he existed only for her.

"I asked you to touch me last night." She pressed his hands downward, skimming them down her rib cage then around her waist, allowing his fingers to brush over her skin—introducing him to her warmth with slow, directed skill. "You barely did."

The muscles in his forearms ached with paralyzing tightness. One reaction, one reflex, and he could caress her curves completely—touch her, please her, pleasure her—in every delicious way. "I wanted to touch so much more."

He'd admit that much because it was the truth. He couldn't claim that he'd resisted exploring her body last night for a good logical reason because, at this instant, he couldn't for the life of him remember what that good logical reason could possibly have been.

"But you didn't," she replied. "Because of Drew, maybe. And now you know, he has nothing to do with us. And maybe you didn't because of what happened in the past. Which is just that—in the past."

She guided his hands in a circular motion to the lowest portion of her hips, then pulled up over her abdomen, between her cleavage, over her throat and chin to her lips. She kissed each of his palms, softly, caressing her cheek against his fingers.

"What do you want now? Right now. Not tomorrow, not next week, because the future takes care of itself. I'm a 'live for the moment' kind of gal, Brandon. You know I always have been. And in this moment, living means making love with you."

He grabbed her face, held her still, searched her irises for any sign, any indication, that she'd regret her seduction in the light of the day. Because if he made love to her, he'd do so all night. To make sure she never forgot. To make sure he always remembered the night his greatest fantasy came true.

"What'll it be, Brandon? Live or run?"

He dipped his head and captured her lips, muttering the last words he intended to speak for a long while.

"Chance men *never* run."

CHAPTER TEN

FOR A KISS THAT started with a slow, deliberate tease, the pace accelerated instantaneously the minute Brandon accepted her challenge. With one hand still on her cheek and the other flat and hot and strong against her lower back, he pressed her full against him and devoured her mouth. With a sigh and a thrill, Serena surrendered, released his hand and untucked his shirt.

She slid her hands upward, marveling at the rock-hard tension in his muscles and the erotic skill of his tongue. Her senses reeled. She didn't know what felt better—her fingers curled with the hair on his chest or her mouth entwined with his. He was so hard. She was so soft. She wanted to feel him fully against her. Inside her.

She forced him to break the kiss long enough to tear his shirt over his head. He bent forward to take her mouth again, but she stepped back, sloshing water high against their knees and thighs.

She shook her head and undid his button fly. He grabbed the marble statue for balance, his chest heaving with barely checked control while she worked his jeans and boxers off his body.

Lord, he was magnificent. She couldn't help but stop and compare the lines of the carved stone with the living, breathing counterpart that leaned against it. She couldn't help but run her hands first over the marble to steal the cool moisture dribbling across the curves, then over Brandon's body—arms first, then down his back.

He turned as though to step out, but she stopped him.

"Don't move. We have all night. I just want to feel you."

His back still to her, she scooped up a handful of water and released it at his waist, then watched, fascinated, as the rivulets swirled over his backside and down his powerful legs. Then she followed the drops with her hands.

She didn't shy from touching him. He didn't shy from groaning his approval of her exploration or from seeking out her mouth, branding her with a probing kiss of his own.

"You got me all wet," he said.

She searched his eyes for humor, but found only a glimmer of amusement in the blackness of his gaze.

"Just a little damp," she answered, her lips, swollen and aching for his, curled into a tiny smile. She had to tilt her head back to look at him directly and he immediately sensed the discomfort that caused.

His hands, wet from his hold on the statue, slipped down her back with a slowness that mirrored her touch, but when he reached her backside, he cupped her and lifted her onto the fountain, sliding her full against marble, her feet poised along the lower edge. Her curves nearly fit with complete perfection, as if she'd let the artist mold the stone against her naked body.

"Now I know why this fountain is so erotic," he murmured, looking down to how the tiny seat in the stone spread her legs just so wide. "It's shaped for a woman." His gaze met hers. "For you."

"I'm sure it's a coincidence," she insisted, but heat pooled between her legs as he lifted her right arm and draped it over a jutted curve, then did the same to her left, leaving her like an open offering to him.

Which she was. In every single aspect of her being, fountain or not.

"I don't believe in coincidences."

"What do you believe in, Brandon?" She couldn't help ask because she really didn't know. Minutes ago, she didn't care, but now, she was vulnerable to him. To his touch and his control over the desire throbbing through her veins and over skin like a pulsing, living heat.

He leaned forward and kissed her temple. "I believe in knowing every inch of you, *chère*. I believe in soft kisses and wet tongues and hard nipples and hot centers and loud orgasms. Really loud ones. Ones where you shout my name so the whole Quarter can hear."

She didn't know if she had wanted a more soulful answer when she first asked, but the one he provided suited her just fine. He ran his tongue to her ear, teasing her flesh with hard moisture and heated breath, nibbling her lobe while his hands hovered beside her cheeks.

"I've waited a lifetime to touch you, Serena."

"Don't wait," was all she could manage, her lungs tight with anticipation. She'd waited that same lifetime to be touched by him, to join with him, the only man she'd ever loved.

"I won't. Now don't move."

He delayed no longer, but he didn't use his hands to explore her. First, he used his eyes, followed by his mouth and tongue. He kissed a path down the column of her neck, across her shoulders and over one arm, then back to the base of her neck. He stepped back and quickly assessed her position.

"Here," he said, grasping her chin and tilting it just a smidgen to the left.

When he did, a splash of running water crossed over her shoulder and down her breast. Her sharp intake of breath thrust the nipple forward and he wasted no time capturing it in his mouth, lapping the water as he covered her sensitive flesh with his warm mouth.

Serena pressed her lids closed. The sensation made her eyes hot with tears, hot with blinding need. He sucked and teased and laved and kissed with a pace just quick enough to make her relish every sensation—and just slow enough to mourn the loss of his mouth when he slid down to his knees and braced his hands along the outside of her thighs.

The fountain's water bubbled beneath her, ran down her back with cool caresses, contrasting with Brandon's hot hands skimming over her legs. His fingers teased. His eyes feasted. Serena held her breath, praying he'd taste her soon, before she lost her ability to speak.

He started at her knees and nibbled his way up. He took a deep breath, then blew hot warmth across her curls. When he finally tasted her, she swallowed a desperate cry. It wasn't enough. Delicious and delectable as his rigid tongue felt against her swollen, pounding flesh, she wanted more.

"Brandon." She spoke his name in yearning, unhooking her arms from the marble to raise his head.

He looked up with eyes darker than a bayou sky. "I said, don't move," he chastised, lust and devilish intentions curving his mouth into a mock frown. "Can't you ever listen?"

"But…" Her protest died a pleasurable death when he wrapped his full mouth against her and flicked her words out of her mind. She was his. For now, all his.

And she told him so. Loudly.

When he finally stood and kissed away the last vestiges of her climax, she regained her ability to think. Soon, very soon, they were going to make love. And they'd need protection.

"There's a box of condoms in my office." She whispered

the fact against his lips, praying she wouldn't destroy the magical mood.

"I was going to ask you about that." His voice brimmed with gentle teasing. He'd obviously somehow found time in the past two days to rummage through her things. "Is there something you need to tell me about the massages you give at this place?"

She laughed because she knew he was baiting her, teasing her. Because that's what they did, she and Brandon. For as long as they'd known each other.

But the amiable ribbing took on a delicious naughtiness now, making her nipples tighten and her heart flutter when he gave her a playful wink.

"Why tell when I'm having so much fun showing you?" she answered.

"Good point. I'll be right back. Don't move."

She waited until he splashed out of the fountain before she slid down the marble and into the water, cooling her hot flesh against the mosaic tiles. She tried not to think about the consequences of what they'd just done, of what they were going to do. She'd allowed Brandon access to so much more than just her body. She'd pay a steep price for her sensual candor.

But as she leaned back on her elbows, submerging her flaming skin in the fountain's cool waters, she knew she'd have no regrets. Not with Brandon. She no longer lamented the years they'd lost since that night in the gym, the friendship they'd sacrificed. She now saw it all clearly as a path to precisely this spot. This moment.

This ecstasy.

He was in and out of her office in record time. He ripped a condom out of the box, tore the foil packet with his teeth, tossed it onto the edge of the fountain and joined her in the water, crawling over her but holding his body rigid and aloft as if he was about to start a repetition of push-ups.

"You moved," he protested.

"I plan on moving a lot in the next few hours. I'm not a passive lover, Brandon. At least, I don't think I am."

"Don't think? You've done this before, right?"

She grinned, certain she wasn't going to tell him one single secret about her sex life. "Not here." She leaned up and kissed a corner of his chin. "Not like this. Not with you."

"Your first time should have been with me." He let out that feral growl of his and pressed his lips to her temple, then down her cheek.

She managed only a breathy "yeah," before he covered her mouth with his. She grabbed his marble-hard biceps, noting the restraint he used to keep from drowning her in either the water or the fullness of his desire. She knew Brandon. She knew when he was holding back. And he now had an industrial-strength wall of restraint in place, keeping him in check. In line. Unlike the way he'd been all those years ago.

Unlike the way she wanted him to be right now.

"Come here," she said. She scooted back on her elbows, wickedly tracing his body with her toes as she slipped away.

He cleared his throat before he asked, "Where?"

Pushing back with his arms, he allowed her room to slither away like a sensual sea creature of ancient myth. She rolled onto her belly, treating him to a tantalizing glimpse of her pale, bare bottom before she disappeared behind the fountain. He didn't think he could grow any harder, but he was wrong. His hands ached to hold her close, to spread his tanned fingers and roughened palms over her incredible curves, to bury himself inside her and let loose the fullness of his desire.

Serena was all that was feminine, but he'd never call her

delicate. She possessed a strength that was physical and spiritual and sensual all at the same time.

And yet, he wondered if even she could match the raging need tearing through him. He'd never realized how strong his passion for her was, how intense. Though she moved away from him, an invisible connection much like a steel towline cranked a painful tension between his heart and hers.

He heard her stand, saw the droplets of water splashing as she climbed the back side of the marble.

"If you thought that side of the marble was interesting—" she noted.

First, he saw one calf, then the other, and just above, an ivory swell of flesh beckoned him like a golden light leading him home. He sloshed gallons of water over the sides of the fountain when he retrieved the condom and cursed the wetness while he forced the latex on.

But force he did.

She leaned on a small, tilted tableau just perfectly shaped and angled to support her belly and rib cage, then curved along the top to caress her breasts with cold, wet marble.

"Look what I found," she said.

He eased up behind her, emboldened by her sharp intake of breath when he pressed his full sex against her derriere. She stretched her hands behind her and grabbed his hips.

"You still think the artist didn't design this fountain for lovemaking?" he asked.

Thigh to thigh, he slipped his feet between hers, easing her legs apart while he bathed the back of her neck in kisses.

"Think?" She rolled her head forward and grabbed him tighter, pulling him so close, he had no choice but to slip between her legs to meet her demand. "Who can think?"

She leaned completely against the tableau, nestling herself

so close to him, Brandon knew the minute he could no longer operate on logic or reason or thought. Instinct—primal and ingrained into all of him that was male—overtook him in a rush of pure need. He wanted to drive himself inside. Take her. Brand her.

But her coo, soft and feminine and lilting with pleasure, gripped his heart and led him inside more slowly. He relished the feel of her warmth surrounding him. Wet. Welcoming. Like velvet. Like silk.

He explored her with his hands while he strummed a gentle rhythm. Her breasts were warm and heavy. She encouraged his touch with a litany of words. *Yes. Touch me. Brandon.*

Some words were more erotic.

Some were unintelligible, but it didn't matter. Just the sound of her voice, coming from the place deep inside her, where he needed to be, guided him, urged him.

She relaxed her shoulders and swayed her hips, rocking him deeper, sealing him to her, proving she wanted all that he could give. And yet, when he came, he wanted to look into her eyes and watch the precise moment when she took all he had in his soul.

Leaning full against her, he slipped both arms around her waist lifted her off the tableau. He loved her breasts with his hands while he backed them up to the edge of the water, then adored her nipples, neck and mouth with his lips and tongue as he turned her around, sat down and guided her onto his lap, pressing back into her tight warmth.

She didn't speak. She only smiled, folded her legs around his waist and her arms around his neck, pulled herself up and then back down to restart their elemental rhythm.

She never closed her eyes. His peripheral vision blurred as they rocked, but he found a steady center in her sea-green gaze, discovered the full breadth of Serena's power as they pumped toward the edge…then spilled over, drop by drop, jet by jet, into a sparkling pool of release.

SERENA FOLDED the fluffy terry-cloth robe around her as she puttered around inside the spa, warding off the chill of Brandon's departure. He'd only gone back to the garden to retrieve the box of condoms, and yet she felt his absence with an emptiness she had no business feeling. Tonight wasn't about happily-ever-afters or marriage proposals or houses on Lake Pontchartrain complete with green lawn, carport and whitewashed fence.

But as she poured hot, freshly brewed tea into two porcelain cups and inhaled the relaxing aroma of chamomile and the sense-enhancing aspects of cloves, she knew tonight hadn't been about just mindless sex or unrequited lust.

She and Brandon had made love like two souls joined by more than passion. More than trust. More than love, if that was possible.

But now that she'd had Brandon inside her, she honestly considered believing that anything was possible, anything at all—including a future for them. Together.

Until this moment, she'd never really allowed herself to think about the future beyond the next day. She'd never dreamed about the perfect husband or imagined becoming a mother or wife. Her devotion to simplicity required she put her faith in making the most of the day at hand and letting the future take care of itself.

But if Brandon was the future's idea of her ideal mate, she wondered if her faith had been incredibly well placed or inherently misguided.

Brandon had once been a loyal friend. Now he was the

most magnificent lover. But he still held back a part of himself from her—an integral part, the driving force of who he was deep down. Even in the years of their childhood friendship, he'd never allowed her that close. Pride and bravado and good humor had always waylaid her, tricked her into believing she knew more about him than she actually did.

Even now, when she felt certain she knew him better than any other woman ever had, she didn't fool herself.

Brandon Chance was still a mystery—one he guarded with more vigilance than he'd ever use to protect a client. Even her. And she wasn't entirely sure she knew how to solve the complete puzzle. Or if she wanted to.

She drizzled some honey into her cup and stirred her tea, aware of the exact moment Brandon entered the spa behind her. She'd spread a blanket of towels over the carpeted area in the center and lit rows of candles along the walls.

During the day, this was a soothing but efficient place of business. But in the shadows of the Quarter, when the antique clock in her office chimed the three o'clock hour and Brandon filled the room with his heat, the space became a personal, erotic haven filled with possibilities that undid the soothing effects of even her strongest herbs.

"David said you didn't like tea," she said, slipping her fingers beneath the saucers and lifting, "but I don't have much else to offer you."

Turning, she started at the sight of him, naked and glorious and grinning like a thick-maned lion sated by the meat of a fresh kill.

"You've offered me everything I could ever want, Serena."

A shy grin bubbled to her lips before she could call it back or mold it into a smile more beguiling or seductive. Even in the afterglow of orgasms that had indeed echoed right over the marble stones of her garden wall, he could still evoke that part of her that remained a precocious child.

He accepted the tea and then followed her when she sat on the towels.

"Does that mean you're done wanting me?" She tried to inject her voice with playful seduction, but his expression hardened and the corners of his lips tilted downward in a deep frown.

"I'll never be done wanting you, Serena. Never. But that doesn't mean…"

"That we can have anything beyond tonight. I know. Well—" she wrapped her palm around her cup and slid the saucer away "—I know that you believe we can't have anything beyond tonight. And I respect that."

"But you don't understand it." He set the tea on the floor and then moved behind her and sat, drawing her between his legs so that her head rested against the crook of his shoulder and her back pressed into his chest with natural ease.

"Your logic was always beyond me, Brandon."

His chuckle warmed her insides before her swallow of tea slid down her throat. "I don't think that's the case, Serena. My logic is too simple for your complex thought patterns. You're way beyond me, sweetheart."

"You really think I'm smart?"

"I think you're brilliant. Wacky and quirky and nuts most of the time, but other than your insistence on subjecting yourself to me, I think you're damn remarkable."

"What's so wrong with subjecting myself to you?" She snuggled closer to him, reveling in the feel of his hard warmth and the mixed scents of sated passion, brewed herbs and sweet honey.

He slid his arms around her and buried his face in her hair, which had dried in haphazard ringlets that undoubtedly resembled a kitchen mop.

"Nothing is wrong, absolutely nothing. I've missed you, Serena. There were so many times I wanted to call or write, stop pretending that you'd done more than just put me in my place as you had every right to."

"Then why didn't you?"

Brandon smiled and inhaled before he answered, loving the heady smell that was hers and hers alone. She simply didn't understand the concept of guarding her thoughts or reining in her emotions. Serena operated on a level above and beyond most everyone he knew. When she wanted, she figured out a way to get. When she didn't want, she denied. He'd seen both sides of her.

He most definitely liked the wanting-taking side better.

"We're not good for each other," he answered.

She snorted in a decidedly unfeminine way. "Excuse me? You expect me to believe that after..." She waved her hand toward the garden and he knew precisely what she meant.

Their lovemaking had been incredible, the stuff of erotic fantasy and undeniable trust and exploration. They'd utilized each and every curve of the statue at the center of the fountain—more than once—and wondered if the sculptor had been an absolute genius or a complete deviant. They'd run through the garden nude and unfettered, like children unleashed on Eden, then coupled on the soft grass like lovers with eternity at their disposal.

But they didn't have eternity. They had only tonight. And Brandon had to make sure Serena understood, before he did something despicable like break her heart.

"I didn't mean we're not good for each other *that* way. I've never made love with a woman like I have with you, Serena."

"But…"

Because he couldn't help himself, he undid the tie on her robe and slipped his hands inside, skimming her satin skin with hungry hands.

"But beyond lovemaking and double dares, we're trouble together. This may sound really dull to someone like you, but I need to find a woman who will rein me in, keep me in line."

"You want to marry a drill sergeant?"

She laughed, but her comment, fraught with sarcasm, couldn't be ignored. He flattened his hands against her stomach and took a deep breath.

"If you'd met my drill sergeant, you wouldn't joke about that," he answered, suddenly uncertain if Serena really was totally wrong for him. He'd pondered the question for years, made his decision and focused on it for so long. Considering another path now seemed foolish, childish, as if he was allowing his hormones to influence his actions. He'd done that once too and had hurt her horribly.

"I'm not joking," she said, running her fingernails over his knuckles. "You have this plan for your future, a plan that doesn't include me. I'll deal with that, but I'd like to know everything you want. I never plan for the future. Life is more interesting when things just happen."

"Like tonight?"

She snuggled against him again, slid her hands completely over his and restarted his exploration by guiding him down to her lap. "Exactly like tonight."

"You don't think about what kind of man would make your life more complete?"

For a brief instant, her hands stilled and her back stiffened, as if a chill ran up her spine before she shook it away. "Tell me what you think I need, Brandon. What you think *you* need."

He closed his eyes. "We each need someone who will balance us. Keep us in line. Keep us out of trouble. Serena…"

I love you, but…

He swallowed the sentiment. He wouldn't say those words just to contradict them. They could have this night together. They could even have a friendship if she wanted to in the light of the next day. But that's all he could promise with any certainty of remaining true to his word.

"You're like a match to my wick," he said.

She nuzzled her backside against him. "I like your wick."

"Serena!"

She laughed and turned, draping herself across his lap, her eyes alight with naughtiness and insatiable intentions. Any seriousness he'd heard in her voice before was now nowhere to be seen.

"What? I do."

With unabashed candor, she wrapped her palm around his sex and stroked with unhurried care, scooting so she could lay her cheek against his thigh.

"Serena…" As she massaged him, logic and reason and plain old common sense began drifting away. He shook his head, willing himself to hold on more tightly to his train of thought. He needed her to understand.

But how could he, when all his arguments melted away at her heated ministrations?

He opened his mouth to speak, but she rolled and kissed a trail up his inner thigh, shedding her robe as she moved.

"I know what you mean, Brandon. Tonight is about tonight. So unless you're going to use that mouth for something other than talking," she warned between nips of her teeth and soothing swipes with her tongue, "I'd keep those lips closed."

When she took him in her mouth, he leaned back in the soft towels, slid her atop him and considered only the most pleasurable uses for each and every part of his anatomy.

CHAPTER ELEVEN

SERENA WINCED as she lifted her feet from the cobbled tiles dotting her mother's garden patio to the wrought-iron chair across from her. When her ankles sank into the downy cushions, she sighed, relishing the pleasant ache in her muscles. The memories of exactly why she felt so sore renewed the heated tingle that had haunted her all morning. She and Brandon had, in her opinion, reinvented the art of lovemaking.

They could write a scintillating addendum to the *Kama Sutra*. She imagined the accompanying illustrations while she sipped her mug of café au lait. She hadn't added enough sugar. She didn't care. She'd had enough sweetness the night before to last a lifetime.

"You look *too* happy." Samantha emerged from the house with a basket of muffins in one hand, coffee in the other and a suspicious, narrow-eyed grin curving her lips. Her hair, still streaked with blond strands from the California sun, was pulled back in a loose ponytail. Sweat-curled ringlets formed around her scrubbed-clean face and along the underside of her long neck, telling Serena she'd recently returned from her workout.

"Is there such a thing as too happy?" Serena pondered, knowing full well that her glee would be short-lived. Brandon had dropped her off at her mother's house just after sunrise, without a single promise that he'd somehow try and find a way to fit her into his carefully laid, I-just-got-out-of-the-military plans for the rest of his life.

Instead, he'd kissed her and agreed only to retrieve her no later than noon. She couldn't blame him. He'd tried to be honest with her, tried to tell her why he couldn't love her the way he should, and she'd seduced the words away. She hadn't wanted to hear his reasoning again, about fire and wicks and bad influences and the need for balance.

She was too afraid he was entirely right.

Sammie knocked Serena's legs off the other chair and sat down, bursting what was left of Serena's bliss.

"Too happy is usually a symptom of delusional behavior," Sammie noted. "Saw it all the time in Hollywood."

"Well, since most people already think I'm delusional," Serena pointed out, taking a brief sip of her chicory-and-milk brew and then fishing a hot corn muffin from the basket Sammie had laid on the table, "I'm going to enjoy being too happy. Today, anyway."

"Yeah, well, enjoy it while you can. Mother just returned from her morning consultation with the senator and she's going to make a beeline out here to find out where you've been all night, what's going on with the threats and why Brandon, your supposed bodyguard, left you unattended all morning."

That he'd been willing to part with her had surprised her a bit. She did very little arguing with him this time, only pointing out that Sammie would be over at first light and her bedroom at her mother's house was on the third floor, well out of harm's way. Besides the fact that Brandon undoubtedly remembered that Miss Lily kept a hidden baseball bat in nearly every room and that her son, Franklin, was the six-foot-six caretaker of the property, she couldn't imagine why he'd finally heeded her pleas to suspend his bodyguard duties, even for a short while.

Except that he *needed* to get away…from her.

She twisted her lips in a tight grimace as she thought, causing Sammie to shake her head.

"Too happy doesn't last long, does it?"

Serena bit into a muffin, silenced at first by the sweet buttery taste of Miss Lily's secret recipe.

"Ask me after you've eaten a muffin."

Sammie broke a steaming, golden cake in half, then popped a quarter in her mouth. She groaned with satisfaction, reminding Serena how she herself had made similar sounds last night—from tasting things that made even Miss Lily's muffins seem like prepackaged, convenience-store fare.

Her smile faded. She and Brandon had shared an experience beyond anything she'd ever, ever imagined. They'd learned things about each other—things physical, psychological, even spiritual. But the knowledge hadn't been enough to make him stay, to convince him to toss his investigation aside and carry her off to some secret hideaway where they could be alone and forget, for one more day, that someone had thrown a brick and a copycat threat through her window. She'd made the suggestion as they dressed, but Brandon had refused, insisting he had to find out who was threatening her as soon as possible.

And while Serena couldn't deny that his diligence and determination were part and parcel of him, she also couldn't deny that as soon as her stalker was caught, Brandon would leave her. For good.

Because she couldn't be the kind of woman he thought he needed.

Serena shook her head, forcing herself not to think about

all the reasons Brandon had given her during the course of the night why their relationship could only be short-lived. He was entirely right that she acted like kerosene on his fire, and he did the same to her. They couldn't help themselves. Couldn't change who they were or the chemistry that had bound them since the moment they met. They'd proven their combustibility on the floor of the spa and then in several other locations, including the roof of her building where anyone and everyone could have spotted them had the night provided just a little more light.

Together, they tempted fate, they pushed limits, denied boundaries.

But the thrill couldn't last.

She understood better than anyone that Brandon desired and deserved stability in his life. His parents, notorious gamblers, showered their children with love, but during more than one stretch of time, they left Brandon and Kell to fend for themselves while they played the ponies in Vegas or hiked the Himalayas with T.J. in tow. They'd encouraged equally risky behavior in all their boys, buying them the toys they needed: airboats for the bayou, motorcycles to cruise the Quarter and beyond, rappelling equipment and airline tickets to the world's deepest caves and highest peaks.

If not for Aunt Tillie and her devotion to the three brothers, Serena wondered how Brandon, Kell and T.J. would have remained alive all these years. Risking it all—gambling for the big payoff—was second nature to a Chance man.

But Brandon seemed tired of immersing himself in that lifestyle. She'd been clued in to that weariness since she'd first stepped into his office. He'd left the military behind, even though he'd loved the service. He'd chosen a new line of work that was admittedly dangerous, but he'd come home to set up shop in the one area of the world where he'd grown up feeling safe and comfortable.

While he might tempt danger during the day as a body-guard, when he went home, he wanted to know that his wife and x-number of kids were waiting for him at the dinner table—not off concocting a new tea blend or parked in Jackson Square trading stories with the street musicians until well after midnight. He needed someone who would ease and settle his wandering, reckless ways—give him what he deserved, what he'd been denied his entire life.

Serena, unfortunately, did not have a calming effect on people. And after last night, she most definitely knew she didn't have that effect on him.

"Earth to Serena."

Serena snapped herself out of her thoughts, which had grown more and more depressing—and more and more clear—as she mused.

"I'm sorry. I didn't get much sleep last night."

Sammie's smile was pure sin and envy. "I gathered. Care to talk about it? I don't mean the details, mind you," she clarified, "but that happiness sure beat a quick path to the door."

"Yeah. Just like Brandon will as soon as he figures out who threatened me."

"What makes you so sure? Sparks fly between the two of you. It's sickening," Sammie added, never allowing her cynical nature to hide for long, "but it's special. Even Brandon is smart enough to know that."

Serena ran her fingers through her hair, curving the haphazard strands around the back of her ears. "Brandon is also smart enough to know that we're not good for each other. We never have been."

"He dumped you?"

Samantha was halfway to standing, undoubtedly ready to go beat some sense into Brandon herself, when Serena grabbed her hand and pulled her down. "No! I mean, not yet. Look, Sammie, Brandon and I are great as friends. We make life interesting for each other. We spark each other's flame, so to speak."

"Sounds like a perfect recipe for lovers," Sammie answered.

"Yeah, it does." Serena allowed herself a moment to be wistful, to remember the fire they'd stoked last night, to imagine the conflagrations they could ignite if only given the chance. But Serena had to come to grips with the fact that such a blaze more than likely wouldn't burn again. "But Brandon…and I…both want to find someone who's more than a great lover."

Until this morning, Serena never really thought about what she wanted. Little by little, the idea of marriage wasn't so bad anymore, provided she found the right person. Someone exciting. Unpredictable. Someone who might think she was crazy, but didn't mind so much. Someone strong and handsome and…

She groaned. She wanted Brandon, the one man she couldn't have.

"This is just an affair," she continued. "It'll end. Soon. As soon as his job is over. And that's okay."

Serena tossed in that last line just to see how it sounded rolling off her tongue. She sipped her coffee, but even the bitterness of the chicory didn't offset the bad taste in her mouth. Samantha watched her over the rim of her own cup, assessing her sister with her incredibly alert gaze.

Surprisingly, she didn't press further. She frowned, shook her head, then set down her cup and folded her hands on the table. "So, what's going on with the investigation? Any leads on your brick-thrower?"

The air in the garden seemed to lighten, and Serena briefly considered the irony that discussing the threats on her life was more comfortable than talking about her affair with Brandon.

"Brandon's eliminated Drew as a suspect," she answered.

Sammie snorted, then popped more muffin in her mouth. "About time. He didn't really think Drew would be that clever?"

"Clever?" Serena sat up straighter, intrigued by her sister's choice of words. "How would threatening me make him clever?"

Sammie waved her hand while she chewed and swallowed. "You know, he threatens you so you'll feel scared and then marry him to be protected. Classic woman-in-jeopardy plot."

"That's ridiculous. I'm not the 'run to my man when I'm in danger' type."

"You've never been in danger before. Who'd know how you'd react? It might have been a decent plan, if Brandon hadn't come back to town."

"But he did, didn't he?"

Drew's voice echoed over the tiles, despite his usual soft and even volume. He stood just inside the gate, then swung the iron hinges closed behind him.

Sammie forced a swallow and picked up her coffee. "Now there's an exit cue if ever I heard one. I'll be just inside, sis."

Serena nodded, but didn't watch her sister leave. She was too shattered by the resigned expression on Drew's face. Resigned and sad. She pushed her own drink away, and the corn muffin she'd devoured suddenly felt like a stone weight in the pit of her stomach.

She scooted her chair out to stand, but he stopped her with a flattened palm.

"Don't get up. Serena, we need to talk."

He joined her at the table and sat motionless for a moment, looking at her hand as if he wanted to take it in his. She realized then that only a few days ago, he would have wrapped his fingers around hers while they spoke, without hesitating, without thinking first.

And she would have accepted that intimacy without a second thought. They were friends. Best friends. She couldn't understand why he ever wanted anything more from her. She had always been certain she'd never done anything or said anything to give him the notion she might entertain, even for an instant, the prospect of becoming his wife.

"Drew, I'm…"

"Don't apologize. I've made a royal ass out of myself over the past year, Serena. I don't know what I could have been thinking."

She shook her head as she spoke. "Just that you care about me. Just that you want to be happy. You want me to be happy."

He looked long at his lap. "It was more than that." When he met her gaze, the sorrow lingering in his blue eyes pushed the stone in her stomach up to the back of her throat. "I knew he'd come back."

"What? Who? Brandon?"

"Tillie didn't just share her gossip with your mother. She seemed to take particular pleasure in torturing me." He grinned when he spoke, acknowledging his exaggeration. "A while back, she made a comment to me that Brandon had been inquiring about office space in the Quarter. She asked me to recommend a reputable commercial real estate agent."

"When?"

"About a week before I booked the church."

Serena sighed as her heart broke and the craziness that had ruled her life over the past ten months finally made sense. "So all this 'you have to marry me whether you like it or not' was about Brandon coming back to town?"

"Can you blame me? You've been pining for him for fifteen years."

She sat up straighter and thrust her hands on her hips. "I don't *pine!*" Lord, had she been that obvious? First, her sister, who'd just moved back to town, and now the man she spent most of her free time with. They couldn't both be wrong.

"Okay, *pine* is a bad word choice," Drew admitted. "Other women pine. You ignore. You escape to this little world that exists only in your mind where you could care less about Brandon Chance or what happened the night he shattered your illusions of him. You dated. You socialized. But you never got involved with anyone. You never risked your heart."

"So what? I'm picky. Heck, I didn't want to marry you, and you're fairly perfect."

Drew impaled her with a look so brimming with common sense and pure practicality that even she couldn't deny that what he implied was true. And she knew it. She'd admitted as much to Brandon the night before.

"Okay, I *pined,*" she admitted. "Sue me."

He did take her hand then and the warmth that enveloped her skin flushed straight to her heart.

"I'm not going to sue you. But I am going to bow out. I don't want to break your heart or anything," he said, all serious and yet incredibly sheepish, "but the engagement is off."

Serena exhaled, then inhaled, empowered by the scent of baked goods, coffee and magnolia…until she glanced up at the window to her mother's room. "Are you telling Endora or am I?"

"I already told her," Drew assured. "I think she's upstairs in her workshop mixing up a potion or casting a spell."

"She's a psychic, not a witch—you know that," Serena re-assured him. "Now, if she calls Cousin Theodora, you're in really big trouble."

He laughed, then pulled her into his lap and gave her a brotherly hug. Serena enjoyed the sensation, knowing at once that she and Drew could finally regain the friendship his marriage quest had nearly destroyed.

"Who said the spell was for me? Endora always liked me. Brandon Chance is another story altogether."

Serena kissed Drew on the forehead and then returned to her chair. "Brandon Chance is another planet altogether. But she doesn't have to worry. After Brandon finds out who's threatened me, he'll be out my life again."

Drew's features twisted into a perplexed question mark. "Come again? You mean I'm stepping aside so you'll be alone?"

"No, you're stepping aside so we can stay friends. Brandon doesn't want someone like me in his life. Not for the long haul."

Drew shook his head. "You keep talking like that, and I'm going to start agreeing with everyone who thinks you're crazy. I saw you and Brandon together at the restaurant. I had a beer with the man yesterday. You haunt him, Serena. You always have."

Serena swiped muffin crumbs off the table and scattered them into the nearby bushes. "Except for the people my mother hangs with, haunting is not a good thing. I can't deny that we're incredibly attracted to one another, but I'm not what he needs or wants in his life. He wants someone to settle him down. Keep him home and content and happy. Someone who cooks and cleans and, I don't know, knits doilies."

When even conservative Drew blanched at the mental picture she painted, Serena wondered if Brandon had any idea what he was asking for. She couldn't imagine a man like him satisfied with a life that was predictable or stable to the point of being typical or average.

But still, it was his dream.

Who was she to burst his bubble?

"What about you? What do you want?"

Serena folded her hands in her lap. She and Drew hadn't had such an intimate conversation since college, when they'd escape to the Blacksmith's Shoppe on Bourbon Street and drink voodoo margaritas and talk about life. And as much as she wanted to share her heart with him and renew that friendship all over, she no longer knew the object of her heart's desire.

She'd wanted Brandon, heart and soul. Last night, she'd had him, and the connection was every bit as overwhelming and passionate and fulfilling as she'd imagined it would be.

But it couldn't last. Not if he truly deserved the happiness he sought, a happiness she couldn't give.

For the first time since she met Brandon on the playground, Serena honestly no longer knew what her future held, or even what she wanted it to hold.

"I want to find out who sent me that threat and have them arrested. I want to return to going where I want to go when I want to go, to not looking over my shoulder or having to drive everywhere when walking is quicker. I want to stop assessing all my customers and friends as potential criminals. I want to be free again."

Free from the threats. Free from the fear.

Free from Brandon Chance and a relationship that could never last.

BRANDON HUNG UP the phone, tapped his folders into a neat and orderly pile and stared at the clock. Just before noon. According to Samantha, Serena had been dutifully waiting for him to return and plot their next move. He assumed she was talking about the stalker. He should have been thinking only about the stalker, about discovering the nut's identity, about fixing the situation so Serena could go about her business and live her life without him and his stupid, impossible needs.

But they were his needs, damn it. His dream. No matter how incredible Serena made him feel, no matter how extraordinary their lovemaking had been, he couldn't let go of the life he so desperately wanted. The wife and home and hearth. The average, typical, comforting family. All the things he'd missed growing up.

When the phone rang, he took a minute to script his greeting. He'd only been in business for three days.

"No Chances Protection. May I help you?"

"Brandon? Honey, is that you?"

"Mom?"

The line crackled with static and an annoying echo that told him Lynn Chance was either out of the country or using a cheap cell phone. Depending on his parents' current run of luck, he was never sure which.

"I'm in Florida."

Cheap cell phone. Monte Carlo must have been a bust.

Once his inner sarcasm subsided, he realized there would only be one reason his parents would be in Florida.

"Where's Kell?"

Kellan, a Navy SEAL, was assigned to MacDill Airforce Base in Tampa. Brandon hadn't spoken to his brother in over a month, but with him leaving on covert missions or training exercises, lack of contact wasn't unusual. His parents traveling to the Sunshine State when jai alai and greyhound racing weren't in season—that was unheard of.

"He's okay. He's in the hospital, but the doctors say he'll recover completely."

While his mother prattled on about the details, all of which meant little to Brandon so long as he'd still have his brother in one piece and functional at the end of the recovery process, Brandon swallowed a knot of regret. They'd been meaning to get together. They met up in Orlando once while Brandon trained in Miami, but that was no substitute for a real relationship.

Just like your affair with Serena, his conscience whispered. No substitute for a real relationship.

"Can I see him if I come?" Brandon asked.

His mother paused, then asked a nearby doctor about visitors. "He'll be up and around in a few days, but you know your brother. He's mad as hell that we came. He forgets that he was once a helpless baby and that I used to bandage his scrapes, not to mention diaper his butt."

Which effectively meant that Kellan didn't like anyone seeing him so prone and vulnerable. That, Brandon could understand.

"Tell him I love him," Brandon said, "and that I'll be there if he needs me."

"He won't need you, Brandon. Your brother likes to think he doesn't need anyone. But I'm sure he'd like to see you as soon as he's up and about. Can you track down T.J.? Your father and I have no idea where he is. We've tried to leave messages on his cell phone, but he's in the mountains…"

Brandon jotted down their number, and before hanging up promised he'd find his youngest brother, who last he heard, had taken a job as an extreme-sports guide at a resort in Idaho. He knew he had the name of the place back at his apartment. And so long as Kell wasn't in any danger of death, he saw no reason to use his mother's request as an excuse to avoid collecting Serena and dealing with all that had happened between them.

On his way back to the Garden District, he reviewed what he knew about Serena's case—which wasn't much since his initial suspicion of Drew was completely off base. Whoever had thrown that brick had to have access to Serena's house to find the fake threats and then copy them. And they had to have a motive to want to harm her.

The motive threw him. Except for some sick obsession, the stalker couldn't have any real reason to hurt a gentle, free spirit like Serena. It was time to start focusing on strangers. Though Serena's antique lock on her front door was hard to open with a key, there was no telling what a talented locksmith or criminal could do with the modern lock in the back.

As soon as he collected Serena from her mother's house, he was going to begin a serious interrogation. Take her through a typical day—if she ever in her life experienced one—step by step and person by person until they came up with a new suspect. He grabbed the computer printout David had made him of spa clients and, by referring to a copy of her appointment book, he would focus on the patrons who frequented her business a little more than necessary. There had to be something he was missing, something that would lead him in the right direction to ensuring her safety.

If only he could find some way to guarantee she'd be safe from him, but his gut instinct told him that no matter how unhappy they might eventually make each other, he wasn't going to be able to let her go.

CHAPTER TWELVE

"SHE'S NOT OUT HERE."

Brandon's heartbeat raged in his ears. He swallowed the lump that had lodged in his esophagus, so his next words came out in a rasp. "Serena's not in the garden," he repeated.

Samantha looked up from her copy of *Bodyguard* magazine unfazed, the arches of her bare feet casually perched on the marble-topped coffee table. "What do you mean she's not there?"

"Damn it, Sam. She's not outside!"

Annoyed, Samantha slapped the magazine down on the cushion beside her and shot past the open French doors, muttering about Brandon's failing eyesight. She returned quickly, apparently convinced that Brandon hadn't somehow missed Serena in Endora's rather large but fenced and gated interior garden. "She's been here all morning."

"Alone?"

"Drew was with her, but he left over a half an hour ago. I walked him to the door myself."

"Why weren't you outside with her?" Brandon clenched his fists, tamping down the urge to grab her and shake her. "You were supposed to be watching her, Samantha!"

"I *was* watching her!" She pushed around him and shot up the winding staircase in the foyer. "She must have just gone to her room the back way or something."

They searched and found nothing. They called the spa on the off chance she might have simply and conveniently forgotten to stay put and had gone in to work. David assured them that neither he nor any other member of the staff, all of whom were present and working, had talked to her all day. Brandon took deep breaths, questioned Miss Lily, who'd been in her kitchen baking while Franklin, her son, repaired the refrigerator right beside her. They'd seen nothing.

Endora also hadn't seen Serena. After talking to Drew, she'd sensed that Serena wanted to be alone. Surprisingly, she'd given her her space, picking a damn fine day to rein in her motherly meddling.

"Calm down, Brandon. She's fine."

"You don't *know* that, Endora."

Sitting behind her ornate, gold and filigree French Renaissance desk in her library, Endora inhaled deeply, closed her eyes and placed her palms flat on the glass top. Her multiple rings and acrylic fingernails tapped the shiny surface. Apparently, she was consulting her psychic sources. Brandon shifted his weight from foot to foot. He didn't buy Endora's mumbo jumbo, but he'd take any lead he could get.

"I know," Endora said just as he was about to turn and leave. "She's unharmed and out of any danger—physically. Emotionally—" her eyes popped open like twin emeralds, flashing with unspoken accusation "—that's another story entirely."

Brandon shrugged off her lucky guess.

"I don't suppose Casper and his friends can tell me where she is?"

Her gaze dropped as she proceeded to tidy the collection of scarves and beads and bottles that littered her desk. "Ask Samantha."

Samantha?

He rushed out and down the stairs, nearly colliding with Serena's sister on the bottom landing.

"I found this in the mailbox." She thrust the quarter-folded sheet of white paper at him. Even before he read the entire threat, his heart stopped. Hot bile surged up the back of his throat and his eyes burned with bound fury.

"'Home is where the heart is…and other body parts.'" He followed the twisted cliché with a string of expletives that made even jaded Samantha flinch.

"Do you want me to call the police?"

Brandon shook his head. Think. Think! He didn't have time to wait for the cops or the patience to turn the investigation over to anyone else. Not yet. *He* was the one who'd promised to protect her. *He* was the one who loved her.

"The stalker wouldn't have left a note for us if he didn't want us to find her. *Home is where the heart is…home is where the heart is,*" he repeated.

He conveniently left off the threatening part, knowing that stoking his fear wouldn't help him rationalize. If he acted quickly enough, he would find her, unharmed, all body parts still intact and assembled in the unique and irreplaceable form of Serena Deveaux.

Serena Deveaux, the woman he loved, with everything that was his and him.

Damn it.

"Home…home…*home* is the key word. Whose home?"

"Not this home. We've searched everywhere," Sam assured him.

"Then we have two choices—the stalker's home, or Serena's. He knows where she lives, and he knows we know. That's where he found the original messages to copy, where he tossed that brick to let her know he knew where she lived. I'm outta here."

"I'll come with you!"

"No! Call the police and then follow."

Brandon was out the door and in his Jeep, engine revving and tires peeling, before he realized that when he'd left, Samantha Deveaux had flashed him her best Hollywood smile.

SERENA BUSIED HERSELF cleaning up her living room to the sound of Cajun music on the CD player. Her tiny, old house felt entirely too quiet. Maurice wasn't snoring in the corner. Tabby wasn't meowing for milk in the pantry.

Brandon wasn't watching her every move, teasing her with his magnetic gaze, daring her with his incredible body… torturing her with a future that would never, ever be.

With the exception of her copycat stalker, her plan to reset the direction of her life had completely succeeded. Drew had called off the wedding and didn't hate her for not loving him the way he deserved. She'd had a glorious, unforgettable night of passion with Brandon, the one man she'd always desired and truly loved, thus undoing all the negative karma of the past fifteen years. They couldn't be together for much longer, but she had accepted that from the beginning and she couldn't change the inevitable.

By all accounts, she would soon be marching on with her live-for-the-day, enjoy-the-moment lifestyle. The universe was righted; the forces of negativity and evil would soon be vanquished; simplicity and tranquillity fully restored.

So how come she felt so miserable?

She wandered to the front window and scratched off a leftover smudge of glue from the fresh installation of glass. Scanning the empty street, she saw no sign of either Brandon or Samantha. She thought it completely odd that Brandon would ask her sister to bring her home and then leave her alone, but she trusted he knew what he was doing. He'd ordered new, shatterproof windows and installed multiple locks on all the doors. Sammie promised to remain somewhere nearby, out of sight, watching her, proving to Brandon what a clever and attentive bodyguard she would make if he'd give her a chance.

For all Serena knew, Brandon had figured out who'd copied her threats and broken her window and was now filing a statement with the police, saving her the red tape. On the other hand, if Brandon didn't know the identity of her stalker yet, she halfway hoped the maniac would come after her, so long as Sammie and Brandon had planned the whole afternoon around catching the crazy and putting him or her behind bars. She didn't mind being bait, though she'd rather she knew about it in advance. But a plan as wildly dangerous as that was definitely up Samantha's movie-magic alley. And with Brandon so desperate to get out of her life, he might just agree to such risky theatrics.

She ran the vacuum for as long as she could stand to, then returned to the pile of dusty board games her sister had left at her house. She pulled out a long black cylinder, uncapped the end and rolled out the leathery lambskin playing board and flattened, colored-glass playing pieces of Pente. She and Brandon had spent hours playing this game after Aunt Tillie bought it for Brandon's twelfth birthday. Tucking her skirt beneath her knees, she sat on the hardwood floor between her living room and kitchen and set up the board, lining the emerald-green stones in the appropriate squares, but cupping the claret-colored set in the palm of her hand.

She toyed with the cool glass, rolling them across her skin, likening the tinkling sound and icy feel to droplets of cold water from her fountain. Determined not to relive that particular memory so soon, she scattered the pieces onto the board and tried to remember how to play the game.

Something about trapping your opponent. She wondered if Brandon remembered the rules or if they could, after he arrived with the good news of her freedom from her stalker, while away the rest of the afternoon in a friendly game.

Trouble was, she and Brandon didn't have the capacity to have a friendly game any more than they could manage a longer-than-one-night affair. For them, competition was endless and cutthroat. Stakes soared and passions ran hotter than the fire in a kiln. From that very first dart game she'd challenged him to just three days ago, to their lovemaking at the spa last night, they'd pushed each other over the brink of reality into the world of extraordinary. They'd each tested and tasted the sweet-spicy flavors of victory, climax and passions most intense.

At least when they made love, nobody lost. Serena had never felt such fulfillment or satisfaction. And she was one hundred percent certain that Brandon hadn't walked away wanting either. Now that the passion was sated, now that she knew how desperately he wanted a future that couldn't include her, the games were truly over. But no matter how the affair ended, neither one of them could claim a long-term prize. If they stayed together much longer, they'd burn each other out. If they parted, her heart would be utterly broken, and she was fairly certain Brandon wouldn't walk away entirely unscathed either. Yet they'd recover as they had before.

Just as she scooped the last of the flat red marbles and slid them into a velvet drawstring pouch, her front door burst open in a shattering hail of splintered wood. Gun drawn, Brandon charged across the foyer, jumping her credenza and scooping her up by the waist. He thrust her behind him and threw her back against the wall. Shielding her with his body, he panted with rage and fear and bravado as he surveyed the empty house with the barrel of his gun.

"Where is he?"

"Where is who? Brandon, what the hell are you doing? I know you didn't like my front lock, but that's no reason to go kicking in my door!"

She tried to sneak around him, but he swung her back against the wainscoting and blocked her path. "Where's the stalker?"

"Didn't I hire you to answer that question?"

Brandon lowered his gun slightly, indicating that he had relaxed, but Serena saw no other evidence, from the pressure he used to hold her against the wall to the glare of anger in his black gaze. "You were gone. We got this note." He grabbed a crumpled sheet of paper from his pocket and thrust it at her. "Weren't you kidnapped by the stalker?"

Serena read the threat, but felt none of the danger the words implied. Not with Brandon pressing so close to her. Not with his gun drawn and his testosterone pumping and his eyes flashing as if they were about to make love. He really was the most magnificent man she'd ever known.

God, she was hopeless!

She swallowed a sigh and refolded the note, shoving it back in his pocket. "Kidnapped? Not unless Samantha is my stalker. She told me you asked her to bring me here. I assumed she was watching from a distance."

Her explanation hung in the air while the dust settled. Her heart, which she suddenly realized was racing, stabilized into a more regular beat. Then, the truth dawned like a brilliant sun over an eastern bayou—slightly hard on the eyes, but impossible to miss.

"Samantha?" he asked, holstering his weapon and dropping his shoulders along with his jaw. "Samantha is your stalker?"

Serena stopped to think. It all made absolute sense—especially because Samantha was a Deveaux and subscribed to a different form of logic than the average person. "Of course she is. How could I have missed it? That little minx!"

"Minx? She threatened your life, Serena. Maybe your sister harbors some serious resentment because you stayed in New Orleans with your mother and she was shipped off to L.A. with dear old brilliant, but broke, Dad."

Serena leveled him with a look of impatience. "Brandon, you know my mother. What kind of resentment could Samantha possibly feel for not having grown up in Endora's shadow? For goodness' sake, Daddy wasn't always broke. He gave her the world and the Hollywood sign to boot. That isn't what this is about."

Serena pushed Brandon aside, which was surprisingly easy now that he'd been officially stunned to silence by the infamous Deveaux way of thinking. She marched past the scattered Pente board and stood in front of what was left of her door, now lying half on the floor and half against her portrait of Miss Lily's favorite cousin, Sarah Blythe.

"I guess I'll have to replace the lock *now*."

She bent to pick up the door and lean it against the shattered frame, but Brandon came up behind her and did the job himself. When the phone rang, Serena stalked away with a frustrated sigh and picked up the portable.

"You owe me one front door, Sammie," Serena said, knowing even without her mother's psychic powers who was on the other end of the line.

"He kicked in the door? Cool! That must have been a sight to see. It looks easy in the movies, but it's really hard on the knees."

Brandon stopped his handiwork to watch her talk, but she

marched across the room for a private conversation. "Is this the part in the movie where the villain explains the details of her plan and then leaves the hero and heroine to meet their fate?"

Samantha chuckled on the other end of the line. "I always knew you were more clever than people gave you credit for. You know what I did and why I did it, though you'll probably have to explain it to Brandon. He's fairly bright, but he *is* a man, and by nature they're damn stupid about these things."

Serena turned her back to Brandon, sure that if he saw her concurring smile, he'd think she and Samantha had planned this ruse together from the start.

"One question," Serena posed.

Sammie laughed. "This is so like a B movie. I love it. There's always the one question. Shoot."

"You obviously pilfered Mother's key to the house without telling me, but why were you looking through my casket? All I keep in there are random pieces of paper, most of which I eventually throw out." She bent to retrieve a green Pente stone that had shot across the room in the melee. "Of course, I'm assuming you found the notes by accident and then figured out what I was up to with the fake threats on my life."

"As Mother would say, there are no accidents, only twists of fate. Remember that sweater you bought me for my birthday?"

"The purple one with the feathers on the neckline? It looked fabulous on you!"

"Yeah, well, feathers are your fashion accessory, not mine. But I knew you loved it and the store wouldn't take it back without a receipt..."

Serena laughed until she felt Brandon's presence behind her, hovering, heating her with a warmth that was a potent mixture of frustration, anger, relief and desire.

All vestiges of laughter retreated. Her sister's plan had

worked, but not in a way either of them intended. Brandon would be fit to be tied when he heard what Sammie had done. And what Serena was about to do.

"Uh, Samantha…I have to go."

Her sister's chuckle echoed in her ear. "If you get a chance, remind Brandon that I must be incredibly elusive to fool him. Elusive and creative. Maybe even creative enough for him to hire for his firm, license or not."

Brandon slid his palms beneath Serena's elbows and turned her around. His gray eyes smoldered as the rage slowly dissipated and another emotion—raw but volatile—twisted his face. The lines of his jaw were tight, but his hands cupped her with a loving softness that spurred Serena to disconnect the call without saying goodbye.

He took the phone from her and set it down.

"Sam did this to force us together," he said, apparently more practiced in traversing the maze of Deveaux logic than she'd first thought.

"She drove me to your office the other day, and between that conversation and finding the false threats when she was searching for a receipt, she put two and two together. I guess when it looked like I was going to come clean and you would leave, she took over."

"To keep us together."

Serena nodded, and swallowed. God, how she wished her sister could do something now…something dramatic and bold and magical that would somehow waylay the inevitable parting she and Brandon now had to face. Unable to match the intensity of his gaze any longer, she slipped away from him and pretended to inspect the precarious position of her door, propped into the frame and held in place by the antique secretary he'd slid away from the side wall.

"She's very inventive, your sister."

Serena nodded in agreement. Now wasn't the time to talk about Samantha. Now was the time to say goodbye. The mystery was solved. The game was over. She couldn't, wouldn't, bear another minute in his life if she couldn't have forever.

"Looks like you can't use the front door to leave."

"Maybe I don't want to leave."

The words played on her shattering heart; with a hot shiver, she felt the walls and crevices vibrate, as if they would soon meld back into place. But the foundation was tentative—and wouldn't last. She turned to retreat, but he blocked her path, taking her hands in his.

"I've been on some of the most dangerous covert missions ever concocted by the United States Army, and you know what? Until today, until I thought that someone might have taken you from me, I never really knew the taste of fear."

His fingers massaged hers and the fiery friction made her want to kiss him long and deeply, to learn the taste he spoke of, to brand the essence of him into her own senses. But kissing him would only prolong the inevitable. It was time to move on.

"I'm fine, Brandon." She flipped her hands around and took control of his ministrations, stopping his touch before she lost her mind. And body. And soul. "I'll be fine," she assured him—and her—again. "The danger's over. We're over. I'm safe now. You're free to go."

He held her hands tighter. "We'll never be over, Serena. Didn't these fifteen years…didn't last night…teach you anything? I want you in my life."

She shook her hands free and marched away, determined to put some distance between them. Faulty or haphazard though her logic might sometimes be, she knew she was right this time. "Maybe it's not about what you want." Perching her knuckles on her hips, she faced him and reconsidered her argument. "No. That's not right. It's all about what you want. I can't be the woman of your fantasies, Brandon. I can't be your anchor, your ball and chain. That's not who I am. But I also know you deserve that future, if that's what you need to be happy. Warm with a fire in your big stone hearth, dog on your lap, wifey baking barefoot in the kitchen."

She gestured wildly toward her own barely used cooking area and tried to remember the last time she'd even lit her stove without Miss Lily or her mother constructing the meal that was cooked there. She'd made her choices along a different path and she wasn't about to start regretting them now.

Since Brandon kissed her fifteen years ago, she'd rarely allowed herself to truly fantasize about her future beyond the next few days…the next few moments. She'd never planned to be anyone's wife, much less anyone's mother. Over the past few days, she'd learned she wasn't as averse to the idea as she had once been, but that didn't change the fact that her vision of marriage and Brandon's were as different as night and day.

Beyond wanting Brandon—a man she honestly thought she'd never have—three days ago, she would have said her plans for the future were to have a life free from hurt and heartbreak. No life mate. No complications. Friends, family, a prosperous business. An occasional trip to somewhere exciting. An affair now and then to remind her she was a woman.

Simplicity, simplicity, simplicity.

Yet here she was, pushing away the keeper of the other part of her soul. There was nothing simple about this, nothing at all.

Brandon's lips tilted into a grin—half-wistful, half-condescending. "I had a real cute fantasy, didn't I? Naive, definitely. Sort of goofy, if you really think about it."

"Goofy? Not to you. You never had that kind of stability

in your childhood. And I certainly can't give it to you now."
She looked around her eclectically decorated home, at her out-
landish clothes, lifting her arms that jingled from the length
of bracelets she wore. "I wish I could."

"No, you don't. At least, I don't." He stopped, instantly realizing that his words stuck in her heart like a thousand hot
stickpins. "That's not what I mean."

Grabbing her by the waist, he swung himself onto the
couch, then pulled her onto his lap and secured her in a tight
grip. "Just sit still and let me explain."

"You don't need to—"

He cut her off by kissing her. Hard. With every inch of his
mouth. With every curve of his tongue. No matter how she
knew she should pull away, she couldn't. One last taste, she
told herself. One last ride on a wave of torrential sensation.

Yet before the pleasure crested, he pulled back, panting
with more ferocity than when he'd busted through her door.

"You think I created that fantasy with the wife and kids and
two point three dogs because of what I lacked in my childhood. Don't try your hand at conventional rationalization,
Serena. It's not your forte."

She knew she should probably be offended, but with his
hands stroking her arms and back with rhythmic heat, she
could do nothing but listen to his explanation.

"I loved my childhood. I thrived on unpredictability and
risk and chance...until my stupid risks tore us apart. So I
created this picture after I enlisted that couldn't include you.
Made it pretty safe for my ego, constructing a future that I
knew damn well you wouldn't want to be a part of."

"What are talking about?"

"I'm talking about the means by which men and women
build walls and shape paths to keep the hurt out. Even after

last night, even after we shared each other in ways I never imagined, I still couldn't allow myself to dream that we'd find a way to make a future work. How could I? If you denied me, I'd have a part of me missing again. The part that's yours. Is yours. Has always been and will always be…yours."

He slid her right hand over his heart, urging her to measure the rapid pounding as a gauge of his love. She shook her head.

"So I make your heart pound. I turn you on. You do the same to me. But you can't build a future on that."

"Why not?"

"Because…" She paused, not knowing the answer. Conventional wisdom subscribed to the theory that a lasting marriage didn't have good sex as its basis. It was about friendship, trust, honesty. Three things she and Brandon now had together, in addition to the great sex.

"Well?" he pressed.

She huffed. Brandon was offering her everything she wanted. Why couldn't she just accept that?

"Sex isn't enough, Brandon."

His eyes lit with a flame that stopped her protest dead before she could elaborate.

"Wanna bet?"

CHAPTER THIRTEEN

"WHAT ARE YOU talking about?"

She didn't know what he was implying, but she saw the very instant his Chance charm kicked in. Brandon's grin spread so wide across his lushly male, recently kissed mouth that Serena thought his whole gorgeous face might split in two. She didn't know whether to be excited or very, very scared.

"I'm talking about the language we both understand best."

"Sex?"

When she said the word, his eyes darkened. His body grew hard and hot beneath her thigh. Trapped in his arms, she fought the instinct to squirm in his lap or she'd further kindle a flame best kept unlit. They'd already proven their compatibility in the sex department. Never in her entire life had she felt so uninhibited, so wanton and brazen and one with the universe, than she had with Brandon in her erotic garden. But even then, she hadn't considered, hadn't even entertained, what would happen beyond the next morning, beyond the next moment. Hoping would only break her heart.

And yet, she realized now, she couldn't help herself, no matter how irrational and naive hoping for a future with Brandon was.

"Serena, do you remember last night? The way you opened yourself to me?" He slid one hand over the crevice between her knees, then up to her thighs, using his hands to illustrate his point—an unnecessary action if ever there was one. "The friction of my skin against yours? The pressure of me inside you?"

She willed herself not to blush, but damn it if a prickly heat didn't spread from her belly to her cheeks, then lower, initiating a gentle throbbing of moistening flesh that could be her undoing. "That's not enough to build a relationship on."

"Maybe it isn't…maybe it is. But I don't think that's all we have together. And you don't, either."

Her mouth dried. Her heart thudded against her rib cage, so hard she wondered if he could see her quake. She slid her hand between her breasts and willed herself to calm down, then suddenly realized that touching herself in such close proximity to Brandon only tightened her nipples with a hungry ache.

"I don't like where this is leading."

Brandon knew the moment she'd become aroused the same way he knew that he'd have to pull out all the stops to lure her to his way of thinking. Some notions, some phenomena, like the two of them together—forever and for keeps—were too far-fetched for even her to believe. But he wasn't going to let her scoff and dismiss the possibility just because he'd told her his stupid fantasy—meant specifically to keep her out of his future, something he now knew was impossible.

He held her steady, stroked her slowly, teaching her with hands and gaze and hold that he had no intention of releasing her so she could run or hide or pretend the way she had for her entire adult life.

Living for the moment and in the moment had served her well in the past—but they'd buried the past. Now it was time to fly into an uncertain future. The topsy-turvy sensation of the vast emotional unknown made him thankful he held her tight. Her eyes betrayed her intention to push out of his arms at the first opportunity and run, run, run.

"Not so full of bravado when faced with hard reality, are you?" he asked.

"What hard reality?"

"That you and I are great together."

"In a physical sense."

His face lost all its laughter, his body all its casual mirth. He turned her slightly so she couldn't help but look him straight in the eyes. She could see straight into his soul if only she dared to.

She struggled. He pulled her closer. Nearly nose to nose, she inhaled. He grinned. He wanted her to smell the musky, natural scent of him, mixed with the aroma of torn wood, dust and fear. Fear of her coming to harm. Fear of him losing her forever.

"You don't really think that's all we have, do you? I love you, Serena."

She shook her head, closing her eyes to offset the wild dizziness swirling around her. "I love you, too. I always have. But that doesn't mean…"

The moment he released her, she rolled off the couch to dash…where? Lord, her house was small! No matter where she went, he'd follow. No matter what she said, he'd persist. From the moment she walked into his office—no, even before then—from the instant she heard he was coming back to New Orleans, back into her life, she'd set a course of events in motion that now she couldn't stop.

She stood immobilized in the center of the living room, quivering when she heard the creak of the couch, the soft shuffle of his feet across the rug. He stopped just in front of her, touched her chin with one finger, tilting her face just enough so she could once again witness the depth of his veracity.

"What do you want, Serena?"

Right now, she wanted him to leave. No, that was a lie. She didn't want him to leave. But she didn't want to have this conversation, didn't want to delve into the chamber of her heart where she'd long ago stored away her love for him—a chamber he'd broken into without even trying, a chamber that now leaked pure desire into every aspect of her body and soul.

"I don't understand," she whispered, shaking her head, wondering how he could unravel her with one single touch, wondering how she'd kept herself in one piece so long without him to hold her together.

With his finger, he drew a soft line from chin to cheek, then curled a strand of hair behind her ear in a sweet, guileless gesture. "I told you what I wanted from my future. And today, I realized that the fantasy I'd created was just a way to keep me from loving you. That plan crashed and burned, *chère*. I know now that I want you, need you, have always wanted and needed you. But what do *you* want?"

She couldn't lie to him. Not again. Not anymore. She didn't have the strength. Perhaps the truth would send him packing just as it almost had two nights before.

"I've only ever wanted one thing, Brandon. You. But for so long, I accepted that we'd never happen—not for the long haul. How could a friendship that ended so easily and an affair that came out of the blue—how could that last? I don't usually think about my life beyond tomorrow, but I can't live that way anymore. I can't lose you again. I can't."

"You won't."

"You don't know that."

"I'll prove it."

"How?"

"Marry me."

"What?"

He dipped onto one knee and stole her hand, cradling her palm in his. "Serena Jeanne Deveaux, be my wife. Be my partner. My life mate. My instigator. My rival. My navigator. My heart."

He shifted closer, grabbing her other hand and pressing them both to his lips. "Be my soul. It'll be a crazy ride, but we're both daredevils. We'll survive."

"I don't want to be a daredevil in marriage."

"Serena, that's all either of us knows. Marriage is a risk, the ultimate risk. But we can't back down. I love you. You love me. We don't have a choice."

"Life is all about choice."

"And about challenges."

"Brandon…"

"That's it!"

To hell with the traditional bended-knee and sappy pour-out-your-heart crap. Brandon stood and lifted Serena in one movement, beating down the impulse to haul her over his shoulder, and cradling her against his chest instead. Serena Deveaux had always operated on a different plane than the rest of the world, but it was time she faced regular old three-dimensional reality—Chance style.

"What are you doing?"

Her voice rose with protest, but she didn't struggle nearly enough to convince him to put her down, which he ultimately did, once they'd reached her bedroom and he'd kicked the door shut behind him.

"You want me to work for this, don't you? I'm game, Serena. I'm always game. There are two languages you and I understand. One is sex. Duly noted. The other is challenge. So here it is."

He rolled with her onto the bed, pinning her beneath him.

She was as soft as her purple satin comforter, but the slick material was cool compared to the heated temperature of her skin. He captured her wrists, held them next to her ears and issued his proposal again—this time in words he knew she couldn't resist.

"I dare you."

"You *dare* me? To what? Sleep with you? I did that."

"Technically, no, you didn't. We made love, we had sex," he amended. "But we didn't wake up in each other's arms, not like married people do, knowing that morning isn't the end, but just another beginning. We wanted each other for the moment. This time it will be different. I love you. I know you love me. I dare you to spend the next twenty-four hours with me, in this room, in this bed. If you decide you want to walk away from me tomorrow, you're free to go. If you still think I could ever walk away, I'll do just that. I'll even up the ante. I'll leave New Orleans."

"No!"

"Then you accept my challenge?"

"Brandon, this is ridiculous."

Dragging her arms over her head, he captured her wrists in one hand, then shifted his weight so he could run the other across her forehead, down her cheek, along her throat. He slid his fingers between her breasts, then skimmed the curves beneath them, watching her nipples pucker through the snug cotton of her sleeveless blouse.

"I double-dare you." He whispered the words against the base of her throat, sliding his palm downward, deviating only to warm the bare flesh of her belly at the hem of her shirt. He felt her tremble. He heard her sigh.

"Brandon, this isn't the time for games and bets," she said, but the sweet sound of resignation urged him on. She knew he would win, but that didn't make the challenge any less invigorating. She was Serena, after all.

"This is the perfect time for games, sweetheart." He dragged his hand over the filmy cotton of her sarong skirt, first where it hugged her hip, then to the slit that had invariably fallen open to invite his hot touch against her sweet, bare thigh. "Am I going to have to triple-dog-dare you or is there another way I can ensure your agreement?"

The sensations of his touch blinded her. The power of his words set her heart aflame. How could she deny this man? How could she deny her heart? She loved him. She wanted him. In her body. In her life. For all time. As his wife.

Yes! Complications be damned. If life were meant to be simple, the masters of the universe wouldn't have brought her and Brandon together.

Fate couldn't be denied. Love couldn't be ignored.

But she didn't have to tell him that—yet. Not with a challenge on the table.

She tugged her wrists free with ease since his concentration seemed to center on untying the knot on her skirt rather than holding her still. With a single push, she rolled him over and straddled his waist, just as the knot unraveled and her skirt fell aside to reveal nothing underneath but soft curls and bare skin. In a flash of pure wantonness, she ripped her tank top over her head and threw it aside. She was atop him, naked and fired and free.

And not yet ready to tip her hand.

"What are your terms again?" she asked, folding her arms across her chest.

Brandon groaned when her pose enhanced the size and shape of her breasts. She was trying to distract him again. And she was seriously succeeding. After taking a moment to caress her with his gaze, he folded his hands behind his head and smiled as if he was merely holding a royal flush over his lap instead of a glorious, naked woman.

A naked woman who loved him.

"The simplest terms we've ever dealt with. We make love. We talk. We eat. We make love. We pull out that Pente game I nearly tripped over, ice up those marbles, draw a grid on your belly and see where it leads."

He started unbuttoning his shirt, but she slapped his hands aside and worked the buttons herself.

"So we bet our whole future on a game of Pente?"

"We bet our future on the morning. If you aren't the most satisfied, most deliriously happy woman that ever existed in New Orleans or beyond, I leave, no questions asked."

He leaned forward, shed his shirt, wrapped his arms around her waist and buried his face in the curve between her breasts. He inhaled deeply, then blew a cool directed breath across the tips of her breasts, licked them, then blew again.

Serena arched her back and closed her eyes while sensations wild and wicked stole through her. He kissed her, caressed her, stroked, teased and pinched until all her fears unraveled into gossamer threads of desire. She sighed and concentrated, willing herself to form at least one more coherent thought before she completely and totally surrendered to the magic he wove.

"And if I am the most satisfied, most deliriously happy woman in New Orleans and beyond in the morning? What do I lose?"

He chuckled as he rolled her back beneath him, shed his jeans and briefs, grabbed her by the knees and slid her down the slick surface of her bedspread so her legs dangled over the side.

"All your inhibitions?" he offered, tugging on the edges of

the Mardi Gras boa collection she kept wrapped around her bedposts. He tossed the emerald and gold ones aside, lifted her leg and tied the thin, purple downy one around her ankle.

While he fastened the other end to the footboard, she drew her toes across his midsection and teased the tip of his straining sex. "I don't have any inhibitions." She grabbed the discarded emerald boa and cast the strand of feathers over his shoulder like a fishing line. "Not with you. What else can I lose?"

He secured her legs, then bent over her, tasted her lips, her earlobes, her throat while he stole the golden boa from her grasp and teased her nipples with the glittered tips of the feathers.

"What about your heart?"

"It's already yours, Brandon."

"Then I have nothing left to win and you have nothing to lose."

"Seems like a win-win situation to me. Why even bother with the game?"

"Oh, I don't know. A dare is a dare and a bet is a bet. You wouldn't want a man who'd welsh on a wager, would you?"

She would have said no if she'd still controlled her power to speak. But when his mouth and body drifted downward, loving her inch by slow inch, she could only moan and sigh and surrender, knowing that this one time forfeiting her soul would produce the most glorious win of all.

EPILOGUE

SERENA AND BRANDON awoke to a cacophony of thunder, lightning and charging rain. The darkness of the storm extended the night into morning. Good loving stretched the morning into the afternoon…then to the evening. By seven o'clock, Serena finally left her bed. She'd admitted "defeat" in Brandon's sensual game hours ago, but as the most satisfied woman in New Orleans, she didn't care about losing one bit.

Her sister borrowed Endora's key one last time and on the kitchen table left a Crock-Pot full of jambalaya, the name and number of a good carpenter and a manila envelope filled with travel brochures perfect for a honeymoon.

After scoring two spoons and a bottle of wine, Serena hefted the jambalaya back into the bedroom where she and Brandon ate, kissed, drank, touched and planned a few months into the future.

"I've always wanted to go to Tahiti," Serena mused before Brandon shoveled a spoonful of spicy rice-and-meat mixture into her mouth. She chewed a morsel of shrimp, inhaling at the heat of the cayenne Miss Lily used with a generous hand.

Brandon slipped the brochure from her fingers and stacked it in the "yes" pile atop Casa de Campo, Rio de Janeiro and Monaco. He'd claimed to enjoy the traveling most of all during his tour in the army—and Serena was quite certain she'd make a hell of a better bunk mate.

"That's four places," he counted. "One week in each and a little in between for travel. Should we charter our own plane or do it like real tourists?"

"Looks like we're heading for the full tourist treatment, complete with the debt."

Brandon grinned and took two more ravenous bites. "Don't worry about debt. My parents weren't the only ones to make a little mad money at the roulette tables. I sunk a chunk into the business, but I didn't buy more than the essentials, so I have cash to spare."

"And you do have my fifteen hundred dollars," she reminded him, slithering across the well-rumpled and well-warmed sheets to retrieve the nearly empty bottle of Beaujolais they'd been sipping like soda with dinner. She took a swig and then handed the rest to him.

"True," he concluded, grinning slyly at his own lack of remorse for taking her money. Well, he *had* saved her. From herself. From her silly notion that they weren't absolutely meant for each other. That was worth at least a couple of thousand.

He chugged down the last of the wine and sorted through another colorful trifold advertisement. "Let's add Aspen, too. We can recover from sunburn on the icy slopes."

She shook her head as he tossed yet another brochure to the growing pile, the remnants of her purple boa dangling from his wrist. She anticipated replacing the feathery string at Carnival next year, and the thrill of experiencing all that was New Orleans with Brandon imbued her with an excitement she hadn't felt in years. This was the way things should have been. And now they were.

So simple.

"I can't leave the spa this long, Brandon. And you just started your business."

He moved the Crock-Pot from the center of the bed to the floor, palmed the winning brochures aside with all the skill of a card shark and scooted the rest away in a flutter. In an instant, she was pinned beneath him, naked and full from good food and wine, yet hungry and thirsty for him and him alone.

"We'll get married just before summer break and David can run the spa while you're gone. As for No Chances Protection, I figure Samantha has earned her shot."

"Really?"

She encircled his neck with her arms and pulled herself up to peck him on the cheek. If Brandon was willing to take a chance on her sister after the stunt she'd pulled, she owed him a lot more than just a kiss. Actually, they both owed Sammie a great deal. Giving her a new job seemed the least they could do. As soon as they returned from their honeymoon, Serena was going to find her sister a man of her own. She simply didn't know what she was missing.

"Thank you, Brandon. Sammie will do a great job, you'll see."

He groaned his halfhearted agreement, but made it clear with exploring hands and lips that he wanted a lot more than an innocent kiss for his trouble. She decided a sweeter price had never been paid.

He claimed her mouth greedily, touching her, arousing her, until she was dizzy with need and begging him to slip inside and turn her world from thunderstorm gray to orgasmic white.

And just like a Chance man, he rose to the challenge.

For my wonderful aunts, Rose, Fae and Anita—women I admire and love with all my heart. I count myself incredibly lucky to have been born into a family that includes you.

And for "Nana" Caroline LaRocca and "Nanie" Velia Leto. You showed us all what love and family loyalty are all about. I miss you both.

INSATIABLE

CHAPTER ONE

"COULDN'T YOU just eat him up?"

If Samantha Deveaux heard the question one more time this morning, she was going to puke. After two weeks on the job at Louisiana Superdome security, her assignment at the SuperMarketing Expo was testing her mettle most. Last week's Wrestlemania had been a cakewalk next to this. At least there she'd known what to expect. Screaming. Cursing. A tussle or two. Just enough unpredictable rowdiness to keep her busy.

But since the Supermarketing Expo's eight o'clock opening, she'd gone from rolling her eyes to groaning aloud at the increasingly bad puns. In four hours, every female in the Dome, and a few men for that matter, had strolled through the wide section of wall-less, corporate-sponsored booths and eventually stopped to make a comment in front of the display by LaRocca Foods. Their snickers and sly remarks relied on a combination of food imagery and naughty sexual innuendo.

All for the man looming across from her position at the end of the aisle. Not in person, fortunately, but on a gargantuan aluminum and enamel replica of LaRocca Food's best-selling pasta sauce in a jar—the centerpiece of their display— complete with a huge label stretched across the middle.

In the label's center, a bare-chested man, sketched with lifelike precision, glistened with sweat as he toiled in the middle of some Mediterranean olive field. He had all the classic features of a Sicilian supermodel: ebony hair worn long and windblown, eyes tinted the color of green Italian marble, and a chest, arms and legs that would put Michelangelo's *David* to shame.

He's hotter than his marinara sauce.

He can toss my pasta anytime.

And then the succinct, but equally charged, *Mmm, mmm, good*.

Samantha had seen his type many times before, but even her jaded attitude didn't deter her gaze from roaming back to that label.

His eyes drew her. Not just because of their Kodachrome color, but because an elusive, alluring emotion charged his emerald gaze with power, intensity. The man had attitude. Presence. Even in still life, he demanded attention.

His grin, sly enough to be sultry and subtle enough to make her wonder what he was *really* thinking, said, "Eat this, I dare you. And if you do, I'll give you an equally delicious reward."

As if the man on the label had leaned down from his rustic field and murmured his challenge only to Samantha, a spark of awareness flared as a fantasy formed in her mind. A wicked tryst. A delicious dalliance. Her thighs clenched, instinctively attempting to sate the hot tickle deep inside her, an all-too-frequent reminder that she hadn't had a man in her life for *way* too long. She closed her eyes for an instant, battling to block the flash of flesh and folly that haunted her lately. Day and night. Asleep or awake.

Unfortunately, her once-indistinct fantasy lover now had a face and a body—a face and a body she obviously couldn't resist. She closed her eyes to block his image, reminding herself that he was nothing more than the artistic rendering of some obviously anatomically obsessed artist, but the sensual stream of heat continued its course upward, quivering in her belly then tightening her breasts. Her self-imposed celibacy, enforced for almost a year, had taken its toll. Sam pressed her lips together and fought the sensations—determined to stay focused. Success would be a valiant feat for a girl who'd discovered her sexuality way too early and only recently recognized that her wild past had actually been a blind search for love and acceptance.

And a few sinful dreams were tolerable as long as she managed to put herself back on track. With her attention on the neon-lit soda logo directly across from her, she began silently reciting the techniques she'd learned in her Internet course on how to disarm a crazed stalker.

Despite the repetition, the unspoken invitation from the man in the olive field still echoed loud and clear.

"So, it's the new girl who rates the choice spot. Enjoying the view, Deveaux?"

Samantha's attention snapped to her left and connected with Ruby Gumbert's wry smile. The retired cop, barely ten years older than Samantha, viewed the world with a laid-back cynicism that Samantha couldn't help admiring. They'd become fast friends, though Sam would never admit just how choice she considered her vantage point across from LaRocca Foods to be. She didn't have to. The minute Ruby slid her *Terminator*-style sunglasses down her nose, she let out the most impressive catcall whistle Sam had ever heard from a woman.

"Who'd you sleep with to get this assignment?" Ruby asked.

"Who'd I sleep with?" Samantha counted back six months to her move from Hollywood, California, to her return to New Orleans. After adding another six months to account for brooding after her breakup with Anthony, Sam shook her head. No wonder the Pasta God had her on the sexual edge of insanity. In this entire year, she hadn't slept with anyone but her older sister's cat, Tabitha II. Unless she counted Maurice. Which she didn't. He was Serena's mixed-breed sheepdog, and unlike her Himalayan feline, he preferred the cool floor to the cozy bed.

"I figured I must have insulted someone," Sam quipped. "Listening to all the *oohs* and *ahs* isn't exactly my idea of an ideal workday." *Neither is swallowing my own* oohs *and* ahs, *thank you very much.*

Samantha forced her gaze away from the damn label that inspired all the appreciative groans. Some women were such suckers for a pretty face. Even she had been once, dating some of Hollywood's heartthrobs, even living with Anthony Marks, the biggest cardiac arrester of them all. Thanks to her father, famed action-flick director Devlin Deveaux, she'd met and mingled with every male celebrity ever chosen as *People* magazine's Sexiest Man Alive, and more future coverboys than she cared to count.

And yet, this Pasta God had her fantasizing about new and interesting uses for extra virgin olive oil just from a pencil-drawn ad.

"If you want a lesson in bad pick-up lines," Sam concluded, "you should trade places with me." Sam watched another gaggle of suited, female conventioneers leer and snicker as they strolled by the sexy label. "If you want excitement and mayhem, unfortunately, this isn't the place."

Ruby's smile curled with ageless wisdom. "Life ain't like the movies, Deveaux. Mostly, this job is standing around, looking tough and politely asking people to follow the rules. Not to mention giving directions to the bathroom."

Samantha stepped down from the box dais that provided a clear vantage of her area and wished she hadn't made such a disparaging remark. She already strongly suspected that once again, this job wasn't going to work out. She'd tried approximately four other professions in the past six months and nothing kept her interest. Except for becoming a personal bodyguard. That one really had her blood pumping. If only her brother-in-law, bodyguard Brandon Chance, would come home from his honeymoon with her sister so they could get to work. He'd already put her on the payroll, but with Brandon out of the country and no clients to serve, Sam had done little but earn some of her certifications and licenses and spend the petty cash on neat gadgets. She'd taken the security job at the Dome for two reasons—to pay back the money Brandon had originally budgeted for office rent and electricity and, at Brandon's suggestion, to garner some experience.

So far, all she'd learned was that her attention span was shorter than even her second-grade tutor would have imagined. Oh, and that she could now be aroused by a pencil-drawn hottie on a pasta-jar label.

"I don't mean to insult the job, Ruby. I know you love it. It's just…"

Ruby pushed the sunglasses higher on the bridge of her nose. "Not what you expected. Never is, 'specially with your background. Pretty girl like you. Working in the movies, living the good life…"

"Define *good*," Samantha interrupted, well aware that Ruby was teasing. They'd had this conversation over coffee at Café du Monde after last week's Julio Iglesias concert. During her Hollywood childhood, Sam had always had food in her belly and a roof over her head—if take-out Chinese and trailers on movie lots counted. Her father had loved her in the way only a self-absorbed genius could, meaning that he showered her with affection whenever he didn't have something more important to do.

A child thrust into an adult world from the age of five, Samantha was lucky to have escaped relatively unscathed— at least on the surface. She was only now starting to repair the damage to her heart. Her life in Hollywood could not be described as *good* unless the standards were incredibly shallow.

Ruby's chuckle lacked humor. "*Good* always is a relative term. For today, *this* is a good job. No worries. Easy money. Who knows what tomorrow will bring?"

Samantha frowned, knowing full well what she'd encounter tomorrow—another day of watching conventioneers stuff food samples into their mouths while planning to cut out early and hit the bars on Bourbon Street. Samantha had wished this temporary job would work out, but she had her heart set on a career whose main benefit would be excitement. A little danger. Maybe she'd be lucky and there'd be a scuffle over the free tortilla chips or a grab for the Godiva. Anything to keep her from hijacking the next flight to Brazil so she could drag her brother-in-law back to the States.

"You sound like my mother," Samantha said. "Sometimes I think she forgets that she stole 'Tomorrow is another day' from Scarlett. Unfortunately, I've always been a *now* and *today* kind of person. You're less disappointed by life that way."

"Are you? Less disappointed?" Ruby shook her head and grinned, her bob of raven hair not daring to move from where she'd gelled the strands in place. "Just wait until Signore Gorgeous makes his appearance. That ought to liven things up."

Samantha swallowed her shock.

"The LaRocca model is coming here?"

"That's the scoop. They'd be stupid to keep him under wraps. He's the hottest draw I've seen in the Superdome since Mike Ditka coached the Saints." Ruby lowered her shades. "Whoever he is, the man's a god."

Samantha felt inordinately annoyed she couldn't argue that point without sounding like a big fat liar. Gorgeous men, real or in pictures, simply weren't on her agenda anymore. She was done equating lust with love—with allowing her passions to triumph over cool thinking and common sense. She'd banked on coming home to Louisiana to find her focus. But since her job experience consisted of baby-sitting her father—a creative prodigy who could barely balance his checkbook—and stunt work that kept Devlin's high-priced actors out of harm's way, Sam wasn't exactly a good candidate for the secretarial pool.

Her life had always been about adventure. Thrills. Discovery. When Devlin left her mother and sister in New Orleans after the divorce, Sam had followed, anxious even at five to see the world with her father, to live on location and mingle with the stars. She'd even appeared in a few films until she hit those awkward teenage years. By then, Sam had already begun to despise the celebrity spotlight. Becoming a stunt double had been the perfect profession—anonymous but exciting.

Then she'd been injured. She'd moved in with Anthony, followed a few months later by their heart-wrenching breakup. Returning to New Orleans after twenty-three years hadn't been easy, but she'd come determined to heal all her wounds—physical and emotional—start over and reconnect with her family.

She'd made some headway. Her agility and strength were at one hundred percent. She no longer thought about Anthony every day or about the choices she *should* have made. The future beckoned.

Unfortunately, even romantic, outrageous New Orleans had held little promise by way of truly exciting career choices, until her sister married Brandon. Too bad the eldest Chance brother, in addition to his military background, had an insatiable sexual appetite that kept the couple on their honeymoon four weeks past their scheduled return date. Or maybe Sam should blame her sister. Surrendering to passion seemed to be a genetic trait.

Aw, hell. She couldn't blame either of them. She'd never been one to deny her own desires—and she'd never even really been in love. Sam couldn't begrudge her sister or Brandon their wedded bliss, but she still wished they'd be blissful at home.

In the meantime, Brandon had suggested that Sam pull some security gigs for hands-on learning. Nothing too risky, he'd insisted. Her stunt-work training gave her physical agility and mental preparedness, but the movie sets, speeding cars and fireball explosions had been controlled. Carefully planned and painfully executed. She needed to experience the unexpected—learn to trust her gut.

Somehow, she doubted the Supermarketing Expo fit the bill.

"Samantha, this is Mitchell. Respond please."

Samantha unhooked the walkie-talkie from her belt and turned from the chatter and music echoing through the professionally designed booths and displays. "Deveaux, here."

"The CEO of LaRocca Foods is on his way to his booth. He's a major player. Tim's with him. Stand tall."

Samantha smirked. Another executive type headed toward his company's booth and another opportunity for the security staff to play Secret Service to people whose importance hardly warranted professional protection. Except for the guys at the front assigned to allow entrance to paid conventioneers, the Expo was hardly high-risk. Now, if Mr. Model-licious did indeed plan an appearance as rumored, Sam might get her wish. Mass hysteria and raging female hormones could cause a very dangerous mix.

She knew that firsthand.

"Gotcha, boss."

"And tell Gumbert to return to her position."

Ruby slipped her glasses back onto her regal nose. "I guess the ogle-fest is over. Back to ice-cream land. How the heck do they expect me to stay on this diet when they keep handing me samples of mint chocolate chip? Still want to trade?"

Samantha shook her head. She had few weaknesses in the world, but one was definitely butter pecan ice cream, which she knew they were also serving at the booth near Ruby's station.

"Fat chance."

Ruby patted her flat tummy. "Fat is right. Have fun with the big shot."

Samantha saluted then snapped the walkie-talkie back onto her belt, slipped her hands behind her back and waited for the corporate executive to rush by and ignore her diligence. She hated this job. She hated hating this job. So far, the only good thing to come of her move was being closer to her sister and mother—and again, the definition of *good* came into question.

Her sister, when not honeymooning in some South American country, was a trip in herself—and gave new meaning to the term *unconventional*. Her mother, a world-renowned medium and self-proclaimed New Orleans spirit guide, defied any and all definitions. But so far, Endora had been supportive of Samantha's return, even when she'd taken this "rent-a-cop" deal to supplement her income instead of accepting Mommy's proffered handout.

Which she wouldn't need if her father hadn't reinvested the money he owed her from her last job into his upcoming film. He'd named her as a producer and assumed she'd be thrilled. She could end up obscenely rich if the movie proved a hit. Too bad Sam didn't care about vulgar wealth. She just wanted to be comfortable, stable and self-sufficient. A couple of months under her brother-in-law's tutelage and she'd be a fully licensed, salary-earning bodyguard. She'd already obtained her concealed-weapon permit and had begun her coursework over the Internet. Now she needed some on-the-job training.

But four weeks after their first scheduled return date, Brandon and Serena were still sunning and loving on a beach in Rio de Janeiro. Never mind that Sam had bought and installed a state-of-the-art computer system. Never mind that she'd used next month's office rent to invest in several tracking devices, night-vision goggles and the smallest communications mechanisms she'd ever seen. They'd be the best-outfitted outfit in the personal-protection game.

If they didn't go out of business first. Okay, that was an overstatement. She'd only spent a couple thousand of the petty cash and next month's office rent. But if she didn't restore the treasury soon, she'd have to call Brandon and ask for more money—and admit she'd spent *slightly* more than he'd authorized.

A growing disturbance near the west entrance caught her eye, sending her senses to alert mode. Flanked by two security guards, a threesome of somber-faced suits made their way through the crowd. Sam recognized the first man as Tim Tousignant, the dynamic young executive at the helm of the massive Expo and the man who'd approved her assignment. Good-looking and driven, he impressed Sam with his desire to run any event with smooth precision. Not enough to accept his invitation to dinner, but Sam didn't mix business with pleasure. Not anymore.

The woman on his left, a tall, dark beauty with luminous olive skin clutched a stack of presentation folders and barely contained a wry smile as she glanced at the growing crowd. She leaned nearer to the man in the center and said something she obviously thought was hilarious.

Nearly a head taller than the others, the CEO of LaRocca Foods obviously didn't agree. He shot his companion a sharp look and muttered a few words that caused her laughter to die a quick death. He watched his feet and held his hand up to the growing number of followers in a gesture more like a "stop" sign than a wave.

Samantha's skin prickled.

Lured by the presence of this reluctant Pied Piper, people left the other displays to follow the hulking executive and his burgeoning entourage toward Sam's end of the aisle near the north exit. An electric buzz rippled through the Superdome until waves of convention goers, mostly female, rushed toward the five-hundred-square-foot area reserved by LaRocca Foods. Mitchell said the CEO, right? She glanced at the label again, then back at the man in the middle of the swarming horde.

Her heart skittered, but then she smiled. A few moments ago, the man's incredible looks and intense gaze, captured on the pasta label, had affected her like a virulent potion. Now she had the perfect antidote—his obvious arrogance.

If he wasn't the end-all, be-all of shameless self-promotion, she didn't know who was. Mr. Chief Executive Officer, sans the top half of his pressed Italian suit, was indeed the sexy hunk-o-rama on his newest product.

Samantha started to laugh, but stopped when the security guards approached, their eyes wide as the swollen throng closed in. A few women squealed. Manicured hands reached across the guards, grabbing at the CEO who still walked, head down, until the mob stopped his progress.

"Oh, God, it's him! Dominick LaRocca!" someone shrieked.

"You can dig in my field anytime, Pasta Man!"

"I'm hungry for more than sauce, hot stuff! Over here!"

For an instant, Sam thought she'd been transported onto Bourbon Street during Mardi Gras. A middle-aged woman in a silk blouse lifted her shirt and bra to the delight of every man within leering distance. The crowd, effectively incited, surged, pressing the small group of five to the wall. Sam jumped onto the dais to regain her fix on LaRocca and company.

Time to work.

She radioed for backup, then shouted at the two security

guards ineffectively trying to hold the women back with drawn nightsticks. Folders scattered as the pretty olive-skinned woman twisted in front of her boss to put one more barrier between him and the tentacles of hungry hands. Sam lost sight of Tim altogether, but figured protecting the man at the center of the disturbance was priority one, especially since he was the one *causing* the melee.

She couldn't wait for the guards to lead him closer to the exit. She tucked her hair under her cap and slipped into the crowd, diving low and pushing through the writhing mass until she reached her colleagues. They begged the women to stand aside, using minimal force despite the growing danger.

"I called for backup," Samantha yelled before pressing between the ineffective wall they'd formed to keep the CEO from harm. "Keep them back!"

"One heck of a security plan you have here," LaRocca growled.

She ignored him and grabbed his elbow.

"Follow me."

"Wait. Where's Anita?"

Samantha felt certain Anita would fare better once the object of these women's desires was removed from the hall.

"She'll be fine once you're safe."

"Wait!"

Undoubtedly used to calling the shots, he dodged her attempts to pull him out. Samantha knew better than to argue, especially when only about every third word could be heard over the fervent screaming, blatant offers of sex and even a marriage proposal or two, if you counted "marry me, marry me!" as a true invitation. Instead, Sam twisted around him and used her full body weight to shove him to the exit. The sheer velocity of her push sent the crowd fumbling and tripping over one another, allowing her the split second she needed to squeeze him through the heavy security door.

She slipped in behind him and immediately threw her back against the door to attempt to close and lock it.

"Which one are you, anyway?" she asked, annoyed. "George, John, Paul or Ringo?"

A growl tore from her throat as she met with resistance from the other side.

Sex-crazed bimbos! Desperate, man-stupid teenyboppers!

"Don't be shy," LaRocca said between pants. "Tell them what you really think."

She'd tossed him into the hallway so forcefully, he'd hit the opposite wall with a grunt. The loosened knot in his tie had flipped over his collar and the left hip pocket of his jacket hung loose at his side. His nostrils flared as he gasped for breath, then he used the opposite wall to launch himself against the door.

Against her.

The contact cracked the air around them with a pop nearly inaudible with women screaming on the other side of the door. But the surge of static electricity burned Samantha from the outer layer of her skin straight through to her heart. She shook her head, trying to dispel the resonating tingle, and pressed her back to the door. She dug in with her powerful legs, legs now tangled between the Pasta God's marble thighs. His scent was as crisp and clean as his starched white shirt, as if he'd just stepped out of the shower. The image of him in nothing but a fluffy white towel immediately sprang to mind.

"Did I say that out loud?" she asked, hoping like hell that he'd interpret the flush of her skin as natural exertion, even embarrassment at her mouthy tirade. She refused to look up in his face, though gazing straight into his chest wasn't any less dangerous when she knew, thanks to the sauce label, exactly what his chest looked like bare.

"Loud and clear. But I'm not arguing. You'd think these

women had never seen a man before." He struggled to help
her close the door, but hands and fingers, even an ankle or two
stuck through the six inches of space between the steel barrier
and quiet freedom. Over the noise from the other side, Sam
finally heard the arrival of reinforcements.

"Back. Back. Move back!"

Hands and feet disappeared from the doorway, but the
press from the other side remained constant, probably from
the guards struggling to clear the doorway. They wouldn't be
safe until they closed the door, and her counterparts on the
other side apparently had their hands full just blocking the
exit.

Glancing down at her for approval, Dominick LaRocca
took another deep breath. "On three."

She nodded, bracing herself for further impact. The rush
of adrenaline snapped her head up. *Good Lord. He's going
to throw his weight against the door. Against me!*

He counted, "One…"

His eyes mirrored the color of freshly crushed mint.

"Two…"

His jaw looked chiseled from flesh-toned granite.

"Three!"

Pressed Italian silk didn't hide an erection worth a damn.

An Important Message from the Editors

Dear Reader,

Because you've chosen to read one of our fine novels, we'd like to say "thank you!" And, as a **special** way to thank you, we're offering you a choice of <u>two more</u> of the books you love so well **plus** an exciting Mystery Gift to send you — absolutely <u>FREE</u>!

Please enjoy them with our compliments...

Pam Powers

Lift here

Peel off seal and place inside...

What's Your Reading Pleasure...
ROMANCE? *OR* SUSPENSE?

Do you prefer spine-tingling page turners OR heart-stirring stories about love and relationships? Tell us which books you enjoy – and you'll get **2 FREE "ROMANCE" BOOKS** or **2 FREE "SUSPENSE" BOOKS** with no obligation to purchase anything.

Choose **"ROMANCE"** and get **2 FREE BOOKS** that will fuel your imagination with intensely moving stories about life, love and relationships.

FREE!

Choose **"SUSPENSE"** and you'll get **2 FREE BOOKS** that will thrill you with a spine-tingling blend of suspense and mystery.

FREE!

Whichever category you select, your 2 free books have a combined cover price of $11.98 or more in the U.S. and $13.98 or more in Canada.

And remember... just for accepting the Editor's Free Gift Offer, we'll send you 2 books and a gift, ABSOLUTELY FREE!

YOURS FREE! We'll send you a fabulous surprise gift absolutely FREE, just for trying "Romance" or "Suspense"!

® and ™ are trademarks owned and used by the trademark owner and/or its licensee.

Order online at
www.FreeBooksandGift.com

The Editor's "Thank You" Free Gifts Include:

- 2 Romance OR 2 Suspense books!
- An exciting mystery gift!

Yes! I have placed my
Editor's "Thank You" seal in the
space provided at right. Please
send me 2 free books, which
I have selected, and a fabulous
mystery gift. I understand I am
under no obligation to purchase
any books, as explained on the
back of this card.

PLACE
FREE GIFT
SEAL
HERE

ROMANCE
193 MDL EE3N   393 MDL EE4C

SUSPENSE
192 MDL EE3Y   392 MDL EE4N

FIRST NAME

LAST NAME

ADDRESS

APT.#

CITY

STATE/PROV.

ZIP/POSTAL CODE

Thank You!

The Reader Service — Here's How It Works:

Accepting your 2 free books and gift places you under no obligation to buy anything. You may keep the books and gift and return the shipping statement marked "cancel." If you do not cancel, about a month later we'll send you 3 additional books and bill you just $5.24 each in the U.S., or $5.74 each in Canada, plus 25¢ shipping & handling per book and applicable taxes if any.* That's the complete price and — compared to cover prices starting from $5.99 each in the U.S. and $6.99 each in Canada — it's quite a bargain! You may cancel at any time, but if you choose to continue, every month we'll send you 3 more books, which you may either purchase at the discount price or return to us and cancel your subscription.

*Terms and prices subject to change without notice. Sales tax applicable in N.Y. Canadian residents will be charged applicable provincial taxes and GST.

CHAPTER TWO

NICK THREW HIS FULL weight into shutting the door. In his mad rush, he trapped the sapphire-eyed security guard beneath him. The latch caught and a sensation not unlike an electric shock snapped all around him. Instantaneous stimulation surged through his blood and rushed straight to his groin.

He hadn't expected the spitfire in uniform to have anything soft about her, anything luscious or feminine. He'd been wrong. Just the brief contact stirred the primal male urge he'd kept in careful check for so long—a self-restraint made especially difficult with women of various degrees of desirability making offers any sane man couldn't refuse. Yet, as she pushed the deadbolt into place, the lush warmth of her curves hugged him straight through his jacket, shirt and tie, making him wish he could forget his responsibilities to his family. Just this once.

"Sorry." He rolled aside, straightening his suit, trying to ignore that his skin tingled as if he'd just been struck by lightning. His grandmothers often mused that a thunderbolt would probably strike him dead before he met a woman who could stir him out of his rigid, business-and-family-first way of thinking.

For once, Rosalia LaRocca and Rafaela Durante might be wrong.

"I'm the one who should apologize." Her eyes reflected blue like the sun-sparkling water of a swimming pool. On a scorching day. One hundred and ten degrees. In the shade. But before he drowned in her liquid irises, she turned aside, patting her slim waist as she checked the presence of her nightstick, walkie-talkie and keys. The moisture in Nick's mouth evaporated.

"The Expo isn't really prepared for mass hysteria," she added, chastisement totally undisguised. "Don't you have personal security?"

Her snippy tone reminded him of the reasons *why* he'd been without a lover for so long—why his body was primed for sexual games he couldn't afford to play. Ever since his picture made it onto that label, women he'd never met had been offering to do things for him—to him—that even his ex-fiancée would consider depraved. He'd received naked snapshots in the mail, wrapped in lacy panties that had obviously been worn. Just last night, a woman in a bikini had ambushed them at the airport, throwing herself spread-eagle over the hood of his hired limousine.

His family had been hounding him to employ a body-guard, but the last thing he needed was some goon in a dark suit following him around as if he were John Gotti or Al Capone. No thanks. He had enough trouble with Italian stereotypes without traveling with hired muscle.

"I'm a businessman, not a celebrity."

"Care to tell that to the women on the other side of this door?" She turned and moved to undo the lock.

"No." He rushed to grab her hand, stopping short when she smiled, winked and released the latch. He smoothed his palm over his hair, attempting a nonchalant recovery. Too bad there was nothing nonchalant about the wave of disappointment that rolled over him because he couldn't touch her again. Ever.

Man, he had to put a stop to this hysteria soon. The barrage of willing women, coupled with his decision to neglect his personal life and personal needs, at least until the European distribution deal solidified LaRocca Food's solvency, threatened to undo him.

And the adorable pucker on the security guard's lips wasn't helping one damn bit.

"*That* mob shouldn't have happened," he insisted, jabbing his finger at the door in an attempt to regain his trademark snarl.

She shrugged. "Shouldn't have is one thing, but it did. What did you expect anyway? Your picture on that label is more provocative than most *Playgirl* centerfolds."

Nick jammed his hand through his hair again, reminding himself that this woman's haughtiness and her all-too-true observation were insufficient reasons to lose his temper. The label *was* provocative. He had the sales figures to prove it.

"That picture was not my doing."

She crossed her arms and shifted her weight to one leg. The pose was disbelief and sassiness potently combined. "You are the CEO of that company, aren't you?"

"CEO, but not chairman. Some decisions can be made without my knowledge. Or at least, they could *before*."

"This isn't just a little bit about your ego? All those women screaming? Tearing at your clothes?"

His eyebrows shot up. He wasn't used to talking turkey with a stranger. "You don't mince words, do you?" he asked.

"No point. I'm a call-'em-like-I-see-'em kind of gal."

And he usually didn't find that trait desirable.

Usually.

"Well, you're seeing this one all wrong."

His grandmothers, the joint chairwomen of the LaRocca board of directors, had schemed with marketing and production to come up with the new label with his picture on it, enhanced to make him some sort of romantic hero. Before he could fire the artist, sales skyrocketed. All the traditional leaders in the sauce business were still scrambling to catch up.

In the midst of a marketing coup, Nick had hoped this trip to New Orleans would allow him to recapture his once iron-hand grip on his personal life. But not only had his grand-mothers seen fit to put his image on the label, they'd included some rather clever copy lamenting his single marital status and celebrating his estimated net worth.

He hadn't known so many single women lived in the United States. Women in every demographic group had flooded the mailroom with offers of marriage. Eager brides congregated in the lobby of his headquarters on Chicago's Walker Drive. It was only a matter of time before they set up camp at his Lake Shore condominium.

He'd come to New Orleans eager for a little peace and quiet, not to mention anonymity. The last thing he needed was another headstrong female in his life, even if she had just saved his hide from the desperate throng.

"I'm featured in that booth because ever since that damn label was introduced, *without my knowledge,*" he added a second time, "sales have gone up forty-seven percent in the past two weeks alone."

"Ah, the bottom line," she said with a nod. "I can under-stand that."

Great. Another woman with dollar signs in her eyes. Won-derful. Too bad that insight didn't diminish his growing fas-cination with the gently bowed, slightly glossy shape and texture of her lips.

"Is there a way out of here?" he demanded. "A private way?"

The security guard looked around to catch her bearings. He noticed that the gold tag on her shirt read "Deveaux."

"Are you staying at the Hyatt next door?" she asked.

"Yes."

"Then follow me. There's a lower tunnel reserved for au-thorized personnel. It'll lead you out the back and all we'll have to do is cross a parking lot."

She swept her hand forward then started toward a stairwell that would take them to ground level. Her step was light and trouble-free, saucy and sexy and dangerous as hell. Her hips rocked with a rhythm only she could hear—but Nick tuned in, despite his best efforts not to. Queen during their hey-day. Joan Jett and Pat Benatar jamming with the Bangles.

He moistened his lips, wondering if he'd ever met a woman who could make him regret so much and want so much, so fast.

"Thank you for taking control out there," he said, knowing he owed her some genuine gratitude and hoping a little more conversation would tamp down his growing physical interest. He reminded himself that she had a sharp tongue and decisive opinions—two strikes for any woman he wasn't related to by blood. As much as he'd tried, he couldn't change the LaRocca women or their daughters. And as much as he loved them, he didn't need another head-strong woman trying to lead him by the nose.

"The guards assigned to me didn't seem to know what to do," he added.

"Yeah, well, they're guys," she concluded quickly. "They probably figured too much force and they'd hurt someone."

Nick chuckled. "I don't doubt that you could do some serious damage if you wanted to."

"Considering my height and weight, it takes a concerted effort for me to hurt someone." She spoke brusquely, totally oblivious to the double meaning to his comment.

Or at least, he assumed she was oblivious. He wasn't so sure when he caught her sharp glance and a fleeting grin. "Women in my field compensate with speed, agility and, well…brains."

Not to mention soft curves, dark blond hair and bright blue eyes. The woman who'd saved him, he decided, was as close to lethal as strychnine.

"Have you been a security guard long?" Nick knew he shouldn't have asked the question, shouldn't have invited more conversation. The more she talked, the more he wanted to know.

"About two weeks," she said, her voice softening as she admitted her inexperience. He never would have guessed she was a rookie. His fascination with her jumped a notch. "But this is just a temporary job. Until my boss gets back from his honeymoon." She paused, biting her bottom lip before admitting, "I'm a protection specialist with No Chances Protection." Her claim grew louder as she spoke, as if she was trying the label on for size.

"Protection specialist?" he asked.

"A bodyguard."

After his brush with the screaming crowd, Nick couldn't begrudge his savior her choice of occupation. In fact, he was having a damn hard time begrudging anything at the moment. Just walking behind her, watching the alluring swing of her hips, catching the light in those impressive blue eyes whenever she looked over her shoulder, did amazing things to his outlook. His cousin and assistant, Anita, had started calling him the ogre at least ten times a day. Right now, he felt like the prince who slew the ogre…all for the sake of a sexy blond princess.

And he didn't appreciate the feeling one iota.

Everything about Miss Deveaux should have gone against his grain. She was tough. She spoke her mind. She took control and did what had to be done without regrets.

A fine combination for a lover, ordinarily, but a horrible mix when he couldn't afford to extend an invitation to his bed unless it was attached to a marriage proposal. And though Miss Deveaux stirred his blood like a chef with a swift wooden spoon, this woman's medley of sassy confidence was the last thing he wanted to deal with for a lifetime.

Nick knew his preferences for a bride—sweet, submissive,

maybe a little shy—were about a century behind the times, but he'd yet to meet someone who inspired him to change.

And though he was the last heterosexual man on earth who *wanted* to get married, he couldn't deny that very, very soon, he'd have little to no choice.

When his grandmothers decided last year that they wouldn't retire and turn the company completely over to him until he settled down and started a family, he should have popped the question to the nearest single adult female and been done with it. Instead, he'd dug in his heels and refused to let them dictate his private life.

Only, his private life consisted of endless family obligations—weddings, baptisms, birthdays—an occasional jog down Lake Shore and, perhaps, a night out with his CFO and vice president of retail sales so they could discuss business under the guise of relaxation.

Their latest discussion was the conundrum his grandmothers had created with their declaration. If Rose and Fae died before he married, LaRocca Foods would be sold in pieces to various family members. The conglomerate he'd worked so hard to build would cease to exist. All the market power he'd amassed since he joined the company just out of college would be lost.

The LaRoccas and Durantes had never been wealthy before. Until he took over the business, they had struggled through two generations of barely making ends meet, of not sending children to college if they couldn't win scholarships, of doubling up on living arrangements to make sure every mouth was fed. But when the family's restaurant fell on hard times and his grandmothers started supplementing the family income by selling their pasta sauce from behind the register, it had been Nick's idea to build a display case for the West Monroe Street entrance. He'd been the one to organize and offer mail order to tourists and, after completing his course of study at the University of Illinois, he'd personally pounded the pavement to introduce their products to grocery stores. And just seven years ago, he'd spearheaded the promotion campaign that pushed their private stock into the public marketplace for a premium price.

And all without putting his own picture on a single label.

Nick quickened his step to match Miss Deveaux's momentum. "I can make it to my room alone, thank you. Just tell me which door leads to the stairwell."

She shook her head, a few more strands of blond spilling out to brush her shoulders. "That's not the way we do things in Louisiana," she said proudly, adding a Creole lilt to her accent-free voice. "This is a Southern state, remember? Hospitality and all that."

"Yes, well, I'm from Chicago. We do things just fine on our own. The last thing I need is another woman clamoring to hold my hand."

She stopped her progression down the hall and impaled him with a look of utter disbelief. "I've met lots of people from Chicago and not one was downright rude. Excuse me for pointing out the obvious, but I did just save your hide. And I didn't touch your hands in the process."

He didn't want to think about what she *had* touched. And how that touching had sent his pulse rate skyrocketing.

"You have my gratitude." He reached for his wallet, but the widening of her azure eyes to the size of jar lids stopped him from offering money for her service. He pocketed his eelskin billfold. "If you could just point me to the right door?"

The sassy security guard with the name Deveaux stitched above her left breast—a rather pert, curvaceous breast—slid her cap off her head, releasing the full, bouncy tumble of her hair. She eyed him head to toe, a growing distaste skewing her bowed lips into an unattractive sneer.

"The blue door at the end of the hall."

He nodded to her curtly—just to make sure she didn't follow him—and proceeded in the direction she'd indicated. Insulting women hadn't been a mainstay of his behavior until recently, when Nana Rose and Nana Fae schemed to make him the most eligible bachelor on the Fortune 500. With the gleeful help of his cousin, Anita, they'd successfully transformed him from a driven businessman into a cynical, overbearing slave driver. He had no right to take his frustration out on Miss Deveaux, but she had the unfortunate luck to be the nearest woman in range of his anger. He'd dictate a letter of commendation to her superiors as soon as he found Anita.

Yanking at the latch on the door she'd indicated, he turned his thoughts from the woman behind him to plotting how he could reschedule his appearance at the booth. He'd planned to glad-hand some of the industry's largest chains into awarding his products more shelf space and additional end-cap promotions. He'd be damned if he'd abandon his short-term goals for the Expo just because his grandmothers intended to make him the Fabio of the grocery business.

As he walked across the threshold, a distinctly feminine squeal snapped up his head.

"It's him! Marry me, Pasta Man!"

Nick glanced over his shoulder at the slowly closing blue door. She'd said "blue," right? Yet he was now standing in the registration area of the Expo instead of a stairwell to his hotel. And one by one, recognition dawned on the faces of several women just a few feet away.

Here I go again.

SERVES HIM RIGHT.

From behind, Samantha watched LaRocca's fists clench. His shoulders tightened. She could only imagine the look on his face—and the horror she pictured gave an extra curve to the smile bowing her mouth. Some men had to learn the hard way. Samantha Deveaux was not a woman to be dismissed. Someone might do it once. But twice? Not likely. Not anymore.

Disheveled and distraught, the women being escorted out of the Superdome struggled against the careful grasps of several annoyed security guards. As Sam figured, her co-workers had reached the main lobby to escort the rowdiest women out of the Expo Hall to cool off. She'd just stoked the flame by misleading the lion right back into the den.

She considered letting the blue door slam shut behind Dominick LaRocca, leaving him at the mercy of the hormonally charged females on the other side, but her duty to protect him intruded on her fun. Pushing the door open at the last possible minute, she allowed him to slip back into the hall before the crowd attacked again.

"Did I say *blue?*" she asked once the door slammed shut, sugar dripping from each syllable. "I meant gold. The gold door is the stairwell, the blue door leads to the lobby." She pointed to each as she spoke, as if willing herself to remember facts she obviously knew perfectly well.

A storm swirled in his eyes, reminding her of a deadly waterspout in the gulf. "That was uncalled for," he snapped, once again trying to straighten his tie and jacket despite that he looked as if he'd just…well, as if he'd just escaped a screaming crowd of crazed women clamoring for his bod.

"I beg to differ." Samantha planted her fists on her hips. "I'd say it was completely called for. You were rude and I *won't* be treated like a groupie. My job—in addition to saving your butt—is to escort you to safety. If you won't let me do that job, then I can't be responsible for the consequences."

He stood straighter as he caught his breath, and Samantha suddenly found his height imposing. If it weren't for the twinkle of amusement dancing in his green eyes, she might have backed down. "So you led me back into the ring? Revenge, quick and simple. That's a concept I understand."

She shook her head. "I don't believe in revenge." Samantha considered that claim for a minute and decided it wasn't entirely truthful. It had been. Once. When she didn't know better. "No, that's not true. I do believe in revenge. In fact, I kind of dig it."

"*Dig it?* How old are you?"

"Old enough to have a father who still says 'dig it' and 'groovy.' And for the record, it isn't considered polite to ask a woman her age."

"Well, aren't you just New Orleans's answer to Miss Manners. I suppose it's the height of proper etiquette to throw a drowning man back into shark-infested waters?" He gestured toward the blue door, his expression incredulous.

She pursed her lips. "We could call it even."

Despite his best efforts, a tiny grin broke through his scowl. "Very reasonable. Now, if you'd be so kind, Miss Deveaux, would you personally escort me to some quiet exit so I can return to my hotel?"

"Name's Samantha. And I'd be delighted to see you safely out of the Dome, Mr. LaRocca."

He hesitated, then thrust his hand forward in a businesslike pose. "Nick. Please."

Sam glanced at his eyes first, then his hand, assessing the threat of touching him. The feel of him against her still resonated throughout the full length of her body, still lingered along the edges of her skin. But her newfound independence and determination wouldn't allow her to refuse.

She concentrated all of her strength into giving him one hearty handshake, but was ill prepared for the electric shock that crackled between their palms.

"Ow!"

He pulled back, glanced at his hand and then at her.

"Sorry. I'm one of those people who conducts a lot of electricity," she explained, trying to remember the last time she'd shocked someone on such a warm and humid day.

"I'll just bet you do." His comment was cryptic, but the deepened crease of two slashlike dimples told her he implied something sexual. Yet the fanciful glint disappeared quickly, leaving her to wonder if this man had just flirted with her or if her celibacy was finally driving her mad.

He gestured for her to lead the way, following a few steps behind when she opened the gold door across the hall, checked that the stairwell was empty and secure, then ushered him downstairs.

Leaving the Superdome without escort posed a greater threat now that a crowd had formed outside, so once they reached the lower level, Sam radioed for instructions. Tim Tousignant, the SuperMarketing Expo executive who'd also been caught in the crush, met them in the security office to ensure that Mr. LaRocca was indeed well and would return to give his presentation as soon as additional security measures were in place. Tim offered his personal limousine to deliver the Chicago food magnate back to his hotel, with Samantha as escort.

"I don't think that's necessary, Tim. The hotel is across the street," Dominick reasoned.

Tim shook his head, his face pinched and his gaze insistent. "There's a growing crowd out front. We'd just about calmed them down when something riled them again." He checked his watch, missing the look Dominick shot to Samantha. "The hotel lobby will be busy this time of day. Samantha can escort you through the service entrance." He turned his gaze directly on Sam. "See him safely to his room. I don't want his safety jeopardized again."

Samantha didn't like Tim's accusatory tone, but she bit back her sharp retort and nodded instead. She didn't figure

Tim for the sass-me-and-get-away-with-it type. Like it or not, she needed this job until she could find something better—or until her brother-in-law and sister returned from Rio.

"I'll see to his safety."

Dominick shook his head, obviously chafing under the protective orders. "Miss Deveaux has been very effective, but I can manage on my own."

"I'm afraid I have to insist," Tim said, his tone conciliatory yet firm. "It won't be good business for the Expo if one of our top exhibitors is accosted outside the Superdome."

Nick eyed Samantha skeptically. Either he didn't trust her to do her job—which she doubted since the man didn't seem to be a fool—or he simply didn't want her around. She didn't blame him. As a bodyguard, resentment of her presence would be a common response. As nice and accommodating as her own childhood bodyguards had been, she'd disliked living under their watchful eyes from the day after her father's first megahit made him a celebrity, until she turned twenty-one and fired them herself.

Dominick's stare lasted a long moment, but then he nodded his acceptance of the inevitable. "Can you arrange tightened security by this afternoon?"

"I'll get right on it," Tim answered. "Samantha, radio Mitchell to send my driver around back. I apologize again, Mr. LaRocca. I had no idea…"

Dominick silenced the apology with a flattened palm. "Neither did I. Obviously, there's no accounting for some women's taste."

Self-deprecating humor looked good on him, Samantha decided, though if she hadn't already spent it, she'd bet next month's rent that he didn't employ such self-mockery often. Still, Dominick LaRocca seemed an interesting mix of contradictions. Gorgeous men like him didn't usually come in multidimensional models, at least not in her experience. Maybe there was more to him than met the eye.

Though the part that met the eye was pretty damn appealing.

While Dominick flipped open his cell phone to call his assistant before they left, Tim pulled her aside.

"Good job, Samantha. I didn't mean to jump on you. I just don't want Mr. LaRocca to think we take security lightly."

"No problem." She glanced at Tim's hand, still lingering on her elbow. He stepped back and shoved both hands into the pockets of his pressed and creased Armani slacks.

"Look, I know you took this job for the money. That's cool," Tim assured her, suddenly looking every inch the twenty-something marketing wunderkind he was. "Looks to me like Mr. LaRocca could use someone like your brother-in-law until this hype dies down."

Despite her many jobs, Samantha had never mastered the art of interviewing. At the time, she'd second-guessed her decision to be completely up front with Tim, but she was now impressed by his supportive attitude and excellent memory. He was probably trying to stave off any bad publicity, but Samantha sensed this wasn't the time for cynicism. "Thanks, Tim. But Brandon's still out of the country."

"If you say so." Then he winked. "I just thought you were dying to get your feet wet in the protection game yourself. You dipped your toe in today and did damned good. Remember that."

Tim nodded, then shook hands with Mr. LaRocca before jogging down the hall and back to work. Tim was a go-getter, all right. He'd moved up the corporate ladder by finding opportunities—not by waiting for them to find him, or worse, by waiting for some member of his family to hand him the brass ring. From the time her parents had divorced and she'd gone to California with her father, Sam had been programmed to put her life on hold until Devlin Deveaux found her focus for her.

He'd cast her in her first film, guided her into stunt work, even had a major hand in her doomed relationship with Anthony.

For all intents and purposes, wasn't she now transferring that dependence from her father to her brother-in-law? Waiting for him to direct her?

Sam could indeed learn something from the way Tim's mind worked. Luckily, she was a quick study.

CHAPTER THREE

SAMANTHA INSISTED on stepping off the elevator first, trapping Nick and the two men from hotel security behind her. With her hand firmly flattened against his chest, she scanned the hallway. Nick knew she was just doing her job by keeping him from disembarking until she was convinced the path was clear, but he couldn't help grunting in frustration.

Even without a jolt of static electricity, her touch ignited an incendiary spark that he suspected would leave him with third-degree burns. Now was not the time for him even to *think,* much less fantasize, about a woman who's entire history and personal background hadn't been checked and double-checked. Thanks to his grandmothers, he was currently a hotter property than any man had a right to be. While he didn't intend to let the attention go to his head, he also wouldn't fall victim to some money-grubbing *femme fatale.*

Not that he had any reason to consider Samantha money-grubbing. But *femme fatale?* Oh, yeah. If she didn't remove her hand in the next few seconds, he was going to die a particularly slow and painful death from testosterone overload.

"Well?" he prompted, causing her to swing around, startled. His body instantaneously recalled the sensation of pressing against her and a pleasant heat stirred low in his groin, shooting sparks of sexual awareness to the tips of his fingers. She'd removed her hat when they entered the hotel, and her hair, a dark-blond hue that reminded him of the butterscotch sauce he loved to drench his ice cream with, fairly begged to be combed through. By him. In bed. After a champagne seduction and mind-blowing sex.

Which, unfortunately for both of them, wasn't going to happen.

"Deserted," she announced, tearing her hand away.

"No one to attack me? That's a switch." He dug his hands into his pockets and shrugged. But despite the bluster of his complaint, he didn't want to insult her again—or worse, sound conceited.

"Maybe you should recall all that pasta sauce," she teased. "Put a big fat tomato on the label instead."

He burrowed his fists deeper into his once carefully creased slacks. Amusement lit her eyes to the color of blue curaçao, a liqueur he could never refuse. "And sacrifice sales? Never. It's a small price to pay."

She shook her head. "Privacy comes with a big price tag in my book."

One of the hotel security guards who'd joined them in the elevator cleared his throat. Surprisingly, Nick had completely forgotten their presence. He was too busy trying to figure out why now, in the safety of this deserted hall, he didn't yet want Samantha Deveaux to return to her duties at the Superdome. He couldn't remember the last time someone had intrigued him so completely, especially someone without a single tie to the business he'd devoted his adult life to. The little socializing he did was either with family or friends, all in the restaurant or food business and all dependent on his expertise and business acumen to guide their futures.

Despite that they had nothing in common, he couldn't break the eye contact that held her still and kept him captive. She was like an infusion of fresh herbs in a dish laden with heavy cream. She not only added flavor to his morning, she lightened up the entire crazy experience. A glint shined from within her eyes, a sharp, focused gleam that reminded him of himself. At least, the self he was five or six years ago.

Lately, he reacted to the world with dour severity rather than with the relaxed, irreverent humor he'd once embraced—before he became Dominick LaRocca, the half-naked man on a pasta sauce label. Back when he was just Nick. The guy who hung out on Taylor Street. Who played stickball with the guys then flirted with the girls while they shared Italian Ices outside Mario's Lemonade Stand.

The guard behind him coughed again.

Without turning, Nick stepped off the elevator and sent them away. "Please see that your staff keeps my room number private."

Thus dismissed, the elevator door slid shut, followed by the mechanical whir of the descending cab.

"You want me to check out your room?" Samantha asked.

More than you know, he thought, marveling at this unexpected, invigorating attraction. She was *not* his type. For one, she spoke her mind whenever she wished. Women from his grandmothers to his cousin to his mother did exactly the same, without heed to his preference for feminine compliance and good old-fashioned peace and quiet. Second, she was too curvy. He preferred his women waiflike, willowy, even if they did threaten to break on any of the rare occasions where his passion flamed unchecked. Samantha Deveaux could clearly handle the unbridled, unhampered desire every man fantasized about.

"Actually, I thought I'd find Anita and determine when I could return to the Expo. You can coordinate the security plan before you leave."

She laughed while following him down the hall. "After our little fiasco this morning, I don't even know if I'll be employed by this afternoon."

"Tim seemed complimentary, when he thought I wasn't listening." He slid his card key into the gold box beside a double set of doors at the end of the hall.

She rewarded his covert eavesdropping with a sly smile. "Tim approved my hire, but he's in charge of the Expo, not the Dome. Maybe he has a lot of pull and won't let them fire me."

The lock clicked softly and he pushed the door open. "Fire you? Because you saved me from a crazed mob?"

"That mob should never have formed in the first place."

She dug her hands into her pockets, shuffling her feet, curling her bottom lip outward just enough to elicit exactly the correct amount of sympathy and guilt she obviously intended. Luckily for Nick, he'd dealt with more than enough scheming, conniving women in his lifetime to let her ploy work. And he'd thought her different from the women jumping onto the hood of his limousine or hiding in the mail cart at the office. Yet, here she was, attempting to play him for a sucker with her tiny little frown and averted eyes. He should be disgusted, even disappointed.

Instead, he couldn't help but grin like a fool.

So she did want something after all. And for some reason completely at odds with logic or common sense, Nick couldn't wait to find out what.

"You're very good," he said. "Very convincing. The little lip thing is a perfect touch. I suppose now is when I offer to make a call on your behalf? Demand your promotion? A raise?"

"That's a bit much, but thanks. I have a better offer in mind." Samantha stepped in front of him, casing the room as she walked. Windows lined the curved foyer, leading past a wet bar to a large room with a conference table, six chairs, two fax machines, an active laptop computer and stacks of papers and LaRocca Foods brochures and promotional materials. Behind the table, a sitting area—complete with twin recliners, an overstuffed couch, a coffee table bearing the remnants of a room-service breakfast and an entertainment center—occupied the largest part of the room.

"Nice digs." She bit back asking if the door on the other side of the stored Murphy bed contained his bedroom or was just another exit into the hall. She'd already opened herself up to more than one sexual connotation this morning. Asking about his sleeping arrangements could prove unnecessary unless she convinced him to hire her as his private bodyguard.

"You don't want a promotion, huh? Hmm, let me think." He tossed his key onto the table and clicked the keyboard on his laptop, summoning the current stock-market statistics to flow across the bottom of the screen. "You did say this security job was temporary. Lay your proposal on the table, Samantha. I'm all ears."

"You need personal security. That's my gig."

"I thought your boss was out of town."

"He is. But we could still work out a mutually beneficial arrangement. You can hire me as your bodyguard—" she slipped around the entertainment center and glanced into the bathroom, which appeared to be empty "—at a discounted rate since I'm not yet fully licensed, and I'll make sure no one gets close enough to rip your clothes off."

"What's in it for you?"

"A chance to get out of this god-awful uniform."

He arched an eyebrow.

She frowned. She'd done it again. "You know what I meant."

"Actually, Samantha, I don't know. My grandmothers put more than my picture on that pasta label. In the small print, they listed my company position, the fact that I am still single and unattached, as well as a generous estimate of my net worth."

She pressed her lips together to contain another grin at his expense. "What were they trying to do, marry you off?"

His grim expression told her she'd hit the nail on the head.

"You're kidding!" And she thought her mother was bad, what with the gris-gris bags left on her doorstep and rows of candles lit at St. Louis Cathedral in hopes Samantha would finally find a man and settle down. "Very ingenious women, your grandmothers." No hocus-pocus for them. Just good old-fashioned bribery. "They have a conduit to the general public, a product to sell—" she gestured toward him "—and at the same time, they increase sales by forty-six percent."

"Forty-seven," he corrected, not bothering to disguise his grouse as he tore off his striped tie and threw it on the couch.

"Forty-seven," she conceded, her gaze riveted as he twisted open the buttons at his collar. When he stopped at his breast-bone, she glanced away, disappointed. Suddenly, she wanted another peek at that full-size pasta label, live and in person. "I'd like to meet your grandmothers sometime. But let's keep them away from my mother, okay? I don't want them giving her any ideas."

She motioned toward the bedroom door. He nodded his agreement to allow her search. No time like the present to demonstrate her diligence, especially when it would keep her from making a fool of herself by staring.

Flipping on the lights, she scanned the bedroom for unlawful entry and found none. The door to the outer hall, a secondary entrance so the room could be rented as a single when the suite was not in use, had an automatic lock. As far as she could tell, even the maid hadn't yet arrived. The bed, a rumpled storm of sheets and pillows, appeared untouched by anyone but Nick.

A copy of Mario Puzo's last hardcover lay on the night-stand, draped by a pair of thin gold, wire-rimmed glasses. Without much effort, she pictured the spectacles sitting on the bridge of Dominick's regal Grecian nose as he lay in bed, propped up by the half-dozen silky shams that littered the bed in sensuous disarray. Bare-chested, with a sheet draping him from the waist down, just enough to make her wonder exactly what, if anything, he wore to sleep….

"I bet you would."

She jumped at the sound of his voice. "Bet I would what?"

He leaned against the doorjamb, no less dressed than he was a moment ago, yet sinfully more sexy. "Want to meet my grandmothers?" He straightened, apparently misinterpreting the alarm on her face. "Do you see something out of place? Has someone been in my room?"

She shook her head, wondering if offering her services was a huge and horrible mistake. Here she thought she was immune to good-looking men like Dominick LaRocca. More like addicted, judging from her behavior so far. Standing in his bedroom, even one he'd rented for a few nights, heightened his presence. His cologne clung to the air. A damp towel, no doubt from his morning shower, was draped over a chair. A drawer in the dresser, not completely closed, cradled clothing that had once, or would soon, cling intimately to his skin.

"Everything looks fine." She slipped past him, holding her breath to keep from inhaling his scent when her shoulder touched his. "Except the maid service runs slow around here. I'll want to talk to hotel management about who they plan to send here and when." She stood beside his computer and crossed her arms over her chest. She simply needed to assume a more professional demeanor. If she was going to be an effective bodyguard, she had to stop thinking about his body.

"That's if I hire you," he reminded her with a boyish, mischievous wink that managed to clip her steady heartbeat.

Oh, no. She wasn't falling for his charm *that* easily.

"Why wouldn't you hire me? Because I'm a woman?"

Thankfully, he sat in one of the overstuffed chairs opposite the couch instead of joining her beside the conference table. Negotiations had begun and she needed the distance to think clearly.

"Precisely because you're a woman, and I don't mean that

in the way you think. Don't you think your offer to protect me is a bit too convenient, in light of my circumstances?"

"You think I'm scheming to marry you?"

Sleep with you, maybe. Marry? Not in your wildest dreams, pal.

"A month ago, I'd expect to be slapped for such presumptuousness. But after being swarmed at the Expo, attacked at the airport and flashed by women wearing starched lace collars and prim business suits, nothing surprises me about the feminine gender anymore."

She nodded, understanding his reluctance. She was, after all, single and not totally invulnerable to his combustible combination of roguish good looks, power and charm. Hell, she'd have to be dead to ignore this man's Mediterranean magnetism. But despite her current need for a serious cash influx, his millions were probably a drop in the bucket compared to the return investment she'd receive from her father's next film.

"Have you ever heard of Devlin Deveaux?" she asked.

He repeated the name a few times. "Hmm. Hollywood type? Won some sort of award."

"His films have won twelve Golden Globes and he's been nominated for two Oscars."

"Oh, yes. The director. Does those action films. Why do you ask?"

"He's my father."

He stared at her blankly.

"He's *really* rich," she explained.

He still didn't get it.

She spoke slowly. "I don't need to marry for money."

He nodded, but smirked, obviously not convinced. "You don't have his money now, or you wouldn't be working as a security guard."

"True. I invested a hunk of cash in his next film and spent

the rest moving back to Louisiana," she explained, leaving out the little detail that investing in Devlin's film was neither her idea nor her preference. Her father had once again found a way to keep her in his life through the money he owed her for her stunt work. "Once *Honor Guard* hits the theaters, I could end up with enough money to buy your company."

Her bravado inspired his quirky grin—one she instantly discovered she liked. A lot.

"The film-going public can be fickle," he pointed out.

"True again. But if this movie doesn't make it, his next one will. The fact is, if I ever really needed to, I could ask my father for money. Or my mother. She's very comfortable. I don't need to sacrifice my freedom to live the high life, which, by the way, I don't want to live. Been there, done that. My interest in you is purely professional. My goal is to be a body-guard, not a temporary security guard or, God forbid, someone's wife."

Dominick leaned back in the chair and assessed her coolly. "And you think my hiring an inexperienced bodyguard is a wise choice?"

She couldn't help admiring the pace of the man's thinking. He was quick, but so was she. "That inexperience saved you today, didn't it? I've been around celebrities all my life. I know what bodyguards do. I had my own bodyguard until I turned twenty-one. I'm a black belt in tae kwan do, I'm licensed to carry a concealed weapon and I have completed courses in threat assessment, security systems and access control."

He balanced his elbows on the armrests of the chair, steepling his fingers as he considered her speech. "You have a fine résumé, but what if I don't want a shadow wherever I go?"

"Better a shadow than potentially dangerous women."

He nodded, clearly still deliberating as he dialed Anita's cell phone and instructed her to find Tim Tousignant and tell him he needed Samantha until the Expo Hall was prepared for his rescheduled appearance at three o'clock. He then dialed room service and ordered fresh coffee.

He cupped his hand over the receiver. "Would you like anything?"

"Am I staying for lunch?"

"Your proposition has merits, but requires discussion."

"Do they have jambalaya on the menu?"

He asked and assured her they did.

"It probably isn't very good. Hotel food, you know."

He asked and assured her it would be excellent.

"I'll have the jambalaya."

He grinned, ordered two servings of jambalaya, a pound of steamed crawfish and a large hunk of praline cheesecake with sweet bourbon sauce.

"That's an awful lot of food for a man who just had breakfast." Especially for a man who looked like a walking, breathing advertisement for the local health club.

"I love food. It's not just business to me. Besides, that wasn't my breakfast. Anita ordered in."

Was Anita sharing his room? Samantha would have to know that, for entirely professional reasons, of course. "She's your assistant?"

"Yes, and my first cousin. Her father and my father are brothers."

He didn't need to add that tidbit of information, but Samantha found herself relieved that he did. She'd finally started to like the guy and didn't want it ruined by the knowledge that he slept with women he employed—as her father did, more times than she cared to count. When the last starlet started making stepmother noises, Samantha knew the time had come to split. She realized then that she'd spent her entire adulthood, not to mention a sizable chunk of her childhood, taking care of her father, catering to the genius director's whims and putting her interests second. Unfortunately, she'd only escaped as far as actor Anthony Marks's bed before he took his turn trampling her heart.

So now, she'd resolved to take care of strangers—on her own terms—and draw a salary at the same time. And she'd come home to New Orleans to reconnect with her mother and sister, both fiercely independent women that—with the exception of wanting her to find a man to settle down with—didn't attempt to run her life in any significant way. Coming home had been easier than she'd ever imagined, thankfully, since she'd never figured out how to work long-distance relationships. And she'd done her share of trying.

Dominick pulled a file folder off the coffee table onto his lap, then motioned for her to take a seat on the couch. "I like to start my day early. Anita's not a morning person, so she ordered her breakfast from here."

She slid a company brochure off the conference table behind her and flipped open the trifolded, high-gloss color pamphlet. On the cover, a posed crowd of over thirty people ranging in age from toddler to octogenarian lifted their glasses in a hearty *salute*. She recognized Anita just a little left of center, standing beside a woman who, judging by the resemblance, had to be her mother. Dominick was just behind her, bracketed by two gray-haired ladies holding tight to each arm—undoubtedly, his grandmothers, ensuring he stayed put for the photograph. The caption identified the crowd as LaRocca Foods, LaRocca Family.

She flashed the picture at him. "You've given a whole new meaning to the word *nepotism*."

"That's not nepotism." He picked up his own copy of the brochure from the corner of the table. "That's a family business. It's only nepotism if the family hired isn't qualified."

"Anita's good?"

His chin protruded with an adorable smidgen of pride, as

if he was more than partially responsible for Anita's success. "The best. She loves this company almost as much as I do. Devotes her life to its success."

"Then why is she just your assistant and not a vice president of something?"

The nerve she hit must have been pretty darned raw, from the way his green eyes darkened to nearly black, and his scowl prickled gooseflesh along the back of her neck.

"She's in the position she's best suited for. Fancy titles don't mean anything."

"Oh, really? Then why don't you just call yourself a secretary? Or the maintenance guy?"

Nick's smile returned. "Actually, I tried mailboy once, but the paper cuts were hell."

Samantha sat back, shaking her head as the man effortlessly disarmed her indignation with unexpected humor. He was good. "I guess CEO does sound better, doesn't it?"

"Definitely. Tell me, is it part of your services as a bodyguard to stick your nose where it doesn't belong?"

"Only if it affects your safety."

"Then let's drop this subject. Anita isn't likely to be a threat to my safety."

She might be if you continue to undervalue her worth. For once, Samantha kept her comment to herself. She'd already skated on thin ice with him and she quickly remembered that she wasn't his bodyguard—yet—and even if she were, he could send her packing without much cause.

"Sorry. I speak before I think way too often. It's just—"

"A *lagniappe?* That's the word, isn't it?"

His tease caught her completely off guard. Not only did he know the popular New Orleans term for "something extra," but he considered her big mouth a bonus? One minute, he was all stern seriousness, the next he inspired a reluctant smile to tilt the corners of her mouth.

"Something like that. I'm not very familiar with the workings of close-knit families or family businesses. I have a lot to learn."

"What about filmmaking for the Deveaux? Did you ever work for your father?"

She returned her gaze to the brochure, perusing the lengthy list of products, from pasta sauces to salad dressings, his company produced. "Unfortunately, yes."

"You were an actress?"

An edge of distaste clung to his words, as if he eschewed the spotlight of celebrity as much as she did—which she honestly doubted. Men were men, after all. Most males she knew coveted the spotlight. Secretly lived for the sound of screaming fans and golden accolades. Even Dominick was currently mirrored in a life-size portrait across the street and on countless grocery aisles throughout the nation. "Small parts as a child, as an extra mostly. Then I did stunt work."

"That's very dangerous."

She shrugged, feeling a tenuous pull in the shoulder she'd dislocated on the set of *Blue Blood,* the film where she'd also earned a moderate concussion and two broken ribs. "That was part of the thrill, I guess."

"The thrill didn't last?"

When her stomach growled, she tossed the brochure onto the table. She hadn't eaten before work, and the enticing photos of steaming Italian delicacies had heightened her hunger. "Thrills rarely do."

"Depends on the nature of the thrill, don't you think?"

Suddenly, Samantha's hunger wasn't about food. His voice, already deep and throaty and hinting of that distinct Italian flavor that spiced his foods, dropped an octave and skirted on the edge of a whisper. Samantha's polyester uniform suddenly felt heavy, hot and binding, but she'd be damned before she let him know that.

"The newness wears off," she claimed, trying to stay on the topic of her former job as a stunt double, but succeeding in critiquing the sad progress of each and every relationship she'd ever found herself in. "Reality sets in. Fear comes into the picture and, bam, you're—" *alone* "—out of work."

She glanced aside, careful to ignore the narrow assessment in his gaze.

"Being a bodyguard doesn't scare you?" he asked.

"Not so long as you promise not to fall off a fifteen-story building and stay out of cars wired to blow up when they hit their mark."

She flashed a smile meant to disarm his personal questions, but he deflected her attempt with a roll of his eyes and a shake of his head.

"I'll do my best. I suppose personal security is safer than stunt work."

"If the bodyguard is good and the subject is—" she knew better than to use the word *compliant* "—cooperative. The key to effective protection is threat assessment, followed by quick and decisive action. Combine that with collaboration with the subject, and a bodyguard has the easiest job on earth."

"Cooperation, huh? That could be a problem."

She snorted, not the least concerned that the sound was decidedly unattractive. With all the awareness crackling between them, she'd probably done herself a favor. "I've already factored that into my plan."

"Have you?"

She'd tossed her hat on the bar when she'd entered, but only now ran her fingers through her hair, wincing at the tangled mess. Standing, she caught her reflection in a nearby mirror and tried to work some order into the ponytail that had fallen apart.

"It's cool if you're a control freak, so long as you realize you'll have to throw some of that control my way to keep your privacy and safety intact."

More resigned than satisfied, she loosened the clip dangling at the nape of her neck, smoothed her hair back into place, secured the barrette and swung around. "One of those marriage-and-money-hungry women might be the if-I-can't-have-him-no-one-will types. Could get ugly."

He grabbed a pen from the table and jotted some figures into the margins of a contract as they talked. "That's your worst-case scenario?"

She laughed. "Nick, if you want worst-case scenarios, you'd better pour yourself a bourbon. I've got moviemaking in my blood. I can come up with some doozies."

He scribbled his signature on the highlighted lines, then closed the folder and tossed it back on the table. Clearing his throat, he leaned back into the chair and considered her from head to toe, nodding almost imperceptibly, as if satisfied with what he saw.

"Let's leave the fantasies to your father. My problem has escalated since I came to New Orleans."

"You didn't have problems in Chicago?"

"Back home, I know the turf and could take precautions. Here, I'm at a disadvantage. To add fuel to the fire, a few of the television newsmagazines picked up on the story of my grandmothers' marriage plan before I left. No doubt their reporters are lurking, though, thankfully, the Expo was closed to the media today. Which is precisely why I planned my presentation for today."

She leaned forward to retrieve the pen he'd tossed aside, along with a blank legal pad. "You mind?"

He shook his head. "I'm talking about a temporary assignment. The Expo ends on Sunday afternoon."

"Two days?" A decent chunk of change at the going rate, nothing to scoff at even with a discount. She'd at least be able to pay the rent on the office without running to either of her parents for cash. She calculated her cost in the margin. "I'm available."

"You'll have to quit your security job."

"Not exactly a problem."

"And it's not just the Expo I have to attend. I have several events around town—business meetings, dinners. A swamp tour with the president of our largest retailer. I'm not sure of the details. That's Anita's department."

Samantha frowned while she listed the scenarios she'd face. "Crowds will make it tough, but it can be done. I'll need your full itinerary, a phone and a place to work. I can put a plan together by this afternoon."

"Good. But I need a bit more than just a short-term plan. I'd like to tone things down before I return to Chicago. Answer some of the burning questions about my love life so those desperate women will crawl back into the woodwork."

He thought ahead. An admirable trait.

"Very smart. Make some kind of big splash here in New Orleans—employ the help of the media, even—make yourself old news by the time you go home. That's actually quite brilliant. You sound like my father's publicist."

"Thank you. I think. But…" He leaned forward in his chair, braced his elbows on his knees and looked up at her with a glint in his eye.

"But?" she prompted.

He wet his lips. "I'll need your help."

Samantha folded one leg beneath her, ready to spring off the chair. Something in his eyes told her to beware. Something in the fullness of his lips and tilt of his half smile triggered alarms in the deepest part of her belly.

"That's what you'll be paying me for."

"I'm not talking about hiring you as my bodyguard."

"What *are* you talking about?"

He moved from the chair to the edge of the coffee table, relieved her of both pen and pad and locked her hand into his. The studied, serious demeanor of the man who ran an empire melted away to leave only a man with eyes the color of emeralds and lips that could kiss a woman into unconsciousness.

"I'm talking about you, Samantha Deveaux. About hiring you not as my bodyguard, but as my lover."

CHAPTER FOUR

NICK WATCHED Samantha's eyes. He'd wrangled enough tough negotiations to know that her initial reaction would map how he proceeded. Yet he almost felt like a novice going one-on-one with Samantha. She was tough, confident and sassy. And sexy. *Oh, yeah.* Sexy as sweet, silky oysters served with the finest Italian wine. Yet an elusive vulnerability lingered, teasing him like a secret. He didn't fool himself into thinking that recognizing her allure would counteract the mind-numbing effects. Women like her always had a trick up their sleeve.

Her thick-lashed lids narrowed. The irises he'd considered exotic, blue like a tropical liqueur, darkened to a fascinating, faceted sapphire, clear of any anger or insult from his purposefully bold, charged-by-design suggestion. In fact, he couldn't read her reaction at all. But, just in case, he held her hand tightly, prepared to deflect a slap.

When she glanced down, he realized that Samantha Deveaux didn't have to use her hands to punish his presumptuous proposition. She shifted her knee ever so casually.

Fortunately for his family jewels, she had a sense of humor to go with her proclaimed black belt. Her expression turned from cool to amused, forcing him to replay the words in his head one more time. He'd been trying to disarm her with an outrageous idea, but his words rang a little too cocky and arrogant, even for him.

She obviously didn't seem to mind. By the time he released her hands with a groan, she was laughing out loud. Which knocked his naturally bred arrogance down a substantial peg.

"I didn't mean that exactly the way it sounded," he said, grumbling.

"I should hope not. I mean, do I look like Julia Roberts in this get up?" She took a deep breath to tamp down her laughter. "'Cause you, pal—" she pointed for emphasis "—ain't Richard Gere."

Nick met her smirk with a reluctant, albeit agreeing grin. No, he wasn't Richard Gere. He never wanted to be Richard Gere or any other celebrity for that matter. He just wanted to run the family business and turn their healthy profits into steady millions. He wanted to expand the product line. Make LaRocca a household word for pasta sauce like Kleenex was for facial tissue. Ensure that everyone who shared his blood had a chance at a prosperous future.

Since his appointment as CEO, he'd schemed and planned and jockeyed to put his company, relatively small and still privately operated, into the leagues where only conglomerates dared to tread. Big dreams, but he was so close to achieving them. He just needed more time—more single, unattached, undistracted-by-a-wife time.

Samantha could buy him his needed reprieve. And maybe a little excitement, too. Excitement that had been sorely lacking in his life for way too long, a reality this sexy security guard effortlessly proved.

"If I'm going to get any business done, I need a bodyguard," he said, determined to clarify his point. "You've convinced me of that. If we lead everyone to believe that we are an item, that would give you a reason to be with me all the time, which would—"

She nodded as she took over his sentence, her laughter dying as business encroached. "Save your big male ego from admitting you need protection."

"Yes, well," he admitted, wondering how this stranger knew him so well in less than an hour's time, "my big male ego does sometimes need saving, but I have a higher payoff in mind. If the public believes that I'm no longer available…that half of my net worth will soon be spoken for…"

Sam applauded. "Nice twist. You convince all those single women that you've made your choice, and they set their sights on the next rich bachelor." After a moment, she wrinkled her nose. "But you know, if I'm going to play your bimbo for the whole world to see, I think I'll rescind the discount offer. We'll call it danger pay. I do have a reputation to protect."

Nick grinned. He'd had no idea that Samantha would be so easy to convince. She either seriously needed the money or she didn't want to wait to become a bodyguard. Either reason, he respected her lack of self-doubt.

They were two peas in a pod. Which added a layer of protection to his plan. Nick might no longer be entirely clear on the kind of woman he *really* wanted to marry someday, but he was quite certain he didn't want a woman who operated exactly the way he did. Career first, money second, reputation third—and in a succession that ran so close, the distinction between each goal was acutely hard to decipher.

"Samantha Deveaux has a reputation?" He hummed his interest, wiggling his eyebrows to make sure he needled her sufficiently. "It's been a long time since I hung out with a girl who had a rep. One of the DiCarlo sisters, if I remember correctly." Now wasn't the time to point out that he never had and still did not date "bimbos." Even the DiCarlo sisters back in high school had just been looking for a little harmless fun. But he didn't want Samantha to think that he rarely dated anymore, true or not. And he'd expect such an assumption.

Why else would his grandmothers have stirred the wild single masses in the first place?

Unfortunately, Nick couldn't remember his last date. He'd broken off his engagement to Sophia over two years ago, and hadn't seen anyone else since, first out of respect for Sophia and then because he didn't have the time. Dating required way more effort than he was willing to expend, especially since he no longer knew what he wanted.

He'd dated a lot during college, but as soon as his company went public seven years ago, he'd met Blair, the sophisticated daughter of a Chicago entrepreneur who should have understood his devotion to business pursuits, but didn't. She was too cool, too calculating and required way more attention than he had time to give. Sophia, a friend from the old neighborhood, should have been perfect. She embraced all the traditional values he thought he treasured. She ended up driving him crazy and he doubted he was any picnic for her, either.

He suspected Samantha Deveaux would drive him crazy, too, but in an entirely different, entirely desirable way.

"So tell me about this reputation of yours," he said. "I'm utterly intrigued."

Samantha stood, her lips pressed tight but her eyes smiling. "I'll bet you are. But," she said with a sigh, "this is the unfair part of the protection game. I get to know everything about you and my life is off limits."

Nick had no idea if she realized that she'd just issued a delicious challenge, but he guarded his expression. He nodded as if he agreed to her terms.

One quick call to his attorneys, who would in turn contact their private investigation division, could garner him each and every detail of Samantha Deveaux's life within an hour or two. If he gave them a whole day, the high-priced sharks he kept on retainer could write her biography, complete with photographs of her twelfth birthday and an interview with her third-grade boyfriend.

But damn, it would be so much more fun to discover her secrets himself.

A knock at the door gave him pause to wonder what the hell he was doing toying with his new bodyguard when he had work to do. He started to answer the door when Sam placed her hand on his shoulder, popping him with another electric shock.

"Ow!" he said, exaggerating the pain, but not the intensity of her touch.

"Sorry." She snatched her hand back and shoved it in her pocket. "I don't know what's up with me today. I'm not usually this electric."

Oh, I doubt that. "You should work for a hospital. You'd save them a bundle on defibrillators."

She merely grinned but she might as well have stuck out her tongue. He swallowed a chuckle.

"It's too soon for room service," she said. "Let me answer the door." She straightened her unwrinkled uniform before she disappeared around the corner.

Nick sank into the chair, wondering what the hell was coming over him. Yeah, his plan had a damn good chance of working. A few high-profile photographs of him and Samantha together, perhaps with her wearing a great big flashy ring, and the novelty of his grandmothers' scheme might die a quick death. He couldn't imagine there was a woman alive who'd want to compete with Samantha Deveaux for his attention. At least not a sane woman.

He could only hope that sane or insane, those women who'd been compelled to buy his products because of the *Playgirl* label would actually taste some of his grandmothers' secret recipe and be won over. The last thing any of them intended was to lose business because he was getting married.

Which he wasn't. Getting married. Not really.

He clapped his hand on his forehead. The stereotypical Italian phrase *Mama mia!* rang loud and clear, even if he'd never actually heard any Italians he knew say it. Fact was, the sentiment fit.

He could at least take comfort in knowing that Samantha Deveaux would provide ample protection from any more crazed single women intent on capturing his attention and ripping off his clothes. It wasn't so easy to concentrate on business with women baring their breasts in his face and snatching at his crotch. He entertained no fantasies that Samantha would bare or snatch. At least not without *a lot* of encouragement on his part, which he most certainly couldn't afford to give. Maybe he'd finally be able to forget about this mess and concentrate on the European distribution deal.

Too bad all he seemed able to concentrate on was Samantha.

That baffled him. She was *so* not his type. She was neither reserved and icy, like Blair had been, nor quiet and demure like Sophia. He'd once had high hopes for both relationships—if he'd only had time to pursue them. But Blair ended up being way too high maintenance and Sophia too clingy. He couldn't concentrate on business with them around.

And unlike today, he hadn't been distracted from a stack of contracts or a pile of phone messages by thoughts of hot, sweaty sex with a woman who carried handcuffs on a daily basis.

No, the distraction Samantha offered was entirely different from his issues with his former lovers.

Blair had constantly interrupted him at the office to show him the booty from her latest shopping spree. To share some inane gossip. To fill his calendar with social events more boring than waiting for his grandmothers to play their ritual game of canasta before every board meeting to determine who banged the gavel.

Sophia, on the other hand, had called once a day at precisely the same time to remind him that she was home, waiting to do whatever he wanted her to do, whenever he wanted her to do it. She bought his socks and had his shirts ironed. She attended family gatherings and dutifully sent out all his birthday, anniversary and condolence cards until she'd so endeared herself to the family that their breakup had nearly caused a holy war.

Never again, he'd promised himself. He was better off alone, he'd decided. Until his grandmothers issued their ultimatum.

Until Samantha Deveaux hurtled into his life.

He listened as Samantha argued and denied entrance to whoever was at the door. He stood up and stepped into the hall when he heard a suspicious creak in the adjoining bedroom.

"I told you, we didn't order filet mignon," Samantha insisted. "You just wait right here…Jimmy…while I call down to room service and get this cleared up."

"Oh, no, ma'am. Please. I'm on, like, probation with the hotel. I can't mess up again."

He imagined her sapphire eyes narrowing with suspicion. "Then why don't you sneak back downstairs, get our correct order and come back up?"

"Um, um…"

Samantha seemed to have the stuttering waiter under control, so when he heard the rustle of material from within his bedroom, he decided to investigate himself. Probably just the maid entering through the side door, he thought. The side door he'd instructed the hotel *not* to use.

He stopped just outside the bedroom door. He didn't have to be a rocket scientist to realize this was precisely the type of situation where he should alert Samantha and let her investigate. The thought turned his stomach more than he expected, churning up the humiliating memory of being nine years old and spooked by a celebrity who'd brought his entourage to the family restaurant for dinner. He'd hidden behind his mother's apron. Literally. The sickening swirl of hot embarrassment coursed through him again, as if the incident hadn't happened twenty-five years ago.

It didn't help that his cousins, uncles, father and grandfather loved to retell the story at each and every family gathering—or whenever they suspected the power of running the business had gone to his head. It also didn't help that, yet again, his life was being molded and shaped by a woman. First his mother, then his Nanas, and now, in a sense, by Samantha.

He pushed into his room. The door, a side entrance into a private hallway, was locked and bolted from the inside. He didn't remember doing that, but guessed Samantha had taken that precaution when she'd searched the room. He glanced at the bed and then to the closet. Nothing seemed amiss. He was going crazy, that was all. Certifiably nuts.

"What's wrong?"

Samantha appeared behind him and reached forward, then pulled her hand back before she shocked him again. Thank God.

"Nothing," he answered, berating himself for being so jumpy over what was probably the sound of the air conditioner kicking on. "Who was that at the door?"

Sam shook her head and pursed her lips, a habit she had that he sorely wished she'd break. All that pink softness puckered and primed was the last thing he needed to see every time she had a deep thought. Which was way too often for a woman as beautiful as she was.

"He *said* he was from room service," she answered.

"You didn't believe him?"

"His jacket was too big and he was incredibly nervous. And he got the order completely wrong, as if he'd swiped the cart. This is a Hyatt. They may forget the ketchup every once in a while, but they don't screw up that royally, especially not on an order for a VIP suite. I got rid of him, but I'll call down and check it out."

He expected her to head for the phone, but instead she stepped closer. Her hand lingered near his arm so that he could feel the charged crackle that seemed to emanate from her fingertips.

"You sure you're okay?"

He cleared his throat. He wasn't anywhere near okay. He was distracted, disheveled, and now, apparently, paranoid. "Why?"

"Because you look like this." She mirrored his cranky expression—furrowed brow, narrow eyes and grumpy chin.

He couldn't help but laugh out loud. "God, I hope not. I'll never sell another jar of pasta sauce again if that expression's on the label."

She backed away, somewhat flustered, if he could believe that anything or anyone could fluster Samantha Deveaux.

"Well," she said, "there's always the big fat tomato."

THERE'S ALWAYS the big fat tomato? Not exactly the most witty response she could have come up with, but with Nick switching from dangerously worried to laughing with a sexy rumble that still reverberated straight to her toes, it was the best she could do.

She hurried to the phone and dialed the restaurant that handled room deliveries. The hotel did employ a waiter named Jimmy, but not only was he off for the day, he was pushing sixty and African-American. Definitely not the barely twenty-year-old Caucasian who'd shown up. She dialed the hotel manager immediately. He insisted on bringing their order up himself and assured her that hotel security would search for the impostor without delay.

She hung up the phone, reeling. This was a real job. A *real* bodyguard assignment. Mr. Dominick LaRocca, multimillion-dollar CEO, was honestly and truly being stalked. By a twenty-year-old *male,* no less. She doubted marriage was on the kid's mind, making her wonder what he'd wanted by trying to weasel into Nick's room.

The possibilities were endless. And damn exciting.

But not nearly as exciting as watching Nick march around the conference table, tapping the keyboard on his laptop without sitting first, flipping open files, stacking and reorganizing papers as if the survival of the world depended on his next deal.

The thrill took a decidedly cooling turn when she remembered who he reminded her of.

"My father never sits when he works, either," she said, once again saying something aloud that she meant to bemuse privately.

"Your father is an extremely successful man. I'll take the comparison as a compliment."

"You would," she said with a laugh.

He stopped, letting a thick file slap back onto the polished table. "What does that mean?"

Anita's voice intruded. "She means that you're an arrogant SOB. Or maybe *conceited* is a better word."

Samantha watched Anita pocket her key as she rounded the corner of the long foyer. Sam needed to get her mind back in the game. She should have heard Anita come in, even if the woman was shoeless and had her own key.

"Samantha has only known me for an hour. Takes at least two before my conceit truly shows," Nick said matter-of-factly, though he winked playfully at Samantha, causing another surge of blood flow from her heart to her outer limbs.

Anita waved her hand at him. "She'd only have to know you for about two minutes to figure out that your head is bigger than the vats we cook our marinara in."

"She loves me, can't you tell?" Nick strode to Anita, spun her around for a quick once-over, then kissed her on the cheek and went back to his paperwork. "The barefoot look is interesting. Trying to start a fashion trend?"

Anita swore when she noticed a hole in her panty hose. "Very funny. If you don't get married soon, I may end up in the hospital after another riot like today's. Maybe you should do a talk show or something. If those women knew how boring you were, they wouldn't be so hot to marry you."

Samantha watched and listened. She'd known Dominick LaRocca for only a brief time, but she'd never describe him as dull. Or predictable. She'd already made the incorrect assumption that he didn't appreciate women like her who voiced their opinions without hesitation—good, bad or insulting. Apparently, he liked Anita a whole lot. Sam did, too. His cousin apparently practiced less diplomacy than Sam did, which could keep Sam out of trouble for once in her life.

"Crazy to marry me?" Nick asked. "I'd say they're just crazy. This is Samantha Deveaux, by the way," he introduced.

Anita accepted Samantha's offered hand.

"Anita LaRocca. Thanks for jumping in back there. If you hadn't removed the meat from the feeding frenzy…" Anita glanced over her shoulder to wait for Nick's objection to her metaphor, but he ignored her. She shrugged. "Anyway, I lost a perfectly matched pair of sling-back Monolos and our supply of presentation folders in the fray, but fortunately—" she patted her long dark curls "—no clumps of hair this time."

"This time?"

"Didn't Nick tell you about the airport?"

"Not exactly."

"Let's just say that the woman who nearly commandeered our limousine last night mistook me for Nick's girlfriend and tried to make me look like Sinéad O'Connor."

"It might have been a good look for you, Anita," Nick offered, though he'd appeared to be ignoring them while he dialed about twenty-five numbers into the phone.

"Well, you won't have to worry anymore," Sam assured her. "Nick's hired me to provide protection for him." She tugged on her uniform. "This security-guard gig was temporary. I also work for No Chances Protection, a local bodyguard service."

Anita blinked, wide-eyed. "Oh, really?"

"You don't approve?" Sam asked, unable to interpret Anita's arched eyebrows and slightly agape mouth.

She shook her head. "Approve? I think it's great. Hell, with you following him around, no one will notice me. Especially if you ditch the uniform. You know…"

Anita's dark eyes, saucer-shaped and chocolate brown, widened as an idea struck her. She raised her finger to preface her brilliant pronouncement, when Nick hung up the phone.

"We're one step ahead of you. Samantha has agreed to ditch the uniform and play my girlfriend for the next few days."

The exchange between the cousins was nearly nonverbal as Anita slapped her hands together triumphantly and beat a path to the phone. They apparently shared the same wavelengths and thought patterns, but Samantha suspected their intentions meshed on the surface only. She distinctly remembered Nick telling her that Anita has been a coconspirator in his grandmothers' scheme. Notwithstanding her desire to keep all her hair attached to her head and her five-hundred-dollar shoes intact, Anita's instantaneous excitement over their scheme made Sam incredibly suspicious.

Rude though it might have been, Sam listened intently to each and every word of Anita's phone call.

"Nana Rose? Hi! How's everything going?…uh-huh… give her a kiss for me. Okay. Yeah. Listen, did you hear? You did…Rick from Sales called? Yeah, not surprised. No, we're both fine. This beautiful security…" Anita tossed a glance over her shoulder at Samantha while her grandmother apparently interrupted the rest of the story. "Yeah. Blond, late-twenties, athletic. Very pretty…no, probably not Italian… but…uh-huh…yeah, I'll let you know what happens…okay. *Ciao*."

Anita chuckled as she hung up the phone, but Sam couldn't contain a frown. She didn't like to be talked about. She never had. Especially by some scheming Italian grandmother who, despite being hundreds of miles away in Chicago, already knew what had happened at the Dome only an hour ago.

"Let me guess," Nick said, amused. "They'd already heard a full report."

"Thanks to Rick, the suck-up," Anita said with a disbelieving nod. "And here I thought I was their best spy."

"So, what do they think?" The sheer interest in Nick's gaze denoted the importance of his cousin's conversation with their grandmother. Made sense. If the Nanas didn't buy that Nick was genuinely interested in Samantha, the ruse wouldn't work. The grandmothers were the first line to the press and the general public, and Samantha surmised that these women weren't pushovers. Women didn't found and run multimillion-dollar companies by being easily fooled.

Anita turned back toward Samantha and took a step forward as if she planned to circle and assess Samantha's suitability before answering. Suitability for what, Sam didn't care to know. She stopped Anita with a pointed stare, so Nick's cousin slid into a chair instead.

"She's not Italian," Anita said, twisting her mouth as if Sam's heritage was a stumbling block to success. "Are you?"

"Not according to my mother, no." Sam shoved her hands into her back pockets. "My heritage is completely Creole, French-Canadian with a touch of Spanish, I believe, though what it has to do with my ability to be Nick's bodyguard, I don't understand."

"But you're not going to be just his bodyguard, now, are you?"

Samantha squirmed. She hadn't minded Nick's plan so much when it was just his idea, presented with his cool logic and clear desire to rid himself of his celebrity-bachelor status. Anita's gaze was entirely too ripe with unspoken schemes and possibilities. Schemes that went way beyond fooling the public, especially now that the infamous Nanas were involved.

Samantha crossed her arms. "That's exactly what I'm going to be. A bodyguard. Period. The rest will just be a cover. It'll help me navigate through his appearances, and if it helps him with his problem, that's fine, too. But…" Sam felt odd saying more in front of Nick, but she had no choice. "But don't get any ideas that this is more than an illusion. A ruse to take the heat off your cousin."

Anita nodded way too complacently. "Oh, of course. It's all a sham. But it's brilliant. And could definitely benefit us all."

A knock on the door once again broke the tension. Nick returned his attention to the laptop; Anita grabbed a pen and paper and started scribbling. Samantha marched to the door to greet the hotel manager, accompanied by a tray that proved to contain their correct lunch order.

Unfortunately, she wasn't hungry anymore.

She rolled the cart to where Anita and Nick now leaned over a spreadsheet of tiny numbers and graphs.

She cleared her throat. "Lunch is served. Hotel security is parked in front of your door until I get back. Don't leave this room without an escort."

"Where are you going?" Nick asked, eyeing the cart that he'd ordered for them. Luckily, Anita was there to enjoy her food for her. Sam knew there was no way in hell she would eat a bite until she stopped her head from spinning and her stomach from churning.

Incredible reactions, both of them. She could jump off a fifteen-story building with barely an accelerated heartbeat.

But playing lover to Nick LaRocca? A heart attack was surely imminent.

"To give my notice at the Dome, change clothes and finalize all the arrangements for your appearance at your booth this afternoon. I'm sure Tim will help me work out the details. Then I'll be back."

Anita was already lifting the metal lids off the food and making yummy noises over the cheesecake. "You sure you don't want to stay and eat?"

"No, really. Go ahead. I have work to do."

Better to act and sound efficient if she wanted to command respect for her protection skills, she decided. Luckily, her drama talents weren't as rusty as she might have guessed.

Before she'd even left the room, Nick and Anita were muttering about cost projections and shelf space as if she'd never been there. *Good.* An effective bodyguard had to become invisible when the situation warranted.

Too bad she hadn't thought about that an hour ago, when Nick LaRocca crowded into her life.

CHAPTER FIVE

"HOW DID YOU LUCK OUT and find her?" Anita asked the moment the door clicked behind Samantha.

Nick shook his head as he grabbed a steaming bowl of jambalaya and napkin-wrapped utensils from the cart. "You said it—pure luck."

Luck and something Nick could only describe as poetic justice. Here he was avoiding single, attractive women as if he were under consideration to be chosen as pope, and the most irresistible female he'd met in years rescues him from disaster. "When she offered her services as a bodyguard, I thought I'd try a different tactic to beat Nana Rose and Nana Fae at this little marriage game they've concocted."

Anita ignored the spicy rice and crawfish that he'd ordered and went straight for dessert. "You should know better than to try and beat them, Nicky. They've been around too long. They know all the angles." She dug her fork into a huge hunk of cheesecake, swirled the ivory triangle into the caramelized bourbon sauce and then slid the sweet morsel in her mouth with a loud groan. "This is delicious!" Her words were muffled by her mouthful. "We should do desserts. I've always said we should do desserts."

"Don't change the subject," Nick insisted, accustomed to the turn in Anita's focus. His cousin had a sweet tooth the size of the Sears Tower and, like him, she had trouble separating business from pleasure. "I'm going to need your help to make this work. No double-agent crap this time." He pointed his fork at her while she licked hers clean, swallowing a chuckle as her brown eyes darkened to nearly black.

For a brief instant, he wondered what he'd have to serve to darken Samantha's eyes that way. More than cheesecake, he'd bet. But before he could imagine the details, he shook the thought away.

"Are you with me, or with them?" he demanded.

Anita immediately skewered another bite of cheesecake, avoiding his stare while she hummed her gastronomic pleasure. Nick knew he was playing dirty, making his cousin choose between her loyalties to their grandmothers and her loyalty to him, but he didn't have a choice. If she blabbed that Samantha was only his bodyguard and not his lover, his plot would be ruined. He wouldn't get a better chance to divert the unwanted attention on his marital status back to the quality of LaRocca Foods' products. Getting to know Samantha better at the same time was just another stroke of luck.

"Anita? I need to know. Right now."

She sliced into her cheesecake again, but kept the morsel balanced on her fork. "It's too late to issue ultimatums, Nicky. I already know your plan. I could blab right now."

"You could have blabbed on the phone a few minutes ago, too. But you didn't. Can I take that as an 'I'm with you, Nick'?"

Nick knew she'd only gone along with their grandmothers' label scheme more as a practical joke than because she had any real interest in whether or not he got married. She knew that the future of the company, and consequently her future, rested in his hands.

If this plan failed, the corporation could end up broken into so many small companies that even *if* Anita were given one to run, her chances of achieving true success would be next to nothing. Not that his cousin wasn't smart or savvy enough to run a business. She just wouldn't have the capital to break out of the pack. Slowly, big food conglomerates would swallow each division. The LaRocca products would become homogenized and lose the homegrown charm and authentic appeal that made them a success in the first place.

He wouldn't let that happen.

And he bet Anita wouldn't, either. And though he also knew his grandmothers didn't want that outcome, they wouldn't live forever. He had to convince them to change their minds about making his marital status an issue or he'd lose the business for sure.

"Unless you don't want me to continue as CEO?" he asked, trying not to sound as arrogant as Anita constantly accused him of being. Arrogance didn't drive him this time; confidence did.

Anita sighed. "You know I want you at the helm, Nicky, but our Nanas do have a point about this die-hard bachelor status of yours. This line you give them about holding out for a nice quiet wife with no opinions of her own is a load of bull. Sophia was *exactly* that woman and you couldn't wait to break free of her."

"Sophia was too clingy," he snapped, knowing the distinction was tenuous. "She wanted my approval on what dry cleaner to pick. What laundry detergent to use."

"No opinions of her own," Anita said, shaking her head. "Just like you ordered."

Nick stirred his rice. An aromatic steam drifted from his plate, promising a kaleidoscope of flavors that might undo his increasingly foul mood. He dug in his spoon. "Next time, I'll make my order more specific. No opinions of her own *about me and my life*. And she can pick her own damn laundry detergents."

Anita shook her head as she grabbed two goblets of ice water from the room-service cart. "Sooner or later, you'll have to settle down with someone. You love family way too much to stay single forever."

"I could say the same for you," he countered.

"But you won't." She stabbed her fork in his direction. "You know damn well that if I get involved with a man, I won't be available 24-7 to run your life."

"If I get roped into marriage, maybe I won't need you to run my life."

She was incredibly quiet and expressionless while she chewed and swallowed. "Don't tease me with pipe dreams. Look, you know I think you're the best person to run LaRocca Foods. Nana Rose and Nana Fae think so, too. But you need a life beyond the business. Although I only met her for a minute, I like Samantha Deveaux. I'd hate for her to get hurt in any of this."

Though Nick knew Samantha was as different from Sophia as sugar was from salt, he couldn't squash the memory of Sophia's teary-eyed departure from his life, the love letters she'd sent for weeks after he'd told her their relationship was over. He hadn't meant to—hadn't intended to—but he'd hurt her nonetheless. The only thing that had saved him from a lifetime of guilt was knowing she'd become engaged to Anita's brother, Carmine, less than two months later. Carmine was a softhearted, attentive man who put business second and his happiness first. It didn't help make him top sales rep for the southeast division, but he'd probably win Husband of the Year.

And though Samantha was as different from Sophia as she was from Blair Davenport—who'd reacted to his breakup by shrugging her shoulders, kissing him coldly and moving immediately along to a richer, more powerful CEO—he doubted Sam would fall victim to any man, much less him. She had a strength about her, a nearly-but-not-quite jaded outlook that would probably keep her heart effectively insulated.

"You don't need to worry about my bodyguard. Her interests are purely professional. She seems entirely immune to my charm."

Anita cracked a grin. "You have charm?" She chuckled at her own quip before finishing off her cheesecake in three quick bites. "Okay, I'm stuffed. Time to hit the workout room."

"No way," Nick protested. "You need to put together some new presentation folders, make an anonymous call to the press about my chance meeting with the security guard who saved me, and then wait here for Sam's call to finalize the logistics for my appearance at the Dome. You only have a couple of hours."

He slipped his spoonful of jambalaya into his mouth, groaning with pleasure at the sudden burst of spicy flavors and diverse textures on his tongue—hot cayenne pepper, sweet rice, chunky sausage. He'd had Cajun food back home in Chicago, but it just wasn't the same. Something about this city, even cooped up in a hotel room thirty stories above the ground, communicated a festive atmosphere of sights and sounds—plastic beads, gold coins and hot jazz.

Of course, he felt quite certain that his run-in with New Orleans-born Samantha Deveaux had something to do with his romanticism. She may not have been raised in the city, but she summoned her drawl on command, walked with an innate rhythm and evoked alluring images he'd forever associate with the Crescent City.

Anita slid her plate, practically licked clean, back onto the cart. "What are you going to do while I'm working my fingers to the bone?" she asked, protesting more out of habit than because she resented the tasks he'd just assigned.

"I'm going to finish this delicious jambalaya, then change into a suit that isn't torn."

She eyed him skeptically. "That'll take a few hours?"

He chewed his next bite slowly, relishing the taste of the Cajun concoction the same way another man might enjoy a kiss. He didn't have much experience with kisses lately, but if the act could prove half as hot as his lunch, he might actually try to change that fact.

Samantha's generous lips, pursed and thoughtful, immediately popped into his mind.

Anita cleared her throat to remind him she'd asked a question. He had planned, after eating lunch and choosing a new suit, to spend a few hours finishing his memo to the marketing department regarding their presentation to the European distributor. But with Samantha on his mind, his body wouldn't be satisfied by just a hearty lunch. Anita had given him a better idea.

"I think I'll take your spot in the workout room."

"Pig," Anita snapped, then laughed and shook her head with resignation. "I don't know... Samantha told you not to go anywhere, and even with an escort, you'll be half-dressed and sweating in the gym. It's a public place. You could start another stampede."

Nick smiled to acknowledge her teasing lilt but, unfortunately, she wasn't entirely wrong. Still, he needed an outlet to burn off his sudden surge of energy or he'd never manage to appear cool and in control when Samantha returned.

"Then call the hotel manager and arrange for a step machine to be brought to the room. I've *got* to exercise."

Anita pushed away from the table, her smile entirely too smug. "I don't suppose shapely Samantha Deveaux has anything to do with your need to pump something, does it?"

That settled it. He and Anita spent *way* too much time together. His cousin could read him like a book in most situations, so she'd know to back down if he barked loud enough.

"Just get me the equipment."

"Yes, sir." She saluted, grabbed her glass of ice water and retired to the desk tucked in the corner of the room, out of his way.

Good. He liked a woman who knew when to back down.

Unfortunately, he doubted Samantha Deveaux possessed that particular talent. If she, for whatever reason, did turn her sights on him, he'd be lost for sure.

"I'M BORROWING your purple suit." Samantha tucked the phone beneath her chin and used both hands to pull the outfit out of her sister's overstuffed hall closet. She wobbled and recovered, stepping over Serena's sheepdog, who'd parked his wide, half-asleep body in front of the door.

"I own a suit?" Serena asked from the other end, thousands of miles away, her voice crackling in and out from a beach in Brazil.

"Apparently so." Samantha pulled a name tag off the slim lapel. "You wore it to some convention."

"Oh, yeah. I have to warn you, it's not very professional. The skirt is short—really short—and the jacket doesn't take a blouse."

Sam sighed as she laid the creation in question over the guest-room bed, her sister's assessment ringing true even while she heard her new brother-in-law making some sexy comment in the background. She'd have nowhere to hide her gun in this getup. She'd have to opt for a purse, which would slow her response time if things got hairy.

"There's more material in a bath towel than this outfit," Sam said. "Why did you buy it? It's not your style at all." Not that her sister dressed the least bit conservatively. Serena favored long, sexy sarong skirts, tie-dyed tank tops and lots and lots of noisy jewelry. But while her mode of dress was alluring, the breeziness denoted a casual nonchalance that matched Serena's sensual personality perfectly. This suit was way more overt. More *here I am*.

More like their mother.

"I didn't buy it, Mother did," Serena confirmed. "She swapped my suitcase on the way to the airport for the convention. Left me a seduce-me-quick wardrobe. You'll find an interesting collection of miniskirts, low-cut blouses and ridiculously high heels in that closet."

"You kept them?"

"What else was I going to do? Donate them to some charity for streetwalkers?"

Sam chuckled. She hadn't really looked at the other outfits, but while this suit was indeed short and snug, she doubted any hookers would be interested. A high-priced call girl? That was another matter.

"You know Mother," Serena continued, her tone half frustrated and half bemused. "She was hoping I'd go to Vegas and catch me a man. You should see the lingerie she bought to go with that stuff."

"Didn't you take it on your honeymoon?" Sam teased.

"Are you kidding? She bought me a whole new collection for my trousseau. The old stuff's in the mahogany chest of drawers next to the window. They're all yours if you want them. Never been worn."

Samantha eyed the dresser in the corner, but rooted her feet to the floor. She'd never taken an interest in sexy lingerie before. She thought they were pretty and whiled away her share of time thumbing through catalogs, but her lifestyle demanded sports bras for support and thongs that wouldn't show through her wardrobe. And the men in her life hadn't minded.

But meeting Nick, touching Nick—even briefly—had initiated a sudden fascination with peek-a-boo lace and slick, silky satin. He seemed like a man who would appreciate the extra touch of femininity, the hint of romance.

She took a few steps toward the mahogany chest, and then glanced back at the outfit she'd chosen from her sister's closet. The fleeting image of her wearing a scant and sensual silk panty beneath the minuscule suit while sharing space with Dominick LaRocca filled her with a mixture of excitement and wantonness that she hadn't felt in a long, long time. And with good reason. In the past, Samantha's libido had often overridden her common sense. She had to squash this attraction soon, or her bodyguard assignment would prove more torturous than exciting. Unfortunately, she knew of only one effective way to derail sexual tension.

Sex. And that was out of the question.

Wasn't it?

"Don't you have anything more conservative?" Samantha asked into the phone, begging for a reprieve from what just might be inevitable.

"I have the black dress I wore to Cousin Arthur's funeral."

Sam shook her head and shivered. "The one with the ostrich-feather collar?" Her sister had somehow looked elegant in the simple silhouette of a dress with plumes, but Sam had no doubt that she'd end up looking more like a sick peahen. "Never mind. This'll do. I can't believe I gave away all my designer duds when I moved down here! What was I thinking?"

"That you wanted to start over. That you wanted to buy your own clothes, not wear the stuff designers sent just to hear their names mentioned at award shows. That you..."

Serena cut off her litany and Sam wasn't sure she was thankful or not. She missed her sister. Free-spirited and open-minded, Serena loved her unconditionally—even after Samantha had schemed and manipulated and downright lied in order to make Serena and Brandon see how they were meant for each other. Of course, she'd been right.

But even before then, Serena had always given Sam advice honestly and from the heart, whether she was talking about clothing or matters more personal. Like whether or not to pursue Dominick LaRocca, which they hadn't yet had a chance to discuss.

Brandon, her brother-in-law, suddenly commandeered the cell phone. "What trouble are you getting me into now, Samantha?"

She huffed loudly. "Why don't you come home from your

honeymoon and find out? You do have a business to run. And in less than an hour, you're going to have your first client."

"So I heard. Care to fill me in on the details? You aren't licensed yet…"

"Yeah, yeah. I know. He knows. I was completely up front with him. He's willing to take a chance on me since I saved him this morning from that rather scary crowd."

Brandon chuckled, having heard the tale by eavesdropping on her account to Serena. "I guess you were right when you claimed you had the instincts for this line of work. Any questions?"

Oh, she had a million questions. How does one carry a weapon when nearly naked? How would she go about crowding close to a man who sparked her flame, without letting him in on her intimate secret desire?

"No," she said, exhaling all her fear. Whether he knew it or not, Brandon needed her to succeed—for the sake of the business. And she needed to succeed for the sake of her own self-worth. That and her bank account. And his. "I don't think protecting Nick will be a problem. It's only two days, and Nick's assistant and I have worked out his schedule very carefully. I've even arranged backup in two locations with that friend of mine I told you about, the ex-cop. She's even going to watch the animals while I'm at the hotel."

"Good. You've got to know when to ask for help. Call me if you need anything. I guess we could head home…"

His voice died away, but by the sound of the pleasured groans that replaced it, Sam knew she couldn't ask him to cut short his honeymoon, even if they were four weeks overdue in returning to New Orleans.

"Have fun," she insisted. "Come home when you feel like it. I seem to have everything under control."

She disconnected the call and unknotted the sash of the robe she'd stolen from Serena's closet after her quick shower.

Serena's long-haired Himalayan cat lit onto the bed beside the suit, scaring Sam with her quick, unexpected appearance.

"Damn, cat. Can't you wiggle your nose or something before you do that, Tabitha?"

Tabitha II's wide blue irises reflected complete indifference to Sam's scolding tone. Despite her aversion to animals of the feline persuasion, Sam reached out and scratched the cat beneath her chin and was rewarded with a loud, rumbling purr. The trill surprisingly calmed her nerves.

She had less than an hour to dress and meet Dominick and Anita at the hotel. Soon, she'd make her first official appearance at Nick's side as the woman who had saved him from bodily harm and then supposedly captured his heart. Only the three of them would know that the pairing was purely professional. The rest of the world would speculate and gossip about every look they exchanged, every touch they shared. She had no chance of keeping her identity secret—particularly not in New Orleans where her famous mother lived and practiced her psychic skills. Sam had no choice but to play the role of Nick's new lover to the hilt.

She tossed the robe aside and headed for the dresser where Serena kept her lingerie.

"What the hell, Tab, right? If I'm playing the girlfriend, I'd better make it real. Maybe he'll give me a bonus."

And for the briefest instant, Sam wasn't thinking about cash.

NICK SHOOK his last hand at precisely five o'clock. For two hours, he had mingled through a crowd of carefully screened convention attendees, each having passed through the tight security perimeter that Samantha, Anita and Tim had efficiently arranged. He'd then given his presentation on the new products LaRocca would be introducing in the next year, stilling any unnecessary applause at the end by timing the dozen waitresses Anita had hired to appear just as he spoke his last sentence. Dressed in tuxedos and wide, friendly smiles, they handed out samples and small glasses of wine so that his listeners' hands and mouths were full and occupied with his food and drink.

He didn't want applause. He wanted increased sales. More shelf space in the stores. Better placement on endcaps and in Sunday advertisements.

Oh, and he also wanted Samantha Deveaux in his bed, but that was another matter entirely.

While the crowd savored and sipped, he glanced over his shoulder where Samantha sat on the dais beside Anita. She bent close to his cousin as if they were sharing some secret, but her gaze—alert and on guard—was trained on him. This time, he stared back. Starting at her feet, he worked his gaze upward, looking his fill while he kept his expression stoic. He didn't feel stoic, but he'd practiced the look so often he could call on his nonchalance even under the toughest circumstances.

Like when he was attempting to keep his arousal to himself.

Samantha dressed the part of sensual siren as if she was born for the role. Dainty heels, not high but strappy enough to be incredibly sexy, hugged her feet and launched his gaze slowly up incredibly toned, sinfully sculpted legs to that incredible skirt. The one that scarcely covered her thighs. The one he could make love to her in by barely lifting the material.

He turned aside to shake hands with another business associate before he had time to assess the snugness of her top. Had she dressed like that to play her part, or was she purposefully trying to torture him? Or both?

She slid behind him and slipped her hand beneath his jacket, settling her palm on his back with a simmering, electric crackle.

He winced, but hardly moved, becoming accustomed to her high-voltage touch. Now, if he could just adapt his intimate responses to her touch so easily.

"Ready to go?" she purred.

Nick eyed the crowd then glanced at his watch. At the moment, he'd spoken to all the people who needed speaking to, shaken hands with the power brokers who needed to be acknowledged. He had a dinner meeting scheduled in less than an hour at a French Quarter restaurant called Irene's, one Sam had claimed was well known among the locals and small enough for her to keep him out of harm's way. While he actually looked forward to sampling the award-winning cuisine and discussing business with the Japanese food broker who'd invited him, he didn't much anticipate the gauntlet they'd have to walk first.

"Are the television cameras out front?" he asked.

Samantha's smile was pure devotion, but her eyes betrayed, for an instant, the drama behind her expression.

"Oh, yeah. Two local news stations. One's an affiliate for *Entertainment Tonight* and the other shares a network with WGN. By the eleven o'clock news, your once-single marital status will undoubtedly be in question."

"WGN, huh? There's a Cubs game tonight. Won't my grandmothers be surprised if they break in with a news flash?"

A tiny frown formed on her plum-painted lips. At least it wasn't a pucker or purse. If she did that, he'd kiss her for sure.

"Are you certain you want to go through with this? Lie to your grandmothers, I mean."

Nick did feel an inkling of guilt over that part of the plan. But what was the cliché? *Turnabout is fair play?* Loving and well-intentioned though they probably thought themselves to be, his Nanas deserved a taste of their own pasta sauce after deceiving him about the label.

Besides, they really weren't the focus of his hoax. He was more concerned with the press and marriage-minded crazies—like the women disguised as nuns who'd staked out the lobby of his hotel earlier. If not for Samantha's efficient planning with Hyatt security, he would have been rushed once again before they'd arrived at the Expo for a second try at his presentation.

Nick shivered. Rushed by a half-dozen women wearing habits and *nothing* else. The image of them disrobing, wimples and habits flying, promised to give him nightmares for years to come.

"My grandmothers deserve to be a little misled. Once all this hoopla settles down, I might be able to talk some sense into them. Particularly if I can swing that European distribution deal in the meantime."

Sam nodded. He'd filled her in on his business goals during the car ride over. Discussing the details with her wasn't his preference, but he'd latched on to that conversation in hope of derailing his blatant stares and sensual speculation about what, if anything, she was wearing beneath her suit.

"Well, if swinging deals is your gig, we'd better get moving."

Sam made eye contact with a dark-haired security guard posted nearby, and then with Anita, who was remaining behind to field questions and supervise the booth. In an instant, a detail of guards appeared, ready to escort Nick and Sam to the exit where a mob of reporters awaited their first amorous appearance.

"That's very impressive," Nick complimented as he watched her coordinate their escape without saying a word or lifting a finger. "You make people move with just a look."

She was moving him, too, though he hoped she didn't notice.

"Subtlety is always a useful tool in this business." She took his hand and coaxed him toward the security detail, her gaze flirtatious and her smile disarming.

Her tone and expression were seductive and brimming with heat, as if her whispered words were pillow talk rather than informational instructions. "There's a small group of women around the reporters, about fifteen at last count." She tapped her ear and he noticed she wore a tiny listening device, visible only because the wire was slightly lighter than her dark blond hair. "Two off-duty policemen are standing by at the car and two are positioned at the exit. I think we can make it outside with all our clothes intact."

Nick nodded. Clothes while walking to the car were good. However, once they were alone in the back seat of the limo, he definitely had other ideas—ideas he'd most certainly have to keep to himself.

CHAPTER SIX

SAMANTHA FOUGHT THE URGE to bite her fingernails, which was weird since she'd never bitten her nails before. She was more likely to fidget when she was anxious. Luckily, walking at a fast pace eased her nervous energy. With each step she took, her thoughts cleared, focused on her goal.

Act the part. Be the bimbo. But as she, Nick and their security detail approached the bank of glass doors that led outside, the blinding gleam of television lights and the popping flashes from 35mm cameras threatened to wreck her resolve. She grabbed Nick's arm tighter and held her breath.

Both actions made her nearly dizzy. For a moment, she forgot who was protecting whom. A barrage of questions and comments fired as rapidly as the sharp clicks and screeching whirs that attacked from every imaginable angle. Sam fought flashbacks she thought she'd long since buried, memories from her high-profile past.

"Mr. LaRocca, is it true Ms. Deveaux saved your life?"

"Over here! Over here!"

"Have you finally found the woman of your dreams?"

"She's not really blond. You can tell she's not really blond!"

Now she remembered why she hated celebrity. Yet another reason why she'd left Hollywood.

"Ms. Deveaux, does he really look as good as the picture on the label?"

That one snapped Samantha back into character and forced her to focus on Nick. She could talk about Nick so long as she didn't have to talk about herself. She subtly pulled him to a halt beside her, her grin both sly and coy. Out of pure habit, she turned her face toward his, ruining a good shot of her but putting him in the center of the frame. She'd learned that trick from Anthony. Unfortunately, she'd also learned that some men would barter her and her privacy for the sake of publicity.

She blinked, wondering why she had so much trouble putting Nick into that category.

"That drawing on the label isn't nearly as impressive as the real thing. I should sue him for false advertising," she purred, leaning in close as if she intended to kiss him right there, but she turned back to the press at the last second. "But I won't, of course."

"Hey! Samantha! How does your mother feel about your new lover?" a female reporter asked, her tone genuinely interested, as if she was one of Endora's many devotees. "Does she predict marriage in your future?"

Samantha's stomach turned to leaden lava. She reminded herself that she'd suspected this would happen. But what else might they dig up? Something about her past? Her "youthful indiscretions," as her mother liked to call them?

Samantha shook her head, determined to deal with that potential disaster later. For now, she pulled a pat answer out of the practiced repertoire she thought she'd left behind on Sunset Boulevard.

"My mother is a strong believer in fate. I have no doubt she'll see my meeting Nick as exactly what it is."

A big fat lie.

"Mr. LaRocca, are you finally giving up bachelorhood?"

Sam watched Nick intently, for the sake of her act, of course, wondering if the nature of the question or the increasingly blinding lights caused the sudden, tense set of his shoulders. Either way, she sighed with relief, glad the reporters' attention shifted back on him. She tilted her head, attempting to scan the crowd and bright lights for danger. She glanced toward the limo, which was still a few more paces away than she would have liked. She started easing Nick toward escape with tiny side steps that resembled natural attempts to keep her balance in the surge of people.

Nick stopped their retreat by yanking Sam straight into his arms. She slammed against his chest—all muscle and rock-hard warmth. Rumbling reverberations echoed from deep within her, stealing her equilibrium and hampering her ability to think.

The instant his crushed-mint gaze met hers, the sounds of the media faded. Power emanated through his gaze, as if he owned a mute button on the entire world—and a play button right in her very center. He slid his hands to the small of her back. His fingers splayed over the curve of her backside, possessive, needful. Thrilling.

He lowered his face to hers and moistened his lips with a dart of his tongue. Samantha held her breath, nearly drowning in Nick's unique scent. Fine-milled soap. Spiced cologne. Aged wine. Man.

Oh, God. He was going to kiss her. Right here. Right now. In front of the entire world. And there wasn't a damn thing she could do about it. If she pulled away, she'd blow their cover. If she allowed him this intimate touching of lips, she'd detonate her tentative control over her libido.

At the last moment, Nick turned to face the cameras, allowing her the instant she needed to grasp and hold on tight to the fact that this was all an act. A ruse to fool the press. A scheme to thwart his grandmothers.

Unfortunately, the little details didn't erase the overwhelming truth—that she wanted Nick LaRocca with every fiber of her womanhood and every taut thread of her most secret desires.

"Bachelorhood is highly overrated," Nick said to the reporter, then turned his attention back to her. Again, the world around her seemed to freeze-frame.

"Don't you think?" he finished.

Sam knew his aside was meant for the press, so she didn't attempt a response. Truth was, she couldn't think to save her life. Or his. As his mouth neared hers, all she could do was close her eyes and welcome the sensations.

His mouth hot and urgent. Her surrender sweet and willing. Tongues twirled, briefly, as the camera flashes captured the moment for the whole world to see.

The minute he broke away, Sam instinctively pulled him closer to the car, hoping to look like the anxious lover she could never allow herself to be. Questions and shouts, and sounds Sam finally registered as jealous boos and hisses spurred her to hurry. Their lover act forced her to enter the limousine first, but with her security friend, Ruby, behind her holding tight to the door handle, Sam knew Nick would be right behind her.

He jumped in, his face immediately hidden by shadows. As the driver eased away from the curb, Nick leaned back into the plush leather seat across from her. A shaft of light from a street lamp streaked inside the car but revealed nothing in his expression.

He crossed his arms over his chest. Arms that had just held her close. Arms that under any other circumstance, she might have broken for embracing her so tightly—tightly enough to crumble the wall she'd built around her heart.

"I should have warned you," he said finally, his voice low and intimate, "about the kiss."

His words didn't actually form an apology, but then, they didn't really need to. They had a deal. She'd agreed to sacrifice her personal space to play the part of his lover.

So how come she felt as if she'd forfeited so much more?

She shook her head, then remembered not to be too emphatic in her denials. It was a dead giveaway. Casually, she plucked a tendril from behind her ear and twisted the curl around her finger.

"The kiss—"

What? Didn't mean anything? Hadn't affected her? Was simply part of their arrangement? Even she couldn't tell that large of a lie.

"—that's not what freaked me out. I'm sorry. I wasn't being a very good bodyguard, was I?"

Nick wore his confusion plainly and slid across to sit beside her. "What are you talking about? You planned that whole escape. Maybe you didn't notice, but your friend Ruby was right beside us the whole time."

Sam pursed her lips. No, she hadn't noticed, not until just before they'd gotten into the car. She'd been too taken aback by the cameras, the flashes, the questions about her mother. *Nick.*

"Don't do that."

His whispered command, throaty yet pleading, snapped her gaze to his. The streetlights and shadows played across his rugged face, making his expression hard to read, but highlighting his expressive eyes. She saw a clear warning in the dark green irises. An omen most sensual.

"Don't do what?" she asked.

The darkness masked his touch, so she felt his fingertip on her lips before she registered that he'd lifted his hand. He traced along the bottom of her mouth, awakening the tingle from his kiss outside the Superdome, renewing the swirl of awareness spawned deep in her center. Tendrils of pure need pulled her nipples taut, then slipped into her lungs and captured her breath.

"You purse your lips when you're thinking," he said.

She swallowed. "I do?"

"It drives me crazy."

"It does?"

She watched the bob of his Adam's apple as the car pulled to a stop outside the bright lights of Harrah's Casino on their way to the French Quarter. Was his mouth watering the way hers was? She forced herself to focus on the riot of neon outside rather than on the intense, unguarded look on Nick's face. This time, the passion she saw there wasn't for the benefit of the press, but only for her. For them. Alone. In the back seat of a car more than roomy enough to accommodate a spontaneous response to their mutual desire.

Samantha scooted toward the door. She'd been that impulsive once, with Anthony, a man she'd hoped to someday love. They'd been so passionate for each other, so overwhelmingly connected, they'd never imagined his limo driver would install a camera to capture the intimate event and then sell the stills to a tabloid. But it had happened. Although Anthony Marks, sex symbol of the moment, had the clout, cash and attorneys to bury the pictures after the first print run, Sam had learned a hard lesson about fame, fortune and celebrity.

She'd lost something precious in the process. First, Anthony. Then her sense of privacy. But most of all, her faith in herself, in her ability to judge the difference between pure lust and potential love.

Like right now.

"Then I won't purse my lips anymore. I was just thinking about my mother."

As intended, her admission knocked the desire right out of his gaze. He returned to his seat across from her.

"Your mother, the psychic?"

Sam relaxed as the pull between them slackened. She'd thank her mother later for having such a dependable and well-timed effect. "My mother is more than just a psychic around here. New Orleans takes its supernatural history seriously.

Madame Endora LaCroix Deveaux is not just a celebrity sooth-sayer, she's an icon. Government officials consult her. The police use her regularly to solve tough cases. Movie stars and dignitaries don't leave town until they've had their audience."

Nick nodded, but in the darkness, Sam couldn't gauge if Nick was as impressed as most people. But listening to herself, she realized she wasn't so doubtful of her mother anymore. All the things she'd said about Endora were true. Here Sam had her own personal conduit to the unknown, and she spent most of her limited time with her mother playing the skeptic. Pretending her Hollywood worldliness somehow saw through Endora's lame excuse for breaking up their family.

"If she's so accurate," Nick said, his tone confidant, "she'll know what our relationship is. Or do you think our stunt will upset her?"

Sam shook her head. She wasn't worried about her mother being upset, per se. She'd been upsetting her mother on a daily basis since she was five and begged to go live with their father in California only two months after he'd left the family to pursue his dream. Endora hadn't understood why a five-year-old would want to leave her own mother. She hadn't understood how Sam's child's heart had ached for the man who promised her wild adventures around the world, boundless excitement and limitless fun. Besides, Daddy had needed someone to take care of him. Mother no longer wanted the job. Serena was nearly two years older, but Sam's sister wouldn't have left New Orleans even if the Mississippi had surged and drowned the city.

Disappointing her mother yet again wasn't her concern. But the added media attention on her because of her mother's renown—that had her squirming.

"We'll get a lot of local press, that's all. Because of Mother. Her phone is probably ringing off the hook right now."

"And this is a bad thing…why?"

"I don't enjoy living under a microscope, Nick. Been there, done that."

"With your father?"

Sam rolled her lips inward, smearing what was left of her lipstick and not caring. She'd told Nick she wouldn't share too much about her life, but since the reporters would more than likely dredge up her past with Anthony anyway, she figured she might as well tell him herself first. He needed to know. Should know. The truth might put a permanent damper on this burgeoning, wonderfully invigorating attraction.

"Devlin protected me from the press when I was a child. Which is why I had bodyguards. But when I got older and started doing stunts…" she smirked. "The novelty was too much for the tabloids to ignore. Then, about two years ago, I started dating Anthony Marks."

"Anthony Marks? Anthony…Marks, huh?"

Sam chuckled. Nick was so out of touch with Hollywood, the name meant nothing to him.

"Oh, wait. Wasn't he in that space movie? The astronaut who never wore a shirt?"

"He's the one." *Space Race* hadn't made much at the box office, but Anthony's shirtless scenes instantly made him a star. "So, you saw the movie?"

Nick frowned. "I haven't seen a movie since college. My niece has his picture hanging in her room. He's quite the heart-throb, I understand. No wonder you don't like the spotlight."

You don't know the half of it.

"But, I can handle it for a few days. It's what I agreed to. And I'm a woman of my word."

Nick left it at that. He whipped out his cell phone and called Anita while Sam gazed absently out the window. Landmarks blurred past—Jax Brewery. The Moonwalk. Street performers and vendors hawking dreams on Jackson Square.

As they waited to turn onto a side street, Sam realized that her affair with Anthony seemed a hundred years ago, when really, less than a year had passed since she walked out. While the relationship had ended at that moment, just after the incident with the photographs, she realized what she and Anthony had shared had never been a real relationship at all.

That had always been her biggest problem. She'd once again injected more into her affair with Anthony than had existed, and once again ended up disappointed and hurt. If only she'd seen their time together for what it was—a brief, fairly enjoyable fling—she might not have had so many wounds to lick when she returned to New Orleans.

And she might not be so reluctant to explore the attraction she shared with Nick, client or not.

Thanks to light traffic, they arrived at the restaurant quickly. Samantha had been careful to guard the location of Nick's dinner from the press, out of respect for the business associate who'd invited him. The small crowd gathered in front of the popular eatery seemed more impressed with the menus they read and the drinks they nursed than with anyone arriving in one of the many black stretch limos tooling around the city on a Friday night.

After they parked, Samantha slid across the seat toward the door. Nick stopped her before she could flip the handle.

"Wait, Samantha." He disconnected the call and pocketed the phone. "I don't want you to…"

Huffing with impatience, she impaled him with her best glare. She didn't want his sympathy, for God's sake, or his genuine concern. She couldn't battle them and her insatiable desire to make love to him all at the same time.

"Please. Don't. Don't play nice and all concerned about my feelings. I'm not your problem. I'm being so unprofessional here I'm surprised you haven't fired me on the spot. I'll deal with the consequences of my actions. Don't worry about me."

Nick chuckled, and as much as she tried to ignore the sensation, the rich sound rumbled through her like retreating thunder. As if the danger was over. As if the storm would soon subside. She knew better. She knew because Nick LaRocca turned her on and Sam was never one to deny her passions. Not even when danger stared her straight in the eye.

"A man would be a fool to worry about you, Samantha. I've never met a more capable, more in-control woman in my entire life. And that's including my formidable grandmothers."

Samantha smiled, grateful when the driver came around and opened the door. If Nick wanted to buy into the persona she so carefully exuded, then so be it.

Capable? Oh, yeah. She was capable right now of sliding to his side of the limo and showing him a lot more than just her pursed lips. In control? Barely. Only by clenching her hands into fists beneath her thighs was she keeping them to herself.

But his total confidence in her cool command of her emotions would play to her benefit. In the long run. But not now. Now, she was shaking. Shaking with frustration and recrimination and regret. Not because Nick had kissed her for the whole world to see, but because she couldn't ask for a private repeat performance.

DINNER WAS AS delicious as it was uneventful. Their Japanese host had married an exuberant British woman who entertained them all with fascinating stories and lively chitchat— and didn't seem the least bit concerned with who Samantha was, who she'd been, or if she and Nick were currently lovers. Sam spent the evening grinning, nodding and covertly watching for potential interlopers or reporters. Since they weren't spotted by anyone who knew Nick or by anyone who cared that he could offer a wife a weekly allowance worth more than the annual education budget of New Orleans Parish, Sam mostly sat back and tortured herself in silence.

Against her better judgment, if she had any judgment left at all after his mind-shattering kiss at the Dome, she watched Nick intently all evening. She watched how he savored his food, eating slowly, testing textures and inhaling aromas with each and every bite. She grew fascinated with the slow undulation of his mouth, the smooth way he retrieved his wineglass and sipped, all the time listening with intense interest to Mr. Ishimi and his wife—as if they were the only people in the room.

But that wasn't entirely accurate. Not once did he make her think he'd forgotten that she was sitting across from him. He didn't miss a single opportunity to suggest a choice from the menu, ask about the quality of her meal or inquire about her desire for anything else. His eye contact with her might have been brief while he focused on his official host, but the meeting of his gaze to hers was no less charged. Brevity made the looks intimate. Subtlety concentrated them with forbidden power. Had she any excess money in her bank account, she would have bet he was attempting to seduce her with his eyes.

Wager or not, he was succeeding.

After dropping his hosts at Le Pavillon Hotel, Nick quietly instructed the driver to return to the Hyatt. Though they'd discussed the night's accommodations that afternoon, Samantha now squirmed about the overnight bag she'd left in Nick's room. For the sake of anyone who might be watching them and keeping score, she'd spend the next few nights on the Murphy bed in his businessman's suite. She'd packed the floppiest, most unappealing sleepwear she could pilfer from her sister's collection, but she couldn't help thinking about the sinful lingerie she'd impulsively worn beneath her suit.

Or how she so much preferred sleeping in the nude.

"I bet you can't wait to get to bed," Nick said, breaking the silence.

"Excuse me?" She might have had a wistful thought or two, but she felt quite certain she hadn't let her fantasy show.

"You look as tired as I feel," he clarified, chuckling at her assumption that he had implied something else. Obviously, he had not. "It's been a long day."

"Oh, yeah. Well...I don't need a lot of sleep. Four, five hours and I'm fine."

"Really? Me, too. Drives everyone I know crazy. I'm usually in bed by midnight and then I'm ready to go by 5:00 a.m."

Sam glanced at her watch. It was barely eleven o'clock. Just what would Nick do while she got into her jammies and prepared for what might very well be a sleepless night? Take a shower? Read his book? Order a nightcap and then attempt to seduce her?

Yeah. You wish.

"Is there anywhere you want to go first?" she asked. "Any place in New Orleans you wanted to see? Your schedule is pretty tight after tonight. Bourbon Street is probably just getting revved up. We could put in a very public appearance." Her suggestion sounded a bit more anxious than she'd intended, but the anticipation of being alone with Nick in his hotel room, with nothing to do and nothing to think about except the full breadth of her attraction, made her more than nervous.

When he didn't answer, she pursed her lips, trying to think of an alternative to partying in the French Quarter. He cleared his throat. For an instant, she didn't know what his chastising look referred to, until he drew his finger to his own mouth and tapped twice.

She rolled her lips inward and shrugged. "Sorry."

It was the last word spoken until they arrived at the hotel. They entered through the main lobby so anyone who cared would note that she was accompanying him to his room. The place was eerily quiet. Even the women who'd been stalking

Nick for the past two days had apparently been drawn to the revelries across town.

"Ms. Deveaux!"

The hotel manager, waving a small, brown-paper-wrapped box, slipped away from the front desk just as they were about to enter the elevator.

Sam tensed, her instincts alert. She pushed Nick inside the elevator, but he slammed his palm against the side so the doors wouldn't close. She frowned impertinently, but his replying scowl won their brief contest of wills. Sam bit her tongue and waited for the manager to catch up.

"This came for you about an hour ago," he said, panting. "I waited past my shift to make sure you got it."

He grinned at Nick, who granted the eager manager the nod and smile he so obviously desired. Nick went for his wallet, but the manager shook his head. "Please, Mr. LaRocca. After the mix-up with room service this afternoon…"

Sam took the box and examined it. She had absolutely no experience with explosives, so she did what she saw actors do in the movies—she held it to her ear. When she did, she heard nothing ticking, but the distinct, blended scents of jasmine, magnolia and a rare Caribbean spice her mother used in her favorite tea tickled her nose. She turned the box over to see her mother's unique wax seal, an elaborate "E" in the center of a double-edged diamond.

"Thank you," she said to the manager, entering the elevator and tapping Nick on the elbow to release his hold on the door. Nick pressed the number to his floor.

"I take it nothing dangerous is inside."

Samantha gave the box a shake and could hear nothing recognizable. Her imagination instantly conjured an endless list of possible items her mother might find interesting to send along to her wayward daughter now that the news of her supposed love affair was all over the airwaves.

A gris-gris bag aimed at enhancing romance.

Dried and ground chicken claws to sprinkle around the bedside to ward off negative spirits.

Condoms?

Or worse, Grandmother Lizabeth's engagement ring, the elaborate ruby Endora had promised to Samantha since her third birthday.

"Dangerous? There's no telling," she answered. "It's from my mother."

"Open it," Nick encouraged, his humor perked by the chagrin Sam didn't bother to hide.

Samantha sniffed the box again and remembered that her mother had been collaborating with her sister, an aromatherapist, on a signature massage oil for Serena's spa. Serena's contribution, a unique blend of ingredients she kept secret from even her own sister, promised to enhance lovemaking. Endora's part, a charmed additive of unknown origins, would supposedly encourage commitment, even from the most reluctant lover.

She eyed him pointedly. "If your grandmothers sent you a box like this, out of the blue, after you'd just kissed someone on the late news, would you open it in front of me?"

CHAPTER SEVEN

NICK INHALED. He tried to make the action appear innocent as he slid the key card into the lock, but the sound of his quick intake of breath immediately drew Samantha's attention. She had to be the most observant woman he'd ever met. While he usually would have admired that trait, right now he was having a damn hard time hiding anything from her, least of all his elemental, inborn response to her standing so close.

Especially with that alluring scent emanating from the shaken box.

"Got a cold?" she asked, her tone just sassy enough to show she was well aware of his attempt to steal a whiff from the box.

"Actually, I *am* feeling quite warm."

"Maybe it's a fever." She eyed his forehead, but made no move to touch him.

Damn it.

"Maybe it's just New Orleans." *Maybe it's just you.* He swept his gaze over her once again, as he'd done so many times tonight, and this time he didn't bother to hide his interest. Why attempt the impossible? "This city gives a whole new definition to the word *hot*."

She slid around him when he pushed the door open. Her thigh briefly brushed against his leg, and though he didn't get a shock this time, the air crackled. His body thrummed.

"Luckily, your room is air-conditioned," she said oh-so-innocently. "The heat can make people do crazy things."

He followed her inside, and when she swung around to lock and bolt the door behind him, he had her trapped. God, she was gorgeous. She smelled like a freshly baked cinnamon creation steeping in a warm oven, injecting the air with a mouthwatering scent. He braced both hands on either side of her, waiting for her to turn around, waiting to find out if she tasted as sweet as she smelled.

Their first kiss had been too quick. He hadn't had enough time to recover from the jolt of pure desire to register all the flavors, or to savor the sensations.

And Nick was a savoring kind of guy.

"What kind of crazy things?" he asked, not really needing an example from her since he was clearly acting the part of the madman, despite the cool temperature in his suite. The aroma from the box was nothing compared to the fresh scent of her butterscotch hair, swept up in a loose twist, elegant in style, but erotically glamorous. He longed to kiss the soft curve of her exposed neck. Taste the extracts seasoning her skin.

"Like thinking you can trap your bodyguard this easily." Before he could react, she'd twisted and ducked out of his reach, darting into the room to turn on lights and check the closets and bathrooms for uninvited guests.

But she was not as immune to him as he'd thought this afternoon. The coy glances they'd exchanged at the restaurant, her instinctual reaction to his kiss at the Dome, the fire-hot tension simmering during the car ride back to the hotel told him all he needed to know. They may have made a deal to only act like lovers for the benefit of his grandmothers and the general public, but Nick hoped to sweeten the arrangement with some real interaction—for their personal enrichment alone.

"Everything all clear?" he asked, knowing he should bide his time. Samantha was now on the defensive. He needed her to relax. He needed to relax. He was wound so tight, he imagined he'd completely unravel if he didn't take things slowly.

And Dominick LaRocca didn't unravel. He was in control. Of his words. Of his actions. Of his desires.

Except now. Except when Samantha Deveaux was marching around his suite in a snug, sexy suit that did amazing things to her already amazing legs. He'd never experienced the brink of lustful insanity before.

Invigorating.

"I need to check out your bedroom," she answered, marching toward the door with utter efficiency.

"Fine with me," he murmured as she swept by him.

She frowned before she entered the dark room, attempting to impale him with a sharp stare.

"Yeah, I figured."

Unfortunately for Samantha, her eyes were a little too dilated, her voice a little too breathless for her verbal swipe to cut his teasing mood.

He slapped his hand on his chest anyway, pretending to be offended. He liked this game they played. Amorous cat to saucy mouse. Besides, teasing her from a relatively safe distance tamped down his instinct to follow her inside his room to show her just how fine her presence in his bedroom could be. "What are you implying, Ms. Deveaux?"

She eyed him narrowly from the threshold, then gave up with a two-handed wave. "I'm implying that your arrogance is showing. Not every woman alive thinks you're some sort of gift to the feminine gender. Anita tried to warn me about you."

"Anita's been warning girls about me since I was ten and she was six," he said, shrugging out of his jacket and folding it over his arm. "And for the record, she was kidding then, too."

Samantha rolled her eyes and disappeared into his bedroom, leaving a trail of heat in her wake. Electricity wasn't the only fire she generated, but before he could complete one step in her direction to discover how hot a blaze they could stoke in his bed, she popped back out with a terse, "All clear."

"You barely checked," he accused.

"I checked enough. The door to the hall is still locked and bolted from the inside and there's no one hiding in your closet. So, here's the rule—you go to your room, I stay in here. I'll see you at 5:30 a.m."

"What if I want to work before I retire?" He gestured toward the work he'd left on the conference table in the center of what had just become *her* room.

She marched to his laptop and flipped down the top, then tidied the papers and files into one efficient stack.

"Aren't laptops an amazing invention? And the cell phone! Both so portable. They go everywhere, including bedrooms."

She leaned back on the table, causing the neckline of her suit to gap just enough to give him a peek of a shiny purple satin strap. Then she pushed off his makeshift desk, slipping away before he had a chance to completely visualize the entirely different use for the smooth, flat table that had come to mind.

"Anita also told me you work too hard," she said. "And I'm sure she wasn't kidding about that. Why don't you forget about work tonight? You have a long day tomorrow."

He shook his head, trying to dispel the image of him luring Samantha onto the tabletop and forgetting all about work for more than just tonight. But there really was no use flirting with such a determined woman, especially when he wasn't sure where he wanted that flirting to lead. Okay, he knew where he *wanted* it to lead, he just wasn't sure that enticing his bodyguard into his bed was the best idea. For either of them.

He surrendered with a polite good night, then went into the bedroom and closed the door behind him.

The bed, crisply turned down, with silver-wrapped candies on the pillows, immediately drew his attention. He peeled a mint and popped it into his mouth, hardly registering the cool, rich flavor on his tongue.

He could only taste Samantha, from a kiss that happened hours ago but still tortured him with hints of flavors and sensations utterly exotic and rare.

She thought he had a long day tomorrow? It would be nothing compared to the rest of the night.

SAM WAITED until she heard his door close with a resounding click. Then she breathed. The man was lethal! She slid into the leather chair, exhausted. Tempering her responses to his blatant sensuality sapped all her energy. He flirted with his eyes. He seduced with his words. When he'd trapped her against the door, his chest to her back, only an inch away from touching, from feeling his erection against her short-short skirt and the lacy panties she wore underneath… She forced herself to breathe again. They could have had sex right up against that door. Mind-shattering, borderline illicit lovemaking that would have knocked the double steel doors right off the hinges.

But she'd pushed away.

Fool.

When she heard the shower from his room turn on, she bolted into action. Now was the time for her to shower, when he was safely under his own stream of hot water and unable to accidentally walk in on her. She grabbed her overnight bag and her mother's box of surprises and tossed them into the guest bathroom while she tore off her suit and closed the door tightly behind her.

She stopped in front of the mirror and shook her head, removing the clips that held her hair in the sexy, slightly tousled chignon she knew made her look glamorous when she was honestly anything but. Hair down, loose and unbound, Samantha acknowledged that she was what she was—a woman with needs, simple desires.

But then, not so simple.

˙ She traced the edge of her purple lace bra with her fingertips, watching, fascinated, as her nipples tightened and pushed
her darker aureoles up from the low-cut cups. But she knew
her touch wasn't responsible for the instantaneous physical
reaction, the thrilling prickle of sexual desire shooting straight
from her breasts to her belly and below.

Nick did this to her. Nick and his come-ons. Nick and his incredible but all-too-brief kiss. She was primed. Aroused.
Charged as if they'd spent the past few hours engaged in
foreplay.

Which in a sense they had.

She smoothed her hands down her rib cage and stomach,
wondering why she worked so damn hard to keep slim and fit
at the same time she worked so damn hard to prevent any man
from sharing the fruits of her labor. She wondered if Nick liked
his women thin and willowy, plump and soft, or like her, somewhere in the middle with a muscled edge from her hour of tae
kwon do in the mornings, followed by her five-mile run, and
then her weight workout every other afternoon. Her physical
routine began years ago as training for the rigors of stunt work.
She'd kept up the practice after quitting the business, first as
a means to heal from her injuries, then to occupy her time. And,
finally, to prepare for her new career as a bodyguard.

But there *were* other payoffs she could explore. Other uses
for her tight abs and slim thighs. Not to mention workouts for
the parts of her body that didn't get nearly enough attention,
that now resonated with the force of her heartbeat throbbing
between her thighs.

If only she had the courage to walk across the hall.

A sound drew her to the door. A shout? Nick! Alarm
dashed her desire along with her modesty, sending her scrambling out of the bathroom. She managed to think enough to
grab her gun from her purse before she slipped into his
bedroom, which was, *oh God,* completely dark.

NICK TURNED the shower on the hottest setting, watching the steam rise off the slick marble tile and coat the shower doors with a haze of hot moisture. In the grayness, he imagined a feminine silhouette—compact, yet curvy—emerging from the fog. Blond hair dampened to the color and texture of rich caramel. Eyes flashing like polished cobalt, dark and wide with desire.

Nick rolled his eyes and turned the faucet as icy cold as he could get during a New Orleans spring. He was losing his mind. It was pure insanity—caused by excessive testosterone and unrequited lust. He'd have to ask his doctor if such a diagnosis was medically possible. No, Nick realized as he tore off his clothes, he knew the ailment was possible. What he needed was a cure…and one that didn't include seducing Samantha Deveaux.

At least, not tonight.

Nick winced as he stepped beneath the surprisingly brisk shards of cold water, but by the time he'd soaped up and rinsed, his erection was no less pronounced and his brain was no less befuddled. Sure, Samantha was beautiful, in a sassy, what-do-I-care-if-my-hair-is-a-little-tousled sort of way. And her body, while not thin like Blair's or soft like Sophia's, seemed to find a happy medium in a toned fitness that she undoubtedly worked hard to maintain.

That's what confused him. Everything about Samantha was the opposite of what he'd believed for so long was his ideal woman. She was brash and opinionated. She knew what she wanted and didn't need him or anyone else to tell her. She also knew quite clearly what she didn't want. Or at least, what she wouldn't allow herself to have. Nick didn't doubt that she was just as attracted to him as he was to her. He'd felt her instantaneous, unhindered response, quick though it was, to his kiss. She just had a much better handle on keeping her desires in check.

He adjusted the water temperature to a more comfortable warmth, then braced his hands on the shower wall and let the water sluice down his back. He closed his eyes, allowing the sensation to conjure the imagined feel of Samantha's hands trailing a similar path over his shoulders, down his spine, across his buttocks. The ache in his groin increased, but the feel of her touch, completely fantasized, was too delicious, too forbidden, to shake away.

It had been so long.

Too long between women. Too long since he'd even allowed himself the luxury of self-gratification to ease the sexual hunger he now fixated on Samantha. Under the circumstances, finding another woman to alleviate his lust was out of the question. He'd just have to take matters into his own hands. So he did.

"Don't," a female voice whispered, stopping his stroke. "Let me."

The bathroom light clicked off. A gentle glow from a scented candle flickered from the vanity. Nick couldn't believe this was happening. He'd never imagined Sam would come to him. Why would she? He had nothing to offer her but wild, lusty sex…and he felt certain that was way below her standard.

"Sam?"

"Shh." The shower door opened, then clicked closed behind a female form slightly smaller than Nick expected. The hairs on the back of his neck prickled over wet skin.

"Don't talk, Dominick. Let's just make love."

The minute she touched him, he knew. This wasn't Samantha.

"Who the hell—?"

The stranger grabbed him and began massaging. Roughly. He jumped back, nearly slipped, and banged his head against the showerhead. "Ow! Let go!"

"Come on, baby. Don't be shy. You know you want it. I've

been waiting underneath your bed since this morning. She isn't going to give it to you. I'm willing. I'm here."

The bathroom light flashed on at the same time the shower door crashed open.

"Not for long. Let go of him and back off. Slowly."

With water stinging his eyes and a madwoman holding tight to his family jewels, Nick blinked, unsure if what he saw was real or some glimpse into his erotic fantasies. If this was a dream, he had definitely watched too many porno flicks in his youth. The sharp click as Samantha released the safety on her gun convinced him this was no triple X-rated film. The dark-haired stranger, more angry than guilty, released him and backed to the opposite side of the stall. The white satin teddy she wore clung wet to her skin, revealing cocoa-brown nipples on an ample bosom.

But she was nothing compared to Samantha. Blond hair wild and finger-combed. Nipples pouting from the edges of a sinfully sexy purple bra. Bare midriff. Plum panties that barely covered the sweet center of his torment. And the gun. Gleaming silver and cocked for business.

His best wet dream come to life.

The stranger thrust her fists on her hips. "What are you, the sex police?"

"No," Samantha answered calmly. "I'm just the body-guard holding the gun. Come out of the shower." Sam gripped her pistol in one hand and motioned to the stranger with the other.

The woman shook her head and crossed her arms over her chest. "No way. I'm not going anywhere. Mr. LaRocca invited me here."

Nick opened his mouth to protest, but Samantha tossed him a towel and rolled her eyes, obviously in no need of an explanation. He shut off the running shower and covered up, pleased that Sam didn't believe the ridiculous lie.

"Is that so? Do you always call your lovers by their proper name? *Mr. LaRocca?* Unless he's a client and you're a…"

"I ain't no hooker. Mr. La…Dominick and me…we're going to be married."

Sam lowered her weapon and nodded for Nick to come out of the shower. He complied just in time for security to burst into his room, through the unlocked door he distinctly remembered was bolted before he'd gone into the bathroom. The first guard holstered his weapon as soon as Samantha flashed her gun. The second guard followed close behind, holding tight to a struggling young man wearing an ill-fitting room-service uniform and holding a camera.

Sam gave the woman an exaggerated frown. "Oh, looks like the banns won't be announced as planned. Unless you can arrange it from jail."

The first security guard grabbed a towel and wrapped up the intruding woman, then cuffed her behind her back.

"We caught this guy about to enter your room, Mr. LaRocca. The door was unlocked." When the guard, graying at the temples but obviously not blind, dared to eye Samantha while he detained their trespasser, she shifted her weapon a little higher. She lowered the gun when the man politely looked away.

With the situation now under control, Sam crossed her arms but made no other move to show that she was the least bit uncomfortable with the situation. "This is the young man who pretended to be from room service earlier, probably casing the place. Now he's got a camera and she's broken into Mr. LaRocca's room wearing next to nothing? Looks like a blackmail setup to me."

The woman and her camera-toting accomplice remained silent, but Nick agreed with Sam's assessment. Pictures of him engaged in a sordid tryst, setup or not, could be both valuable and damaging. Once again, Sam had saved him.

Nick cleared his throat. "Take these people out of here and call the police," he instructed.

"The NOPD will want a statement from us," Sam informed him.

The last thing he wanted to do tonight was talk to cops. "We'll press charges and file a report in the morning. Not before."

Nick's tone elicited decisive nods from hotel security.

"And keep this quiet," Sam added. "I don't think your hotel or your manager would appreciate the bad press." She followed her implication with a quick little grin and said, "Thank you and goodbye" in one brief flash.

They made a great team. By the time the room emptied and the door slammed shut behind him, Nick realized he was standing in the middle of his bathroom, holding a towel around his waist, dripping wet, and completely stunned by what had just happened.

Samantha was obviously no better off. She'd just broken up a possible assault on his very naked person. And in her underwear, too.

Incredibly sexy, sewn-for-seduction underwear.

She slid the gun onto the countertop and combed her fingers through her hair in a hard thrust. "God, Nick. I'm so sorry."

He slammed his lips together, suddenly aware that he was gaping, openmouthed, at the woman of his fantasies, nearly naked, packing heat and...apologizing?

"For?"

Rushing by him to lock the door from the inside, Samantha shook her head and plopped down on the bed. "I'm so not ready for this job. Brandon's going to kill me for screwing this up."

Nick's muddled brain snapped clear. *Woman in distress.* This he could do. He shrugged into the hotel-supplied robe, then grabbed a second one from the closet and wrapped it around her shoulders as he sat beside her on the bed.

"Samantha, you rescued me again. And just in time, too."

Sam shook her head, apparently not ready to hear his positive spin. "How'd she get in? I *know* that door was bolted from the inside. I checked when we got back."

Nick realized the rustling sound he'd heard that morning had *not* been the air conditioner or a figment of his imagination. "She said she hid under the bed since this morning."

"Under the bed? That I didn't check." Sam pulled the lapels of the robe closer as she noticed Nick's proximity. "That guy with the camera was the same one who brought up the wrong room-service order this afternoon. The chick in the teddy must have used the side hallway to break into the bedroom. The room-service ploy distracted me so I wouldn't hear."

Nick wasn't about to admit that he *had* heard something and his well-documented male pride hadn't allowed him to tell her. "That private hallway was supposed to have been locked before I arrived."

"She could have stolen a passkey with the waiter's uniform. Or picked the lock."

Sam's frown was repentant, and nearly as maddening as her most thoughtful pucker. "I guess I should have looked under the bed."

Her honest admission of her error grabbed him right in the middle of the chest. She might have checked under the bed had he told her that he'd heard something suspicious. But who screwed up when wasn't important now. He only wanted to remove the embarrassed look from her face.

"Who checks under a bed for a grown person?" he asked. "Besides, most hotels have those kickers on the bed frames so you don't lose your socks."

Sam's tiny grin warmed the chill the air-conditioner was wreaking on his wet skin. "You almost lost something more valuable than socks." She glanced down to the front of his barely closed robe. "That woman had a death grip on the future LaRocca progeny. Are you all right?"

Wanna check for yourself? Nick nearly let the invitation fly, but his instincts told him Sam's pride and confidence were still too wounded to deflect such an innuendo. "I'd rather not think about it. So, what? They planned to get me in some compromising position and then blackmail me into marriage?"

"Marriage…money. No telling. You know, she must have waited under that bed all afternoon until we left for the Dome and then hid again when we came back." Sam slipped off the side of the bed and ducked under the edge of the comforter to look under the bed. Big mistake. Her robe fell open just at the perfect angle to renew the throbbing in Nick's groin—the throbbing that had absolutely nothing to do with the physical assault on his person.

"She must have really wanted you," she said.

Her assessment sounded too much like a personal admission—too much like those hypothetical scenarios where someone talks about themselves in the third person—for Nick to let her comment go. He extended his hand to her, inviting her to stand when he did.

"I know what it feels like to want someone that badly," he said.

She licked her lips.

He thought he'd die.

"You do?" she asked.

He answered with a slow nod.

She pursed her mouth. Pink. Moist. His entire body tensed with the rigid need he wasn't sure he could contain much longer.

"I asked you not to do that," he whispered, reaching one finger to press on the center of her tightened lips.

She gently guided his hand to her cheek. "Because it turns you on?"

"Oh, yeah."

She smiled, then pressed a tiny kiss in the center of his palm. He sucked in a breath, sure she was torturing him, sure she was determined to drive him utterly insane.

"I can't seem to help myself," she answered. "I wonder why that is."

CHAPTER EIGHT

THE RINGING SOUND barely registered in Samantha's ears until Nick swore. She moved to grab the receiver, but he pulled her back into his personal space.

"Let it ring," he said.

She shook her head, half of her thankful for the interruption, half of her mad as hell. "It could be the police. If we don't answer, they'll come up and check on us."

With a growl, he tore away from her and snatched up the phone with a loud and curt, "What?"

His sudden absence hit her like an icy wind, throwing her off balance and weakening her knees. Luckily, the bed caught her when she sat to think. To regroup.

Good Lord. Had she just propositioned her client? The man she was supposed to protect? The man she'd just seen in all his nude and perfect glory, while she'd pranced to his rescue in underwear too racy even to be Victoria's best-kept secret?

Of course, if she'd done her job right, Nick wouldn't have needed rescuing. From their kiss at the Dome to the tension in the limo, she'd battled her overwhelming desire to make love with him. She'd hurried through her search of his bedroom earlier in hopes that a good night's sleep would unwind the tense coil of need he'd spun with his sexy banter and skilled kiss.

She *had* checked the closets and bathroom, as well as behind the curtains and even inside the tall armoire. But the bed? Oh, no. She'd given that particular piece of furniture a wide berth. Certain his scent lingered on the sheets, she'd utilized every ounce of her control just to keep from burying her face in his pillow. Her brief glance at the bed had instantaneously hit her with an erotic flash-forward vision. Nick beneath her. Above her. Unclothed and carefree, rolling and laughing and discovering each other over, under and around the soft, feathery comforter.

Had she been able to control her overactive imagination, she might have found the woman hidden beneath the frame, waiting for Nick to get into bed or into the shower, anywhere vulnerable where she could trap him and fulfill her scheme.

Sam braced her elbows on her knees and buried her face in her hands. In all honesty, she didn't know if the woman was certifiable or brilliant beyond words.

Nick's voice coaxed her from her one-woman pity party.

"No, no. It's been a rough night. I didn't mean to bark." His tone calmed from frustrated to professional, but his impatience showed by the way he marched around the nightstand and knotted the phone cord while he spoke—she assumed from the conversation—to the hotel manager.

Sam watched him, amazed at the ease with which he caged his raw power. Unleashed, such energy would make the man a magnificent lover. She already knew from his actions at the restaurant that he was attentive, concerned with her needs. She also knew from watching him at the Expo that he preferred to be in charge. In careful control. To a woman like Samantha, a woman forced by her circumstances to take control even when she didn't want to, Nick's combination of intuition and strength was inherently seductive. Irresistible beyond her wildest dreams.

Sam twisted her fists into the downy comforter beneath her, and the gentle bounce of the mattress reminded her that she was very close to living that particular dream. Too close.

She should get up. Get out. Book the first flight out of New Orleans and go back to the illusory world of Hollywood where she could convince herself that she was content with brief affairs and meaningless sensual interludes.

But she'd come home to New Orleans in search of something more. Roots. A home. People who liked her just because she was Samantha and not because she could get them a job with her father or bankroll their next film. So far, the best thing she'd found in New Orleans was Nick, a man whose obligations and goals would take him out of her life in two days.

But how could she ignore the act of fate that had thrust Nick and her together? Or deny the rush of attraction she hadn't felt in so very long? Sam had learned, from her father and every other Hollywood player she'd ever known, to seize opportunities before they slipped away.

Like right here. Right now.

"No, I'm sure we're not going to sleep anytime soon," Nick said into the receiver. His voice was matter-of-fact, but his eyes sought hers and practically glowed with endless possibilities—glittering sparks of sensual promise that caused an electric shiver to run from her fingers to her spine. The anticipation of a total erotic torrent made her light-headed, as if she was standing on the top of a ten-story building, preparing to jump, aiming for the safety mat inflated below.

"That's completely unnecessary. No…yes, of course. I appreciate your hospitality." Nick hung up the phone. "That was the hotel manager. He wanted us to know that the police arrived, and while they wanted to come up and take a report right now, he convinced them to wait until morning to investigate."

Samantha nodded.

"He's bringing up a nightcap for us, to help us sleep after our 'disturbing incident.'"

She nodded again. "*Disturbing* is a good word."

Tension coiled in Sam's belly, and as the sensation intensified, she bolted off the bed. This wasn't right. She wasn't supposed to be attracted to her client any more than she was supposed to be sitting on his bed dressed in nothing but sexy lingerie and a borrowed robe. Especially not with room service on their way up.

"I'd b-better get dressed," she stuttered, gesturing to the door that separated their rooms.

He shook his head. "Just relax, Sam. The manager is bringing it himself. I can answer the door."

"But it's my job."

Nick hesitated. His eyes narrowed, and this time *he* pursed his lips. She could see why he found her little habit so infuriating. His lips were inviting, full and defined, beneath an incredibly Grecian, incredibly regal nose. If she hadn't stopped herself, she would have puckered her own mouth in response.

"Then I'll finish my shower and join you in a few minutes," he said.

Sam smiled when Nick disappeared into the bathroom and shut the door tightly behind him. He still trusted her to do her job. Why, she had no idea. But his faith in her zapped the last of her regrets out of her head. She'd screwed up once—she wouldn't again. Not with her job. Not with her life.

Fortunately for her, she couldn't think of a single way that making love with Nick could be considered a mistake. Not if she proceeded with her eyes open and her expectations nil. Not if he still wanted her with the same overwhelming attraction she felt for him.

Anticipating the arrival of the hotel manager, Sam nearly changed into her floppy pajamas before realizing her robe and tousled hair would play perfectly into their still make-believe love affair. She chuckled to herself, imagining what the security guards had told the hotel manager about what they'd seen when they came to collect the trespasser and her intended accomplice.

Swear to God, boss. She was holding a 9mm in purple underwear.

She tossed any embarrassment aside. She still wasn't worse than the naked nuns.

That she'd carry a gun when on a date with her new lover would make sense since everyone knew she was employed with No Chances Protection and that she and Nick had met when she was working security at the Dome. An outrageous incident like a nearly naked woman attacking Nick in the shower only for him to be rescued by his scantily clad lover would undoubtedly make the morning talk shows and add nicely to the illusion she and Nick were creating.

Illusion. And she thought she'd left that all behind in Hollywood.

Perhaps she had.

The knock came quickly, and Sam answered the door after checking the peephole. The manager offered profuse apologies, which Sam accepted along with a cart laden with a bottle of cognac, a chilled magnum of Asti Spumante and two dishes covered with silver domes, one on ice and one warmed with Sterno. The manager informed her that he'd posted two guards at the elevator and he offered one for the door, but Sam insisted the third man was overkill.

There was such a thing as too close for comfort.

She rolled the cart into the living room, placing the peace offerings from hotel management on the low coffee table. Familiar aromas emanated from the heated bowl—butter and sugar and fresh, roasted pecans. She was just lifting the top when Nick came into the room, dressed again in his loosely sashed robe. His dark hair was combed and slicked back, making his features even more angular, his green eyes more piercing. Pajama pants, striped blue and white cotton, covered his knees and ankles and added warmth to his cool yet potent masculinity.

"That smells incredible," he said.

She took a long sniff. The action sent her spiraling back in time, to Miss Lily's kitchen in her mother's house. She'd been no more than four, begging to lick the spoon while Serena mixed the pecans they'd picked from the tree in the backyard with the melted butter and caramelized sugar Miss Lily had set to simmer in an old, battered pot. They'd drop the mixture onto rolls of butcher paper lining the countertops and listen to Miss Lily tell stories until the praline candies cooled enough to pilfer. They would wrap the rest in colored cellophane to share with the neighbors on All Hallows' Eve.

When Sam opened her eyes, Nick was standing directly across from her.

"Where were you?" he asked.

She smiled shyly. She rarely allowed herself the luxury of childhood memories, because a good one inevitably led her to a bad one, like her first Halloween away from New Orleans when her father had his maid take her trick-or-treating because he had a film to edit. Shaking her head, she plopped down on the sofa. "I was back in Miss Lily's kitchen."

"Miss Lily?"

"She's my mother's cook and very best friend in the universe."

Nick sat on the love seat next to the couch and examined the bottle of cognac. "A cook, huh?"

"The finest in all of New Orleans. You have no idea how much money she's been offered to open her own restaurant."

He set the dark brown bottle aside and lifted the wine out of the ice-packed bucket. He smiled and promptly began removing the foil and wire protecting the plastic cork. "New Orleans has an amazing culinary past. I'm ashamed I've never visited here before now."

Sam eyed the bathroom, wondering if she should excuse herself to shower. But the soft terry cloth of the robe felt lush and warm against her skin, a sensuous contrast to the soft chafe and subtle pinch of the purple lace. Despite their mutual state of undress, or maybe because of it, Samantha had no desire to leave.

"Can I pour you a glass of Asti? This is my favorite," he admitted, his grin somewhat boyish, as if he was sneaking a glass of alcohol during his parents' dinner party.

He showed her the label and she smiled. "That doesn't cost more than fifteen dollars in a grocery store."

"The best things aren't always the most expensive."

Samantha laughed, then slid a chilled, empty flute toward him. She silently agreed that the Italian sparkling wine was delicious, but that wasn't the reason why she wanted to share a glass with Nick. There was an innocent decadence about it, a forbidden indulgence that seemed entirely safer than what she really wanted to do—shed her own terry-cloth robe so she could climb into his. Blaming the heat from the Sterno for the jump in her body temperature, she patiently waited for Nick to pop the cork and pour them both some wine.

"What's hiding under the other cover?" Nick asked, handing her a fizzling glassful.

She retrieved the wine, then leaned forward to reveal a glistening bowl of red, ripe strawberries.

"Oh, my," she said. "You must tip well. This is some spread."

"Are you hungry?"

Sam swallowed a mouthful of wine, knowing full well that a sip would be entirely more genteel and appropriate. But at the moment, she didn't care about propriety. Nick's voice was low and throaty. His dark lashes were lowered, shading his intense eyes just enough for her to know that he meant more than he said. His question brimmed with meaning beyond her appetite for food, and her answer had to match his, or she'd lose out on more than just a contest of wits.

Bubbles filled with courage trickled down her throat.

"I've been told I'm insatiable," she answered, plucking a berry from the bowl.

His expression didn't change.

"So have I. Maybe that's why I'm so good at what I do."

Sam stopped, smacking her lips closed before she took a bite. Okay, she was good at this tease thing, but he was better. Or they were at least evenly matched.

But he smiled when she did, and that knocked the tension down a peg. He was toying with her—and she with him. She shook her head while she took a bite of the large strawberry, closing her eyes as a burst of tart freshness filled her mouth. Nick was not only adept at the game of flirting, he made the interactions fun. Exciting. Charged and unpredictable.

Sam couldn't remember the last time she'd enjoyed such banter. She didn't know how he'd created the illusion, but she actually felt that, for once, she could let go and be herself and lose nothing in the process.

Couldn't be.

Impossible.

"What are we doing here, Nick?" she asked, not sure she wanted an answer since it might destroy the oddly wonderful combination of seduction and camaraderie they'd somehow created.

"So far, we're sharing delicious wine and, soon, a tempting dessert."

"Is that all?"

He shrugged and took a long sip. "The night's young. I told you, I'm a night owl. A hungry night owl."

"So have a strawberry," she said, choosing a second fruit, but this time lingering over the steaming praline sauce, prolonging the act of coating the berry in the delectable concoction.

"Oh, I intend to," he said, tilting his glass toward her before he drew in another measured sip. "But ladies first."

Nick sat back when Sam dragged her strawberry through the praline sauce in slow, undulating streaks, seemingly oblivious to the sensual rhythm she wove. His trained palate conjured the combined tastes of the buttery, browned sugar sauce, the crunchy pecans, and the tart fruit—all before she took a single bite. Before he stole the tastes from her.

His mouth watered. When Samantha licked her lips, then drew the dripping berry closer and closer to her mouth until she finally took a single ravenous bite, his taste buds exploded.

He knew each flavor, each texture, by heart. He knew the nuances well enough to combine them in his brain. Yet, he craved one special essence, one elusive extract only Samantha could add to the mix. A secret ingredient. Alluring. Subtle. Elemental to the union of sweet and sour on the tongue. His tongue with hers.

She bit and chewed slowly, lowering her lashes to half-mast as the heavenly flavors danced on her every feature. "Good God, Nick. You've got to try this."

He took a hearty sip of his Asti Spumante, ignoring the rush of effervescence, then stole the few inches he needed to reach her mouth with his.

"I intend to."

She met his gaze boldly. A tiny, strawberry-stained smile told him she wouldn't protest, propelling his appetite from hungry to ravenous—all for a taste of her.

Her mouth was softer, riper, than the fruit. Her tongue inherently sweeter. She smelled of pralines and perfume. Felt like velvet warmed by a fire. He'd intended to take only the briefest taste of her, but Sam moaned and grabbed the lapels on his robe. He couldn't back away.

But he had to give her one last chance. One final opportunity to stop the momentum.

But first, he finished kissing her. Thoroughly. Until he knew every contour of her mouth, every slick groove in her teeth, every pleasure spot on her tongue and lips.

"I can't believe we just kissed again," Samantha said, making absolutely no move to back away. Nick searched her eyes for any hint of regret, any inkling of anger at him or at herself.

He saw only pleasure. Intense desire.

"Fantasies do come true, I guess. I, for one, am damn glad," he said.

"But what are we doing? Living for the moment and enjoying each other—or believing our own press and taking our fake affair way too far?"

Nick respected every reason she had to question his timing. Their timing. Their motivations. They'd known each other for less than a day, and in that time, he'd shown her only slightly more than his established persona—the Nick even his family thought was the real him. The facade bought him a certain degree of separation, allowing him to operate as he needed to as CEO of the family business. He wore his confidence to the point of arrogance. He feigned flippancy to the emotions that drove a woman's heart.

But Sam's heart? From what he could tell, she protected her heart with all the vigilance of a seasoned bodyguard. She was a painfully private woman in an increasingly public world.

They were so alike, Nick steeled himself against a tremor of pure need.

"I won't be just some conquest…some shot to your ego," she insisted.

He smoothed his hands up and down her arms, hoping to disguise his own intense reaction to her honesty. He succeeded only in eliciting a soft purr from the back of her throat, the vibrations of which seeped straight into his skin. "A nearly naked woman hiding under my bed and accosting me in the shower is enough to last any man's ego for a lifetime."

Sam smirked and, on her, the wry smile looked remarkably sweet, especially so close up. They'd yet to pull away after their kiss and spoke nose to nose, like the intimate lovers they could be.

"Then we're just living for the moment? Enjoying what we have, here and now?"

Nick surrendered to the liquid blue of her irises and touched a kiss just above each eyebrow. Her lashes fluttered, tickling his chin.

"Sounds too good to be true," Nick confessed. "I can't remember the last time I've been with a woman who doesn't seem to *need* anything from me."

"You're so wrong, Nick."

"You don't need my money," he reasoned. Until this moment, he never would have described himself as jaded or disillusioned with women. He'd always viewed his doubting attitude as a practical, logical deduction based on a woman's ulterior motives.

But with Samantha, he didn't care what her ulterior motives were. In fact, he seriously doubted she had any. But if she had them, he suspected he'd willingly provide whatever she wanted just for the chance to slip inside her giving warmth.

"I do need your money," she protested. "I need this job. I told you that from the start."

He brushed his lips over her bangs, inhaling the spicy scent of her shampoo. "You could find something else in a heartbeat. You may need this job, but not enough to sleep with me to keep it."

She glanced down, shaking her head as she laughed lightly. "Then why should I sleep with you?"

Nick smoothed his palms along her cheeks, weaving his fingers into her fragrant hair, tilting her gaze to meet his. "Because I'm offering you one night, just for us." He pressed his lips against her soft cheek, just below where his thumbs caressed her skin. "A man." He kissed her chin, skipped her mouth, and placed a tender peck on the tip of her nose. "A woman." His hands trailed down her neck, dipping into the open collar of her robe. "An insatiable hunger."

Samantha's bold stare never left his. The dilation of her pupils and the slight rasp in her breathing were the only outward signs that she'd even heard his proposal. An expert negotiator, he appealed to what he knew she wanted most.

"No strings, Samantha. No expectations. An utterly discreet and private night for us alone."

Her gaze narrowed as she slipped her hands between them to work the knot on his robe. "You've left out the most important detail, Nick."

He straightened, wondering what he could possibly offer her that he hadn't already voiced. But the glint in her sapphire gaze told him she was toying with him again, manipulating him with the same skill that she used to release the tie on his robe and toss the terry cloth aside.

She nuzzled close, grazing her lips over his bare chest. Instantly, he knew exactly what sensual item he'd inadvertently forgotten to mention.

"Oh, you mean the part where I promise to make all your erotic fantasies come true?"

She stood so close, he felt the thrill shimmy up her spine and light her eyes with hot fire.

"I didn't forget, Samantha. There are just certain things that go without saying."

CHAPTER NINE

WITH A SINGLE GLANCE and a brief caress, a wealth of knowledge passed between them.

That she could trust him.

That the passion surging between them was natural and honest and undeniable.

That she was going to nourish his erotic fantasies at the same time he satisfied hers. And she knew *exactly* how.

She lifted herself on the balls of her feet and placed a brush of a kiss along the base of his chin, where a tiny, almost unnoticeable cleft hid beneath his incredible lips. She had one particular fantasy in mind that craved immediate attention, if for no other reason than to erase the picture of another woman accosting him in the shower.

"I'm feeling a little grimy after our long day." She whispered her confession directly into his ear.

"I should have invited you to share my shower."

She chuckled and shook her head, sliding her palm from his cheek to his chest, then across to his shoulder and down, where she clutched his hand in hers.

"Your shower was a little too crowded," she said, winking.

He rewarded her quip with a reluctant grin. "You're very funny, you know that?"

She wiggled her eyebrows, and he pulled her closer. He kicked his robe away and tried to grab the sash on hers, but she deflected the move with a skillful twist. She wanted Nick. She wanted to be naked with Nick. But the promise of a slow, deliberate seduction, the anticipation of a long-awaited payoff of the most sensual kind, outweighed both their needs to act quickly. Making love with him—tonight, with no promises, no commitments between them—filled her quota for spontaneity.

The rest would be planned and executed with her trademark precision.

Like the bathroom in Nick's half of the suite, hers also had candles on the dresser which she lit while he watched from the doorway. As soon as the fourth and final wick flared, Nick flipped the light switch, bathing the bathroom in a flickering kaleidoscope of warm light. The candles, doubled in intensity by their reflection in the mirror, were unscented, but as the flames warmed the intimate space around the vanity, Samantha smelled the unique fragrance seeping from her mother's brown paper box.

She slid the parcel closer to her as Nick entered the bathroom, shutting and locking the door behind him.

"I can't believe you haven't opened that yet. Aren't you curious?"

Sam fingered the taped edges. Whatever was leaking from inside had now darkened the paper from tan to chocolate. The substance was oily and slick on her skin. Nick came up behind her, examining the package from over her shoulder.

"What's that?"

Sam drew her hand to her nose, rubbing her fingers together as she inhaled the unusual mixture of scents. "Some kind of oil," she answered, and with each word, her fingers grew instantly hot. Her eyes widened. Possibilities most erotic scrambled her ability to speak any further.

"The aroma is so enticing, so—"

Sam turned around and smeared some of the oil across Nick's lips, silencing him. "The aroma is nothing compared to this."

She blew a soft breath on his mouth. The instant the heat flared on his lips was reflected in his eyes. He cooled the sensation with his tongue, and his grin, while narrow, spread effectively across his face.

"It's flavored and it reacts to air by getting hot? I think I'm going to like your mother."

Samantha turned around and unwrapped the box. "Thank my sister. I bet she and Brandon had a great time testing this."

Inside the box, Samantha found a small, antique glass vial of the potent mixture sealed with wax that had somehow cracked just enough to release the undeniable fragrance into the air—enough to spill some of the magic elixir and pique Sam's undeniable curiosity. Sam had no doubt that her mother sent the oil to somehow manipulate her or her present situation, but with Nick standing behind her, nuzzling her neck while his fingers deftly undid the sash on her robe, she didn't care. She took the bottle from the box and popped off the wax seal and tiny cork, both tied with twine made of natural hemp.

Dangling from the string was a pair of foil squares, and her grandmother's exquisite ruby ring.

Two out of three isn't bad, Sam recalled her guess about the box's contents. She plucked the condoms free, realizing they actually had more than two, and handed them to Nick. She hid the ring behind the artful fan of face towels the maid had crafted on the vanity. Despite her mother's cunning intentions, tonight wasn't about commitments or marriage or happily-ever-anythings.

Pleasure was their primary goal. Discovery and adventure and living for the moment, relishing sensations, focusing on nothing but this one erotic interlude—to milk the experience for every last drop of pure excitement.

Kind of like jumping off a building. Or driving a car rigged to explode when the wire is tripped.

Or jumping into a fray of frenzied females to rescue a

man that could, with a single, intimate touch, rescue her right back.

Sam swung around just as Nick snapped the sash out of the loops. He worked the robe off her with no resistance, his eyes alight at the revelation of her wicked purple bra and panties.

He perused her with brazen approval. "You didn't tell me your family dabbles in sex aids," Nick teased, tapping the slippery bottle she held.

Sam grinned, drawing tiny circles around the rim with the tip of her finger.

"With a little imagination, your pasta sauce could be a delicious sex aid."

As the possibility played in his mind, his tongue darted out to moisten his lips. "Have I told you that I like the way your mind works?"

He didn't have to tell her. Judging by the lascivious images popping into her brain with each and every glimpse she caught of his magnificent chest and shoulders, they were operating on exactly the same wavelength. "Have I told you that I like the way your body works?"

"You haven't seen my body work. Not yet."

She tilted one eyebrow as she glanced past him at the shower stall.

"That doesn't count," he insisted, obviously remembering that she'd seen him in the nude when she came to his aid in the shower.

"Sure it does." Sam tapped a small puddle of oil into her palm. "I may have only gotten a brief glimpse, but that's all I needed for inspiration."

She rubbed her hands together and moved to smear the slickness on him, but he caught her by the wrists to stop her assault. "I got more than a brief glimpse of you, Samantha. And you've been inspiring some incredibly sinful thoughts since we first met. Before I ever knew that you favored purple lingerie."

"What? When I tackled you and got you out of the crowd?"

Nick chuckled as he slowly turned her around, wrapping both her wrists in one big hand, so that when she faced the mirror, he could retrieve the other hand and control when she applied the oil. And where.

"Just a bit later," he replied. "When I tackled you against the door."

"That was just the static electricity," she claimed, inhaling sharply when Nick used his teeth to slide down the straps on her bra so they dangled off her shoulders. The demicups loosened and gapped, barely covering her aroused nipples.

"Maybe." Nick pressed his body completely against hers. His erection strained through his light cotton pajama pants, full and hard and long. "But let's see if we can't generate something a bit stronger."

He forced her hands together.

"Close your eyes," he whispered.

She watched his reflection in the mirror, intrigued by the shadows playing across his muscled shoulders, captured by the light flickering in his fathomless, dark green eyes. He dipped his head to deliver his next instruction on a warm breath directed into the shell of her ear.

"Trust me."

She let her lids drop. His strong, thick fingers and wide palms completely covered hers, holding them clasped together. The sensuous slide of the oil in her palms created desires more dangerous than any stunt she'd ever performed, stoking needs no lover to date had ever dared to satisfy.

The infused aromas of the massage oil intensified as her hands warmed the mixture at his command. Floral essences, sweet and exotic, battled with that elusive spice that had no name, but that she'd known her entire life. The scent of comfort. Hot tea on rainy days. Scented flames on sad nights. Soon the aromas meshed with Dominick's natural musk, already heightened and strengthened by a woodsy shampoo. Sam breathed in deeply, allowing the sensations to penetrate her completely, to float in on the warmth from the candles, to seep into her pores.

Nick pulled Sam's hands apart, guiding one hand to rest on her bare belly, the other to her shoulder.

"I bet that oil's feeling pretty slick right now. Is it hot?"

"Just warm."

"Want to heat it up?"

He slid her hand across her collarbone, stopping when her pinky touched the crisscrossed center of two thin cups of purple satin. Her fingers rested on the crest of her breast, centimeters from where her nipples peaked, straining for his touch. Her touch. Any touch.

"Your nipples are getting hard. Don't look," he said when her lashes fluttered. She complied, pressing her lids tighter. The sensations created by his voice, the warmth from the candles, the scents of the oil, overrode her need to see anything. She preferred to imagine.

"Do you ever touch yourself?"

She swallowed. "Of course."

"Have you ever touched yourself while a man watched?"

She attempted to swallow again, but there was no moisture left in her mouth. She managed to shake her head.

"Touch yourself, Samantha," he commanded, releasing her hands to quickly unhook the back of her bra. The material fell away. "Don't look, just touch." He braced his palms on her hips—flat, motionless, but raging with controlled fire that seeped straight from his skin to hers.

"You touch me, Nick."

He kissed a soft path from her shoulder to her neck, nuzzling her hair aside to nip at the lobe of her ear. "I will. Show me how."

For an instant, Sam felt dizzy. Swirls of orange and gold

light danced on the dark inside of her eyelids. Nick's tongue, wet and warm, caressed the tiny spot where her pulse raged on her neck, in sync and in rhythm with the throbbing between her thighs.

She wanted to do this. Touch herself. Not for her own pleasure, that would come when he took over the task, but for his. She had the means to drive him wild with wanting; the power to stoke his pleasure beyond his most decadent imagination.

She concentrated on the feel of her oiled palms against her belly. Slowly, she smoothed a slick path across her middle then upward, coating the underswell of her breasts with a light sheen of oil, cupping and lifting and massaging until the warm glaze covered every inch of her skin except her aureoles and nipples.

Nick's breath, ragged and hot on her neck, stopped when she said, "More oil."

Without releasing herself, she spread out her hands to accept the drops he placed on her fingertips. Licking her lips, she dabbed the hard pebbles at the center of her breasts. Sensation zinged through her, intensified Nick's hardening grip on her hips. She swirled the oil in erotic circles, outward, then back inward until she couldn't contain a pleasured coo.

Nick spun her around, lifting her with ease onto the vanity. Her eyes flashed open in time to see Nick bend his head and blow a thin stream of air directly at her nipple. The oil instantaneously reacted. The burning sensation, concentrated and focused, stole her breath. She grabbed his shoulders as he turned and ignited her other nipple.

Like the lighting of a match, the flare spread. The fire of the chemical interaction assailed her, but when Nick took her nipple in his mouth, he doused the heat on the surface of her skin only to ignite the burning deep within.

He tasted every curve and crevice of her breasts. He teased

and tormented until she combed her fingers, still oily and hot, through his hair and guided his mouth to hers. Their kiss was demanding, wet. Intimate beyond belief.

The flame from a candle nipped at Sam's back, so she slid the votives to the far corners of the vanity. When she turned around, Nick had retrieved the massage oil and was shaking a generous amount into his palm. He eyed her with devilish promise.

She licked her lips. "That's an awful lot of heat you're putting into your hands."

"I have a lot of skin to cover."

"Are you going to oil yourself up for me now?" she asked hopefully.

But when his gaze dipped to her legs, then to her panties, and back to her face, that optimism died a delicious death. He meant to make sure he had touched her completely before he allowed himself the same decadent pleasure.

NICK WATCHED the anticipation light Samantha's eyes. She leaned back against the mirror, naked except for the sheer panties he planned to ask her to take off any minute. She was fearless. Brazen. At ease with her sexuality like no woman he'd ever met. And yet, he spied a hint of shyness in the way she toyed with her bottom lip with her teeth.

The experience of experimenting, of destroying the boundary between fantasy and reality, was apparently as new to her as it was to him. And he couldn't imagine a more perfect partner to share the sensations with.

He clasped his hands together to warm the chill off the bottled oil. He glanced at her panties and without saying a word, she removed them, then rebelliously crossed her legs.

He frowned.

She smiled. "I can't just give you everything you want, can I?"

"You want me to work for it?"

Through the material of his pajamas, she tickled his inner thigh with her toe. "Well, you are a known workaholic. A little effort won't kill you."

He captured her ankle before her foot reached her easy-to-find target between his legs. "I wouldn't be so sure."

Gently, he pressed her foot flat against his stomach, scooting back a few inches so she could straighten her knee. Her calves were toned and sleekly muscled, but the satiny softness of her skin provided a perfect contrast. Nick attended her foot first, massaging her from toe to heel, then her ankle, calf and knee.

By the time he reached her thigh, his control weakened and he had to fight not to pick up the pace and rush to explore the amber curls and slightly swollen flesh torturing him in the candlelit darkness.

Leaning completely against the mirror, her eyes half-closed, her thighs half-spread, she freely moaned and cooed and sighed. She threatened to drive him crazy with wanting. Resisting her was like denying his need to breathe. He splashed more oil on his hands before he caressed the soft inner flesh of her leg, moving closer to the heat he so desperately craved.

Smoothing the oil up to her outer thighs, he slowly moved forward until he stood flush with the vanity, the center of her need only inches away. Her eyes flashed wide open when his thumbs grazed the tawny triangle, thumbnails skimming the sensitive folds of flesh hidden there.

She gripped the edge of the vanity. He leaned forward, kissing her softly, enjoying the taste and tease of her mouth in nips and brushes.

"Relax, Sam."

He swished another kiss across her lips, touching her intimately with his fingers at the same time.

"You'll make me come," she admitted.

He couldn't contain a chuckle. "Yes, ma'am, I will. That's the idea."

She shook her head, grabbing his hand when he moved to touch her again. "No, I mean, if you even *touch* me again, I'll come. Right now."

"You think it's too soon?"

She nodded, biting her bottom lip with such uncertainty that Nick felt his hardened heart crack. Samantha Deveaux, his woman of experience, his woman of power, who not only knew the world, but also could conquer it with a single quip, had no idea what good loving was all about.

"Come for me, Sam. Now. Then again. And again."

With each word, he stroked her. With each successive touch, he sought her mouth. Deepening his touch. One finger. Then two. Deepening his kiss. As she predicted, the quivers started instantaneously, followed by shallow pants of breath and a tightening of her thighs around his hand until she cried out his name.

The most glorious thing he'd ever heard.

He wanted to hear it again. And again.

Slowly, he coaxed her thighs wider, massaging away the tightness in her muscles, the clenched aftermath of her release. He oiled his hands and attended her other leg while she struggled to regain her composure, rediscover her control. He had no intention of allowing that, not when wild freedom was so much more delicious.

He knelt and blew a soft breath behind her knee.

"Nick," she gasped, grabbing his shoulders as he directed the stream up along the inside of her thigh, igniting a firestorm he meant to slake with the moisture pooling in his mouth.

Her fingernails dug into his skin, a bite of pleasured pain that intensified the throb in his groin. He'd never wanted a woman so intensely, so desperately, so much that he was not only willing to wait to have her, waiting was part of the thrill. He wanted to savor her pleasure first. Make her orgasm a potent prelude to his own.

He trailed a path slowly, laving and blowing a haphazard stream of air and fire until he reached her upper thigh. Tugging gently on her ankles, he scooted her forward until her subtle scent, enriched by the aromatic oil, made him dizzy with need. He ached to taste her, but first he'd stoke the flame of her desire with a concentrated current of breath, directed at the oil-slickened cleft he so wished to savor.

"Oh. Nick. So. Hot." She punctuated each word with a writhing whimper. He braced her thighs, held her still and blew again, this time floating her name on his focused exhale.

A needful cry from her lips cut short his protracted tease. He covered her full with his mouth, cooling her at the same time that he suckled the essence of her heat. Her sweetness intoxicated him. Her pleasured cries urged him to drink until she shook again with pure, feminine release.

He stood and kissed a soothing trail from her breasts to her chin. When he met her gaze, the clouds of passion had cleared from her eyes and a seed of embarrassment threatened to shatter their intimacy. Samantha's distaste for vulnerability threatened to sever the connection they'd only begun to build, so before she bolted, he lifted her off the vanity, cradling and caressing her while he tore off his pajama pants and turned on the water.

"Nick, I…"

"Shh…" He touched a slick finger over her mouth. "No regrets, Samantha. What we're sharing is honest. Real. And there's so much more."

She closed her eyes, sighed and curled into him. Her sweet surrender touched him in a deep, uncharted recess of his heart and he hardly had the time now to figure out why. But he knew that abdication and trust didn't come easily to a woman like

Sam, a woman who made her living and her reputation by staying in control. He felt honored. And the sensation nearly stole his balance along with his sanity.

When the water warmed to a pleasant heat, he carried her inside and slid the glass door shut. He dashed them both under the water, startling her into laughter, then kissing her squealing giggle into soft moans.

She broke the kiss, dipping her head back and letting the hot stream thoroughly saturate her hair. Her lashes darkened and dripped mascara down her cheeks, but he found the raccoon look adorable. However, he'd been around women long enough to know to keep that particular comment to himself.

Instead, he handed her a washcloth and soap.

"You can put me down, Nick," she said as she lathered the cloth and spread the foaming bubbles over her face.

"Then I won't be touching you."

"No, but you can watch me bathe."

He didn't need a more erotic incentive. He placed her feet on the slick tile carefully, making sure of her footing before he stepped away.

She rinsed her face clean of soap and makeup, then turned to challenge his expectant stare.

"You're too close."

"There isn't a lot of room for me to work with here, Samantha."

She glanced around him to the ledge in the corner.

"You can sit there. I've got a lot of oil to wash off. I need my space."

She sounded so practical and pragmatic, but Nick knew by the glint in her eye and her saucy smile that she intended to do a hell of a lot more than just remove the oil he'd so carefully placed on virtually every inch of her skin. She was going to torture him.

He sat on the ledge, crossed his arms over his chest…and grinned.

She held the washcloth beneath the showerhead and rinsed away the makeup stains, then lathered again, pushing the showerhead toward the wall so the water produced steam, but left her relatively dry except for the moisture already clinging to her flesh. She stopped before touching the frothy white square to her skin and sought his hungry gaze.

"Hmm. Where should I start?"

Despite the increasing steam, Nick felt his mouth run as dry as a desert lake.

She shifted her weight from one hip to the other, seemingly engaged in perusing her body to see which part needed washing first. Glancing up, she met his gaze beneath clean but thick lashes of dark gold.

"I'm pretty much greased everywhere, aren't I?"

He attempted to swallow, gaining enough moisture to speak. "Your neck."

She slid her hand down her throat, tilting her head and arching her back so her breasts thrust deliciously forward. She raised the cloth and started slow, deliberate ministrations.

From there, she moved to her shoulders, then her arms and hands. She stepped completely out of the shower's redirected stream, so the soap clung to her like a foamy cream. From there, she washed her rib cage and belly, leaving her breasts untouched, her skin dark beside the bubbles, her nipples even darker, harder despite the warmth of the enclosed stall.

She moved to wash her ankle, but made a show of not having enough room. Grinning, she placed one foot directly between his legs on the small tiled ledge, her toes brushing his soft sac.

She massaged her foot with the cloth, brushing against his erection with seeming innocence.

"You really got that stuff all over me, didn't you?" she asked, drawing the cloth up her calf.

"I tried my best," he quipped.

She grinned. "Well, no one can ever say your best isn't good enough."

She washed her knees and thighs, drawing sensual circles on her skin. He watched each rotation, measuring the closing distance to her downy curls, spying the jutting slopes of her breasts while she moved, rhythmically, in a soft rocking motion not unlike languorous lovemaking.

But before she reached her center, she switched legs and began again.

In no hurry, she teased him more boldly this time, sliding her foot beneath him, stroking him as she washed her toes, then cruelly abandoning him to finish her leg. He used the time wisely, slipping on the condom he planned to use very, very soon.

When she stood, two places on her body remained untouched. Two places he desperately wanted to touch again. She'd taken her time bathing, and he imagined years had passed since he'd last run his hands over her breasts or felt the dewy warmth between her thighs.

Licking her lips, she boldly handed him the cloth. He grinned, expectant and pleased. Until she turned and offered him her back.

She drew her hair over her shoulder. "I've left a couple of places for you. That's okay, right?"

He growled as he stood, snatching the cloth a little more roughly than this deliberate seduction dictated. He took a deep breath, forcing himself to wash her slowly.

"You're very, very good at this." She writhed beneath his touch, giving him precisely the incentive he needed. Samantha Deveaux was an amazing woman. Beautiful. Sensual. And smart. She played to his ego and he fell for her compliment hook, line and sinker.

Once her back was completely lathered, he stepped fully

against her, his erection snug against the small of her back, his sacs gently slapping her bottom as he rocked into her. "You're not so bad yourself. You're driving me insane, Samantha."

He wrapped his arms completely around her. She sighed, lifted her arms over her shoulders and slipped her soapy hands into his hair, pulling herself ever-so-minutely upward, so that his erection slid against the soapy curve of her lower back. "I think I like you insane."

Curling his arms, he thoroughly lathered her breasts. The bubbles, a diaphanous lubricant, mingled with the oil already spread on her skin. The slick sheen on her flesh and her mindless, pleasured cries urged him to wash harder, rougher over her nipples. When she whispered his name, he dipped the cloth between her legs.

She answered his action with an unbridled, "Yes!"

He held his breath, closed his eyes and let the cloth drop to the shower floor so he could spread the soap with his fingers. Her feminine folds were slick and hot. The wet warmth that curled around his hand came not from the water or the foam, but from the intimate place deep within her, the place he longed to greet with his own insatiable need.

She bent forward just enough to invite his erection between her legs. She stroked and manipulated his pulsing head into her slippery passage.

Nick groaned as he slid inside. She felt like hot velvet on a cold night, completely enveloping him in a sensation that was comfortable and warm, then instantly turned scalding to the point of pain. The instinct to drive hard—to reach her core and release the delights hidden there—was nearly impossible to fight, but he struggled and won. Gently, he guided her hands onto the marble wall, where the misdirected showerhead spewed a steamy spray that forced them both to close their eyes or be blinded by the shardlike mist.

Then Samantha started to move, rocking with an undeniable rhythm—an irresistible tempo that pulsed straight to the part of him that was nothing but pure and simple male need. He matched her movements, echoed her pleasured cries until even the powerful water swirling around them was no match for the tempest they created.

With unbridled thrusts, Nick gave Samantha every inch of him. With indulgent moans, she took what he gave, then slipped one hand off the wall and wrapped her fingers around the back of his neck, pulling herself closer. Forcing him deeper. Destroying every flailing thought in his mind except one.

Join.

Their climax was loud and long and followed by sensuous strokes and soft words and eventually, a gentle, mutual laughter. Nick pulled the showerhead from the wall and rinsed Sam clean of soap. She did the same to him, then flipped the faucet off. A thick fog surrounded them. Ensconced in the mystic, dreamlike cloud, Nick silently wondered if any of this was real. Samantha. The free, limitless boundaries of their lovemaking.

The emotions raging through him. Admiration. Wonder. Excitement.

Sam slipped her arms around his waist and laid her head on his chest. "That was new."

"You've never showered with a lover before?"

Sam leaned back and glanced up at him with a wounded look so exaggerated, he knew she was simply reverting to her natural inclination to tease him. "How many lovers do you think I've had?"

He kissed her impertinent nose. "Don't know. Don't care."

One golden eyebrow tilted and he could see she wasn't entirely convinced. "What about you? You've never showered with any of your lovers before?"

Nick laughed aloud at the idea of Blair allowing her makeup to run or her hair to get wet—or Sophia agreeing to lovemaking anywhere except the confines of a bed. He'd had other lovers, of course, but none of those women had ever enticed him to share anything so personal, so erotic.

"I can honestly say this was a fantastic first."

The pride that lit Samantha's eyes rewarded him for his honesty. Her next suggestion was a good old-fashioned, New Orleans styled lagniappe. Something extra. Something unexpected.

"Care to try for a second?"

CHAPTER TEN

AROUND 4:00 A.M., they stopped counting. Sam listened to Nick sleeping, her head tucked in the crook of his arm, his hard pectoral muscle softened by a downy pillow. She closed her eyes, determined to sleep, determined to keep her mind from analyzing all that had happened between them—all the intimacies they'd discovered and shared, both physical and spiritual. In between their lovemaking, they'd polished off the strawberries and the bottle of sparkling wine while he told her about his family. About his responsibilities to his family. About his utter devotion to making sure his company was so solvent, so successful, that if anyone in the LaRocca line ever needed anything money could buy, he'd have no trouble providing the cash.

Sam shifted in Nick's sleeping arms, marveling at all she'd learned in one rather brief conversation. From his confident demeanor, she'd assumed the LaRoccas had always had money—always enjoyed success. She'd been surprised to discover that Nick came from humble roots—that his grandmothers hadn't started their business in earnest until ten years ago, when the restaurant they ran in Chicago's theatre district stumbled onto hard times. Fresh out of business school, Nick had helped his Nanas build an empire that not only put the restaurant back on its feet, but also provided incomes for every family member who wanted a job.

He was barely thirty-five, but he had become the patriarch

of a tightly woven fabric of family. No wonder he was willing to work so hard to keep it all together.

A smudge of praline sauce, cool after they'd extinguished the Sterno, had dropped onto her lap, effectively stopping any further conversation. Then a while later, sated by food, drink and sex, they found themselves in his bed and Nick asked Samantha to reciprocate with stories of her own. But she'd effectively distracted him with coos and kisses until tales of her home life were no longer important to him.

Then, he'd fallen asleep, leaving Samantha to wonder how much, if anything, she should tell him when he woke.

Unable to put the matter to rest, Sam slid out of bed and into one of the terry-cloth robes they'd left on the floor. She inhaled the lapel, trying to determine who'd worn the garment last, but their scents were so intermingled, she couldn't tell. The entwined fragrances of his shampoo, her perfume, the massage oil and sweet, browned sugar engendered an immediate melancholy Sam didn't want to feel.

Tonight was about tonight, she reminded herself. No commitments. No regrets. Pleasure for the moment. In the moment.

Despite the robe, she shivered.

She slipped into the outer room, dark except for the lights on Poydras Street glowing through the wall of windows on the other side of the conference table. She poured herself a snifter of cognac and slid her hip onto the credenza beside the window, staring out onto the business district, a portion of the city she barely knew. Yet even if her view was of the French Quarter, she wouldn't have known much more. She'd been away for so long. Too long. She'd come home to find her roots, connections to her family and her past that had been ripped and torn during her parents' divorce.

What she'd found instead was a man she could love, if only he didn't have to leave. If only he didn't have responsibilities and interests that would inevitably and rightfully be more important than her.

She'd lived that kind of life with her father. Devlin Deveaux always had a big studio, a crew of technicians and actors, a career milestone that came before she did on his list of priorities. He depended on her to understand, to pick up the slack and pay the electric bill and fix his breakfast and make sure the housekeeper had his laundry done. She'd developed an interest in the film industry only to be closer to him. Hell, if she dug a little deeper, she'd admit that she'd only moved in with Anthony, the star of her father's latest, highest-budget film, to get a reaction out of Devlin—maybe some anger or a touch of concern that she'd risk her heart with such a well-known heartbreaker.

Instead, he'd been thrilled that she was keeping his headliner happy. Not that she hadn't truly been attracted to Anthony. His perfect features and devastating smile made him impossible for any woman to resist. She'd even grown to respect him as an actor and care for him as a good friend. But when the photos of their limousine tryst came to light, he'd considered allowing their release simply to further his career. Publicity was, after all, publicity. Good or bad.

She'd finally convinced him to change his mind, but the damage to their relationship was done. He was no better than her father, willing to sacrifice her for his own needs.

She'd sworn she'd never again involve herself with anyone—a man especially—who might even entertain the notion of using her to get what they wanted.

Yet, hadn't she invited Nick to do exactly the same thing?

Her thoughts weren't so deep or indulgent that she didn't sense him all the way across the room the minute he appeared in the doorway. After all they'd shared, she knew she'd detect his undeniable presence even in the largest crowd. He paused in the threshold a moment, fully nude and glorious, then strode

ross the darkness as if he wore a designer tuxedo. His self-
surance acted like a magnet to her wounded, restless heart and
e could feel a renewed desire to reach out for his attention.

She shook her head and took a sip of the brandy, suspect-
g she'd need the full breadth of her resistance to fight the el-
ental, emotional pull Nick cast over her. Heat burned down
r throat, settling the quivers that shook her as he approached.

"Aren't you exhausted?" he asked.

"Too tired to sleep, I guess." She attempted a smile, but
e action only provoked a deepening of Nick's furrowed
pression.

"What's wrong? No, wait. Stupid question for any man to
k a woman. You'll just say, 'nothing,' and we're back to
uare one."

As much as she fought the reaction, his dead-on observa-
on evoked a genuine smile.

"You have a busy day ahead of you, Nick. Go back to
eep. I'll just finish this and then join you."

He slipped into the space between the credenza and a
otted palm, his naked thighs brushing against her knees.
You have a busy day, too. Following me around. Pretending
be my lover."

"Guess that won't tax my acting abilities anymore, will it?"

She knocked back the last of the cognac, then handed him
e glass and moved to slip off her perch on the credenza. He
warted her sudden need to escape by caressing her cheek
ith his palm, touching her with a gentleness that held her still.

"Is this about regrets, Samantha?"

Without thinking, she pressed her face closer to his hand.
ithout thinking. Her instincts, primal and strong, lured her
this man like a lioness to her chosen mate. He could sate
r hunger. He could ensure the continued survival of her
omanhood, the element of her body, soul and spirit that
ctated the feminine needs she'd ignored for so long.

"I don't regret making love with you, Nick. But th
doesn't mean I'm certain it was a wise choice. For either
us."

Nick slid the empty snifter onto the windowsill th
brushed a lock of her hair out of her face and twirled it arou
her ear. The sensation of his fingertip, rough against the se
sitive skin, evoked a renewed flame deep within her. A flic
ering pulse sparked between her legs. Her nipples tighten
and she couldn't help but sigh.

God help her. She was farther gone than she realized.

Nick drew a lazy line from her earlobe, beneath her chi
then up until he traced the soft curves of her mouth. "Did v
really have a choice?"

She shook her head, determined to defy the sensual spe
he wove. "We always have a choice."

"Do we? Really?" With each word, he lowered his fac
Inch by inch, his mouth neared hers. She searched his ga
for any hint of machination, any spark of untruth in what I
said or did that would give her the means to elude him,
protect her heart before she fell too far into the well of nee

But just as his lashes closed over his dark green gaze, sl
saw nothing but pure, raw desire. With his kiss, she su
cumbed to the craving—concentrated and intense. She w
too tired to fight, too overwhelmed to struggle.

In the morning, she'd use the dawn to show him that the
had no business opening this Pandora's box of unfettere
desire. Nothing lasting could come of their pairing. After tl
ecstasy wore away, they'd have nothing but emptiness.

In the morning. Because right now, with Nick's han
slowly pushing her robe aside and his mouth trailing a h
path to her breasts, Samantha had never felt so full.

"ROOM SERVICE," the voice responded. After yesterday, Ni
knew better than to fall for that ruse again, but this time the voi

ᵥas familiar. Very familiar. Like a voice he'd been hearing his
ᵢntire life. His lungs clenched. A pit formed in his throat.

No. Not here. Not today.

He said a brief prayer before he peered through the
ᵨeephole, then swore up at heaven for having no mercy.

Nana Rose.

"Dominick Michael LaRocca, you open this door this
ᵢnstant!" When she started muttering in Italian, Nick unhinged
ᵢhe lock, took a deep breath and pulled open the door with a
ᵨatient smile.

"Nana Rose, what are you doing here?"

Her pointed glare erased the bogus grin off his face, though
ᵢe still bent forward for the obligatory kiss on the cheek.
ᵀhey'd barely exchanged the greeting when his grandmother
ᵐade a startling snuffling noise and waved past him. "What
ᵐ I doing here? What am I doing here?" Her volume esca-
ᵢated with each repetition. "I'm sitting in my easy chair, bottom
ᵨf the ninth, Cubs up by one and the scoring run on third base
ᵥhen WGN scrolls a little news flash across the bottom of my
ᵢcreen. Good thing Fae insisted we buy the big-screen televi-
ᵢion for the ball games. I'd have missed it, so small."

"Missed?"

Her harrumph and iced stare told him she knew about his
ᵢnvolvement with Samantha. He started forward to explain,
ᵦut she put a stop to that with one palm-out gesture.

"Stay at the door!" she ordered, her petite form waddling
ᵦeneath a covered tray of *sciaccata,* the thick-doughed pizza
ᵢhe brought with her whenever she visited anyone, anywhere.
ᵀRafaela and Anita are right behind me. They stopped in
ᵢnita's suite to drop off our bags."

She popped the tray right on top of the papers he'd been
ᵢooking over while Samantha showered and dressed in his
ᵣoom. He listened, but from this distance he couldn't hear the
ᵥater running or determine if she knew they were no longer

alone. He'd shut the door for precisely that purpose. He wa
finding it hard enough getting any work done with so littl
sleep and an hour-long interview with the police. Just th
sound of her turning on the water had his body instantly read
to relive the sensuous washing they'd shared the night befor
But he'd already scheduled a meeting with Anita to reviev
the vital numbers for the European distribution deal. Whe
he'd called her room to cancel, even at the ungodly hour o
6:00 a.m., she hadn't answered her phone.

Now he knew why. She'd been summoned to fetch the
grandmothers and hadn't done a damn thing to warn him.

"Anita knew you were coming?"

Rose smiled, flipping off the striped cloth that hid his favorit
food underneath. The scents of garlic, Romano cheese an
olive oil wafted into the air. Real Italian pizza from the Ol
World.

"Of course not. We called her midflight to pick us up."

Nick swore under his breath, but his grandmother scolde
him with piercing eyes nonetheless.

He thrust his hands on his hips and scowled back. Disre
spectful or not, every once in a while he had to remind hi
meddlesome grandmother that he was no longer a little boy
"So you heard about Samantha and couldn't get here fas
enough to check her out."

Rose shook her finger at him. "Watch your tone
Dominick. We're here because we have business to discuss

Nick's spine reverberated with the serious tone of her voice
Nana Rose rarely, if ever, got truly angry. Fits of temper wer
usually left for Rafaela, the younger of the two by a year or so
Though the women only became related when Nick's fathe
married Nick's mother, they'd been inseparable friends sinc
their childhood in Sicily. Their families had come over t
America together just before the First World War. Rose and Fa
had attended the same schools, learned English together, dis

covered cooking in the same kitchens, had even, by their own embellished accounts, been courted by some of the same men.

After Rose married Vincente LaRocca and Fae wed Salvatore Durante, they continued their friendship until they successfully arranged for their two eldest children to fall in love. Nick's parents, who'd remained silent about the grandmothers' scheme to find Nick a wife, often joked about being the last arranged marriage in the New World. But the truth was, they'd been married for over forty years and were still going strong.

Now Rose and Fae had their sights set on Nick, and no doubt, they weren't happy that he'd gone and found a woman without consulting them first.

"There he is!"

Rounding the corner in the hallway with Anita cradling her thin arm, Nana Fae was all smiles and kisses when she crossed the threshold.

"Oh! This is a lovely room. Look at the view, Rose."

"I'd rather look at what Signore Lover-boy has planned for the European distribution of our marinara line," Nana Rose replied, with a tad more snip than his grandmother normally employed.

Nick shut the door, perplexed. He shot Anita a look that begged for some help, but she shrugged her shoulders and shook her head, obviously as confused as he was.

The introduction of LaRocca products into the overseas market had been Nick's idea from the beginning, and until today, his worry. His grandmothers normally concerned themselves more with recipes and promotion, leaving placement and distribution issues entirely up to Nick and Anita. The notion of taking an Italian-American product into the European marketplace—where genuine foods from Italy were commonplace—was a calculated risk, but one Nick was convinced would take LaRocca to the next level of worldwide success.

Unfortunately, to breach the tight market, Nick had to do

business with the most powerful food distributor in Italy, one
Franco Bomini. Though raised in the United States, Franco had
returned to his birthplace in Rome to launch a billion-dollar
brokerage business. Bomini, who grew up in the same Taylor
Street neighborhood as his grandparents, was violently disliked
by both the LaRocca and the Durante clans. Nick never pressed
for details, figuring that the past was the past, and so long as
his grandmothers didn't expressly object, he could solicit the
man's business without worrying about whatever personal
rancor existed between the man and Nick's family.

But now, with Nana Fae oddly quiet at one end of the conference table and Nana Rose practically ranting at the other,
he was worried. Very, very worried.

"You made me promise to handle the Bomini deal myself,"
Nick reminded Rose. "You didn't want to be involved. Why
the interest all of a sudden?"

Rose's dark eyes narrowed into slits. "Because I'm not the
only one who watches the Cubs play baseball."

Nick took over for Anita, helping Fae, who had trouble
with her knees, sit in a comfortable chair, with arms, at the
conference table.

"*Grazie,* Dominick," Fae spoke, patting his cheek lovingly.
"Rosalia, *sederie.*"

As Fae ordered, Rose accepted Dominick's proffered chair.

Anita busied herself making a fresh pot of coffee at the wet
bar. Nick, sideswiped by his grandmothers' sudden arrival,
chose to stand near the window and lean against the same
credenza Samantha had retreated to when he found her missing
from his bed last night. Her look had been sad and pensive, but
she'd responded to his touch with an eagerness that belied his
first suspicion that she regretted their lovemaking.

But if she didn't regret their liaison last night, she surely
would once she came through that still-closed bedroom
door. He tried to devise a means to warn her…then realized

that her presence in his suite, with his grandmothers, the matchmakers, there as witnesses, was *exactly* what he should want.

Suddenly, he was torn. Protect Samantha or thwart his grandmothers' marriage scheme? He didn't realize how conflicting those goals would be. To save him from the unwanted attention of strangers, he'd have to sacrifice Samantha's reputation. He didn't like the cost one damn bit.

But Rose interrupted his thoughts by rapping on the table. "I got a call last night just as that no-good second baseman struck out and left the runner stranded at third."

Nick nodded. The Cubs had lost again, which accounted for part of his grandmother's foul mood.

"And this is related to our distribution how?"

"Franco Bomini—" Rose paused after speaking the name, as if she might spit to remove the bad taste from her mouth "—was in Chicago last night, visiting his new great-granddaughter."

Nick's gut clenched. "Bomini is in the States?"

Rose nodded, her mouth in a grim line. "He stayed up late to watch the game with his son-in-law, when all of a sudden he reads that you are romantically involved with some woman you picked up at the Food Expo."

Nick checked his temper even as his blood raged. He didn't like the tone of his grandmother's voice, the implication that Samantha was nothing but some stranger he'd met in a crowd.

She had been only that when they'd first met— God, less than twenty-four hours ago. But even before they'd made love, she'd already become more to him. How? He had no idea. And he certainly couldn't work the logic through with his grandmothers staring up at him with disapproving eyes.

"First of all, Samantha Deveaux is a lovely woman," he clarified. "She saved my life, no thanks to you two. Your little practical joke has women tearing at my clothes and literally jumping out from under my bed. I won't even tell you about the naked nuns in the lobby."

Fae giggled while Rose crossed herself to ward off any possible blasphemy. Nick looked up in time to see Anita slip seamlessly into his bedroom.

"Well, maybe Fae and I acted a bit rashly, but the truth is, Dominick, you *have* to settle down. Now more than ever. You know how Franco feels about indiscriminate personal behavior."

Nick dug his hands into his pockets. "Yes, he's very European. Marriage is a must. Mistresses are also a must, but should be kept discreetly."

Even Rose sniggered at his true assessment of Bomini's continental attitude. Fae remained quiet. While his grandmother Rose and her husband, Vincente, made no secret of their personal dislike for the man, they knew enough about the food business to know that only Bomini could break their American company into the European market. Fae remained, as always, totally silent on the matter. So far as Nick knew, she wouldn't even speak Bomini's name.

"According to the video on the evening news, you and this Miss Deveaux have not been very discreet. Bomini can't see how he should do business with a man who flaunts his romances on the television."

Nick took a deep breath. Now was not the time to point out, yet again, that he wouldn't be in this situation if his grandmothers hadn't schemed to force his marriage.

"I suppose you want me to fly to Chicago and smooth his ruffled feathers."

"No need," Rose said, waving her hand. "He's coming here."

"To New Orleans?"

Nick asked the question at the same time as Nana Fae. Her eyes were filled with something akin to terror, an emotion he'd never seen in his indomitable grandmother's gaze.

"Why do you think we flew down in the middle of the night? To bring you *scacciata* and meet your new lady friend?"

Nick stared, eyes wide, needing nothing verbal to acknowledge the obvious.

"Well, of course we did that, too. So, where is she?"

As if on cue, the door to the bedroom opened and Samantha emerged, a slight stumble in her first step as if she'd been pushed. Anita poked her head out from behind her, folding her lips together to contain a raging fit of laughter.

Nick shook his head, then massaged his forehead. When he looked up, both his grandmothers were staring at him, perplexed and impatient.

He did the honors with less enthusiasm than he should have. "Nana Rose, Nana Fae, this is Samantha Deveaux."

Sam smiled. "It's a pleasure to meet you both."

Anita scurried to the wet bar to pour cups of coffee and serve them to their grandmothers, still quiet as they assessed Samantha from head to toe. Dressed for their scheduled lunch appointment with the head of a Northwest grocery chain, she wore a black turtleneck and blazer, blue jeans and boots. With her hair pulled back in a ponytail and her face sporting just enough makeup to bring out her luminous eyes and generous lips, she looked as vivacious and athletic as she'd proved to be in his bed, and as casual and comfortable in her own skin as any woman he'd ever known.

He smiled, confident that his grandmothers would like her, then frowned, wondering why in the hell that should suddenly be important to him.

Rose turned and whispered over her shoulder. "She stayed here last night?"

Nick cast an unrepentant grin at his Nana. "This is the twenty-first century, Nana."

"Yes, well, women stayed the night with men in my

century, too," Rose countered. "Difference was, in the morning, you married them, or their brothers hunted you down with a gun."

"Do you have brothers, dear?" Fae asked, not as innocently as she intended. Anita didn't bother to hide a snicker and Rose huffed her disapproval at being thwarted.

Sam had the dignity to hide her smile. "No, ma'am. I have a sister, though. She lives here in New Orleans, but she's on her honeymoon."

"How sweet. *Per favore,* come sit beside me."

Samantha joined Fae without hesitation, giving Rose an extra-wide smile before she sat. "This is a little awkward," she admitted, instantaneously earning Fae's sympathy judging by the look on his grandmother's face.

Nick was impressed. One down, one to go.

"Of course it is. We don't usually barge in on Dominick," Fae said, turning her head toward Rose, her expression brimming with chastisement. "And we won't again. But now that we're here, tell us a little about yourself."

"The news said your mother is a psychic?" Rose asked, her tone slightly skeptical.

Sam grinned. "Yes, ma'am. I'm afraid I don't come from a conventional family. My father is Devlin Deveaux, the film director."

As the conversation grew and expanded, Nick circled over to the bar, watching as Sam slowly but surely won his grandmothers' approval. She was honest, funny, forthcoming and respectful. She asked questions about Rose and Fae's other grandchildren, about their lives in Chicago and their childhoods in Sicily. She even admitted a little more than he expected about her life in Hollywood—and the lack of family ties that bothered her most.

After an hour had passed, they'd shared Rose's pizza, coffee and a good dose of mutual liking. When Sam excused herself to freshen up before they left for their appointment, Nick exhaled a confident breath. If nothing else, his worries about his grandmothers' meddling in his private life, at least for the moment, were over. If they liked Samantha as much as he suspected, they'd soon call off their quest to find him a wife.

"So," he said confidently, "I take it you find her as charming as I do."

"Very much so, Dominick," Fae said, smiling. "It's no wonder you forgot your upbringing and took her to bed the first night you met her."

Anita spat out her coffee. Nick had a damn hard time swallowing the last of his. While Rose was infamous for her straight-to-the-heart-of-the-matter assessments, Fae was usually more discreet.

She silenced them both with a nonchalant wave. *"Va' la, non fare l'innocentino."*

Nick and Anita obeyed, wiping the "so innocent butter would melt in their mouths" look off their faces.

"Things don't work so differently in this twenty-first century of yours as it did in ours," Rose said. "You've bedded her. Ordinarily, that's a private matter between the two of you."

"Ordinarily?"

With a nod, Rose opened her basket-weave purse and produced a folded document. The blue back page told Nick it was something legal. When he took the pages from his grandmother, he recognized the contract he'd signed when his grandmothers appointed him chief executive officer of the company.

"Read section eight, sub-paragraph C," Rose instructed.

Nick tore at the pages until he found the section she indicated. He'd read each and every word of the contract before he signed it six years ago. Hadn't he? The words blurred, first with disbelief and then with anger.

Words like *moral turpitude, scandalous* and *family values* jumped out at him.

"A morals clause?" he bit out. He didn't remember signing this. He knew he had, but he'd probably ignored the clause in deference to his Old World grandmothers and their Old World ideas.

Both Rose and Fae met his outrage with stoic faces. "An insurance policy." Rose stood, her gnarled fingers braced on the table. "Fae and I worked too long and too hard to lose this company to scandal. You made a spectacle of your affair with Miss Deveaux. Now, you'll make it right."

She gestured for Fae to gather her things and then waddled behind her to help her stand.

"What do you mean 'make it right'?"

After Rose was certain Fae had her balance, she looked up and skewered him with a pointed stare. "Has the English language changed so much with the new century? You'll make it right. You'll marry her and keep this scandal from embarrassing the family. You'll marry her or you'll lose your job."

CHAPTER ELEVEN

GET MARRIED? Sam clamped her hand over her mouth. She didn't know whether to feel guilty for eavesdropping or indulge in the hysterics she held tight in her belly. She contained her laughter, not wanting the family to hear her outburst. She was certain that, to them, this situation wasn't the least bit humorous.

She pressed her ear to the bedroom door, trying to decipher the raised voices, then realized most of the conversation had now lapsed into the LaRoccas' native tongue. Since her knowledge of Italian ended at *ciao, baby,* Samantha numbly paced to the bed and sat.

Nick had to marry her or lose his job?

Her wonder at the irony lasted for about ten seconds. With all the talk that had gone around that conference table about this being the twenty-first century, the archaic clause shouldn't be causing any friction at all. The obvious solution to this problem resided with her, and she'd take care of this mess right now, before Nick said something to his grandmothers that he might regret—or vice versa. She marched into the fray with a patient smile and stood there, rocking on her heels with her hands clasped behind her back until Rose, Fae, Anita and Nick all acknowledged her presence with testy stares.

She rewarded them with the sweetest smile she could muster. "Sorry to interrupt." She made sure her voice reflected only a tiny ounce of true apology. Nick and Anita

might be accustomed to being pushed around by their grandmothers, but adorable and well meaning though they were,
Sam couldn't allow her future to be dictated by strangers. She
had enough trouble with her own mother, who'd attempted
to speed Sam's involvement in a committed relationship along
with an engagement ring, massage oil and some condoms.
Maybe Endora was truly clairvoyant. They'd already indulged
in the oil and prophylactics. Now she had a way to use her
great-grandmother's jewelry as well.

"Samantha, you don't have to get involved," Nick assured
her. He swiped his hand through his hair and took a deep, apparently fortifying breath. "I'll handle this."

She didn't doubt Nick could make this situation go away,
but she didn't know what the outcome would do to his relationship with his family. Her method was quicker. Cleaner.

"There's nothing to handle, Nick."

She slipped her great-grandmother's ruby ring off her right
hand where she'd put it this morning for safekeeping. With a
purposeful march, she handed Nick the ring. "Ask me to
marry you."

"What?"

She pursed her lips. When his rage kept him from recognizing her subtle hint, she winked. "You heard your grandmothers.
You don't want to lose your job, do you? Ask me to marry you."

Nick blinked several times. He hesitated, but began to do
as she asked, perhaps out of curiosity alone.

"Will you—"

"Oh, no," she stopped him, simply because she could. A
trill of excitement, of expectant pleasure, surged through her.
This might be all make-believe, but Sam was an expert in that
department. Besides, this might be the only proposal she ever
got. "Down on one knee. I do have my standards."

Behind him, Nick's grandmothers quietly nodded. Oh,
how she hated to disappoint them.

Nick complied, taking her left hand in his. "Samantha Deveaux, will you do me the honor of becoming my wife?"

For the briefest instant, Sam allowed her imagination to shift her into a romantic dream where she had brought Nick to his knees in want of her. Where he lifted her into his arms after her teary-eyed acceptance and carried her to the bed to make mad, passionate love.

Only in the movies, she mused. Except for the mad, passionate love part, which she figured would soon be over for good.

"No," she answered.

"What?" Rose nearly broke a hip thrusting her fists in outrage. Fae, like Anita, merely covered her mouth to contain a laugh.

"I won't marry him. He asked. I declined. He's done his duty by your morals clause. That contract can't force me to become his wife, can it? And really, Mrs. LaRocca, that's a dirty trick to play on your grandson. Especially one who loves you both so much."

With a gentle tug, Sam helped Nick stand. He gazed down at her and his expression stole her breath. Was he disappointed? Amused? Hurt? Damn, she couldn't tell. He brushed a soft kiss across her cheek, then turned to his grandmothers and gestured with a flourish.

"There you go," he concluded.

Rose threw up her hands, thwarted again but not down for the count. She gazed at Samantha intensely, but Sam knew her act of defiance had raised her in Rose's esteem. She could see the respect in the older woman's focused gaze.

"That doesn't solve our problem with Franco Bomini," Rose said. "He may have the morals of an alley cat, but he doesn't do business with people he doesn't respect. Right now, he's looking for an excuse *not* to do business with us."

"Putting Dominick's picture on our pasta sauce played right into his hands." Fae waved to Anita to help her sit again, this time choosing the more comfortable love seat, indicating to Sam that a LaRocca family strategy session was about to ensue.

"I should check on security for your meeting, Nick." Sam noted the time on her watch. Since she'd just declined an offer to officially join the LaRocca family, she thought it best to make herself scarce. "We're scheduled to leave in an hour."

Rose scuttled beside Fae and lowered herself into the cushions. "No, no, young lady. I think we need you here. It's clear you don't appreciate other people making decisions for you. You're a quick thinker. We may need your help."

Sam smiled at the compliment, wondering if she could ever convince her mother of her ample intelligence or her need for independence so easily. She'd come home to attempt to repair the rift her parents' divorce had caused between her and her family, and yet, sitting down with the LaRoccas, obvious experts in family values, she realized that her moves toward true reconciliation with her mother had been nothing more than lip service. To mend the damage, they'd actually have to have a conversation. Maybe even a loud fight instead of sharp barbs and innuendos.

But for now, Sam slid onto the recliner across from Nick's grandmothers, determined to help them however she could, save marrying her grandson and moving to Chicago.

"Is Mr. Bomini a superstitious man?" Sam asked.

Fae looked down at her hands while Rose twisted her mouth in thought. "Of course. No self-respecting Italian man isn't afraid of a good curse. Are you planning to call your mother?"

Sam shook her head. Endora wasn't too keen on curses. She preferred to deal with only positive forces and clean, white magic. *What the hell was she thinking?* Sam didn't believe in her mother's mumbo jumbo. But asking for her mother's help—willingly—might be a gesture to benefit them all.

"I will call her if we need her, but she doesn't really do

curses. But she might, under special circumstances. I was just throwing out ideas. Brainstorming."

Rose nodded, smiling. "Trust me, Samantha. I don't need a psychic to deliver a potent curse. But you should call your mother anyway."

"Why?"

"She's your mother, isn't she?"

Sam nodded, unnerved that Nick's grandmothers had the same intuitive powers her mother owned without all the costumes and drama. Did women achieve some special power just by giving birth? Sam shook her head, confusion and anxiety building with each passing moment. The fact that Nick stood just behind her, silent, didn't help. His pensive vibrations echoed through her—from the tense set of his shoulders to his measured circular pace.

She glanced over her shoulder, attempting a peek at his expression. He turned just as she did, denying her a clear view of his face.

Nick toyed with the ruby ring Sam had handed him, aware that she watched him. Practice allowed him to keep his face emotionless. Stoic. He was angry. Damn angry. Though her spontaneous and brilliant charade of a refused proposal had thwarted his grandmothers and effectively saved his job, the aftermath unnerved him. He simply didn't like it when someone told him no, that was all. Right? Even in pretense, Dominick LaRocca didn't get on his knees just to be denied.

Or did his fury stem from somewhere deeper? For a brief, unreal instant, he'd secretly hoped Samantha would consent to be his wife. Until last night, he'd thought that the woman he'd been seeking for a soul mate was nothing like Samantha. That their affair was a mutually beneficial dalliance. A way to pleasurably pass the time.

In marriage, he'd wanted a woman who was quiet. No opinions of her own, except for those he couldn't be bothered with. Someone who would mold her life to fit his demanding, important schedule.

How boring. How arrogant. As Anita had pointed out yesterday, he'd found his so-called dream woman with Sophia, and while she was admittedly too extreme, he should have learned his lesson. In his mind, he'd conjured up a woman that would be impossible to find so he didn't have to bother with looking. With being disappointed. Or with becoming trapped.

Marriages, even to an amazingly independent, intelligent, caring and compassionate woman like Samantha demanded the one thing Nick had a hell of a hard time mastering—compromise. Sharing. Surrendering his needs to fulfill the desires of his partner. In lovemaking, he handled the concept with relish. Enjoyed it even. But in life? He wanted everything and he wanted it all his way.

He was spoiled. Hardworking and loyal, yes, but spoiled nonetheless. Yet he was trapped at the same time. Snared more firmly than a snake in a tiger pit by a woman who had, with her refusal, held firm to their agreement of no commitments or promises beyond the weekend.

"I have an idea," Nick said, slowly spinning the glittering red-jeweled ring on his pinkie. He closed his eyes and swallowed, only half believing what he was about to suggest. Talk about a gamble. Nick shook his head, knowing that if he thought too hard, he might change his mind. Maybe he needed to take a second lesson from Samantha. As a stuntwoman, she'd had the courage to jump off buildings and hang from window ledges one hundred feet above the ground. But this wasn't the movies. Nick was a man of reality. A believer in the bottom line.

"Are you going to share with the rest of us?" Anita asked.

He was going to share all right. On a trial basis, anyway. He was going to share until sharing killed him. That's how much he wanted Samantha in his life.

"Bomini will only be here for today, right?" he asked. "The Expo ends tomorrow."

Rose nodded. "He has to be back in Rome by Monday. That he told me."

"Then Sam and I can just pretend to be married until then."

"Pretend?" Sam asked.

Nick slid around to the front of Samantha's chair. Determined to work this spin correctly, he knelt back down in front of her, the ring clutched between his fingers.

"It's not like the man is going to demand a marriage certificate. It's not like I'd feel the least compelled to show him one even if he did. But if I tell him we flew off to Vegas last night to marry, he has no choice but to believe me. I'm a man of my word."

"You won't be after you tell him that lie," Samantha pointed out. It was apparent to him that her skepticism ran deeper than her expression revealed. They may have known each other for only a day, but already Nick could sense more about her than he could with anyone else. He read pure unadulterated fear in her gaze. Fear of him. Fear of them together.

Good. He didn't want to be the only one quaking in his boots.

Fae finally spoke up. "Franco Bomini wouldn't know the truth if it bit him on his…" She spat out the Italian word for backside with more spite than Nick had ever heard from his grandmother before. Maybe he shouldn't go through with this. No distribution deal was worth the stress his grandmother obviously felt. No matter how much the pretense of marriage could help him win Samantha's heart and the distribution deal as well, he wouldn't sacrifice his grandmother for either victory. He'd find another way.

"Then let's find someone else to distribute our products," Nick said. "Bomini isn't the only game in town. He's the most powerful, but—"

Fae stamped her foot and pointed at him with a crooked finger. "Don't coddle me, Dominick. Bomini deserves to be lied to. It'll serve him right, the hypocrite."

Nick jerked at his grandmother's poisoned tone, but suddenly felt righteous in perpetuating this untruth. For Rafaela's sake. For the sake of the LaRocca family.

For him and Samantha. If nothing else, the charade could win him one more night in her arms, one more night to brand himself in her heart.

"What do you say? I'm asking again and I'm already on my knees."

Sam drew her bottom lip in her mouth. "You just want me to *pretend* to be your wife. For the weekend?"

Nick held the ring out to her, twirling it so the facets caught the light. "Maybe your mother *is* psychic. She sent the ring, didn't she?"

"Don't even joke about that," she said, the power of her chastising deflated by the sound of genuine fear.

Again, the sound of her apprehension bolstered his determination. If Nick was going to start sharing, he thought it only fair to give Sam half of both the good and the bad.

SAMANTHA SLIPPED INTO the restaurant ladies' room just before dinner, alone, not knowing where Nick had disappeared to during appetizers and drinks, and willing herself not to care. Just before they'd left the hotel for the dinner party Anita had hastily arranged at Brennan's, Nick fired her as his bodyguard. Television and radio stations across the country had announced the end of Nick's bachelor status. Reporters interviewed women who'd been chasing him and noted that the hunt was officially over. Pictures of Samantha and Nick, posing and smiling beneath a floral wedding arch they'd borrowed from the hotel, had made their way onto the Internet. So far as the world knew, she was the new Mrs. Dominick LaRocca.

At least her moviemaking, media-spinning know-how had come in handy. But she swallowed the irony with the same resistance as a thick dose of chalky antacid. She'd come home to New Orleans to escape Hollywood's pretense, to discover what was real and true and important. She'd found love—and it was all a lie.

"The bodyguard hides in the bathroom. That would make an interesting headline."

Samantha turned at the sound of an opening door, not in the least surprised to see her mother enter the small bathroom as if she were a queen entering her royal hall. Her timing, as always, was impeccable. Endora locked the door, then sashayed over to the mirror to check her flaming red, perfectly coiffed and curled hair.

"I'm not his bodyguard anymore. He fired me."

"He paid you first, I hope."

Sam nodded. No Chances Protection was safe from bankruptcy, Nick had seen to that. And since she'd received a call from Serena announcing her and Brandon's arrival in New Orleans by tomorrow afternoon, Sam's professional life was finally looking up. If only her personal life would follow suit.

"How did you know where to find me?" Samantha asked, knowing her mother's crystal ball didn't usually operate as a homing device.

"I received a phone call from a charming woman, Rosalia LaRocca. She invited me to attend the dinner as her guest. I haven't met her yet, but her granddaughter, Anita, told me I'd find you hiding in here."

"I'm not hiding."

"Oh? Then what are you doing, Samantha?"

"Don't you know?"

Endora pressed her red-rouged lips together in a thin line, crossing her arms across her amble bosom with a jangle of bracelets and beads. "Do you want to know what I see when I look at you?"

Sam slid off the porcelain sink where she'd perched. "No, Mother, not really. I may not share your psychic talents, but I'm pretty sure I already know what you see."

"Really? And what is that?"

Sam shook her head, pressing her lashes together tightly to fight the burning tears welling behind her eyes. Of all the places to have this conversation with her mother. The bathroom of a restaurant! On the eve of her biggest heartbreak.

"You see the daughter you love, the daughter who abandoned you, the daughter who can't seem to make anything work in her life."

Endora shook her head and sighed. "Good thing I'm the only one who depends on intuition to make a decent living." Endora opened her arms, but Sam shook her head. She couldn't hug her mother right now. If she'd did, she'd lose control and she feared she'd never get it back.

Endora took her refusal in stride. "You're right on only one thing, Samantha. I do love you. Yes, I resented the fact that you chose to live with your father after the divorce." Her face twisted in an expression half disgusted and half amused. "Five years old and had a mind of your own. But I never meant to make you feel guilty for that."

Sam skewered her mother with a pointed look.

"Okay, maybe I meant to make you feel a little guilty."

Sam nodded at her victory, hollow as it was.

"Do you know *why* I didn't want you to live with your father?" Endora's floor-length swirls of purple dress lightly swished as she spun back toward the mirror. But she wasn't looking at herself. Samantha watched her mother's piercing eyes use the reflective glass as a portal to the past. Her expression softened. The lines of her expertly defined makeup muted with memories. "Devlin was the most charismatic, most handsome man I'd ever met. I fell so hard in love with him."

Endora turned back around and braced her hands behind her on the sink. "But Samantha, he's the neediest so-and-so ever born to the male race. You were such a caring child. I knew if you went with him, you'd take it upon yourself to take care of him. And you did. You sacrificed your childhood. Your dreams. It should have been the other way around."

"It wasn't that bad."

Endora tilted her eyebrows, but didn't question Sam's claim further. "Maybe not. But look at you now. You don't know what you want. You've spent so much time worrying about what Devlin wanted, then what that pin-up boyfriend of yours wanted. And I'd wager Grandmother Lizabeth's ring there that you're hiding in here right now, worrying about what Dominick LaRocca wants."

Her mother couldn't have been more wrong. She was contemplating everything *she* wanted and simply couldn't have. "I'm just taking a breather." Frantically, Samantha pulled the band of gold and rubies off her finger and slapped it into her mother's hand. She didn't need the darned thing anymore. Dinner with Bomini was almost over.

Endora glanced down at the ring, then without comment, slid it into a pocket hidden in the fold of her skirt. "Dominick's a potent man. Reminds me of your father."

Endora didn't make that comparison lightly. Her intense stare only punctuated exactly what Sam had been thinking.

"Yeah, well, luckily for me, Dominick only wanted a pretend wife for the weekend. After he closes this deal with Signore Bomini, he won't need me anymore. He'll return to Chicago and run his empire. Brandon will be back and, by Monday, we'll get No Chances really up and running. I won't have time to think about how much I love that big Italian hunk."

With a melancholy nod, Endora wrapped Samantha in a gentle hug. Sam didn't fight the gesture this time, but bit her lip and willed her self-indulgent tears to remain at bay.

For the moment, she won the battle. No regrets. She'd made that promise to Nick—and to herself. But if all she had was one day left, she would make it count. And she sure as hell couldn't do that while hiding in the bathroom.

She broke away from Endora, but kept her arm wrapped around her mother's slim waist. "Come on, Mother. I'm going to introduce you to Nana Rose and Nana Fae."

"You sure you want to do that? I have a strong premonition that the three of us could cook up some delicious trouble if we're left alone too long."

Sam shook her head and laughed, her mind happily turning from her lost love with Nick to the chaos the three indomitable women could cause. Separately, they'd already done some serious damage. If not for the bounty Rose and Fae had put on Nick with the pasta label, she and Nick might never have met. And her mother's gift of oil and condoms—not to mention the ring—had paved the way for experiences of delight and of woe that still had her reeling.

What the hell. No matter how they tried, they could never conjure more grief than Sam had already worked up for herself by falling in love with a man who couldn't stay with her even if she asked.

She unlocked the bathroom door and ushered her mother through Brennan's glittering dining room to the opulent court-yard outside. The twinkling stars, the soft strains of home-grown jazz, the scents of simmering Bananas Foster, the wobbly feel of the cobblestone beneath her dainty heels—this was New Orleans. This was home.

This was what she wanted. And though she wanted Nick too, with a powerful pull she knew would ultimately tear her to shreds, she couldn't sacrifice one for the other.

She'd already forfeited her own needs in the name of love once for her father. Maybe she'd made the mistake twice, if she counted her dalliance with Anthony when she'd accompanied him on location for his films rather than grabbed a once-in-a-lifetime opportunity to start her own business. No matter how tempted she was, she couldn't allow herself to follow that same path a third time. Not if she really wanted to discover all she was.

To build a solid future, she had to stay here in New Orleans. With her family. With her new career, the first one that actually excited her to the point where she practically wanted to pinch herself and make sure this dream was real.

Luckily for her, she knew coming home to New Orleans was the most real thing she'd done. Just as she knew that her marriage to Nick was nothing more than a story they'd made up—their love affair a fantasy that couldn't withstand the intrusion of hard reality. But for tonight—this one last night— they could relish the reverie, and perhaps, make memories that would last forever.

CHAPTER TWELVE

AFTER SIGNING HIS NAME on the bottom line, Nick handed his ballpoint to Anita and reached across the conference table to shake Franco Bomini's aged but beefy hand. The dinner party had been a total success. After dessert, Nick invited Bomini and his grandson, the vice president of Bomini's operations, to his suite to shore up the deal. They had stayed up all night haggling details so the Italian businessman could make his scheduled flight to Rome in two hours.

Nick had been forced to leave Samantha to sleep, alone, in his bed only a few feet away, but he reasoned that the payoff would be worth the price. The deal done, Nick would have everything he wanted. Well, nearly everything. As soon as the crowd cleared out and he had Samantha to himself, he'd own the whole damn world.

Bomini scanned the pages and, satisfied, handed them over his shoulder to his grandson. "*Perfetto!* We will both make a lot of money, yes, Dominick?"

When Franco scooted his chair back, Nick rose. "That's the plan."

"I never dreamed this would all work out so well, you understand?" Bomini's broken English barely masked the depth of his emotion. The regret in the older man's gaze was impossible to miss. "My objection to you was only a means to force Rafaela to speak to me, to get past your Nana Rose, so I could apologize. I won't live forever. I had to make right what was wrong."

Nick nodded, honestly happy that the bad blood simmering between Bomini and his grandmothers had been settled, thanks to Samantha's mother, Endora. With her probing questions and some otherworldly intercession, she'd brokered peace between Bomini and Nana Fae who, it turns out, was once betrothed to the man before she met Nick's grandfather. In an act of youthful stupidity, Bomini had ended up in the bed of a well-known *pottana,* and rather than deal with the aftermath, he'd returned to the old country and left Fae behind.

His grandmother had been humiliated by his betrayal, but luckily, she'd met Salvatore Durante soon after and enjoyed a long, happy marriage. According to Endora, Salvatore himself had helped arrange the reconciliation—from the "other side." Nick preferred to believe that time simply healed all wounds.

But to Nick, time was now his greatest enemy. As soon as Bomini left his suite with a signed contract tucked in his briefcase, Samantha had no other reason to stay—except for the sensual reasons he planned to unveil, slowly and with complete detail.

"I'll expect you in Rome in, let's say, two weeks," Bomini announced as his grandson snapped his briefcase closed. "We'll have a plan for you to look over, and arrange meetings with the biggest retailers."

Nick nodded. Sounded like the way to go. The Nick he was only two days ago would have started barking orders at Anita right then and there. Setting up strategy sessions with his top staff. Brainstorming new advertising for the European market. Considering a new product or two to add to the line specifically to entice foreign buyers. But Nick couldn't think of a single thing he wanted to do *less* than work. Except for saying goodbye to Sam, which he'd soon have to do—unless he took the plunge.

By the time he responded to Bomini, he was shaking his head instead of nodding. "*Mi perdono,* Signore Bomini, but I won't be going to Rome myself."

He turned and handed his copy of the contract to Anita. "You need to memorize this, cousin." He turned back to Bomini. "Anita will handle the European distribution from this point on. She's just been promoted."

Nick held his breath, hoping Bomini wouldn't protest his selection. Bomini's Old World views were legendary and Anita was, after all, a woman—a shocked-to-silence woman at the moment. Instead, the old man smiled and grabbed Nick's cousin into a companionable hug, complete with a grandfatherly kiss on each cheek. "How lucky am I to do business with such a beautiful and intelligent *signorina?* You know, my youngest son is your age. Maybe you'd like to meet him?"

Anita smiled, but didn't say a word, causing Franco to chuckle again. After their new business associate left, Anita spun away from the door and eyed Nick warily.

"Thanks," she said finally.

Nick smiled. His announcement had indeed dazed his cousin to near speechlessness—a priceless reward if ever there was one. "You're welcome. There will be a job title change, of course. Why don't you pick it and have your business cards printed before you leave? Think you can stand jet-setting to Rome and London every few months?"

"I'll live," she quipped. "Care to clue me in on why you're suddenly handing me the deal you've been working on for as long as I can remember?"

Nick glanced at the closed bedroom door.

Anita grinned, then winced. "She left, you know."

"What?"

"Through the side door. About a half hour ago."

Nick tore into the bedroom, his heart halting at the overwhelming emptiness of the room. Her scent lingered, but her warmth was gone, sending a chill up his spine. He grabbed his jacket and wallet, scanned briefly for a note that didn't exist, then rushed back to Anita.

"Do you know where she went?"

Anita pressed her lips together. She had the crucial information he needed. Nick didn't hide his desperation or impatience, so after a long minute, she told him what he needed to know. "She said she had some cleaning up to do around her sister's house before Serena got home from her honeymoon. The plane lands at eleven-thirty."

Nick's watch read eight-thirty. He had three hours to catch Samantha. To explain. Explain what? That he loved her? That he was willing to try whatever she wanted to make a marriage work for real?

Trouble was, Nick knew exactly what Samantha wanted and needed. She hadn't said so directly, but the bits and pieces of her past that she'd revealed over the past two days added up to one clear and admirable goal—to stay in New Orleans. By doing that, she could repair the damage to her relationship with her mother and sister. See if her new venture as a bodyguard could work out permanently. And all together, restore the confidence in her own independence that had slipped whenever she'd followed a man because of love. First her father. Then that pretty-boy boyfriend.

He could give her what she needed. Space. Permanence. A foundation, like the one he'd received from his tight-knit family since the day he was born. He'd find a way. But he'd need a little help.

He nearly knocked Anita down when he rushed to kiss her for being, as always, incredibly diligent and prepared. He tore to the door, grabbed the knob, then spun back, again nearly knocking her down as she retrieved a slip of paper from her pocket.

Scribbled across the middle was the address to Serena's house.

"You're the best, Anita."

"I want a raise, Nick."

Nick laughed, but didn't reply, knowing now was not the time to negotiate a pay increase with his wonderful, smart-beyond-words cousin. In his current mood, she'd bleed him dry.

"OKAY, TAB, I'm now officially homeless."

Samantha twisted the clasp on her satchel and scanned her sister's guest room for anything she might have left behind. She shooed the cat from her perch on the nightstand so she could read the clock. In a little less than an hour, her sister and her sister's new husband would be home to reclaim their house. Since she'd needed her apartment's security deposit to pay for the night-vision binoculars she'd found on the Internet, Sam had canceled her lease three weeks ago. But living at her sister's while Serena was out of the country was one thing. She wasn't about to impose on newlyweds.

With a deep breath for fortification, she marched into the kitchen, grabbed the phone and punched in the numbers to her father's cell. As expected, his assistant picked up. Also as expected, he made excuses for why Devlin couldn't take her call.

"Tell him it's a matter of life or death," she insisted, finished with being patient and understanding and doormat for her father.

"Whose life or death?"

Sam narrowed her eyes, wishing Devlin's smarmy right-hand man could see her expression. "Yours. I want to talk to my father now, understand?"

Apparently, he did. After a brief wait, Devlin's voice echoed on the other end. "Yo, baby-girl. It's about time you called to check in. How's the gumbo?"

Samantha took a second deep breath. "Expensive. I need my money, Dad."

"Sammie, the film hasn't even premiered yet. I can't start playing favorites. You aren't the only producer on this—"

She cut him off, sure she couldn't stand to argue with his expert reasoning that somehow always worked in his favor. "I'm the only producer who's your daughter."

"Honey, you know how I feel about nepotism," he said, simmering her blood with his practiced, singsong tone.

Sam bit her tongue, then remembered her first conversation with Nick about his family business and thought about all the firsthand examples she'd seen of how family members could indeed work together without ruining their relationships.

"Nepotism has nothing to do with this, Dad. You didn't hire me to do stunts because I was your daughter, you hired me because I was the best woman for the job. Then you made me a producer on the next film to avoid paying me my salary."

"But you could make so much more on your investment," he reasoned calmly.

She shook her head at the phone. If he didn't have the money, she could understand. But she knew damn well he wasn't keeping his new mistress happy with gifts from an outlet mall. The monthly mortgage payment alone on his Beverly Hills mansion was probably equal to what he owed her.

"I don't care about making more money, Dad. I didn't *choose* to put my money into this film. You chose for me. And I'm done with that. Dad, I love you, but I won't let you take advantage of me anymore. I won't allow you to use this money to keep me in your life. I worked hard. I only want what I deserve."

Silence. As more time elapsed, Sam's eyebrows rose over widening eyes. Her father was never this quiet for this long, and since she could hear him breathing, she knew they hadn't been disconnected.

"Baby-girl…Samantha, I didn't mean to take advantage of you. I just wanted to give you more."

A hot rush of moisture coated the back of her throat. "I don't want more, Dad. Not more money, anyway."

But did she want more from herself? Yeah, she wanted everything. And from Nick? She wanted so much more than he could ever, ever give.

After finalizing the amounts with her father and arranging a funds transfer, she spent the next few minutes tallying her income on a scratch pad she found in Serena's kitchen. With Nick's money, she'd already covered the outstanding rent on the No Chances office and made the last payment on the equipment she'd bought.

Now, with her hard-earned money released from her father's film, she had more than enough cash to make a new start. On her own.

She wadded the handwritten spreadsheet into a ball and shoved it in the pocket of her bag. Hefting the bulging satchel into the living room, she tried to tamp down the resentment suddenly rising inside her, anger she should feel only at herself. It was her choice to leave Nick—her choice to run away without even a goodbye.

But spending last night alone, waking up alone, was a cutting example of the life she'd lead if she tried to stay with Nick. First, she'd have to move to Chicago. And once she was there, how many lonely nights would she spend in his Lake Shore apartment while he worked out the details of some business deal or stayed late at the office to work through strategies with Anita?

Sam had a different idea altogether about what her life should be. She was done coming in second to anything or anyone, especially with people she loved.

She tossed her bag into the living room and grabbed a pillow from the couch, leaning her cheek on the brushed fabric while she thought about the cute little house she'd seen for sale last week. Situated on the very end of Bourbon Street away from the tourists and the crowds, the two-story cottage was close enough to both her sister's house and the office for her to jog to both places. A few more blocks up and she could catch the St. Charles streetcar to deliver her nearly to her mother's door in the Garden District. A place like the pink stucco town house—old and intimately small—would be just what she needed to really feel as if she'd found a home in New Orleans.

Especially when her heart was miles and miles away. In Chicago. With Nick. Who'd never even know.

She shifted on the couch, smiling ruefully when Serena's large, mixed-breed dog, Maurice, shuffled from his bed in the corner to lay his massive head on her lap. Ruffling his ears, she wondered how Nick would react when he realized she'd left without saying goodbye.

She honestly hadn't had any choice. She'd spent the entire dinner party fantasizing about getting him alone in his suite, making love with him until they were exhausted, imprinting the feel of him inside her. Instead, she'd remained awake half the night, alone, listening to the muted sounds of Nick dickering with Bomini, making his precious deal, doing what was most important to him. By the time she awoke the next morning, her dreams for a long romantic farewell had been dashed to hell. She couldn't have faced him without losing control.

Too many emotions clashed within her—anger, frustration, admiration, sorrow, grief. She'd write him a letter. Later. Maybe call. After she taught herself how to say goodbye to him, because, in all honesty, she had absolutely no idea how to form the words, much less accept the reality that she'd never see him again.

Maurice lifted his head with a growl, preluding a knock at the door. Samantha blinked, wondering how long she'd been sitting there. Were Serena and Brandon home already? Didn't they have a key? She grabbed Maurice's collar and let him drag her through the foyer.

She opened the door to find two grocery bags—with legs. Long, muscular legs encased in soft, new-looking denim.

"I have just discovered the most incredible grocery store in the nation. An A&P, right in the French Quarter, the size of my old bedroom in my mother's house back on Taylor Street. But, hey, they carry LaRocca products, so I'm sold."

Nick lowered the bags and ended his ramble as Samantha kept Maurice from attacking. Hell, while she kept herself from attacking. She'd never seen Nick dressed so casually and looking so comfortable and talking with such abandon. As if he didn't have a care in the world.

"Are you going to invite me in?"

Sam held up her hand to stop his forward motion, then shut the door in his startled face while she dragged Maurice, whimpering and barking, onto the back porch.

Nick was here? With groceries? Talking with unbridled awe about the neighborhood store where she bought her munchies?

She opened the door to find him leaning against the porch rail, a bag on each hip. His chambray shirt was unbuttoned to his breastbone, allowing her a peek at his incredibly muscular chest—the chest that had caught her eye from the label at the Food Expo—the one she now knew felt like cushioned down when cradling her cheek.

"Your Southern hospitality is slipping," he remarked, barely able to contain a grin Samantha found more and more annoying as each second ticked past.

"My sister and her husband will be home soon," she offered by way of explanation—by way of cowardly escape.

Nick's grin widened. "Actually—" he set one bag down and glanced at his watch "—they are probably just settling in for a first-rate brunch at Brennan's. I sent my limousine to pick them up at the airport. After they eat, I've instructed my driver to deliver them to your mother's house. She's organized a little welcome-home party for them. At my request, of course."

"Why?"

He blinked a few times, but his smile didn't falter. "Because I need to be alone with you."

"Why?"

He set the other bag down on the porch and took a step forward. "Because I love you."

Samantha swallowed, clutching the threshold with one hand and the knob with the other. She should slam the door in his face again. Permanently. Wasn't it bad enough that she loved him? He didn't need to add more heartbreak by admitting that the feeling was mutual.

But he'd spoken the words so softly, on such a powerful wave of emotion that his tone dipped and his volume faded, she couldn't deny the honesty he'd offered. He loved her. Okay. Fine. That didn't mean they could make a committed relationship work.

"I love you, Samantha," he repeated. "Aren't you going to say anything?"

She shook her head, but stepped back so he could come inside. She supposed she should say something, but the obvious response caught in her throat.

Nick retrieved the bags and followed her inside, kicking the door closed behind him. "All right. I'm two for two. First, I shock Anita into near silence and then I shut you up without even trying. The two most opinionated women in the continental United States. Next to my grandmothers, that is."

Sam stifled a grin at his arrogant swagger, at the way he marched into the kitchen to deliver the groceries as if he owned the place. Leaning against the framed arch separating the living room from the kitchen, she watched him unload more food than two bags would ordinarily hold.

Andouille sausage. A full roaster chicken. Dried red beans
Two pounds of rice. A mess of vegetables, some of which she
didn't recognize. A dozen or so spices. Fresh shrimp and
crawfish wrapped in white paper and marked with wax crayon
on the side. A long, crusty loaf of French bread, and a huge
tin of LaRocca's Extra Virgin Olive Oil.

"You're planning to make me lunch?" Sam asked, knowing
this conversation would be easier than addressing those three
little words that had formed his heartfelt confession—the
same three little words she still hadn't said to him.

"And dinner," he acknowledged, sorting the food with confident precision, his grin faltering when he found the eggs—
at the bottom. He turned and sapped her breath with a sexy
wink. "And breakfast, if all goes well."

"I don't think Serena and Brandon want to spend their first
night home at my mother's."

"I didn't think so, either, so I reserved them the finest suite
at the Monteleone Hotel. You said they seemed reluctant to
end their honeymoon. Your mother assured me that they'd be
thrilled to have one more night."

"You can't just come in and shanghai my sister's house!"

Her vehement protest didn't slow him for a second. He
perused the label of the wine he'd bought, then set it on the
rack above Serena's cabinet.

"I intend to make it worth their while," he said.

She jabbed her fists onto her hips. "And what about me?"

Though she didn't mean her protest to carry a double
entendre, Nick's minty-green eyes flashed with desire at the
implied challenge.

"Oh, believe me…" He crossed the room in three long
strides, pulling her into his arms and full against his rigid,
aroused body and crackling the air with a loud, electric pop.
The static charge only intensified his grin. "I intend to make
it worth your while, too."

CHAPTER THIRTEEN

"AND HOW ARE YOU going to do that, Nick?" Samantha forced an impertinent stringency into her tone, forced herself to ignore her instantaneous reaction to Nick's embrace—a response that had her insides feeling like a ball of candlewax left too close to a raging fire. "Will you move to New Orleans? Settle down? Cut your business meetings short because you have a wife in purple underwear waiting for you in bed at home?"

"Sounds delicious."

She pushed herself out of his arms, creating a distance by stalking to the table, grabbing the package of seafood and tossing it into the refrigerator with a loud slam. "Don't, Nick. Don't make this some sort of fantasy. We lived the fantasy." Her voice softened. She couldn't shout about their affair. She couldn't be angry that he'd discovered all the erotic secrets she'd wanted him to find—that they'd shared one night of utter bliss. "I don't regret making love with you. But it's time to move on. It's time for *me* to move on."

Nick moved to step forward, but Samantha held him at bay with her stare—one she'd intended to be intimidating, but felt sure resembled the wide-eyed shock of a possum caught in headlights. She hadn't expected to see him again, to have this conversation.

Coward.

Wisely, Nick slid his hands into his pockets, though not very deeply, thanks to the snug fit of his jeans. She sighed.

I'm hopeless.

"It's time for me to move on, too, Samantha. That's what last night made me realize."

"Last night? Unless you count me sleeping, alone," she emphasized, "in your bed, nothing happened last night."

Nick frowned. "That's just it. Nothing happened. When Bomini was talking cost projections, I was thinking about how I wanted to touch you in the dark. When he adjusted the dates of implementation for his benefit, all I wanted to do was taste you. All of you."

He stepped closer.

She clutched the countertop behind her.

"I wasn't there when you woke up," Nick said simply. "I always want to be there when you wake up."

Samantha crossed her arms, more than aware that her stance was childlike and defensive and completely impotent to keep this man away if he chose to invade the shrinking distance between them. He'd already invaded her heart. He'd plowed straight into her soul and held her, practically powerless to deny her foolish fantasy that they might share a life beyond this weekend.

But she had to hold on to reality. The hard facts. The ugly truth.

"Imagine how you'll feel when you're in Chicago running your empire and I'm here, in New Orleans, finally taking hold of my life. Doing something I love." Samantha slid her hands onto the countertop and boosted herself up. With her feet dangling off the ground, she realized she couldn't run if Nick decided to come for her, wrap her into his arms, press her cheek to his heartbeat and force her to hear how the pounding raged just for her. Good. She couldn't run anymore. She'd have to fight. For a second time today, she had to fight for what she wanted—what she now knew she had to have. Her freedom. Her dreams.

"When I moved to L.A.," she explained, "I just wanted to be with my father. Take care of him. I was the only kid in Hollywood who *didn't* want to be in his movies. But I grew up and turned out to be really good at stunt work. Other directors requested me all the time, but I turned them down. So I could be with Devlin. So I could put him first."

Nick didn't move, but she watched his eyes soften with each word of her confession.

"Then I got hurt and couldn't work. Another director offered me the chance to consult on a film she was doing with a female lead. She wanted to use only female stuntwomen and I would have trained the other women to do what I did. Make a real name for myself. But Anthony came along. He'd just won a part in another big-budget film, and I put aside my dream again. Went with him halfway across the world to sit in his dressing room and wait." She closed her eyes, marveling at how she could finally admit all this to Nick, to herself, at the moment when she least wanted to talk about her past. But she owed Nick the truth. She owed him an honest goodbye.

"I'm not your father, Samantha. And I'm sure as hell not Anthony Marks."

She shook her head, denying that she'd meant to make any comparison between them. Nick wasn't the reason she couldn't leave. Not really. *She* was the reason.

"All my life, I've followed the men I loved at the expense of my needs. My dreams. I do love you, Nick, but loving you makes me want to do it again. I can't. I'm not that same girl anymore. Before you came, before we met, I was just starting to see that I have to put myself first. If we'd met two months ago…"

"We probably wouldn't have fallen in love. I love the woman you are now, Sam. The woman who has to put herself first."

"But I can't go with you, Nick. Please don't ask me to."

"I won't." He stepped nearer then, his hands clasped just in front of him, as if he fought the urge to grab her, shake her, coax her to change her mind. "I wouldn't."

Though she heard the answer she wanted, her heart still cracked within her chest, allowing a hot stream of sorrow to burn into her belly, then up the back of her throat, until it welled up in her eyes.

She pulled in a ragged breath, forcing her words out on a shaky exhalation. "Then there's nothing left to say."

"There's always the part where I tell you that I'm moving to New Orleans."

Her eyes flashed wide. "What?"

He struggled to contain that wonderful, delicious, arrogant grin that made her insides clench with need each and every time. "I haven't worked out the details, but I put Anita on the European distribution. Now I'm thinking about expanding the LaRocca product line, working in other ethnic foods like authentic Creole and Cajun stuff. Maybe enticing this Miss Lily you and your mother keep bragging about to sell us some recipes."

Sam pressed her palm to her chest, certain Nick could see the leap her heart made at the possibility that he was telling her the truth.

"What about your family?"

Nick shrugged. "That's what e-mail and airplanes are for. Chicago is only a two-hour flight away." With that declaration, he dismissed the topic and looked around her sister's kitchen with narrowed, assessing eyes. "We'll need a place with a bigger kitchen. All state-of-the-art. I saw a building a few blocks from here that was zoned for business. I called the listing agent and we're meeting tomorrow. Any preferences on where we might live?"

Sam shook her head, not because she didn't know—she did—but because she was trying to dislodge the fog clouding her brain, marring her ability to think.

"There's this cottage on Bourbon Street…"

Nick's grin nearly split his face in two and for the first time since she'd known him, he laughed. Not a chuckle or a snicker, but an explosive burst from his belly—unguarded, unchecked and totally unrefined. With a wild swoop, he lifted her off the counter and swung her around, making her dizzy with happiness. When he lowered her ever so slowly to the ground, ensuring that every inch of her body slid down every inch of his, the light-headedness turned to irrepressible desire.

He crooked his finger beneath her chin. "I never thought I'd ever fall in love, Samantha. With you, it took less than two days."

She smiled, lifting herself on tiptoe to place a soft kiss on his chin. "Imagine what we could do with the rest of our lives."

Nick swept a trail of kisses across her temple and down her cheek. "We won't have to imagine. But first…" Again he looked around the kitchen, and again, Serena's neat and tidy space wasn't up to par. He released her and looked out the window over the sink, satisfied at what he saw outside.

Until Maurice jumped up from the other side and greeted him with a growling snap.

"Is there somewhere else you can put that dog?"

Samantha grabbed a box of dog biscuits from the cabinet, then enticed Maurice into the guest room, where she dragged his bed and water dish. When she returned to the kitchen, Nick was gone. Judging by the back door, which he'd propped open with a chair, Nick had ventured onto the porch.

She slipped outside, thrilled, excited, giddy with desire and happiness and love. Nick had found a way to follow *her*, to create an entire new business so they could be together. He valued her needs enough to alter his own.

All for her.

The hundred-year-old wood on Serena's back porch creaked beneath Sam's weight, the rubbery squeal echoing in the quiet, walled-in space behind the house. Like most French Quarter residents, Serena had created a wild, intricate garden behind her house, overrun with ivy that climbed up the ten-foot brick walls and dripping with fern and jasmine and big, leafy plants Sam couldn't name. A small, trickling fountain bubbled in the center, providing sweet music for the natural silence. Sunlight struggled in vain to touch the shadows, and Sam was glad. Especially when she stepped off the porch and caught sight of Nick watching her from the base of the stone sculpture that centered the fountain.

When she crossed the stepping stones to meet him, he glanced over his shoulder at the statue, a Grecian couple, naked and entwined. "Your sister has interesting taste."

Sam swallowed a grin. "You should see the fountain at her spa. Most erotic thing you've ever seen."

Nick's smile faded, and heat, male and needful, burned from his eyes. "You're the most erotic thing I've ever seen."

She looked down at her clothing, smoothing her hands from her midriff, bared by her cutoff T-shirt, to the waistband of her soft, floppy knit pants. Her hair was snared in a loose ponytail, which she immediately released. She'd spent the morning cleaning and packing, giving no attention to her appearance.

Yet, reflected in Nick's eyes, she was the most beautiful woman in the world.

"I probably look better in the purple underwear."

Nick's body instantly reacted. A rush of hot need throbbed to his groin, then bolted straight to his brain to flash images and sensations of Samantha rescuing him, Samantha touching him, Samantha opening her body and soul for him to explore. Just two nights ago, he'd learned about giving and sharing the parts of himself he'd buried, protected, denied.

Never again. Not if Samantha accepted the proposal that,

despite his overwhelming desire for her, still lodged in the back of his throat.

"You think? I barely remember the purple underwear. Maybe later, you can remind me. Right now, I have a standard to live up to."

Sam gasped when Nick dropped to his knee and produced her great-grandmother's ruby ring from his pocket. She'd returned it to her mother last night, but before they left the restaurant, Endora had given it back to him. She made him promise to put the ring to good use, muttering something about destiny and spiritual ownership.

Despite his inability to believe in such nonsense, he'd carried the ring with him ever since, tucked in his breast pocket during the meeting with Bomini, and slipped into his jeans pocket during his shopping spree this morning. He'd known he had to give it back to Samantha, but he wouldn't unless he did so the right way.

"Where did you—"

He cut off her question by shaking his head. "Your mother claims the ring's aura is interwoven with mine."

She bit her lip. "I hate to admit this, but my mother's hardly ever wrong."

"Then if I ask you to marry me," he whispered, taking her left hand and slipping the ruby onto her finger to the sound of her sigh, "to be my wife and lover and keeper of my soul, you'll say yes?"

She looked at the ring, examining it on her hand as if she'd never seen the glittering gem before. He watched her eyes glisten, marveling at how the nearly imperceptible increase of shine in her eyes clutched at the recesses of his heart. God, he loved this woman.

She tugged him up to stand, then curled into his arms. He breathed in her scent, spread his hands around her bare middle and stamped her warm body with his needful touch.

"Yes, Nick. I'll be all those things for you. With you."

Nick kissed her, hungry for the taste of her, starving for the spice her simple presence added to his life, to his soul. He could kiss her forever, touch her forever. She was a craving he'd never, ever satisfy—though he intended to enjoy trying.

"But you'll have to promise me one thing," she added once they broke to gasp for some air.

He held her back a few inches, loath to release her, but intrigued by the mischievous lilt in her voice. "What's that?"

With her signature quick reflexes, she twisted out of his embrace and whipped her T-shirt over her head in one smooth and graceful move. His eyes drank in the sight of her, free and aroused and wearing a satin bra cut sinfully to cup her breast, but not cover them.

This bra was red.

His mouth watered and his jeans tightened. With measured slowness, she slid her pants down, over her hips, revealing first her thighs, then knees, calves, ankles. She stepped back to him, leaving her clothing behind, her fingers skimming the triangular top of the equally scarlet panties.

"Seems I inherited a complete collection of naughty underthings recently." She whispered the news as her lips nibbled from the center of his chest, up his neck, to his chin.

He swallowed, watching her nipples brush the material of his shirt while she worked each of his buttons. He managed a casual, "Really?" just before she placed an opened-mouth kiss on the center of his now-bare chest.

"Mmm-hmm."

She swiped a stiff-tongued lick across his nipple, flaming his desire so that he nearly shook trying to remain still.

She popped the top button of his jeans, then slid his zipper in one fluid move, the rasp of the metal accompanying his sharp intake of breath.

"Until my experience in the purple ones, with you, I never

knew how sexy they could make a woman feel. How decadent. How insatiable." Her hands dipped into his waistband and clutched at his buttocks with an intense squeeze.

"Uh-huh," he muttered, noting that somewhere beyond the haze of his need, he was supposed to be agreeing to something she wanted. He blinked, trying to follow her hints, but gave up the minute she dragged his jeans down his legs.

"I'm feeling pretty darned ravenous right now, Nick. Promise you'll do something to satisfy me?"

That invitation he could follow. He kicked his jeans into the undergrowth and lifted Samantha into his arms, eyeing a bench two or three strides away.

Triangles of cool tile bit through his cotton boxers when he sat, but the feel of Samantha wrapping her legs around his waist instantly fired a steady, throbbing heat.

"Satisfying hunger is what I do best, sweetheart. You're going to be the most satiated woman in New Orleans, sexy underthings or no sexy underthings, for the rest of your life."

She licked her lips.

Then licked his.

And the only thing she could think to say was, "Mmm, mmm, good."

Everything you love about romance...
and more!

Please turn the page for Signature Select™
Bonus Features.

New Orleans Nights

BONUS
FEATURES
INSIDE

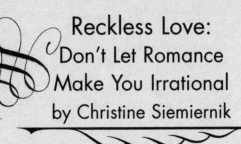

Reckless Love: Don't Let Romance Make You Irrational
by Christine Siemiernik

Are you constantly on edge, waiting for your love to realize you're not "the One"? Find out how romance turns women from rational to reckless and what you can do to stop the insanity!

4   Who ever said falling in love is easy? It seems simple enough: You meet the perfect guy and fall in love. But in reality, you can't seem to get comfortable in the relationship. You're on edge, waiting for him to realize you're not the one for him. Sound familiar?

Well, if it does, you're not alone. Many women cope with feelings of inadequacy, insecurity and a fear of rejection. But, as Dr. Judith Sherven, coauthor of *Be Loved for Who You Really Are* says, rejection is all in our own minds.

"Rejection is an inside job. Nobody really gets rejected by the guy. He may prefer a different kind of woman from who you are, but when we prefer chicken over steak, we're not rejecting steak," she says.

Dr. Sherven, a twenty-two-year veteran psychotherapist, encourages women coping with a fear of rejection to look in the mirror. "Women who live with that kind of fear of rejection need to be clear that the rejection lives inside of them."

Ask yourself where you learned that you weren't good enough. Did a parent, a friend, someone in the community tell you that you were too talkative? Too annoying? Too fat? Too thin? Too whatever?

"Nobody's born thinking they're not good enough," says Dr. Sherven.

Fatal Entrapments

As a result of this insecurity, we women often do some wacky things.

Everyone's got a friend who went off the deep end and did something à la *Fatal Attraction*. Dr. Sherven herself tells the tale of a young woman who took a rather unorthodox approach to eliciting a marriage proposal from her boyfriend.

The pair had been dating about six months when the gal ambushed her guy. "He was coming over to pick her up [and] when she opened the door for him, he was greeted by her naked in war paint. She had covered her body in war paint," says Dr. Sherven. The pair engaged in a water-pistol fight, and when they were finished, she playfully pointed the water pistol at him and asked if he was going to ask her to marry him. As one might expect, he said no, and she was crushed.

"When women throw themselves at men or when women set up really wacky kinds of seductive entrapment, men see through it. They see the desperation, they see the anxiety, and they also see the desire to entrap them," says Dr. Sherven. "And the first thing that men will do is back up. So, the very thing the woman is afraid of, that he'll leave her, she is, in fact, creating."

There's nothing wrong with asking your guy where things stand—just not on the first date. And while there's no surefire way of ensuring that the "Where are things going?" conversation won't freak your guy out, finding out where you stand is always the best way to go.

Try having a mature, adult conversation with your fellow, and use his reaction as a gauge to where you stand, says Dr. Sherven. If he shrugs your comments off, or ignores you, it's a pretty good sign it's time to move on.

Mr. Wrong
And sometimes, he's just the wrong guy. Emily finally realized her longtime boyfriend Michael was wreaking havoc on her self-esteem.

"Throughout our six years together he always made me feel like I wasn't good enough. I was good enough to be on his arm and do social things but I was never equal to his family. He always made me feel like my parents didn't compare to his," she says. And, for a while, she started to believe him.

"We were at his parents' house the first Christmas we were together. One lady asked me my last name. She said she wasn't familiar with that last name, and what did my dad do? I said that he works at McDonald's and walked away," she says. "My boyfriend's mom followed me right into the kitchen and said to not say anything else about my family in front of her friends."

The final straw in their relationship came when Michael went away for a summer to work without telling Emily, until one of their friends brought it up. She took the summer to decide whether she wanted to spend the rest of her life with a guy who put her last.

"When he came over to take me out the first night he got into town, I was so excited. He came to the door and I was excited and nervous, like on a first date. As I opened the door he smiled. For the first time he said, 'Boy, do you ever look good tonight,'" Emily recalls. "I stopped and remembered all the times that my dad would say 'Doesn't she look good tonight?' and he would say 'Yeah' and continue on. I looked him right in the eyes and said, 'The sad thing is that I have always looked this good, you just never noticed' and slammed the door shut. I felt like a new person. I couldn't believe that I did that but it felt great."

And she discovered that she *was* a whole new person. Throughout their relationship, she'd let Michael make all the decisions. In her current relationship, Emily pipes up whenever she's got something to say, and is an equal partner.

Testing the Waters

Dr. Sherven encourages women to take an active role in dating. When she first started dating her husband, she put him through a series of tests. On their first date, when he said he'd like to buy dinner, she said that was fine, but next time she'd like to pay. "I wanted him to know I wanted to see him again. I also wanted him to know I was an employed woman who expected to share the finances of anything we did," she says. And if he had insisted on always paying, he would have been weeded out then and there.

There are two things that women do that really cement their insecurity, says Dr. Sherven. Having sex too soon and choosing men who are either emotionally or legally unavailable. "They jump in the sack way too soon. Now they've made themselves sexually vulnerable without knowing his intentions at all."

Wading through the pitfalls of a relationship can be tricky, but we women have to remember to hold ourselves accountable for our own actions— even the ones we'd like to forget.

Originally published online at www.eHarlequin.com

Here's a sneak peek...

Killing Me Softly
by
Jenna Mills

*Look for this breakout novel in bookstores
May 2006 from Signature Select.*

PROLOGUE

SHE WAS GONE.

New Orleans police detective Cain Robichaud tore through the dense undergrowth, but even as he came to the clearing, he knew he would find no trace of the woman to whom he'd made love less than forty-eight hours before.

She was gone.

After ten years on the force, he was intimately familiar with the taste and feel and smell of lies and deception. He'd become a master at illusion. No matter how viciously he wanted to believe otherwise, he knew the instructions were just a ruse.

Savannah Trahan was gone.

"It's after midnight!" he called anyway. "I did everything you asked, damn it. *Everything.*"

Come alone, the note had instructed. To the burned-out ruins. At midnight. Leave your service revolver at home.

"Where the hell is she?"

Memories pushed in on him, images he didn't want to see. The sheen of her eyes the first night they'd met. The lingering taste of wintergreen the first time they'd kissed. The feel of her blond hair tangled in his hands. The husky cry that had torn from her throat the first time they'd made love.

There'd been no dimmed lights or soft music for them. No bed strewn with silk sheets. That would have been too trite, too tame.

There'd never been anything tame about Savannah Trahan.

He'd tried, damn it. He'd done everything short of locking her away to keep her from stumbling too close to the truth. He'd warned her to quit poking around where she didn't belong. He'd made it clear what would happen if she didn't stop taking risks that didn't need to be taken. Graphically, he'd described the fate of others who hadn't known when to stop.

The memory of a single bullet hole dead center between a pair of open, lifeless blue eyes twisted through him.

Savannah hadn't listened. A hotshot investigative reporter, she'd been too drunk on the need for justice to turn away from the investigation that consumed her. And he...he'd been too drunk on *her* to see through her platitudes.

Now she was gone, and just as Cain expected, nothing but the screech of a lone owl answered his hoarse command. The creature sat high atop a skeletal cypress tree, its solitary form silhouetted by the wavery light of a crescent moon.

Dark urges ripped through him. He was a man of action—the blood of his Cajun ancestors ran hot in his veins. He wanted to be doing something, anything. Run. Punish. But all he could do was make sure he was heard.

"You're making a grave mistake!" he warned, surveying his surroundings. A row of crumbling columns jutted up toward the night sky, solitary remnants of a once-grand plantation. No longer pristine white, the equally spaced columns had faded to a muted ivory, scarred by the fire that had claimed the manor they once embraced. The pillars stood as out of place among the sprawling oaks and towering cypress as Cain did among New Orleans society. Fingers were already being pointed. With every day the darling of the Baton Rouge evening news remained missing, the whispers grew louder.

"You won't get away with this!" he vowed, striding toward what had been the front of the house. A set of wide rounded steps remained, rising from a tangle of ferns and leading to a veranda that no longer existed.

Cain mounted them. "Savannah!"

"R-robi…"

The hoarse cry barely registered above the yammering of the crickets, but it reverberated through Cain like a shout.

BONUS FEATURE

"Savannah!" Heart hammering, he leaped down and ran toward the trees.

"Vannah!" She was the only one who'd ever called him Robi, an abbreviation of his last name. They'd been in bed the first time she'd used it, their legs tangled, hands joined. She'd smiled down at him and said, "More…Robi. More."

Now the leafy canopy stole the light of the moon. The darkness grew deeper, thicker, but Cain never missed a step. This was Robichaud land. He'd grown up scrambling across the gnarled undergrowth and climbing the emaciated cypress trees. He knew every twist and turn. Every hidden trap. Every danger.

"Robi…" Louder. Closer. *"H-help me."*

"Hang on!" Low-hanging branches slapped his face. "I'm here." He tore at vines and stumbled on the knee of an old cypress, shouting her name with each step he took. Until the gauzy light of the moon illuminated a flash of pink—and a puddle of red.

"Vannah!" He lunged toward the old oak and dropped to his knees, violating everything he knew about proper crime-scene management. He grabbed the silk blouse and drew it to his face, not giving a damn about the blood.

"Robi…h-help me."

His heart kicked violently against his ribs. *"Chère,"* he breathed, twisting toward the voice.

The sight of the tape recorder embedded in a nest of Spanish moss at the base of a young oak stopped him cold.

"Robi—please."

Deep inside, the hope he'd been harboring, as fragile as spun glass, shattered. She wasn't here. Had never been here.

"Cain!" The urgent, familiar male voice echoed through the wooded area.

"Where the hell are you?" yelled a second voice, this one older and strained. A creative stream of Cajun swearing came on the warm breeze. "Now is not the time for games!"

Two beams of light cut like knives through the gathering fog. "Cain! Answer me, damn it."

Numbly he balled his hands, still tangled in the mutilated silk blouse, into fists.

That's how they found him. On his knees. Holding her shirt. With blood staining his hands.

Detective Alec Prejean and Sheriff Edouard Robicaud tore through the moss and stopped abruptly, their flashlights aimed like weapons.

"Merde, neveu…what the hell have you done?"

CHAPTER ONE

Eighteen months later

THE SECLUDED BAYOU cottage Savannah Trahan once used as a retreat from the cutthroat world of journalism still stood. There, away from prying eyes, she'd been able to relax and rejuvenate—and rendezvous with the darkly seductive police detective everyone warned her to steer clear of.

Cannas bloomed in an untended rainbow of red and orange and yellow, guarding and inviting, hinting that once, someone had tended the overgrown grounds. Now waist-high weeds crowded out the walkway, the window were dark, the door boarded shut.

A lone tire swung from a rope affixed to a stumpy old oak, the breeze easing it in and out of the gathering fog.

It was still there, after all this time.

Renee Fox drew a hand to her mouth and moved closer, careful not to step on a partially secluded anthill. There was a sadness to this remote corner of the swamp, an aura that extended beyond the stark fall day.

Here, in the farthest reaches of southern Louisiana, fall arrived with little of the orange and red fanfare northern climes enjoyed. Gray skies and cool damp winds slithered in and stripped the trees of their leaves, turning them from green to brown in the blink of an eye.

"This is private property, *chère*."

The disembodied voice came from behind her. Dark and drugging, its innate masculinity struck a chord deep within her. And without even turning to look, she knew who stood behind her.

Her heart revved and stalled, her breath hitched. A protest hammered through her. She'd not meant for him to find her here. She'd not meant for him to find her at all.

The Robichauds didn't take kindly to deception.

Brutally aware of the crossroads she'd reached, she took a steadying breath and turned toward him.

He stood beyond the clearing, a shadowy specter lounging against a cypress tree. Fog licked at his long legs and swirled about his chest, making her question whether he existed at all. But the woman in her recognized this was no mere spirit watching her. No ghost, no phantom, no illusion. She recognized him in a heartbeat, the man who resided in the darkest corners of the need that pushed her from day to day.

BONUS FEATURE

Now he stood dead center between her and the truth she'd come to claim.

Cain Robichaud. She would have known him anywhere, any time. His pictures had been splashed all over the press, even in Canada. The shadows about him were darker, but little else had changed since his days as an undercover detective in the city of sin. Not the midnight-black hair, nor the midnight eyes. Not the square jaw, nor the dark stubble covering it. Not the wide, forbidding shoulders. Not the predatory stance.

He started toward her, his purposeful steps trampling the tall brown grass. "Perhaps you didn't hear me the first time, ma'am, but this is private property."

"I heard you."

He stopped so close, his six-foot-plus body crowded out the rest of the world. "Then that makes you a trespasser."

She'd always enjoyed a challenge, had never been one to back down. That trait had always been her greatest asset and, according to her brother, her greatest liability.

"And here I thought Bayou de Foi was a friendly town," she said with all the sugary Southern charm she could muster. "Is this the way you welcome all strangers, or just lucky ones like me?"

The lines of his face tightened. "If you're looking for hospitality, you should head on back to New Orleans, *belle amie.*"

18

Deep inside, she shivered. This man was not calling her pretty lady as a compliment.

"All a pretty lady like you has to do is name your price."

But not here, she knew instinctively. Not this man. He didn't play by others' rules. He sought to indulge or please no one but himself. "What I'm looking for can't be purchased."

"Everything has a price."

Even your soul? she wanted to ask, but the question jammed in her throat. "Then what's yours?" she surprised herself by asking.

She wasn't sure what she'd expected, but it wasn't laughter. The rough sound broke from his throat and echoed on the breeze. "My price is my penance," he said, then gestured toward the highway. "And like I said, this is private property. It's time for you to be going."

Time changed people. She knew that. So did loss and betrayal. After months of media notoriety, mentions of Cain Robichaud had trickled off to the point where recently there'd been nothing at all. Not even his photography Web site had been updated. It was as though the man had ceased to exist.

"I mean no harm," she said, realizing she had to backtrack. She'd been wrong to play footsy so quickly. "I was just…" Eventually, he would discover her real reason for being here, but the longer she kept him in

BONUS FEATURE

the dark about her assignment, the safer she was. "Someone I knew used to come here."

Something sharp and volatile flashed through his eyes, but other than that he was unnaturally still. "There's no one here now but you and me."

Heat rushed through her, despite the cool fall breeze. He was right. There was just the two of them, a woman no one would look for and a man many believed belonged behind the steel bars of Angola State Penitentiary.

Vulnerable was not a word she liked, but she'd taken her safety for granted before, and it was not a mistake she would make again. "I can see that. I just—" Had to come. To see what remained from that night in the not so distant past. "—needed to come here."

"Needed?" In that moment he sounded every bit the cop he'd once been, renowned for securing confessions. Coercion or seduction, the method hadn't mattered. "Trust me. A pretty thing like you, the only thing waiting for you out here is trouble."

That's where he was wrong. Remnants remained, of a life gone by, a mystery begging to be solved. There were answers here. And truth.

But those words could not be said.

"I wanted to see if I could still feel her," she said, choosing her words carefully. "My friend who used to come here to clear her head." And to make love with the unorthodox police detective who'd made her forget everything she knew about caution and survival.

His expression darkened. *"Who?"* For such a big man, he uttered the question in a deceptively soft voice. "Who is this friend?"

The urge to turn away was strong. Once she spoke the name, there would be no going back. She knew that. If she wanted to walk away, to pretend she'd not stood close enough to Cain Robichaud that she could lift a hand and let the whiskers darkening his jaw scrape her fingertips, she should do so now, before she waded into waters still and dark and deep. She had only to accept that some questions would never be answered, some needs never met.

She could never accept either.

"Savannah," she said, wincing at the way his eyes went cold and flat. "Savannah Trahan."

It was just a name, that's all she said, but the shadow that fell over Cain made it clear she might as well have cursed his soul to perdition and beyond. Because Savannah Trahan would never be just a name to this man, not when half the parish believed he'd murdered his former lover. Buried her on his land, some believed. Submerged her naked body in the swamp, others claimed. Burned her in a bonfire of her pictures, another said, and let her ashes scatter with the wind.

He stood there so horribly, brutally still, the planes of his face tight, his eyes like shrapnel. Even his mouth flattened, turning into a hard, uncompromising line. And in that instant he looked frighteningly capable of the cold-blooded murder she'd read about in the newspapers.

Everything became sharper, more intense, as though someone had taken an eraser and scrubbed away all the blurry distractions, carving out the afternoon in relief—the screech of the egrets, the wind slashing through the tall skeletal trees, the fog soaking into her bones. Even the silence intensified.

He drew the moment out like a death sentence, then shattered it with his voice. *"Who the hell are you?"*

Relief flashed so profound she could taste it. He didn't recognize her. Then reason surfaced. Of course he didn't recognize her. There was no reason he should.

"I asked a question," he said in that same quiet voice. "Don't make me ask again."

An endless valley of lies lay ahead, but right here, right now, she chose to offer the truth. "A friend."

"A friend." He made the word sound like an offense. "Any friend of mine or Savannah's knows better than to come here."

The blade of pain nicked fast and deep. "If you're trying to frighten me," she said, "it's not working."

His smile was sardonic. "I suppose you're not trembling, either."

Refusing to give an inch, she hugged her arms around her middle. "It's cold."

"Maybe on the inside, but not on the out. Try again."

She angled her chin, said nothing. The man could see subtleties and nuances others couldn't. Once, the trait had made him a good cop. It also explained his success as a photographer. His work adorned the walls of galleries in New Orleans, as well as many a coffee table book and calendar. His flare for shadows and light brought solitude to liveliness, sobriety to gaiety.

The quiet spun out between them, thick, pulsing, allowing sounds of the land to spill in. From the darkened copse beyond the clearing, dead leaves rustled and twigs snapped. It almost sounded as though—

He pivoted toward the cypress trees jutting up like a line of soldiers separating land from water. "Don't move." Slowly he edged forward. Each step, each movement, each breath still screamed the caution of the cop he used to be.

Renee's imagination sprinted down a dangerous path as she watched him go down on one knee. "Beautiful."

Heart hammering, she turned to see a great blue heron perched atop the old swing.

"Perfect," Cain murmured as he angled a 35mm camera toward the tire. "Ah…that's my girl. Me, I'm going to be very, very good to you…."

Until his big hands cradled the sleek metal outfit, Renee hadn't noticed the camera hanging from his shoulder. Easy mistake with a man like Cain. His intensity made it impossible to register anything but the man.

Seconds blurred into minutes, minutes into searing intimacy. Cain inched closer to the bird while his drugging voice urged the heron to stay in place.

"Let me have you," he coaxed. "I won't hurt you…just want to make you mine."

The black magic drawl did wicked things to Renee's immunity. How could he shift from suspicious detective to reverent photographer in the space of one broken heartbeat?

24

Somewhere close by twigs snapped. The bird reacted instinctively, lifting its magnificent wings and soaring into the gray sky. But Cain remained crouched, staring at the point where the hero had vanished.

What did he see? Renee wondered. Heavy storm clouds gathering beyond the trees, as she did? Or something different, something no one else could envision.

"You're still here?"

She blinked, saw that he had turned and was moving toward her. "Either that or you're hallucinating."

"My ghosts are my business, Ms.—" He destroyed what remained of her personal space. "I don't believe I caught your name."

"No, you were too busy playing big, bad wolf."

An odd light lit in his eyes. "Do I know you?"

Her heart gave a quick, cruel kick. "That's a question only you can answer," she said with a calm that pleased her. Then she took a leap of faith.

"Renee," she said. She'd known this man and all that he represented would be her greatest challenge, but nothing, not months of preparation, nor layers of scar tissue, had prepared her for the rush of being close to him. "Renee Fox."

"Well, then, Ms. Fox." His gaze flicked down the length of her body in a purely male gesture. He made the return journey slowly, thoroughly, leaving her warm and flushed, as though he'd touched her with those big hands of his. "Shall I walk you to your car?"

"I can manage on my own." Had for a long time. Without another word, she turned and strode toward the rental, refusing to let his less-than-enthusiastic greeting deter her.

"The highway's just a few miles down the road." The falsely friendly words echoed on the breeze. "Don't look back and you'll be in New Orleans before sundown."

Renee ignored the sting and kept walking. No way was she going to give him the satisfaction of looking back. Coming to Bayou de Foi jeopardized the life she'd been quietly building, but she could no longer live without knowing what really happened the night this man was found with his lover's blood on his hands. She would find out, and she would avenge.

Then, and only then, would she be free of the nightmares that made it impossible for her to sleep with the lights off.

...NOT THE END...

Rock and Rolling
by Julie Elizabeth Leto

CHAPTER 1

"OKAY, SO WHERE'S THE FIRE?"

Darcy Michaels, aka "D'Arcy Wilde" to her legions of fans, barged into the French Quarter house without so much as wiping the Bourbon Street stickiness from the bottom of her knee-high boots. She'd paid for the place; she could damn well walk in without knocking. After receiving an urgent call for help from her nineteen-year-old daughter, Cassie, who was living in the house while she attended Tulane University, Darcy had left her band in the middle of a rehearsal. Resilient, clever Cassie rarely needed help with anything, and when she did, her mother was usually the last person she asked.

And when Darcy turned the corner between the foyer and the parlor, she briefly wished Cassie hadn't asked this time, either. Her heart screeched to a halt, along with her feet.

Oh, God.

"Rock?"

Joseph "Rock" La Rocca unfolded himself from an antique settee, looking much like a bull in a china shop. When he stretched to full height, Darcy's breath caught. Beneath her leather-trimmed denim vest, her breasts tightened. Warm moisture diluted the dryness in her mouth. Though Rock would never notice. She'd become incredibly adept at hiding her body's response to this big, gorgeous hunk of male flesh.

Whenever Rock slipped into her radar, which happened more and more frequently since she hired him to run her road show, she forced herself to remember that she wasn't wild Darcy Michaels anymore—a sixteen-year-old kid looking for trouble in Rock's backseat. Now she was the famous and infamous D'Arcy Wilde, contemporary of Madonna, reigning queen of rock 'n' roll, wealthy music industry power broker—and most important, a woman whose world would fall apart once Rock learned the secret she'd kept from him over all these years.

"Why aren't you at rehearsal?" she asked, one hand fisted on her hip.

"Why aren't you?" he shot back, characteristically unfazed.

"My daughter needed me."

"Same here."

Darcy's chest ached. Cassie needed Rock? For what? Several terrifying possibilities flew through Darcy's mind, but only one had the power to turn her cast-iron stomach into a pit of acid.

"Excuse me?"

"Cassie called me at the Dome. Said she had something she needed me to do. I figured she waited until we came to town so I could fix some broken pipe or hook up her stereo. She may be your kid, but she's cheap."

Darcy's eyes narrowed. "She's frugal," she corrected.

"Didn't inherit that from you, did she? Sometimes I wonder if she's really your kid."

She was hers all right. And though Darcy had deferred the day-to-day raising of her child to her much more levelheaded, much more stable sister, she'd worked hard the past few years to build a relationship with the child she'd been way too young to have.

Sixteen. She'd been sixteen. Young, horny, stupid. At least, too stupid to protect herself with means that actually worked while she sweated in the bed of that truck with Rock. She didn't regret giving birth to Cassie—and she definitely didn't regret the sex. The only thing that ticked her off was that she still had feelings for the guy after all this time.

She'd had her share of lovers since, but none had quite measured up to the man who started it all. The man who was Cassie's father. The man who could make her forget the words to a song she'd written herself and sung a hundred times in front of millions of fans simply by taking off his shirt while he and his team built the stage for her latest gig. The man who had no clue that he shared his DNA with the love and light of her life.

"Well, she is my kid, so whatever she needs, I'll take care of it. Where is she?"

Rock crunched himself back into the chair, pretending to be interested in Cassie's chemistry textbook. "Don't know. Said she had to run to the neighbor's and would be right back."

As if that meager explanation were enough, he turned his shoulder and devoted his attention to the book. Darcy stalked out of the room toward the kitchen, then realized after she'd stepped onto the tile floor in the back of the house that she didn't feel any less caged here than she had in the living room.

She hated dealing with Rock like this. Alone. With no entourage to act as a buffer, no business to discuss that would distract her from noticing how tanned he looked after his vacation to parts unknown, or how his raven-black hair seemed to have picked up fiery highlights that did amazing things to his obsidian eyes.

Her cell phone rang, giving her a much-needed distraction.

"Talk to me," she ordered, not bothering to read the caller ID because she really didn't care who'd called so long as it took her mind off the man in the other room.

"Hey, Ma. How's it going?"

"Cassie? Where are you?"

BONUS FEATURE

"Taking care of something urgent."

"Is this the same something urgent that required me to leave rehearsal in the middle of a set with only three days before the opening night of my new tour?"

"You've been rehearsing for four weeks straight. Don't you think you need a break?"

"You didn't answer my question."

"I'm working up to that."

"Cassie, what are you up to? Why is Rock here?"

Darcy heard her daughter's cell phone shake, as if she was covering the mouthpiece. Mumbles followed. Just who was she consulting? Suspicious, she tiptoed into the hallway and peeked in on Rock. He'd graduated from chemistry to economics, but his phone remained clipped to his jeans.

She slipped back into the kitchen, this time shutting the pocket door behind her. "Cassie! What's going on?"

Cassie's deep breath sucked the air right out of Darcy's lungs. "I think you'd better sit down."

This couldn't be good. Darcy reached blindly for a chair and lowered herself into the dainty cushioned seat. "Cassie, don't tell me you've chosen this weekend to tell Rock who he is."

"Okay, I won't tell you that."

Cassie's reply gave her no solace. The kid had a smart mouth.

"Cassie…"

"Don't worry, Mom. I'm not going to tell him."

The silence that followed nearly caused Darcy to pass out. She knew what was coming. She knew. She clenched the phone so tightly, she nearly cracked the casing. "Cassie, don't tell me you want me to…"

Cassie's laugh alleviated some of the terror streaking through Darcy's brain. It would be bad enough if Cassie told him. If Darcy broke the news, he'd likely break her arm. Maybe more. "Relax, Ma. I'm not planning to tell Rock the truth. Not yet. Not if you agree to spend the weekend with him, alone, in the house. It's your choice."

CHAPTER 2

Rock La Rocca closed the textbook he'd been pretending to read, and listened. Just what the heck was going on? His instincts screamed that he'd been lured into a trap, but he didn't know if his former lover and current boss, D'Arcy Wilde, was the designated predator or just another hapless victim of Cassie's scheming. He chuckled. If Darcy ever guessed he'd placed her name and the word *victim* into the same sentence, she'd have his head on a platter. Or other more important body parts.

Unfortunately, he couldn't hear a thing. Wasn't surprising since he'd spent his entire adulthood since age seventeen on the road with rock-and-roll bands who hadn't met a decibel they didn't like. But for the past ten years, he'd been on Darcy's payroll, starting off as muscle in her crew and now, running the complete operation of her world-famous stage shows and international tours. Somehow he'd become her right-hand man—the right hand she never spent time with alone, which was probably good for both of them.

When she was in the studio, he coordinated the musicians, songwriters and technicians. When she was on vacation, Rock ensured that her security was top-notch and her travel and accommodations, sinfully luxurious. But she'd never admit how much she relied on him. So far as Darcy let on, he was nothing more than the hired help and should consider himself damned lucky to have such a high-paying, glamorous job.

He couldn't argue about the choice paychecks, but even if he wanted to work in a job others considered glamorous—which he didn't—working as the biggest cog in the D'Arcy Wilde machine was nothing less than exhausting. And exhilarating. As much as he hated to admit the truth and would never act on it, Darcy stirred his blood like no other woman ever had.

So they avoided one another, particularly when they might end up together alone. Never working too late, never allowing the sensual undercurrent born from their past to overtake them in the here and now. Only for Cassie would he have come today, he tried to tell himself. He'd only met the kid a few years ago and didn't know much about her except she didn't seem much like her mother. He figured she took after her father, but no one seemed to know who the lucky guy had been. Not that Rock cared. So long as the kid hadn't inherited her mother's bossy attitude, which she hadn't, he didn't so much mind having her around.

But apparently she had developed skills in sly manipulation. Cassie had easily lured him away from the last round of rehearsals before Tuesday's opening night with just one phone call—but only because she claimed that Darcy needed him and was too proud to ask for the help herself.

"Mom needs you," she had said simply.

Rock had peeked around a wall from backstage at the rehearsal, certain the sultry voice echoing on the sound system belonged to Darcy. It had. He'd know her unique vibrato anywhere and at any volume. He heard her in his dreams.

36

"Listen, kid. Your mom is on stage right this minute, running through her second set."

"I know," Cassie said, tension crackling over the phone line. "But you know my mom. When she's working, she doesn't think about anything else but wowing the crowd. But in just a little while, she's going to get another phone call and will take an unscheduled break. And when she does, she's going to need you here with her."

That had been enough for Rock to make the arrangements for his assistant to run the show for the rest of the afternoon. A few minutes later, when he'd watched Darcy's secretary skitter across the stage with a cell phone in her hand, he knew Cassie hadn't been exaggerating. He headed for his car ahead of

Darcy, but knew from the paleness of her skin and her frantic gestures that she wouldn't be far behind.

While he'd beat Darcy to Cassie's rented house in the French Quarter, he hadn't had more than ten seconds to talk to the girl before she beelined out the back door to complete some mysterious errand with a neighbor. He'd suspected Cassie had been up to something. And if his instincts were correct, she was now spilling the entire story to Darcy via cell phone.

Unable to sit still any longer, he stalked toward the closed pocket door separating the girly antique parlor and long hallway from the kitchen in the back of the house. Rock liked women, but damned if their decorating choices didn't perplex him. What was with all the flowers? Wasn't it enough to have a garden out back? And the lace. One glance at the doilies displayed in fruitwood frames along the wall and he was transported back to his grandmother's house in Chicago. All that was missing was the perpetual smell of garlic and the inevitable and loud "discussion" as to why he preferred living like a gypsy to working in the family business.

Not wanting that memory to take root, he slid open the door and marched inside the kitchen. Darcy had her back to him, her hand cupped secretively over the phone.

"You can't be serious," she insisted, but the lack of sheer and utter confidence in her voice told him that whomever she spoke to wasn't telling her a joke—and she knew it.

When she finally sensed his presence, she straightened her spine and twisted her neck, slowly meeting his gaze without turning completely around. Damn, but she was one gorgeous woman. She had an incredible sense of rhythm that trickled down to something as common as throwing a dirty look over her shoulder.

She held the phone to her breast, drawing his gaze to the skimpy denim vest she'd been wearing at the Dome. Snug against her age-defying, unbound breasts, the shirt succeeded at what the entire outfit had been designed to do—make any man within a two-mile radius drool with lust and forget anything and everything but her. He thought he'd be immune by now, but damned if he wasn't.

"Do you mind?" she snapped. "I'm having a personal conversation here."

"With Cassie?"

She didn't answer, but the quick dart of her eyes told him the truth. He crossed the room and yanked the small device out of her hand.

While Darcy cursed, Rock held the phone to his ear. "What the hell is going on, Cassie?"

"Rock? Oh! Um, I need to finish talking to Darcy."

"I've got work to do, kid. I ain't hanging around here all day."

Darcy wrestled the miniscule phone out of his beefy hands, but spoke to him instead of to her daughter.

"You will if I tell you to," she proclaimed.

"Oh, yeah? Why? You going to fire me?"

He knew she wouldn't. Not over this. Hell, he'd given her plenty of reasons to can his ass over the past ten years and for some reason, she hadn't. And with her biggest tour ever only three days away, he was gambling she wouldn't now, either.

Darcy lifted the phone, promised she'd call Cassie back, then disconnected the call. In one smoky moment, her stiff spine softened into a sultry curve— one hip jutting slightly to the left, her right boot snaking to the side in a coy pose he'd watched her perfect on the stage. Men more devoted to goodness than he—married senators, pious clergy and right-eous politicians—had fallen prostrate to Darcy's charm with nothing more than her signature sexy stance. So who was he to fight?

"I'm not going to fire you, Rock," she promised, her voice a sensuous purr. "But if you give me a chance, I'll make your stay here worth your while."

CHAPTER 3

"WELL?"

Cassie Michaels pocketed her cell phone, then stared at her friend Samantha La Rocca, not quite sure what had just happened. She'd issued her ultimatum to her mother, but she hadn't received the definitive answer she so desperately wanted.

"I don't know. She told me she'd call me back."

Just over thirty, blond and blue-eyed, Sam smiled. "That's good, right? If she didn't barge right out the door, she must be interested in your…suggestion."

Cassie nodded, trying to contain her hopes. She sighed and relaxed against the wall of the building she and Sam had chosen for their stakeout—kitty-corner to the one her mother had leased for her so she could escape the Tulane University dormitories. Darcy loved buying her extravagant gifts, taking her exotic places and generally making their limited time as mother and daughter as exciting and memorable as possible. Was Cassie so wrong to try to give her mother something so much more precious in return?

Namely, one last shot at her one true love?

Sam laid her hand on Cassie's shoulder, causing Cassie to relax and smile. Cassie's curiosity about her birth father had brought the women together shortly after Cassie's enrollment at Tulane—but it had been kindred outlooks on life that had kept them together. That and the fact that Cassie was seriously in love with one of the waiters at the restaurant Samantha's husband owned—a rare Italian trattoria in the Cajun- and Creole-food Mecca of New Orleans.

The name on the marquee—La Rocca—while not uncommon in New Orleans, had lured Cassie to the restaurant that bore the same last name as her birth father, a man she knew, but didn't know. A man she only recently realized hadn't been just another of her mother's meaningless conquests, but had actually been her one and only love. Cassie's curiosity had not only led her to meet *Rock's* cousin, Nick, and his new wife, Samantha, but in the process, she'd gained a great deal of insight into her birth father's loner personality. Insight she hoped would propel her plan to reunite her parents to success.

Well, not exactly *her* plan alone. Sam had helped. Her distant cousin by marriage had garnered a well-earned reputation for matchmaking. Her specialty involved forcing two people together until they had no choice but to confront their feelings for each other—or at the very least, engage in some fairly mind-blowing sex.

Cassie figured most kids would be freaked out thinking about their parents having any kind of sex, much less the mind-blowing variety. However, most kids didn't have rock-and-roll diva D'Arcy Wilde for their mother—or hunky Rock La Rocca for a dad, even if he didn't know. Yet. But he would soon. How soon depended entirely on Darcy.

"She's definitely interested," Cassie said, "though I'm not sure if her curiosity is out of lust or fear."

"Either one works for me," Sam quipped, reminding Cassie that Sam had told her how she'd once used fear to fix up her own stubborn sister and her now-smitten husband. "So what's the next move?"

Cassie thought a minute. She hadn't expected her mother to agree to her demands quickly, but she also hadn't planned on getting disconnected. Time to move on to Phase Two and hope for the best.

"I'm going to give Darcy a few minutes to think about what she's going to do and how she's going to do it. Then I'm calling in the reinforcements."

DARCY LICKED her lips, tossed her hair and hoped like hell that Rock hadn't developed an immunity to her over all these years. When she'd first hired him on her road crew, she'd wondered how they would manage to keep their hands off each other, working so closely and at all hours of the day and night. But after a few weeks, Darcy realized she'd worried needlessly.

42

Joseph "Rock" La Rocca, once the most hands-on boyfriend she'd ever toyed with, had developed an iron-clad, hands-off policy when it came to her. She guessed that maybe—if she'd really turned up the heat—the sexual tension crackling between them might have burned through his defenses.

But she'd kept the attraction on simmer, certain she'd fare better in the long run. She had, after all, given birth to his child and then decided not to tell him. And however good her reasons had been when she was sixteen and he'd just run off to run sound for a local garage band, the reasons didn't hold up now.

And according to Cassie, her reasons soon wouldn't matter. She was ready to tell her birth father the truth. And shock of all shocks, she was giving Darcy a heads-up so that if she had any unresolved feelings for her former lover, she could put things in order right here, right now.

"We need to stay here for a little while," she said. Rock watched her with wary eyes, but as she neared, she wondered if a spark of desire didn't dance in those obsidian depths, as well.

He folded his arms over that massive chest of his, eliciting a hungry groan from the back of her throat. God, he'd aged well. The last time she'd felt those callused hands on her flesh, she'd been a hormone-ravaged teenybopper with unstoppable dreams of fame. Now she was a woman who'd attained those dreams in her own irreverent style—and yet she still wanted Rock. She'd wanted him for a long, long time…but it took her daughter's ultimatum to force her hand.

"Why? Where's Cassie?"

"She's not coming."

"What's this all about, Darcy? What are you up to?"

She considered lying, but what would be the point? For once in her life, the truth—or, at least, the portion of the truth that most applied to their current situation—could work to her advantage. For nearly ten years, she'd wanted Rock in her bed again. She'd wanted to show him the woman she'd become—the powerful, adventurous, exciting woman that men all over the world clamored to make love to. Men all over the world—except Rock. And while his lack of interest stung, she'd figured it was fair compensation for all she hadn't told him about her feelings for him—and about Cassie.

But now, she had no choice. In a few hours, the truth would be out. And knowing her mother as she did, Cassie had suggested Darcy do whatever it took to come to terms with her feelings for Rock before all hell broke loose. She had only now to take what she wanted—and D'Arcy Wilde didn't need much more incentive than that.

The minute she broke into his tight personal space, she inhaled. Scents of sawdust and motor oil and warm honeyed musk dizzied her senses, causing her hand to quiver oh-so-slightly when she reached up and cupped his stubble-roughed cheek.

"This is called a seduction, Rock. Why don't you just relax and enjoy the ride?"

CHAPTER 4

RELAX AND ENJOY the ride? Rock thought, way more tempted to hop on board than he'd ever admit out loud. He was a man after all. And D'Arcy Wilde was one tough woman to resist.

46 Damn. He prided himself on being the one man on Earth who wouldn't fall to his knees after one sultry look from her—yet the minute she turned her sensual powers on him, his body hardened, his breath left his lungs in a quick rush, his sex throbbed with a need so innate, so natural, he would have hardly thought twice if she'd been any other woman.

But she wasn't any other woman. She was his boss, his high school crush, his favorite sparring partner. She was the siren who haunted his nights with her sensual voice and hypnotic eyes; the harpy who taunted his days with her incredibly high expectations and unreasonable demands. He dropped his arms to his side, curious about why she'd chosen today to rekindle the fire that had once burned white-hot between them. If she pressed closer, he might just find out.

"The ride? You and me would be more like a train wreck."

His quip didn't slow her down, not that she was moving fast. Her hand cupped his chin lightly and, like molasses drizzled over hotcakes, she eased her body to his until the buttons on her denim vest pressed into his T-shirt. Her tiny, leather miniskirt sidled against his thighs. "Train wrecks can be exciting, so long as no one gets hurt."

"Darcy, with you, someone always gets hurt."

Not surprisingly, the truth didn't faze her. "That's a lie and you know it. I don't mess with men who don't understand me."

That made Rock laugh out loud, no matter how his guffaw pissed her off. "Darcy, a whole team of psychiatrists living with you 24/7 couldn't understand you."

She rewarded his ill-timed humor by slapping him on the ass. Damned if it didn't turn him on.

"You may be right. Maybe it's better that way. Trying to understand someone requires work. And I don't know about you, but I prefer to expend my energy in a less cerebral way."

"Sex can be cerebral, if done correctly." He inhaled as she pressed her palm down his chest. The scent of her Parisian shampoo—lightly scented with herbs and flowers—teased his nose. He wanted to

BONUS FEATURE

bury his face in her soft, black hair. Or better yet, with her straddled atop him, the strands could tease him as they dangled in his face. "That is what you have in mind, right? Sex?"

"It's what I always have in mind."

"Not with me," he pointed out.

"You don't really know that, do you, Rock? Not for sure." She stepped back, walked a tight circle around him, her hand never surrendering contact with his body. "We've been dancing around each other for a long, long time. Maybe I'm tired of lusting after you from afar."

Rock wanted to contradict her, wanted to insist she never looked at him with anything in her eyes other than job-related expectation—but he knew he'd be lying. Too many times, he'd caught his gaze drifting toward Darcy when she was on stage, singing some sexy ballad, her eyes trained on him. It had happened during intimate rehearsals in her hotel suite or during concerts when thirty thousand screaming fans howled all around them.

When the moments hit, Rock had been instantly transported back in time to those hot nights when he'd throw pebbles at her bedroom window in the middle of the night, then spirit her away to their secluded spot by the lake so they could make love under the stars.

They'd been kids then. And even though Darcy was the same incredibly uninhibited soul he'd known

48

back then, times had changed. He'd changed. Toying with Darcy now would be a huge mistake.

And yet, when she slid behind him and snaked her hands around his waist, then lower, he knew he'd give her whatever she wanted.

"Darcy, don't…"

"Why not, Rock? I know you want me."

"Why, because every man wants you?"

The throaty sound of her laugh sent a warm shimmy up his spine. She completed her rotation around him, slipping her arms around his neck and pulling herself up so that her lips were just centimeters from his. "Partly. But between us, there's more. You remember those times back at the lake just as much as I do, don't you? You remember how great we were together. Two kids, practically virgins, but still, we never felt awkward or walked away less than satisfied. Maybe that's why I've taken so many lovers over the years, trying to find one who was equal to you."

He couldn't resist wrapping his hands around her slim waist, allowing his fingers to dip over her tight derriere. Her black lashes fluttered when he squeezed her flesh possessively, and her tiny moan testified that the desire she claimed for him was no act, no manipulation. Darcy may have had a thousand and one bad habits, in his opinion, but lying wasn't one of them. Not about sex, anyway.

"Maybe I'm not even equal to those standards anymore. I'm not a seventeen-year-old kid with more hormones than sense."

She swiped her tongue over his lips, spearing her fingers into his hair at the same time. "Thank God. If you were that good when you didn't know what you were doing, I can only imagine how hot you're going to make me now."

Rock combed his hand up the back of her neck, latched on to her hair and tilted her head back with a gentle tug. "Oh, baby. You don't have to imagine. I'm going to show you. Right here. Right now."

CHAPTER 5

THE MINUTE Rock's lips locked onto the hollow of her throat, Darcy jumped into the swirl of pent-up desire she'd been trying to sate for nineteen years. She wouldn't turn back now. Spikes of pure heat slashed through her body, igniting fires from the tips of her breasts to her toes and everywhere in between. Her veins and nerve endings throbbed, surging with a rush of blood and need and ultimately, disbelief.

God, how she wanted this. Had wanted this. For what seemed like forever. Night after night—sometimes when in the arms of another man—this exact fantasy had haunted her dreams. Yet with so much emotional baggage between them—suitcases full of lies and regrets, most of which Rock didn't know about—she'd held back. The woman known throughout the music industry for pushing the envelope and snatching fame and fortune when no one would give it to her in the time frame she wanted—that same woman had waited all these years to taste again

BONUS FEATURE

the magic that in so many ways, had made her who she was.

Rock grabbed her backside and lifted her, her feet nearly dangling while he bathed her neck in moist kisses. Her skirt rode up to her waist, allowing his hands to roam free over skin bared by her thong-style panties. He pressed her hard against his pelvis, and the thickness of his erection sent a second wave of passion coursing through her.

She had his shirt over his head and on the floor in no time. Her vest was next, though half the buttons clattered and shot across the floor, torn from the fabric. When the rush of need subsided just long enough for them to assess their surroundings, Rock wore nothing but unzipped jeans and sneakers, while Darcy dared to tempt him further in her bra, panties and knee-high boots.

Briefly, Darcy realized they were about to do the deed in her daughter's Donna Reed-style kitchen. No matter how she sliced it, she'd leased the house for Cassie, never guessing her supposed golden child would set her and Rock up on the very same property for a wild, mad tryst. Luckily, Darcy knew the layout well enough to lure Rock toward a small back room with only a sly half grin and a half-crooked finger.

The tiny windowless room, no bigger than a closet, was still stacked nearly floor to ceiling with blankets, pillows and sleeping bags. When Cassie's friends showed up to party in the Quarter, she preferred to put them up on the floor rather than send them home drunk. With one shove, two towers of pillows tumbled to the floor and Darcy dove in, unabashed and unashamed.

For an instant, Rock just watched her from the doorway, shaking his head in disbelief though his eyes sparkled. This was just the kind of spontaneous, brazen thing they would have done as kids. By the time she'd unzipped her boots—slipping a condom out of the clever pocket inserted into the design just for that purpose—he'd removed his shoes and jeans and joined her in the pillows.

"You're crazy, Darcy. You know that?"

She grabbed his hand, then with a playful push, twisted until she had him pinned beneath her. "Crazy with wanting you. Nineteen years is a long time for a girl like me to wait."

He rubbed his callused hands over her smooth thighs, eyeing her with absolute hunger. "Then why did you?"

She rolled her eyes, hoping her expression would hide, at least for now, the truth she wasn't ready to share. "You weren't exactly pursuing me, you know."

He laughed. "Since when has that stopped you?"

She moved to deliver a playful punch to his shoulder, but he anticipated her response and grabbed her by the wrist. His aggressive counterattack sent an electric thrill shooting up her arm. "Even a bad girl like me wants to be chased every so often."

He arched a brow. "Like I chased you back in high school?"

With a shift of her knees, she pressed her sex against his. Why she thought the move would punish him, she didn't know. The only one suffering seemed to be her. A sleek moistness seeped through the thin fabric of her panties, and from the darkening look in his gaze, the tale of her arousal spread through his boxers, as well.

"You didn't have to chase me then. Just like I didn't have to chase you. We sort of just fell together."

He glanced around at their precarious position on the pillows. "This is a habit with us."

She leaned down and swiped a kiss over his mouth. "A good one?"

54

His response was to hook his hand behind her neck and press her face to his for a longer kiss. "A great one."

Like a flame doused with brandy, the heat of his kiss seared her, burned her, straight through to her soul. No matter what happened later, they'd have this moment, this adventure, forever.

Slowly, she reached around and unhooked her bra, allowing the dark material to fall away across her pale skin, watching Rock for every degree of dilation in his eyes, every short rasp of breath. He didn't disappoint her, taking the time to adore her with his hands, mouth and tongue until she thought she'd go insane.

In a split second, the last of their clothes were

gone and he'd slid the condom over his thick sex. Unable to resist, Darcy took the flavored latex into her mouth until Rock begged for sweet mercy.

Without warning, he flipped her and pinned her to the pillows. Before she could protest, he captured her mouth. Unable to wait, she parted her legs so he could find his way home.

The minute he entered her, passion took over. She lifted her hips and bent her knees, needing to feel all of him, all the way. He tortured her with a slow, sensual rhythm and refused to increase the tempo until he sensed her surrender to his lead. Then he captured her hands, twining her fingers with his, and oh-so-expertly rode with her to the edge.

At just the last moment, Rock rolled her, wrapping his arms around her like a vise so their connection didn't break, not even for a moment. When they came, together, the past and the present collided in a bright ball of glorious light—leaving Darcy to wonder if this moment could possibly save them from the inevitable destruction sure to come.

CHAPTER 6

ONCE THEY LAY lust-sated and drowsy with satisfaction on the pillows, Rock realized a truth he'd denied for way too long. He wanted Darcy again. And not just "again" in the sense that he intended to hunt down discarded jeans for his wallet and another condom sometime in the next hour—which he did— but he meant "again" in the long-term.

God, nineteen years seemed a lifetime ago. When he'd left their hometown for parts unknown, he'd had nothing but rootless adventure on his mind. His father and all his uncles had been tied into a family business, but Rock never envisioned his future there. The responsibility, the expectations, the day-to-day sameness would have snuffed him as painfully as a screwdriver to the skull. Only now, with Darcy's hair fanned over his chest and her exotic scent stirring his senses, did he realize that what he'd actually resisted was not the restaurant business or the lack of excitement. He reviled the permanency.

And yet, he'd been with Darcy and her tour for ten years. And once on the payroll of D'Arcy Wilde Productions, no two days were ever alike. Her shows took him to the most exciting cities on every continent. When her music required inspiration or she sought an exotic locale for a video, she thought nothing of crossing the equator or several oceans to find the perfect desert oasis or the whitest, sandy beach. Even when she was settled in one place, the constant stream of people, from fans, agents and musicians to artists, celebrities, industry professionals and groupies, changed the atmosphere from moment to moment. She knew everyone—and yet she met someone new every day.

Even Darcy's personality was as changeable as her wardrobe. Some days pensive, some days outrageous, she was, every day, smart and fun and exciting. She was the perfect woman. So why hadn't he realized this until now?

Simple answer. Because until today, his perfect woman hadn't wanted him. Or so he'd thought. Not since high school, when they used to lie in the bed of his truck, staring at the stars and devising a thousand ways for her to escape her poverty-stricken life in the trailer park. Now that he knew the truth—that her desire for him hadn't lessened despite the many years and their many other lovers—he intended to keep her.

BONUS FEATURE

"Well, that was a blast from the past, wasn't it?" she said, her humor uncharacteristically understated as she attempted to move out of his embrace.

He yanked her back down and placed a kiss on her temple. "This wasn't about the past, Darcy, and you know it."

Her muscles stiffened and she pulled away. Only then did he notice the glossiness in her eyes, the pale tinge around the lips. Yes, he'd kissed off all her hot-red lipstick, but wariness made her tremble through her attempts to suddenly escape his touch.

"No, I don't know that at all. I wanted you again. I've had you. Now it's time to bolt."

This time, she scrambled quickly enough to get away. Stunned, he took a few seconds to recover. A burst of angry energy propelled him up and out of the room and he didn't even bother with his shorts or jeans. She, however, struggled to bend herself back into her sweaty underwear. When she caught him watching, amused by her failing attempts to dress, she cursed, then threw on her vest and skirt without them.

"Where do you think you're going?" he asked.

"I have a rehearsal to finish," she snapped.

She rushed past him in search of something, most likely her boots. When she found them, she didn't return to the kitchen to put them on, but sneaked into the living room. Luckily, this house wasn't a big place. Neither was the city of New Orleans. She couldn't outrun him for long, though she'd likely gain more distance since she was dressed and he was not.

No bother. He knew where she was going. He could give her a chance to cool down, then confront her with the facts. Knowing Darcy, this sudden fit of temper and denial was a direct result of the fact that their little tryst meant more to her than she'd planned, more than she wanted to admit.

But before she left, he needed to make sure she understood the future she'd face. He wasn't going to let her go and she was better off knowing that right here, right now.

"So you're telling me you arranged this afternoon just for a quickie? Hate to break it to you, babe, but one time isn't going to get me out of your system."

"I never said you were *in* my system," she declared.

He leaned his shoulder against the doorjamb between the hallway and the living room, suddenly damned comfortable wearing nothing but a cocky smile. "You didn't have to say it."

She finished zipping up her boots, then stood, stamping her feet one at a time on the hardwood floor. "Yeah, well, maybe I didn't. Point is, I'm done. Getting involved with you, beyond today…just wouldn't be…it won't work, Rock. Trust me." She flew past him, grabbing her purse from where she'd roped it on the hat tree next to the front door. "There's too much you don't know."

Without much effort, he trapped her against the door. He was more turned on than he'd guessed. His sex, hard and hot, slid against her leather skirt. The short hem sliced softly across him. If she'd let him, he could likely slip underneath and remind her about what he did know.

"Then tell me."

For an instant, he thought she would. Bold defiance, the expression he associated the most with her for all the years they'd known each other, flashed in her eyes. But an instant later, fear blinked her confidence away.

Fear. In Darcy?

"I can't," she admitted, her voice barely a whisper.

He shook his head, disbelieving. "You're frickin' D'Arcy Wilde. You can do whatever the hell you please."

She used both hands to push him away so she could yank open the door. "Not this time, I can't."

Where Rock expected the door to open to sunlight, instead he blinked at the flash of cameras. Dusk had descended on Bourbon Street, and with it, a swarm of reporters had gathered at the door. He had just enough time to duck out of sight before he heard the first reporter shout, "Hey, D'Arcy, who's that in there with you?"

Then another. "Reports are that you left the Superdome this afternoon enraged. Are you canceling your tour?"

Then the next—and this question nearly coaxed him out of hiding. "Ms. Wilde, your daughter has called to alert us about an upcoming press conference. Just what is that about?"

CHAPTER 7

THE QUESTION INSTANTLY halted Darcy's push through the crowd. She stood, stunned, reporters swarming, flashes bursting, questions assaulting her from every angle. Cassie called a press conference? Oh, God. This couldn't be happening. No way would her mild-mannered, always-polite, "How could she possibly be related to you?" daughter announce who her father was to the press before she told Rock herself. That had been their deal!

Then again, Cassie did possess half of Darcy's brazen blood. She'd do what it took to get what she wanted—just the same as her mother.

Darcy scrambled back inside the house in time for Rock to lock the door behind her.

"What the hell is going on?" he demanded. "Was this some sort of publicity stunt?"

Before Darcy could answer, her cell phone rang. She didn't have to look to know Cassie would be on the other end of the line.

"And you told the reporters I was here, why?" she asked, knowing beyond a shadow of a doubt that her daughter had arranged the raving welcoming committee outside.

"Because I don't want you to leave. Yet."

"I have to," she said, flashing a glance at Rock, who hadn't had the common decency to put on his shorts. She squeezed her eyes tightly shut, blocking out the sight of him, so male, so glorious, so hard she could still feel him inside her. How she was going to do without that sensation for the rest of her life, she didn't know. She'd managed once, but no way would she accomplish that feat again.

Yet once he found out the secret she'd been keeping from him, she knew he'd likely quit his job and devote the rest of his life to trashing her for being a selfish, heartless bitch. And she wasn't so sure he'd be far off the mark.

"You don't have to, Mom. Tell him. Tell him the truth about me."

"Oh, yeah. That'll keep us together longer," she said sarcastically.

Cassie's laugh trilled with nervousness. "I removed all sharp instruments from the house before I left. You'll be fine."

"I thought you were going to—" she paused, aware that Rock remained just a few feet away, listening intently to every word she said. "I thought we decided that you were going to handle that revelation yourself."

"Mom, I was nine years old when we made that deal. Any suggestion you made that sounded like I was in charge was okay by me."

Darcy's gaze darted down the hall, but when Rock's stare followed hers, she knew she couldn't disappear into the kitchen or anywhere else for privacy. She was stuck with him. "So what changed your mind?"

"I got to know Rock last summer on the tour. I watched you watching him all the time."

"I don't…" She pressed her shoulder to the door and cupped her hand over her mouth. "Not *all* the time."

"You do when you don't think he'll catch you. All during my childhood, I thought my birth father was just a sperm donor, another link in your endless chain of lovers. I didn't know you loved him."

"I don't," Darcy insisted.

Cassie, apparently, wasn't going to argue over a fact she knew was irrefutable. "You owe him the truth. From you. It'll either ruin everything or fix everything. But the time is now."

Darcy swallowed the lump in her throat. Damn it, she hated when her kid sounded so frickin' much like an adult. "Okay."

Silence crackled over the phone line. "Okay? You're not going to try and bolt again, are you?

Because if you do, I swear I'll announce it to the press. You think he's going to be pissed now, you just wait until he hears the news from those sharks outside your front door."

Damn, she was good. Here Darcy thought that letting her responsible, loving sister raise her daughter would smooth out the ruthless edges Cassie had likely inherited from her—heck, from both parents. No dice.

"I won't leave," she answered begrudgingly.

Cassie was right. Again. No matter how Darcy had considered herself a progressive parent by deciding her daughter could pick how and when she informed Rock about her existence, confessing this secret was her responsibility. And in a way, Cassie *had* chosen. But to make it interesting, she'd left them alone long enough so her mother could be tortured with an explosive sexual encounter that would likely never happen again.

"But that doesn't mean he won't," Darcy clarified.

Cassie chuckled. "Oh, I don't know, Mom. I'm sure you have plenty of ways to keep him occupied."

Darcy rewarded that tart comment with a string of curse words, then promised to call her daughter back and hit the End key.

"What was that all about?" Rock asked.

"Blackmail."

"From who?" He stood up straighter and fisted his hands on his hips. Oh, great. Just what she needed. Michelangelo's *David* on the warpath.

"Keep your pants on, Hercules. Or I should say *put* your pants on. My blackmailer is just my kid."

A grin cracked his face. "She's more like you than you'd care to admit."

Darcy tossed her phone into her purse and lassoed the strap back onto the hat tree. She walked into the living room and then retraced her steps to the back room, shouting triumphantly when she caught site of Rock's boxers. She tossed them back at him, then flung herself down into a plush chair by the fireplace.

"Yes, my daughter—manipulative, crafty, stubborn and sometimes very, very stupid."

He stepped into the shorts and with a quick tug, covered himself, giving her a brief respite before he crossed the room, knelt at her feet and took her hands gently in his. "Maybe she inherited the stupid part from her father."

Oy.

Darcy dropped her chin to her chest, shaking her head. Laughter bubbled inside her—not the ebullient laughter in response to something truly funny, but the high-pitched cackle of someone just a step from insanity.

"Rock, babe. Don't say that. Don't even think it."

Rock's face twisted in a disbelieving sneer. "What, the guy was a genius?"

Lord, men could be so dense sometimes! "Genius? No. But he's a good guy. The best. Someone that meant a lot to me a long time ago. Still does, though he'd never believe me if I told him."

"Oh." Rock stood, remained still for a minute, then crossed to the back of the house and grabbed his jeans and shirt and shoes. He was half-dressed before Darcy realized that he thought she was talking about some other guy. If only!

"Rock," she said with a sigh, bracing herself for the confession she knew she had to make. "Where are you going?"

"We're done here, Darcy. You've obviously got it bad for Cassie's dad. Under any other circumstance, you can bet your ass I'd fight like hell to keep what happened between us today going hot and heavy. But I don't stand in the way of families."

She jumped up from the chair. "Rock. Pay attention! Can't you see what today has been about? Can't you see why Cassie arranged for us to be alone today? Why she called the reporters? She's nineteen years old. Do the math!"

CHAPTER 8

ROCK HELD UP his hand, palm forward, hoping to God the gesture kept Darcy from saying another word. Before he knew it, that same hand was pressed against his mouth while the other patted the air behind him, hoping something along the lines of a chair or a couch materialized soon. He found himself plopping into the antique chair he'd been sitting in when Darcy first arrived, the hardcover textbook squashed beneath him.

"Listen, Rock," she began, but he quieted her with one quelling look.

Took a minute for that to sink in, too. He'd just quieted D'Arcy Wilde with one look? At least he knew the regret glossing her eyes was genuine. Only real regret would keep her from indulging in a full-fledged hissy fit right now.

"Cassie's my kid?" he asked, just wanting one, very basic verification.

She nodded.

"When did you know?"

She shrugged, but met his eyes before she answered. "About a month after you took off. Around the same time the record company offered me that deal."

Didn't take much to get his mind around why she hadn't contacted him then. For one, she probably hadn't known where he was. Very few people had. For another, at barely seventeen, he hadn't exactly been father material. Had she contacted his traditional Italian family, every male would have been deployed to track him down and force him to take responsibility for his child. He would have cracked under that pressure—and Darcy, more than anyone else, had known that.

But what about more recently? Like ten years ago when she spotted him at an awards ceremony and made him a job offer he couldn't refuse? Had she wanted to check him out? See if he'd gotten his act together? Well, hell…who took ten years to pass judgment?

"Okay." Rock removed the book from the beneath him, tossed it lightly to the floor, then braced his hands on the hand-carved chair arms. "Start talking, Darcy. And don't shut up until I've got all the details."

She complied. Beginning with her decision to let her mother, and later her sister, raise her child so she could pursue her career all the way up to Cassie's graduation from high school last summer, Darcy filled him in on each stage of his daughter's life. He already knew she'd been raised with love and attention. That she was bright, funny—that she loved her mother even if she didn't agree with all her choices.

He'd spent a lot of time with Cassie on the tour last summer, honestly impressed with her levelheaded attitude. But he'd never suspected...heck, he'd never even once wondered *who* the birth father had been. He figured the topic was touchy, since no one, not even the press, ever made reference to the guy.

And now he knew the guy was him.

"So you slept with me today to soften the blow?" he guessed after she remained quiet, waiting for his response to her story.

"No," she answered flatly.

70

"Then why?"

"Same reason I told you earlier. I wanted you. I have for a hell of a long time, but because of this secret between us, I couldn't risk getting close to you again. I knew you'd hate me once the truth came out. And I couldn't bear to face that."

"Hate you? God, Darcy, I've loved you since I met you. Why do you think I put up with your bad moods and incessant demands?"

She threw up her hands in disbelief. "Because I pay you to."

He grinned. "Fringe benefit."

It was her turn to thrust her hands on her hips and stalk across the room. When a flash popped from the other side of the window, Rock turned to chew out whatever photographer dared get so close to the house, but Darcy grabbed his hand and tugged him toward the stairs. "They're probably in the garden in the back, too," she explained, leading him up to the landing.

At the top, he stopped. All that existed upstairs were bedrooms and though he didn't doubt he and Darcy could solve the world's problems between the sheets, the dilemma facing them personally would require much more than sex.

With a huff, she sat on the top step. He stared at her, wondering what she was going to do or say to possibly try to make this right, when she grabbed his hand and tugged him down.

"Okay, let's recap," she suggested, morphing into businesswoman mode. He groaned, knowing he was in deep. Darcy was tough to resist when she was being fun and irreverent and wild. When she turned on the smarts, anyone, male or female, didn't stand a chance.

"You've lied to me for nineteen years," he said, guessing they should start with the most pertinent facts and work down from there.

She didn't agree. "Yes, but I had a good reason."

He leaned sideways to see her face. "Like?"

"I loved you. Love you. Present tense."

"You have some way of showing it, sister."

Her grin was nothing less than feline. "Oh, I have marvelous ways of showing it, if you'll recall."

BONUS FEATURE

He rolled his eyes. "Point taken. So you didn't tell me about my kid because you loved me."

"Once I knew you were still that great guy I'd made love to in the back of the truck, yeah. If I told you, you'd hate me, even though at the time, I had the best reasons for not letting you into Cassie's life. Hell, I hardly let me into Cassie's life. And you know what? She's turned out great. I may never be Mother of the Year, but I knew my sister could be. And Cassie deserved the best."

"Cassie deserved a father."

"I can't deny that. I was wrong, Rock."

He stared at her openly. "Hold on. Should I call one of those reporters inside? Get that on record?"

She slugged him in the shoulder and they dissolved into laughter. A warm comfortable sound that could, with time, wash away all the resentment he knew he should feel. But why? Why throw away a chance with Darcy over past mistakes?

Rock sure as hell didn't like admitting it, but he could understand how and why Darcy made her errors. She'd done some things right and some things wrong—but everything she'd done had been to protect her child.

"You forgive me?" she asked.

"I'm thinking about it."

She smiled. "Anything I can do to help?"

He glanced around. There were no windows up here, and no view from below that could possibly allow anyone to intrude on their privacy. "When's Cassie coming home?"

"Not until I call her. She's staying with friends. She wanted to force us together. Figured we wouldn't be able to resist our feelings if we were alone—really alone."

"She really is a smart kid."

She skewered her bottom lip with her teeth. "Must get it from you."

"Yeah." He laughed, shaking his head. "Rock La Rocca, genius. Can't even do basic math."

She walked her fingers over his hand, then up his arm. His bare skin tingled at the contact. He shook his head, disbelieving. God, he had it bad. He loved this woman enough to forgive her. And even though she'd had a hard nudge from Cassie, Darcy obviously loved him enough to face her mistakes with honesty and apology.

Though, she didn't have to know that he was willing to totally forgive her. Not just yet, anyway.

She tickled her fingers over his shoulders, up the sensitive muscles in his neck.

"Darcy, what are you doing?"

"Touching you. Do you mind?"

"Depends," he answered.

"On?"

He shrugged, then in a flash of impetuousness, he grabbed her by the waist and pulled her onto his lap.

"On if that touching is going to lead to some awesome makeup sex."

Her blue eyes flashed with so many emotions, he wasn't sure which one meant more to him. The relief? The excitement? The love? The desire?

Right now, definitely the desire.

"I don't know," she said, shaking her head with exaggerated doubt. "We have some serious issues to deal with. Making up might take the rest of the weekend, at least. Just think about all the naughty things I'm going to have to let you do to me so you'll love me again."

She snuggled closer, moving so that he was instantly reminded that she wore nothing beneath her skirt. "I never stopped loving you."

"So you say," she said, her brow arched. "I think you have some proof to provide yourself."

Rock wrapped his arms around her, certain he'd never have a dull moment so long as Darcy was in his life. "You're a very bad girl, D'Arcy Wilde."

She rewarded his assessment with a long, sultry kiss. "I know, and you wouldn't want me any other way."

COMING NEXT MONTH

Signature Select Collection
A FARE TO REMEMBER by Vicki Lewis Thompson, Julie Elizabeth Leto, Kate Hoffmann
A matchmaking New York City taxi driver must convince three women he's found their life matches...but it's hardly a smooth ride.

Signature Select Saga
YOU MADE ME LOVE YOU by C.J. Carmichael
For six friends, childhood summers on a British Columbian island forged lifelong friendships that shaped their futures for the better... and the worst. Years later, death brings tragedy, mystery and love to two of them as they explore what really happened.

Signature Select Miniseries
SEDUCING McCOY by Tori Carrington
Law-enforcement brothers David and Connor McCoy find that upholding the law can get in the way of love as they try to convince two women not to settle for less than the *real* McCoy!

Signature Select Spotlight
CONFESSIONS OF A PARTY CRASHER by Holly Jacobs
Though her friends agree that it's a great way to meet men, Morgan Miller isn't comfortable crashing a posh wedding reception. Then again, it's better than not going at all...especially when wedding photographer Conner Danning enters the picture!

Signature Select Showcase
LOVE SONG FOR A RAVEN by Elizabeth Lowell
A ferocious storm plunged Janna Morgan into the icy water of the frigid sea—until untamed and enigmatic Carlson Raven saves her. Stranded together in a deserted paradise, Raven is powerless to resist his attraction to Janna. But, could he believe her feelings were love and not merely gratitude?

SIGCNM0506

Paying the Playboy's Price

(Silhouette Desire #1732)

by

EMILIE ROSE

Juliana Alden is determined to have her last—
her only—fling before settling down. And she's
found the perfect candidate: bachelor Rex Tanner.
He's pure playboy charm…but can she afford
his price?

Trust Fund Affairs: They've just spent a fortune—
the bachelors had better be worth it.

Don't miss the other titles in this series:

EXPOSING THE EXECUTIVE'S SECRETS (July)
BENDING TO THE BACHELOR'S WILL (August)

On sale this June from Silhouette Desire.

*Available wherever books are sold, including most
bookstores, supermarkets, discount stores and drugstores.*

HOTEL MARCHAND

Four sisters.

A family legacy.

And someone is out to destroy it.

A captivating new limited continuity, launching June 2006

The most beautiful hotel in New Orleans,
and someone is out to destroy it. But mystery,
danger and some surprising family revelations
and discoveries won't stop the Marchand sisters
from protecting their birthright…
and finding love along the way.